W9-BUV-185

By the same author

Play Dirty
Chill Factor
Ricochet
White Hot
Hello, Darkness
The Crush
Envy
The Switch
Standoff
The Alibi
Unspeakable
Fat Tuesday
Exclusive
The Witness
Charade
Where There's Smoke
French Silk
Breath of Scandal
Mirror Image
Best Kept Secrets
Slow Heat in Heaven

SANDRA BROWN

SMOKE SCREEN

DOUBLEDAY LARGE PRINT HOME LIBRARY EDITION

SIMON & SCHUSTER
New York London Toronto Sydney

This Large Print Edition, prepared especially for Doubleday Large Print Home Library, contains the complete, unabridged text of the original Publisher's Edition.

Simon & Schuster
1230 Avenue of the Americas
New York, NY 10020

First Simon & Schuster hardcover edition August 2008

SIMON & SCHUSTER and colophon are registered trademarks of Simon & Schuster, Inc.

Manufactured in the United States of America

ISBN-13: 978-0-7394-9753-1

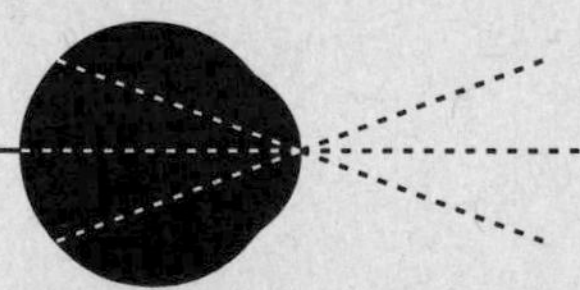

This Large Print Book carries the
Seal of Approval of N.A.V.H.

June 18, 2007

To those brave nine

SMOKE SCREEN

PROLOGUE

Thank God he was still asleep.

Waking up to find herself in bed with Jay Burgess was embarrassing enough without having to look him in the eye. At least not until she had time to collect herself.

As carefully as possible, she inched to the side of the bed and slipped out from under the sheet, trying not to lift it away from him in the process. She perched on the very edge of the mattress and glanced over her shoulder. The draft from the air-conditioning vent above the bed was cold, causing goose bumps to break out on her arms. But although Jay was naked and covered only to his waist, the chilly air hadn't roused him. Shifting her weight from the bed to her feet a little at a time, she stood up.

The room tilted. To keep from falling, she instinctually reached out for support. Her hand found the wall with a smack that might just as well have been a cymbal crash for the reverberation it created in the silent house. No longer concerned so much about waking him as about wondering how in the world she'd got so terribly drunk last night, she remained propped against the wall, taking deep breaths, focusing on one spot until her equilibrium returned.

Miraculously, her clumsiness hadn't awakened Jay. Spying her underpants, she crept to the foot of the bed and retrieved them, then tiptoed around the room, gathering strewn articles of her clothing, hugging each garment against her chest in a gesture of modesty, which under the circumstances was rather ridiculous.

The walk of shame. The college phrase seemed apropos. It referred to a coed who sneaked out of a guy's bedroom after spending the night with him. She was way past college age, and both she and Jay were single, free to sleep together if they chose.

If they chose.

The phrase struck her like the cruel pop of a snapped rubber band.

Suddenly, the shock of waking up in Jay's bed was replaced by the alarming realization that she didn't remember how she'd got there. She didn't recall making a conscious decision to sleep with him. She didn't remember weighing the pros and cons and deciding in favor of it. She didn't remember being wooed until practicality was obscured by sensuality. She didn't remember giving a mental shrug and thinking *What the hell? We're adults.*

She didn't remember anything.

Looking around, she took in the layout and furnishings of the bedroom. It was a pleasant room, tastefully decorated and tailored for a man who lived alone. But nothing in it was familiar to her. Nothing. It was as though she was seeing it for the first time.

Obviously it *was* Jay's place; there were pictures of him scattered about, mostly vacation snapshots with various friends of both sexes. But she had never been in this room before, nor in this house. She wasn't even certain of the street address, although she had a vague recollection of walking here from . . . from somewhere.

Yes, The Wheelhouse. She and Jay had met there for a drink. He'd already had several when she arrived, but that wasn't uncommon. Jay liked spirits and had an amazing tolerance for large quantities of alcohol. She had ordered a glass of white wine. They'd sat and chatted over their drinks, catching up on what was happening in each other's life.

Then he'd said—

Remembering now what he'd told her, she shivered, but not from the cold. She covered her mouth to catch a low moan and looked back at him where he lay sleeping. She whispered a sorrowful "Oh, Jay," repeating the first words she'd uttered when he broke the awful news to her last night.

Can we continue this conversation at my place? he'd asked. *I've moved since I've seen you. An elderly aunt died and left me all her worldly goods. Lots of china, crystal, antique furniture, stuff like that. I sold all of it to a dealer and bought a town house with the proceeds. It's a short walk.*

He was chatty, acting as though they'd been talking about nothing more worrisome than the approach of hurricane season, but his news had been a bombshell. Terrible. Impossible to believe. She'd been staggered by it. Had compassion moved her to affection? Did that explain the lovemaking that had followed?

Lord, *why couldn't she remember?*

Searching for answers as well as for the rest of her clothing, she went into the living room. Her dress and cardigan were bunched up in a chair, her sandals were on the floor. There was an open bottle of scotch and two glasses on the table in front of the sofa. Only an inch of whiskey remained in the bottle. The cushions of the sofa were rumpled and dented, as though someone had been wallowing on them.

Apparently she and Jay.

Quickly she went back through the bedroom, finding the bathroom on the far side of it. She managed to close the door without making a sound, a precaution that was canceled out a moment later when she retched noisily into the toilet. Her stomach was seized by painful spasms as it disgorged what seemed to be gallons of scotch. Never a big fan of scotch, she knew with absolute certainty that she would never touch a drop of it again.

She found toothpaste in the mirrored cabinet above the sink and used her index finger to scrub the film and bad taste from her mouth. That helped, but she still felt rather shabby and decided to shower. When she faced Jay, she would feel more confident and less embarrassed over the excesses of last night if she was clean.

The stall was a tile enclosure with a large, round showerhead mounted into the ceiling. Standing directly beneath the simulated rainfall, she lathered and rinsed several times. She washed carefully and thoroughly between her legs. She shampooed her hair.

Once out of the shower, she didn't tarry. Surely all the noise she'd made had woken him up by now. She dressed, used his hairbrush to smooth out her wet hair, then bolstered her courage with a deep breath and opened the bathroom door.

Jay was still asleep. How could that be? He was a well-conditioned drinker, but apparently last night had been an overindulgence even for him. How much scotch had been in the bottle when they began to drink from it? Between them, had they nearly emptied a whole fifth?

They must have. Otherwise why couldn't she remember taking off her clothes and having sex with Jay Burgess? Years ago, they'd had a brief affair that soon flamed out, ending long before it developed into a bona fide relationship. Neither's heart was broken. There hadn't been a scene or a formal breakup of any kind. They'd simply stopped dating but had remained friends.

But Jay, charming and irrepressible Jay, hadn't stopped trying to lure her back into his bed whenever their paths crossed. "Having a roll in the sack and staying friends aren't mutually exclusive," he'd say with his most engaging smile.

That hadn't been her experience, and she'd told him so each time he tried to talk her into a sleepover for old times' sake.

Last night, he must have persuaded her.

She would've expected him to be up early this morning to gloat over his conquest, waking her up with a kiss and a teasing invitation to have breakfast in bed. She could almost hear him saying, *Since you're here, you might just as well relax and enjoy the full Burgess treatment.*

Or why hadn't he joined her in the shower? That would be a Jay kind of thing to do. He would step in with her and say something like *You missed a spot on your back. Oops, and here's one on your front, too.* But the shower hadn't disturbed him. Not even the repeated flushing of the toilet.

How could he sleep through all that? He hadn't even—

Moved.

Her stomach gave a heaving motion

like an ocean swell. Soured scotch filled her throat, and she feared she was about to be sick again. She swallowed hard. “Jay?” she said tentatively. Then louder. “Jay?”

Nothing. No sigh or snuffle. Not even a slight shift of position.

She stood rooted to the floor, her heart thumping hard now. Forcing herself to move, she lurched toward the bed, hand outstretched to touch his shoulder and give it a firm shake. “Jay!”

CHAPTER 1

Raley pulled open the rusty screen door, its hinges squealing. "Hey! You in here?"

"Ain't I usually?"

A curl of faded red paint flaked off when the wood frame slapped closed behind Raley as he stepped into the one-room cabin. It smelled of fried pork and the mouse-gnawed Army blanket on the cot in the corner.

It took a moment for his eyes to adjust to the dimness and find the old man. He was sitting at a three-legged table, hunched over a cup of coffee like a dog guarding a hard-won bone, staring into the snowy screen of a black-and-white television. Ghostly images flickered in and out. There was no audio except for a static hiss.

"Good morning."

The old man snorted a welcome through his sheaves of nasal hair. "He'p yourself." He nodded toward the enamel coffeepot on the stove. "Can't recommend the cream. It curdled overnight."

Raley stepped over the three hounds lying motionless on the floor and went to the refrigerator that was jammed between an antique pie safe, which served as a pantry, and a drafting table, which served no purpose whatsoever except to collect dust and further reduce the floor space in the crowded cabin.

The handle on the fridge door had broken off, probably decades ago, but if you pressed your fingers just right into the soft rubber sealant in the crack, you could pry it open. "I brought you some catfish." Raley set the newspaper bundle on one of the rusty wire shelves, then quickly shut the door against the mingled odors of cream gone bad and general spoilage.

"Much obliged."

"You're welcome." The coffee probably had been boiled several times and would be the consistency of molasses. Without cream to dilute it, Raley thought it better to pass.

He glanced at the silent TV. "You need to adjust your rabbit ears."

"Ain't the rabbit ears. I turned off the sound."

"How come?"

The old man replied with one of his customary harrumphs that said he couldn't be bothered to answer. A self-proclaimed recluse, he had lived in voluntary exile ever since "the war," although which war had never been specified. He had as little as possible to do with other *Homo sapiens.*

Shortly after Raley had moved into the vicinity, the two had come upon each other in the woods. Raley was staring down into the beady eyes of a dead opossum when the old man came crashing through the underbrush and said, "Don't even think about it."

"About what?"

"About taking my possum."

Touching the bloated, flyblown, limp

body with the pink, hairless tail and horrible stench was the last thing Raley intended to do. He raised his hands in surrender and stood aside so the barefoot old man in stained overalls could retrieve his kill from the metal jaws of the small trap.

"Way you been stampin' 'round out here, it's a wonder to me it ain't you caught in this trap 'stead of the possum," he grumbled.

Raley wasn't aware that anyone lived within miles of the cabin he'd recently purchased. He'd rather not have had a neighbor of any kind, but especially one who kept track of his comings and goings.

As the old man stood up, his knees protested in loud pops and snaps, which caused him to grimace and mutter a string of curses. With the carcass dangling from his hand, the old man looked Raley over, from his baseball cap and bearded face to the toes of his hiking boots. Inspection complete, the old man spat tobacco juice into the dirt to express his opinion of what he saw. "Man's got a right to walk in the woods," he said. "Just don't go messin' with my traps."

"It would help me to know where they are."

The old man's cracked lips spread into a wide grin, revealing tobacco-stained stubs that once were teeth. "Wouldn't it though?" Still chuckling, he turned away. "You'll find 'em, I'm bettin'." Raley could hear his laughter long after he disappeared into the dense foliage.

Over the ensuing months, they'd accidentally bumped into each other in the woods several times. At least to Raley these were chance meetings. He reasoned the old man made himself visible when he wanted to and didn't when he was disinclined to give his new neighbor even a grunt of a greeting.

One hot afternoon, they met in the doorway of the general store in the nearest town. Raley was coming in, the old man going out. They nodded to each other. Later, when Raley left with several sacks of groceries, he noticed the old man sitting in a chair on the shaded porch of the store, fanning himself with his straw hat. Acting on impulse, Raley peeled a cold can of beer from the plastic webbing and tossed it to the old man, who, revealing excellent reflexes, caught it in one hand.

Raley stowed his groceries in the bed of his pickup and climbed into the cab. The old man regarded him with patent suspicion as he put the truck in reverse and backed away, but Raley noticed that he'd popped the top on the beer.

The following morning there was hard knocking on Raley's door. This being a first, he approached the door cautiously. The old man was there, holding a chipped ceramic bowl containing a heap of some raw animal flesh that Raley couldn't identify. He feared it was carrion that even the trio of hounds had rejected.

"In exchange for the beer. I don't like bein' beholden to nobody."

Raley took the bowl thrust at him. "Thanks." His visitor turned and walked down the steps. Raley called after him, "What's your name?"

"Who wants to know?"

"Raley Gannon."

The old man hesitated, then grumbled, "Delno Pickens."

From that morning, they developed a quasi friendship founded on loneliness and a shared reluctance for interaction with other people.

The sum-total value of Delno's possessions wouldn't be a hundred dollars. He was always dragging home something he'd salvaged from God knew where, items he had no practical use for. His cabin was situated on stilts to prevent it from flooding when the Combahee overflowed its banks. Junk had been stuffed into the crawl space beneath the structure, as though to provide a more solid foundation. The area surrounding the cabin was also littered with junk that was never utilized so far as Raley could tell. Collecting it seemed more important to Delno than the articles themselves.

He drove a truck that Raley called Frankenstein because it was made of parts Delno had assembled himself, held together with baling wire and duct tape. It was a miracle to Raley that he ever got the contraption started, but as

Delno said, "It ain't pretty, but it gets me anywhere I want to go."

He would eat anything. *Anything.* Anything he could knock from a tree, trap, or pull out of the river. But whatever he had, once their friendship had been established, he was always willing to share it.

Surprisingly, he was very well read and conversant on subjects which, to look at him, one wouldn't have expected him to have even a passing knowledge of. Raley came to suspect that his hillbilly accent and vocabulary were affected. Like the squalor he lived in, they were protests against a former life.

But whatever that former life had entailed remained Delno's secret. He never mentioned a hometown, his childhood or parents, an occupation, children, or wife. Beyond his hounds, he talked to no one except Raley. Intimate relationships were limited to a stack of old nudie magazines with well-thumbed pages, which he kept on the floor beneath his cot.

Raley shared nothing personal with Delno, either. Not for the first two years of their acquaintanceship. And then one evening at sunset, Delno showed up at Raley's cabin, bringing with him two Mason jars filled with a murky liquid that he'd fermented himself.

"Haven't seen you in over a week. Where you been?"

"Here."

Raley didn't want company, but Delno elbowed his way inside anyway. "Thought you might be needin' a swig or two." Giving Raley one of his scornful once-overs, he added, "Lookin' at you, I'd say my hunch was right. You appear to be in bad shape. Could smell you as I was coming up the steps."

"You're a fine one to criticize someone else's appearance and personal hygiene."

"Who'd you call?"

"What?"

"That blabbermouth that runs the cash register at the store? The one with her hair piled up high, wears long, dangly earrings? Told me you come in there last week, got a handful of change, and fed it into the pay phone outside. Said you talked a few minutes, then hung up, looking like you was ready to kill somebody. Got in your truck and took outta there without even paying for your groceries."

He uncapped one of the jars and passed it to Raley, who sniffed the contents, then shook his head and passed it back. "So, I'm askin'," Delno continued after taking a hefty swallow from the jar, "who'd you call?"

It was dawn before Raley stopped talking. By then, Delno had drained both jars. Raley was simply drained—emotionally, mentally, physically. It had been a painful but therapeutic catharsis. He had lanced a dozen wounds.

With nothing more to say and no breath left to say it, Raley looked over at the old man, who had listened for hours without making a single comment. The expression on the creased, leathery face was one of profound sadness. His eyes were naked and unguarded for the first time since Raley had known him, and Raley knew he was looking straight into the soul of a man who'd experienced indescribable heartache. It seemed Delno Pickens had collected all the misery and injustice in the world and packed it into that one hopeless gaze.

Then he sighed, and in one of the rare times they'd ever made physical contact, reached across the space separating them and patted Raley on the knee. "Go wash your armpits before the stink of you makes me puke up all that good liquor. I'll cook you some breakfast."

They never again referred to anything Raley had told him that night. It was as though the long night had never happened. But Raley never forgot the bleakness with which Delno had looked at him that morning. And this morning when he raised his head from staring into his coffee mug and looked up at Raley, he was wearing that same expression of despair.

"What's the matter?" Raley's heart hitched, automatically thinking *disaster.* A 747 loaded with passengers crashing into a mountainside. A presidential assassination. A terrorist attack on the scale of 9/11.

"Don't go and do somethin' crazy, now, okay?" Delno said.

"What happened?"

Muttering dire predictions about "nothin' good comin' outta this," Delno hitched his chin toward the TV.

Raley went over to the vintage set and turned the volume knob, then fiddled with the rabbit-ear antenna in the hope of getting a better picture.

The video remained erratic and the audio was scratchy, but within moments he had a clear understanding of what had happened and why Delno had dreaded telling him:

Jay Burgess was dead.

CHAPTER 2

"They don't believe me, do they?"

Britt addressed the question to the stranger whom she had retained as her attorney. It was now twenty-four hours since she'd discovered that Jay had died while lying beside her, and still she continued to hope that this was all a terrible dream from which she would soon awaken.

But it was all too real.

Shortly after her frantic 911 call, EMTs and two police officers had arrived at Jay's town house. They'd been followed by the coroner and two detectives, who introduced themselves as Clark and Javier. They had questioned her in Jay's living room while, in the bedroom, his body was being examined and prepared for transport to the morgue. She had gone to police headquarters with the detectives to give them her formal statement. After the last *i* was dotted and the last *t* crossed, she'd thought that would be the end of it, except for grieving.

But this morning Clark had phoned her at home. He apologized for the imposition but told her he and Javier would like to clear up a few details and asked if she would mind returning to the police station.

The request was issued in a friendly, casual manner, but it made her uneasy, uneasy enough to feel it would be advisable to have counsel meet her there. Her dealings with lawyers were limited to tax issues, real estate transactions, contracts, and her parents' estate. She doubted the attorneys handling those matters had ever been inside a police station.

Needing a reference, she had called the television station's general manager.

Of course the lead story on every station last night had been about Jay Burgess's shocking death. Her fellow broadcast journalists had been discreet in their reports of her involvement, but no matter how they'd couched it, it was a hot story: The highest rated news reporter in the market, Britt Shelley, was now the one making news.

From the objective standpoint of a television journalist, she had to admit it was a juicy irony as well as a sensational story.

The general manager had commiserated with her situation. "What an awful ordeal for you, Britt."

"Yes. It was. *Is,* actually. That's why I've bothered you at home."

"Whatever you need. Whatever I can do to help," he'd said. She'd asked him to recommend a lawyer.

"A criminal lawyer?"

She'd been quick to assure him that she was only being prudent, that the interview—she didn't even refer to it as an interrogation—was routine, a formality really. "Even so, I think I should have counsel." He had readily agreed and promised to make some calls on her behalf.

When Bill Alexander had arrived at

the police station, he'd been breathless and apologetic for being ten minutes late. "I got stuck in traffic."

She'd hoped for someone imposing, authoritative, and charismatic, so it was difficult to hide her disappointment when the slight, unassuming, and frazzled Alexander proffered his card and introduced himself only seconds before they were joined by the two detectives.

By contrast, Clark and Javier personified central casting's call sheet for tough detective types.

Yesterday, when the pair had arrived at Jay's town house and realized they were talking to *the* Britt Shelley of Channel Seven News, they'd been dumbstruck and awkward, as people sometimes were upon seeing a TV personality out and among ordinary folk.

The detectives had apologized for having to detain her and put her through the police work on the heels of such a traumatic experience, but unfortunately it was their job to learn exactly what had happened. She'd answered their questions to the best of her ability, and they had seemed satisfied with her account.

This morning, however, the tenor of their questioning had changed, slightly but noticeably. They seemed no longer starstruck. Their inquiries had taken on an edge that hadn't been there yesterday.

Britt was cooperative, knowing that reluctance to cooperate with the authorities usually signaled guilt, at least on some level. All she was guilty of was sleeping with a man who happened to die in his sleep. It was fodder for crude jests about Jay's sexual prowess, and hers.

He went out with a bang. Wink, wink.

Bet he died with a smile on his face. Wink, wink.

He came and went at the same time. Wink, wink.

If these detectives were after details about the sex, they were out of luck. All Britt remembered was waking up and finding Jay lying dead beside her in his bed. She had no memory of anything else happening in that bed. Even after an hour of intense dialogue, she didn't think the detectives believed that.

Moments ago, they had suggested

taking a break, leaving her alone with her newly retained attorney, which gave her an opportunity to better acquaint herself with him but, more important, to get his read on the proceedings.

"They don't believe me, do they?" she repeated, since he'd faltered on his answer the first time she'd asked.

This time, he gave her an insipid smile. "I don't get that sense at all, Ms. Shelley." His tone of voice suggested he was stroking a nervous cat. "They're being thorough, which they must be whenever someone dies under unusual circumstances."

"Jay Burgess's cancer was terminal."

"Yes, but—"

"He'd had a lot to drink. Probably the alcohol didn't mix with the strong medications he was taking."

"No doubt."

"All too often people mix prescription drugs with alcohol and it kills them. Jay died of cardiac arrest, respiratory failure. Something like that."

"I'm sure you're right."

"Then explain to me why I'm being questioned so extensively."

"In part, it's a knee-jerk reaction to the sudden death of one of their own," he said. "Jay Burgess was a decorated police officer, a hero to the men in this department and beyond. Naturally his colleagues want to know what happened during the hours before he died."

She'd covered the funerals of fallen policemen, and had always been impressed by the global fraternity of law enforcement officers, who rallied 'round when one of them died.

Rubbing her forehead, she conceded the point with a tired sigh. "I suppose you're right. But that's just it. I don't know! I've told them I can't remember. I don't think they believe that, but I swear it's the truth."

"Maintain that," he said as though applauding the passion behind her voice. "Or, even better, say nothing at all."

Shooting him a scornful look, she began pacing the compact interrogation room. "Everybody says, especially lawyers, that it's better not to say anything. But as a reporter, I know that people who refuse to talk look like they have something to hide."

"Then don't deviate from your story."

She came around, ready to object to his calling her account of Jay's death a "story," but just then the two detectives returned.

"Do you need a restroom break, Ms. Shelley?" Clark asked.

"I'm fine."

"Can I get you something to drink?"

"No thank you."

He was tall and rawboned with thinning reddish hair. Javier was short, swarthy, and his black hair was as dense as carpet. Physically they couldn't be more dissimilar, yet she was equally wary of both. She mistrusted Clark's politeness, thinking it might be affected to cover suppressed redneck leanings. And Javier's pockmarked cheeks made her think of fatal knife fights. Clark's eyes were blue, Javier's so dark that the pupils were not discernible, but both pairs of eyes were quick and watchful.

Having dispensed with the courtesies, Javier resumed the questioning. "When we left off, you were saying that your memory got foggy after you had a glass of wine at The Wheelhouse."

"That's right." Everything that had happened since she drank that glass of Chardonnay was a hazy, disjointed recollection. Up to a point. Then her memory of events had been completely obliterated. How could one harmless glass of wine wipe clean her memory? It couldn't. Not unless . . . Unless . . .

"Date rape drug."

Until the three men froze in place, she didn't realize she had spoken the words. She stepped back from herself, examined what she'd just said, and was struck with the plausibility—no, almost certainty—that she was right.

"I must have been given one of the substances collectively known as date rape drugs." The two detectives and the lawyer just stood there, staring at her as though she was speaking a foreign language. "They give you temporary amnesia," she said with a trace of impatience. "I did a feature story on them. An incident at Clemson sparked concern about the increased usage of them at parties and bars where young people hang out. They cause a short-term memory loss. Sometimes the memory never comes back. But it doesn't matter, because by the time the effects wear off, the damage has been done."

She looked at each man in turn, expecting them to be sharing her excitement over this credible explanation for her blackout. Instead they continued to stare at her without reaction. With asperity she said, "Blink if you can hear me."

"We hear you, Ms. Shelley," Clark said.

"Well, then? Don't you see? My wine was doctored with one of these drugs. They work quickly. That would explain why I can't remember anything after reaching Jay's apartment."

"How about an empty bottle of scotch?" Javier asked.

"I don't like scotch. I never drink scotch. If Jay had offered it to me, I would have declined it, especially since I wasn't feeling well."

"Your fingerprints were on one of the drinking glasses. Your lipstick on the rim," said Javier.

"You've already examined the drinking glasses? Why?"

The two detectives exchanged a glance. Clark said, "Let's start at the beginning and go through it again. Tell us everything that happened."

"I don't know everything that happened. I can tell you only what I remember."

"Okay, then, what you remember. You don't mind if we videotape it this time, do you?"

Immediately suspicious of Clark's dismissive tone, she said, "Why would you?"

"Just so we have it, so if the need should arise, we can refer back to the tape, get the details straight in our own heads."

Mistrusting his explanation as well as his snake-oil salesman's smile, she looked at Alexander, who said, "It's standard practice, Ms. Shelley. You still don't have to answer any question you don't want to."

"I want to answer the questions. I want the answers myself. Probably more than they do."

Since calling 911, she'd been swept up in the disagreeable technicalities of an unexpected death—the pronouncement of the coroner that Jay was indeed dead, the questioning by police, the paperwork. She hadn't had time to indulge the personal aspects of it. She hadn't yet actually grieved the loss of her friend.

Nor could she now. Not until she got past this unpleasantness. Restating her point, she said, "I'm desperate to know what happened to Jay."

"Then we've got no problem." Javier sat down at the small table and motioned her into the chair facing the video camera. "I sure wouldn't expect you to be camera shy."

His grin made her think again of sharp blades piercing soft tissue. She turned away from it and sat down. Clark checked the focus of the camera, stated the time and date and who was present, then sat down on the edge of the table and began swinging his skinny leg back and forth. "Who called who?"

"What do you mean?"

"Who made the date?"

"Jay. I told you that."

"We can check phone records."

Javier's statement wasn't just that. It was a veiled threat.

Looking him squarely in the eye, she said, "Jay called me earlier that day and asked if I would meet him at The Wheelhouse for a drink. He said he wanted to talk to me."

"Before that, when was the last time you saw him?"

"I don't know the date for certain. Several months ago. When the man accused of child molestation at the preschool in North Charleston was arrested. Jay was at the press conference and addressed questions about the police investigation. I covered it for the station. We waved at each other, but I didn't talk to him. I got my story from one of the arresting officers, not Jay."

"But you and Burgess were friendly."

"Yes."

"More than friendly?"

"No."

The two detectives exchanged another telling glance. Alexander sat forward in his chair, as though about to warn her to be cautious.

"Never?" Clark asked.

"Years ago," she replied with equanimity. Her brief affair with Jay hadn't been a secret. "I relocated to Charleston to take the job at Channel Seven. Jay was one of the first people I met. We went out a few times, but our friendship was always more or less platonic."

"More or less?" Javier's raised eyebrows suggested *more.*

"We'd been nothing more than friends for the past several years."

"Until night before last, when you became lovers again."

"I—" She hesitated. Alexander raised his index finger as though forestalling her from answering. She lowered her gaze to her lap. "I don't know whether or not we were intimate that night. I'm not sure. I can't remember."

Clark sighed as though he found that impossible to believe, then said, "So you met at The Wheelhouse."

"I arrived at seven, the appointed time. Jay was already there. He'd had several drinks."

"How do you know?"

"By the empty glasses on the table.

Have you questioned the cocktail waitress?"

Ignoring that, Clark said, "You ordered a glass of white wine."

"Yes. It wasn't very good." Speaking directly into the camera lens, she added, "I believe something was put into it."

"By Jay?"

Actually, on that point, Britt shared Javier's apparent skepticism. "I don't see how he could have without my noticing. I don't think he ever touched my wineglass. Anyway, why would he drug me?"

Clark tugged on his lower lip. Javier didn't move. Both continued to stare at her. She was aware of the video camera recording every blink, every breath. To anyone viewing the recording later, would she look guilty? She knew that investigators looked for telltale signs of lying. She tried to remain perfectly still and to keep her face composed.

"What did you talk about?" Javier asked.

"I've told you," she said wearily. "This and that. 'How's your job? Fine. How's yours? Do you have any vacation plans?' That kind of thing."

"Nothing personal?"

"He asked if I was seeing someone. I told him no one in particular. He said, 'Good. I'd hate to depart this earth leaving you to some undeserving but lucky bastard.' He was grinning, and it was the teasing kind of flirtation Jay was famous for. I laughed. And then I realized what he'd said and asked him what he meant about departing this earth. He said, 'I'm dying, Britt.' "

Recalling that moment and Jay's somber expression, her voice became husky with emotion. "Then he told me about the cancer."

Pancreatic. Advanced. Not a chance in hell of beating it, so I'm not putting myself through chemo and all that shit. At least I'll have my hair when they bury me.

After a quiet moment, Javier said, "According to Jay's oncologist, he had only a few more weeks. Month or two at the outside. Shocked the hell out of everybody in the department when he announced it. Some people cried for days. Jay offered to surrender his badge, but Chief said he could work right up till . . . well, the end."

Britt nodded, confirming that was what Jay had told her. "He was such a vital individual. He created his own energy field. When he told me, I couldn't believe it."

Clark cleared his throat. "Do you think maybe he was trying to get around to all the women he'd wanted to sleep with one last time before—"

"No," she said adamantly. "When he invited me to join him, he said he needed to talk to me. I got the impression it was about something serious."

Javier snorted. "More serious than terminal cancer?"

Her temper snapped. "A basic part of my job is to evaluate people, Detective. I can sense when someone is holding back the key element of a story because they don't want to be in the news, or when someone exaggerates their role in an attempt to seem more important to the story than they are.

"Jay dismissed my condolences and said he had something much more important to talk about. He said he was about to give me an exclusive that would make my career. And it wasn't a flirtation and it wasn't a come-on. I would have known if it was. Jay was serious. Whatever he wanted to tell me was important to him."

There she paused. Clark leaned forward expectantly. "Well? What was it?"

"I don't know. That's when Jay suggested we leave so we could talk in private." She didn't want to tell them it was at that point that Jay also had seemed to grow nervous. Already her veracity was being challenged. Who would believe that Jay Burgess would ever become nervous?

Apparently the detectives sensed she was withholding something. Clark leaned toward her again. "You had privacy at The Wheelhouse, Ms. Shelley. You and Jay had a cozy little corner in the bar. People saw you. Witnesses said you two had your heads together like nobody else in the world existed."

Witnesses? The word struck a criminal note that was unsettling. "That's a gross distortion," she said. "Jay and I had our heads together very close so we could hear each other above the noise."

"Or to whisper sweet nothings."

She glared at Javier. "I'm not going to honor that with a comment."

"Okay, okay. Uncalled for."

He left it to Clark to continue. "Jay asked you to go to his place."

"To continue our conversation, yes."

"And you went willingly?"

"Willingly? Of course. I thought he was about to give me a big story."

"So you go to the apartment of any man who offers you an exclusive?"

"Mr. Javier!" Alexander exclaimed. "I will not let my client be subjected to insults like that."

"It was a follow-up to what she said herself."

"Let it drop," she said to the lawyer. Actually she was glad to know he was still awake, since he'd said nothing for several minutes. Javier's crack was low, but she had reached the crux of her story and was eager to move it along. "When we left The Wheelhouse, I felt dizzy."

"Had you had a drink before you met Jay?"

"I've already told you that. No."

"Did you take any . . . medication? Cold remedy, antihistamine?"

"No."

"One glass of wine made you tipsy?"

"Apparently it did, Mr. Clark. Doesn't that strike you as odd?"

"Not particularly. Not for a lady who doesn't drink scotch. One glass of wine could make you drunk."

"It's never affected me that way before."

"First time for everything." Javier shifted to a more comfortable position in his molded-plastic chair.

Ignoring him, she said into the camera, "By the time we got outside The Wheelhouse, I wasn't feeling well."

"How so?"

"Well, drunk. Nauseous. Disconnected."

"Anything unusual occur between the bar and Jay's town house?"

"Again, my memory of the walk is hazy, but I don't think so."

"No exchanges with anyone else along the way?"

"No."

"Did Jay ask you to spend the night with him?"

She looked directly at Javier. "Not that I recall."

"Did Jay know you weren't feeling well?"

It was a good question, and she wished she had an answer for it. "I'm not sure. I don't believe I remarked on it. I might have. He might have asked me if I was sick. Honestly, I don't remember talking about anything. We walked to his town house and went inside."

"Then what? What's the first thing you did when you got inside?"

"I remember being embarrassed over my condition."

"Over being drunk?"

"Or drugged," she said with emphasis. "I remember making my way to the sofa."

"So you knew where his sofa was?"

"No. I'd never been to that town house before. I saw the sofa and knew I needed to sit down."

"Did you take your shoes off first?"

"No."

"Your dress?"

"No."

"Did you undress before or after Jay started pouring the scotch?"

"I didn't undress."

"So Jay undressed you."

"No!"

Clark jumped on that. "How do you know if you can't remember?"

Before she could respond, Javier said, "If you didn't undress yourself, and Jay didn't undress you, how come you woke up nude and in bed with him, which, by your own admission, you did? Want me to read back that part of the statement you gave us yesterday morning while they were taking Jay's body to the morgue?"

"No, no! I remember what I said in my statement because it's the truth. What I don't remember is how we got undressed and into bed."

"You don't remember getting blitzed on scotch?"

"No."

"Or taking off your clothes?"

"No."

"Or having sex."

"I don't know that we did."

Javier reached into the pocket of his sport jacket and removed a small plastic sandwich bag. Inside was the foil packet for a condom. It was empty. "We found this among the cushions of the sofa."

Britt stared at it, searching her memory, coming up blank.

"Do you customarily carry a condom in your handbag, Ms. Shelley?"

Meeting his insinuating gaze, she replied coolly, "It must have been Jay's. He could have used it anytime."

Clark shook his head, looking almost rueful. "His maid had come that morning. She said she gave the place a thorough cleaning, even took the cushions off the sofa to vacuum underneath. She'd swear to it this wasn't there then."

Britt asked, "Did you find the condom itself?"

"No. It's assumed Jay flushed it."

"He could have used it earlier in the day. After the maid cleaned, but before meeting me."

Clark shook his head. "Jay was here at headquarters all day. Didn't even go out for lunch. He left at six. Hardly time for him to return home and have sex on his sofa with another woman, then get to The Wheelhouse and down several drinks before you joined him at seven."

He smirked and Javier chuckled, anticipating what his colleague was about to say. "Even Jay wasn't that fast."

CHAPTER 3

George McGowan opened his bedroom door in time to see his wife of four years, Miranda, slipping a terry-cloth robe over her nakedness. The young man in the room with her was zipping the cover around his portable massage table.

Unruffled by the unexpected appearance of her husband, she said, “Oh, darling, hi. I didn’t know you were home. Would you like Drake to stay? He just finished with me.” Her eyelids lowered drowsily. “He was particularly magic today.”

George felt his face grow hot. His fingers tightened around his glass of Bloody Mary. “No thanks.”

Drake hefted his table, essentially doing a biceps curl with it. "Wednesday, Mrs. McGowan?"

"Let's make it ninety minutes instead of the usual sixty."

He smiled suggestively. "I can extend it as long as you like."

Drake's double entendre wasn't lost on George. Neither was the hot, musky smell of sex that permeated the room, or the rumpled satin sheets on the king-size bed. Drake hadn't done his work on the massage table, and the sly look he shot George as he sidled past him on his way out said as much.

He should follow the smarmy bastard, break him over his knee, shatter the bones of his hands, ruin his face, and put him out of business. The oily, Mediterranean-looking prick was beefed up, but George could whip his ass. Maybe he'd gone a little soft around the middle, but he could still make this guy wish his ancestors had stayed in Sicily or wherever the hell they were from.

Instead, he soundly closed the bedroom door and turned to glare at his wife. The silent rebuke was wasted, however, because she didn't see it. She had moved to her dressing table and was pulling a brush through her mane of auburn hair as she admired her reflection in the mirror.

She would dearly love for him to take issue with her screwing her masseur in their bedroom. So damned if he would give her that satisfaction. Besides, something else took priority.

"You need to see this." He opened the doors of the tall armoire and turned on the television set inside. "Britt Shelley is about to conduct a press conference about her and Jay."

"This should be interesting."

"It is. She claims she was given a date rape drug."

Miranda McGowan's upraised arm was arrested in motion. She lowered it slowly. "By Jay?"

George shrugged and turned up the volume just as the local newswoman addressed a question about her relationship with the recently deceased Jay Burgess. "He and I were friends."

"I'll bet," Miranda remarked as she moved from her dressing table to the end of the unmade bed and sat down.

"Shh!"

"Don't shush me."

"Will you just shut up and listen?"

George remained standing, the remote control in his hand, his attention riveted on the plasma screen and the close-up of Britt Shelley as she averred that she had no memory of the events immediately preceding Jay's death. "I have a vague recollection of entering his town house with him. Nothing beyond that."

"Are you accusing Jay Burgess of giving you the date rape drug?" a reporter asked.

"No. But I believe that someone did. My experience matches that of other women who have been given them." George turned and looked at his wife. She shifted her gaze away from the TV and locked eyes with him, but neither said anything.

George turned back to the set in time to hear Britt Shelley's lawyer reply to a question. The man held his fist to his mouth and cleared his throat. As a former policeman, George knew the gesture was a dead giveaway of uneasiness. The man was about to either hedge on something he was unsure of or blatantly lie.

"Ms. Shelley has submitted a urine specimen to be tested for these various substances. However, they disappear from the system relatively quickly. Depending on which drug Ms. Shelley was given, it's possible that too much time has elapsed for it to be detected."

A reporter in the front row said, "So you can't prove that she was given one of these date rape drugs."

"I can't comment until I know the result of the urinalysis."

"Regrettably, I did everything wrong," Britt Shelley interjected, much to the consternation of her lawyer, who frowned at her.

He jumped in before she could say more. "Ms. Shelley didn't at first realize that she'd been victimized. Had she, she wouldn't have showered, wouldn't have used the bathroom until after she'd submitted a specimen for testing."

"In other words," Miranda said, "she's making claims she can't prove."

Without turning, George waved at her to be quiet.

"No, I don't have any idea what caused Jay Burgess's death," Britt Shelley was saying in reply to another reporter's question. "He'd been diagnosed with pancreatic cancer, which he'd been told was terminal. It's assumed his death is cancer related, but an autopsy will be conducted—"

"Do you know when?"

"That's a question for the medical examiner. I hope sooner rather than later. I want an explanation for Jay's death, just as everyone else does."

"Do the police suspect foul play?"

Before Britt Shelley could respond, her attorney whispered something in her ear, and she nodded at him. "That's all I have to say at this time."

"Are the police—"

"Did you and Burgess—"

"What did you drink at The Wheelhouse?"

The reporters continued to shout questions at her and her lawyer as they retreated from the podium.

"Turn it off."

George did as Miranda asked. In the instant silence, ice cubes rattled in his glass as he took a drink of his Bloody Mary. "How many does that make so far today?" Miranda asked.

"You care?"

"You're damn right I care!" she fired back. "I care because you've been drunk ever since we got the news."

"Jay was my friend. Drinking is part of my grieving process."

"It doesn't look good."

"To who?"

"To anybody who happens to be interested and is paying attention," she said, angrily emphasizing each word.

"Everybody is interested and paying attention. Jay's dying is news. He was a hero."

"So were you."

He stared down into his glass for several moments, then shot the last of the drink. "Yeah. A big hero. Which is why you married me."

She laughed softly. "That's right, sweetheart. I wanted a hero"—she spread her robe open from the waist down—"and you wanted this."

There was a time when he would have dropped to his knees, crawled to her, and planted his face in her lap. He would have sent his tongue burrowing into her sex in search of the tiny gold charm that pierced her flesh, a tantalizing trinket that remained hidden until she was aroused. He used to make her crazy doing that.

But then he'd found out who had suggested she get the charm. That had ruined the pleasure for him.

She laughed and covered herself. "Poor George. So upset over Jay's demise he can't even make love to his wife."

"Not when she still reeks of Drake."

"Oh, please. Don't take a self-righteous posture with me. You're in the throes of a ridiculous affair with the teenybopper who hustles drinks at the country club."

"She's twenty-six. She only *looks* eighteen."

If anything could hurt Miranda—and he had a powerful need to hurt her just now—it was a reminder that she wasn't getting any younger. Thirty had come and gone. Forty loomed. It was still a long way off, but she was terrified of it.

In her youth, she'd been Miss Charleston County, Miss South Carolina, Miss This and Miss That. She had more tiaras and trophies than the housekeeper could keep polished. Other girls were winning those titles now. Girls with firmer thighs and perkier tits. Girls who didn't get Botox injections as regularly as pedicures.

Idly, painfully, he wondered if the current Miss Charleston County would have an abortion just to keep her tummy tight.

Miranda's rich laughter interrupted that dark thought. "Does your tacky little affair explain why you're popping Viagra these days?" He gave her a sharp look. "Oh, yes. I found it in the medicine cabinet."

"I'm amazed you could locate it among all the pills you keep in there." He set his empty glass on the portable bar and considered pouring another shot of vodka but talked himself out of it. He'd kept a buzz going for the last thirty-six hours. Miranda was right; it didn't look good.

"If you need a pill in order to keep it up for your new, young girlfriend, you're more pathetic than I thought."

She was trying her best to rile him, to start something or, rather, continue it. Usually he'd get right into it with her and keep it going until she won. Miranda always won.

But today, he didn't want to play their game. He had other things on his mind, life-and-death issues that were weightier than their ongoing contest to see who could inflict the most painful wound.

"We're both pathetic, Miranda."

He went to the window and moved aside the drape, which had been pulled closed, no doubt to create a more romantic ambience for her and Drake. From this second-story vantage point, George could see down onto the back lawn of the estate, where a crew of men were mowing, weeding, clipping. Separated from the formal lawn by a stone-wall border, the irrigated acreage spread out like a green apron. A white wood fence enclosed a pasture where their racehorses grazed.

He could see the roof of the multicar garage that housed his father-in-law's collection of classic cars as well as his own fleet of automobiles, kept buffed and polished and gassed up, ready to roll at his whim.

George McGowan had come from the working class. Money, actually the lack of it, had been a constant worry to his folks. In order to provide for his family of seven, his daddy had worked overtime at Conway Concrete and Construction Company. It was hot and dusty work that killed him well before his time. He'd dropped dead one August afternoon while working an extra shift. The doctor said he hadn't felt a thing.

Who would ever have guessed that his oldest son, George, would wind up marrying Miranda Conway, only child of the owner of the enterprise, the most desired girl around, because she was not only the most beautiful but also the richest. She was a debutante, a beauty queen, and an heiress. She could have had any man she wanted. She had wanted George McGowan.

"I can't go back and undo it," he said quietly as he watched the Thoroughbreds graze, taking their life of privilege as their due. As Miranda did. "Even if I could, I wouldn't. God help me, I couldn't give all this up." He let the drape fall back into place and turned toward her. "I couldn't give you up."

She tossed back her hair and looked at him with exasperation. "Stop being such a crybaby, George. For crissake. Jay Burgess died in bed with a naked lady beside him. Don't you think he'd rather go that way than die of cancer?"

"Knowing Jay like I did, yeah, he probably would."

She gave him her smile, the one that would make a man sell his soul to have her. "That's my boy. That's my hero. That's my strong, handsome George." She stood up and started walking toward him with a feline gait, slowly untying the belt of her robe and letting it slide off her.

When she reached him, she pressed her lush body against him and boldly began massaging him through his trousers. "Are you sad, baby? Worried? I know how to make you feel better. You've never needed Viagra with me, have you?"

She caressed him with a know-how that could only be achieved with practice. Lots of practice. He gritted his teeth and tried to reverse the rush of blood funneling toward her stroking fist, but resisting her was a lost cause. He cursed her to hell and back, but she only laughed and unzipped his trousers.

"Georgie Porgie, puddin' and pie. Kissed the girls and made them . . ." Coming up on tiptoe, wrapping one long leg around him, she bit the lobe of his ear, then whispered, "Make me cry."

His soul was lost already, too far gone to ever hope for redemption. So, what the hell did it matter?

Roughly, he thrust himself into her.

"Mr. Fordyce, they're replaying it now."

"Thank you."

Attorney General Cobb Fordyce's personal assistant withdrew, leaving him alone in his office. He'd asked her to alert him if Britt Shelley's press conference was aired a second time.

He swiveled his chair around to face the walnut cabinetry behind his desk and used a remote to switch on the television set, to watch what had been broadcast live during the lunch hour, which he'd missed because of a meeting.

Cobb didn't know Britt Shelley personally, only professionally. She'd been a fledgling reporter during the election that put him in this office, and she'd advanced just as he had. Often she covered the state capitol for the Charleston station, and he'd seen her on-air work there.

She was a tough but fair interviewer, far superior to the station's other reporters, better than the station's news operation altogether, and he'd often wondered why she hadn't been snatched up by a larger TV market.

He'd also wondered if she purposefully downplayed her attractiveness so it wouldn't be a distraction to the story or a drawback to her credibility. When a hurricane had been threatening

Charleston last year, she'd covered it live, dressed in a jacket with the hood drawstring tied tightly beneath her chin, her face washed clean of makeup by the torrential rain. Hardly glamorous.

She was no prima donna and no pushover. She certainly didn't look like one as she faced an audience of her colleagues and stated she didn't remember anything beyond going into Jay Burgess's town house. Then she alleged that she'd been given a date rape drug.

She was articulate, earnest, believable. But if her urinalysis came back negative, her attorney would have a hell of a hard time proving that she'd ingested a drug that would cause total memory loss.

The lawyer seemed to realize that. He looked uneasy and uncertain about his client's claim. He looked constipated. He appeared to be the kind of timid defender who actually helped prosecutors get convictions.

She, on the other hand, was confidence personified. Of course, she was adroit at playing to a camera. Cobb had experience with that himself. She knew how to evoke a self-serving emotion from her audience. He could relate to that, too.

The press conference ended with her saying that she wanted to learn the cause of Jay Burgess's death. She said it with enough conviction that, despite his skeptical nature, Cobb Fordyce believed her.

He was about to switch off the TV when the local news station went live with a follow-up story. The Charleston PD public information officer had been asked if Britt Shelley was under arrest. "Absolutely not," he replied. "Up to this point, there's been no evidence of any wrongdoing."

Standard-issue statement, Cobb thought.

"Jay Burgess died in his sleep. That's all we know at this time."

Cobb doubted that. That wasn't all they knew. They had something. Maybe nothing more than a hunch. But something had spooked Britt Shelley, or she wouldn't have made a preemptive strike by calling the press conference to claim friendship with Jay Burgess and express her deep regret over his untimely death—in effect to profess her innocence.

The CPD were fools for letting her get the jump on them. They should have kept her under wraps, or issued a gag order. That was a giant blunder on their part, letting her use her media advantage to state her defense before it even became a criminal case.

Again he was about to switch off the set when a local reporter was shown standing outside the state capitol. If Cobb looked out his office window, he'd probably see the news vans parked along the boulevard.

This was exactly what he'd dreaded and had hoped to avoid.

"We've tried to contact Attorney General Cobb Fordyce this afternoon for a statement on the unexplained death of Jay Burgess, but Mr. Fordyce was unavailable for comment. As many of you may recall, Fordyce and Burgess were two of the four men who valiantly saved lives, at tremendous risk to their own, during the Charleston police station fire five years ago."

Cut to file footage of the building in full blaze, surrounded by fire trucks spraying water on an inferno that had burned out of control. Then, appearing on the screen was a photo of himself, Jay Burgess, Patrick Wickham, and George McGowan, oxygen masks strapped over their smoke-stained faces, their clothing charred, hair singed, heads bowed, and shoulders slumped in abject fatigue.

That picture had made the front page of *The New York Times* in addition to every newspaper in the South. National magazines had printed it with stories that extolled their bravery. The photographer had been nominated for a Pulitzer.

"Attorney General Fordyce was working for the Charleston County DA's office at that time," the reporter explained when they came back to him on camera. "The other three men were police officers. Jay Burgess is the second hero of that day to die. Patrick Wickham, tragically, was killed in the line of duty barely a year following the fire.

"Yesterday, I spoke with George

McGowan, now a businessman in Charleston. I asked him to comment on his fellow hero's death. He declined to appear on camera but told me that Jay Burgess was the best friend a man could ever hope to have and that he will be missed by everyone who knew him."

The reporter then pitched it back to the anchors in the studio, who commented on the poignant and dramatic elements of the story. The segment ended on the legendary photograph, the studio camera going in for a close-up on Jay Burgess's face, where there was a reflection of the flames in his eyes and tear tracks in the soot and smoke stains on his cheeks.

Cobb clicked the remote, and the image blinked out. He loathed that damn photograph. Because of the boost it had given his career, people expected a framed copy of it to be prominently displayed in his office. And that was precisely why he didn't have one.

He left his desk chair and moved to the window. As expected, news vans were lined up along the curb; reporters from various stations across the state were doing stand-ups with the capitol serving as backdrop.

The police station fire. It was like a recurring nightmare. Every so often it would come around again. This time, Jay Burgess's death had resurrected interest in it. Cobb wished for nothing more than that it would never be mentioned again. He wanted it kept out of the media, which seemed to relish replaying footage, retelling the story, showing that damn immortalized picture. He wished for voters not to be reminded that, were it not for that fire, he might not occupy this office.

Most of all, he wished not to be reminded of that himself.

CHAPTER 4

Following the press conference, Britt spent the remainder of the day at home.

She fielded telephone calls. Some were from acquaintances, others from reporters. All wanted the lowdown, the nitty-gritty on her night with Jay Burgess. Her acquaintances were only slightly more subtle in their approach than the brash reporters. They expressed shock over her situation and outrage that she was being placed on the defensive. But behind their commiserations she sensed a raging curiosity to know what had *really* happened. Weary of repeating herself, she stopped answering the phone.

The only person she wished would

call was Bill Alexander, telling her that her urinalysis had revealed traces of Rohypnol, one of the very effective date rape drugs, which sometimes remained in the individual's system for as long as seventy-two hours.

When the anticipated call did come, that wasn't his message. "I'm sorry," he said, cutting straight to the chase. "The urinalysis was negative for any of the suspected substances."

Curled up in the corner of her sofa, cell phone in hand, she expelled a long breath. "I didn't really expect otherwise. They act quickly, hit hard, and soon disappear. That's the beauty of them for the son of a bitch who puts one in a woman's drink."

"Yes, well . . ."

He went on to say that he'd received a harsh dressing-down from the chief of police, as well as the district attorney's office, for conducting the press conference. "They said I might have cleared it with them first. I reminded them that you are not a suspect of a crime, that, indeed, it hasn't yet been determined that a crime was committed, and that you were exercising your First Amendment right to free speech."

"Ooh. I bet that scared them."

Apparently he knew she was being droll. "The point is," he continued peevishly, "you're not a favorite among officers of the CPD, especially Detectives Clark and Javier. They suggested to me, in very stern language, that you deliberately impeded their investigation."

Calling the press conference had been a calculated risk. She'd realized it probably wouldn't go over well with the police department. But she'd wanted to go on record—public record—that ingestion of a drug was the most plausible explanation for her lost memory of the night Jay died. Now that the urinalysis had come back negative, she was especially glad that she'd gone public with her suspicion.

"If I have to, I'll submit to an MRI to prove I don't have a brain tumor or some other affliction that caused me to black out."

It was the lawyer's turn to be droll. "There was the scotch."

She started to ask him whose side he

was on but decided not to waste her flagging energy. "Jay was my friend, and I grieve his passing. He had terminal cancer and died in his sleep, which many would consider a blessing. But because I'm a TV personality, and he was a hero, and we apparently slept together, his death has been turned into a media event. For his sake, I resent that. It dishonors his passing."

"But you can understand the police department's duty to determine exactly what happened to him."

"Certainly. What I can't understand is why that duty doesn't extend to determining what happened to *me.*"

"The significant difference is obvious, isn't it? You're alive."

That conversation left her feeling angry and dejected. If her own lawyer didn't see her as a victim, how could she convince the police of it? Maybe she shouldn't have been so quick to judge the motives of the friends who'd phoned her today. Perhaps their concern was genuine. Maybe she'd only imagined that their calls were ill-disguised fishing expeditions for salacious details.

She was in desperate need of staunch allies who wouldn't question her claim of a memory loss or, more important, her integrity. She didn't have the standard support group—parents and siblings, a spouse. She didn't have a chaplain to give her advice and assurance.

But what she did have was a list of prominent people who owed her a favor. In addition to hard news reports, she often did personality profiles or human interest stories. The subjects for these reports were people who, in her opinion, deserved recognition for a job well done. Rarely, if ever, did she cash in these IOUs. But now was the time.

She called the first name on her list.

"Judge Mellors's office."

"Hello. Is the judge available?"

"Who's calling, please?"

She identified herself and was told to hold on. When the assistant came back on the line, she was effusively apologetic. The judge had a very full schedule for the remainder of the afternoon. "So much is happening, with the presidential appointment."

"I'm sure," Britt said, sensing a brush-off. When the president had nominated Judge Mellors for the U.S. District Court, Britt had covered the story, including a lengthy interview. She'd wrapped up the story by saying, "The Senate vote on Judge Mellors's nomination is sure to be only a matter of protocol."

Apparently the judge wished it to remain only a matter of protocol and didn't want even the slightest association with someone caught in a scandalous news story.

Next Britt tried to speak with the owner of a private insurance company who had exposed the deliberate errors and omissions of giant insurance carriers. His allegations had resulted in lawsuits and costly countersuits. When he ultimately won, Britt did a news feature on him, extolling him as a David who'd gone up against Goliath. He'd said, "If there's ever anything I can do for you . . ."

But when she called, like the judge,

he was too busy to speak to her. Or so she was told.

A surgeon who devoted half his time to indigent patients. A couple who'd begun a foundation for juvenile diabetes following the death of their child. A pilot who had safely landed a disabled airplane, sparing the lives of all onboard.

She worked her way down the list. To no avail. Either everyone in Charleston was incredibly busy that afternoon or she had gone from superstar to leper the moment she woke up in bed with Jay Burgess dead beside her.

Finally, she called the general manager of the TV station, to thank him for responding so quickly to her plea for help that morning. "Mr. Alexander was a godsend." That was a huge stretch, but she said it with as much sincerity as she could muster.

"This is a messy business, Britt."

"Yes it is. I'm not enjoying it at all."

"I gave my okay for our station to cover the press conference. I question that decision now."

That surprised her. "Oh? Why?"

"People could accuse us of partial reporting."

"Our reporters' questions were as direct and incisive as any."

"Some don't see it that way."

"Like who?"

"Police department personnel. People in local government. Jay Burgess was a hero. Folks don't take well to him being accused of drugging a woman to get her into bed."

"I made a point of *not* accusing Jay."

"That's what you said, but folks aren't stupid. They can read between the lines."

"I never—"

"Anyhow, I'm glad you called. I was going to call you later this evening."

"I appreciate your concern."

There was a brief but significant pause. "Actually, Britt, I was going to call and tell you not to bother coming to work tomorrow."

What they said about the rug being jerked out from under you was an apt analogy. One moment, she was simply worried. The next, she was falling, flailing, knowing that rock bottom was somewhere beneath her and she was closing in on it fast.

She was stunned beyond speech, or breath, or thought. Of all the things he could have said to her, this was the most unexpected. Surely she hadn't heard him correctly. Was he truly asking her—no, *directing* her—not to report to work as usual?

Finding her voice, she said, "I'm touched by your thoughtfulness, but I'm fine. Honestly I am. I want to work. I need to."

And that was true. If she didn't continue doing her job, people would assume that she was hiding, that she had something to hide. She didn't, and she didn't want it to appear that way. Besides, she would go mad if she spent another day cooped up inside her house, waiting for something to happen.

"Take some time off, Britt," he said. "Take a leave of absence. Until further notice."

Her mouth opened and closed several times before she was able to ask, "Are you firing me?"

"No! Hell, no. Did you hear me say that?"

I'm not stupid. I can read between the lines. "How long will this leave of absence last?"

"For however long it takes to clear up this mess. Let's wait and see what happens in the next couple days. Then we'll regroup."

The escape hatch he'd left for himself was bigger than the Grand Canyon. He then became parental and expansive, offering his and the station's unlimited help with anything she needed. "During the leave, you'll be paid full salary," he assured her. Just before saying goodbye, he encouraged her to eat well and get plenty of rest. Had he been there in person, he might have given her a patronizing pat on the head before beating a hasty retreat.

She hung up, furious over his hypocrisy. Britt Shelley had been caught in a compromising situation. Locally, that was big news. Her station would have the inside track, giving their newsroom a distinct advantage over its competitors as well as an instant boost in ratings.

The GM was licking his chops over the furor she'd caused while at the same time distancing himself from it. If something really unsavory was forthcoming, his news staff would be first on the scene to cover the story, but he wouldn't want her shadow of disrepute to fall on his station.

But in addition to her anger, she felt abandoned. Without her work, she truly was at loose ends and lacking any bastion of support. She watched the highlights of her press conference on the evening news and concluded that she'd come across as sincere in her sorrow over Jay's sudden death, and truthful in her allegation that she couldn't remember anything because she'd been drugged.

But she wasn't naïve. People were more likely to suspect the worst than to believe the best.

Darkness fell, and her spirits sank further. Telling herself she was hungry, she heated a Lean Cuisine but finished less than half of it. She took a long bath but couldn't really relax. Her mind returned again and again to that night. She'd already gone through it a thousand times, from the moment she entered The Wheelhouse until she woke up the following morning.

Hours of time were missing from her memory, hours during which anything could have happened. She didn't remember having sex with Jay, but she didn't remember drinking the scotch, either, and obviously she had.

If Jay hadn't given her the drug, who had? And for what purpose? The possibilities caused shudders of revulsion. Did she want to remember? Or was it a blessing that she couldn't recall what had been done to her while she was stripped naked and incapable of protecting herself?

She had gone to her gynecologist and requested an examination. Britt had insisted the doctor prepare a rape kit, in case the need for it should ever arise. The doctor did as she requested, swabbing her mouth, vagina, and anus, all the while telling Britt that the chances of the swabs providing any conclusive evidence of rape were slim. She had showered. Too much time had passed.

At least she was comforted to learn that any sexual congress hadn't been violent. She'd suffered no apparent physical damage.

Even if she hadn't been sexually abused, she'd been emotionally and psychologically violated, and because she couldn't remember it and deal with it, the assault continued. Sitting in her bathtub, knees to her chest, her head resting on them, she cried so hard her sobs echoed off the walls. She cried until she had no tears left.

Eventually she got out of the tub and prepared for bed, then went through her house turning out lights. She peered out her front windows to make certain that some resourceful reporter hadn't discovered where she lived. It would have been difficult, because Britt Shelley was a professional name, not her real one. All her tax records, deeds, debts, and such were in her legal birth name.

Her phone number wasn't listed under either name, and she received her mail at a post office box. Only her most trusted acquaintances knew her address. She'd been able to elude reporters when she left the police station after being questioned the last time, so she didn't think she'd been followed. Nevertheless, she checked to make sure.

The street was dark and quiet.

Later, she would marvel that she had managed to go to sleep at all, much less fall into a slumber so deep that she hadn't heard the chirp of the alarm when the contact was broken, hadn't sensed him looming over her bed, hadn't been signaled of his intrusion in any way until he clamped his hand over her mouth.

"Turn it off." A growl close to her ear. *"Turn it off!"*

He shoved the portable keypad into her hand. Terrified, she fumbled with the rubberized digits, trying to remember the duress code, which would signal the monitoring agency that she was indeed being forced to disengage the alarm. But she couldn't remember anything except her standard code.

How long had it been chirping? When would the actual alarm go off? *Please, God. Now! Now!*

"The code." His breath was hot on her neck. "Do it."

Over the back of his gloved hand she could see the lighted numbers. She punched in the correct sequence, and the chirping stopped. He relaxed, marginally, but the hand across her mouth did not.

With his free hand, he tossed back the covers and jerked her from the bed. She stumbled, fell, hard and hurtfully, but freely. His hand no longer over her mouth, she screamed, then scrambled across the floor.

He grabbed her hair, causing her to scream again. "Shut up!" he commanded as he hauled her up by her hair and clamped his hand over her mouth again.

She thrust her elbow back as hard as she could and got some satisfaction from his grunt of pain.

That was the last thing Britt heard before her world faded to black.

When she came to, she was lying down on her side.

She ached all over and her head was

throbbing. Additionally, every hair follicle had its individual pinprick of pain. Her feet were bound, her hands tightly secured behind her back. She had been gagged by something fabric, maybe a handkerchief, that had been twisted into a tight rope and placed in her mouth like a horse's bit. She could push her tongue against it, but she couldn't work her jaw.

Something had been placed over her head like an executioner's hood. Or like the hood of one about to be executed. The thought filled her with terror.

Instinct told her she was in the backseat of a car, although it wasn't moving. Had she come to when it stopped?

Must have been, because seconds after she regained consciousness, a car door opened near her head. Through the cloth hood, she felt the shift of air, which she gratefully breathed in through her nostrils. Besides blinding her, the hood made her claustrophobic.

She remained still and limp, feigning unconsciousness. Besides, to try to fight would be futile. She couldn't move her limbs at all.

Hands gripped her under her arms

and hauled her out of the car, then left her lying on the ground. Beneath her bare legs she could feel dirt, pebbles, dry, spiky vegetation. She heard footsteps, the jingle of keys, another car door being opened. Then he was back, sliding his arms beneath her shoulders and knees and lifting her. She was carried a short distance. This vehicle was larger, taller than the first; she could tell that because it was an effort for him to hoist her dead weight into the front seat. She allowed herself to slump to her left side.

"Stop faking it," he said. "I know you're conscious."

All the same, she lay perfectly still, listening, trying to do what women were advised to do if ever in this situation.

Don't get into the car with your abductor. She already was.

Try to get the keys from him and use them as a weapon. Impossible.

Use your senses to follow your trail. With her hands bound, she could touch nothing except the upholstery of the seat. Leather. Which she could also tell by the smell. She couldn't see. She could taste only the gag, but that didn't tell her much except that it was clean. It tasted slightly of detergent.

However, she could hear, so she concentrated on cataloging the sounds.

A car door closed. More footsteps. The driver's door on her left opened and he got in, obviously behind the steering wheel, and set something in the foot well in front of her. He shut the driver's door.

Suddenly his weight was pressing down on her and she thought, *This is it.*

But he was only leaning across her to reach the seat belt. He slid his other hand beneath her and groped around looking for the other part of the buckle. "You could make this easier if you'd sit up."

She didn't move or give him any indication that she'd heard, believing her only defense right now was to remain completely passive, even if it meant being manhandled.

"Suit yourself." He groped some more. Finally finding the other half of the seat belt beneath her left breast, he clicked the latch and moved off her. She heard him fasten his own seat belt, then he started the car.

"It's a ride from here."

The road was rough. The vehicle jounced along over potholes and bumps. Several times she would have fallen out of the seat were it not for the seat belt around her. If he'd planned on killing her, at least right away, he wouldn't have taken the precaution to fasten it. Would he?

Who was he? Why her? Ransom?

She was a celebrity, of sorts. Was he a nutcase trying to make a name for himself before taking her life and then his own in a dramatic final act? Or was this a completely random abduction?

Horror stories, some of which she had reported on herself, flashed through her mind. Sometimes psychos treated their hostages kindly, even lovingly, before slaying them by the most brutal means.

Damned if she would go down without a fight.

But how to fight? Unfortunately she didn't know how long she'd been unconscious before he'd stopped to switch vehicles. It could have been minutes or hours. She could detect nothing of where this switch had taken place, knowing only that the road to it was unpaved.

Identifiable sounds hadn't given away the location. She hadn't heard the swishing noises of cars speeding along a nearby freeway, or the slapping of water against a shore, airplanes taking off and landing, or anything else that gave her a clue. Nor could she determine the direction in which they were traveling now.

However, now that she was conscious, she could keep track of time to approximate how far they traveled. She began counting out a fifteen-minute interval.

Before she reached fifteen minutes, the vehicle turned off the rough road onto one that was much smoother.

It was hard to keep count. He'd tuned the radio to a country music station that played its repertoire without commercial breaks. But she focused her mind on her counting and tried to tune out the beats of the various songs.

The first fifteen minutes passed. Then another fifteen.

Well into the third segment, she lost count. The effort of holding herself perfectly still had caused her muscles to cramp. The seat belt buckle was gouging her. Her head hurt. Her hands and feet were numb from lack of blood circulation.

When she thought she couldn't stand these discomforts any longer and was thinking about wiggling to let him know she was conscious, the vehicle went into a sharp turn that tightened the seat belt around her. They were on another bumpy road. But they didn't go far before they slowed, then came to a full stop.

Her whole left side, from shoulder to ankle, tingled from lying in the same position for so long, but still she didn't move, not even when he slid his hand beneath her again to release the seat belt.

He got out. Besides his footsteps, she could hear a loud chorus of insects and amphibians. He opened the passenger door. "Want to sit up now?"

She didn't respond.

He sighed, then grabbed her around

her right biceps and hauled her into a sitting position. Her head teetered as though it were about to roll off her shoulders. Nerve endings screamed in pain. She bit into the gag to keep from moaning.

He lifted her from the vehicle and carried her up a set of three steps. He had to juggle a bit in order to open a door, then with her still in his arms, went through it sideways like a groom carrying his bride.

The air inside was hot and stuffy. The floor beneath his footsteps sounded as though there was hollow space beneath it. She heard something being dropped with a thud. Then she was deposited ungently into a hard chair.

"You can sit up, or play dead and fall out onto the floor. Where you'll lie till Doomsday, because I'm not lifting you again."

She remained sitting up and heard a snuffle of amusement, along with the soft snick of a light switch. The hood was suddenly pulled off her head. The light pierced her eyes. Reflexively she squeezed them shut, then slowly opened them and blinked her abductor into focus.

He stood directly in front of her, unyielding and unsmiling. “Long time, no see, Ms. Shelley.”

CHAPTER 5

At first, the beard threw her off. Then, looking past it, she recognized the face. Putting a name to it took a moment longer, but finally one emerged from distant memory. Gannon. Raley Gannon.

Identifying him didn't allay her fear. In fact, when he extended his hand toward her, she recoiled, which caused him to frown. He hesitated as though waiting to see just how spooked she was, then reached around to the back of her head, untied the gag, and removed it.

She moistened her lips. Or tried. Her tongue and mouth were dry. When she tried to speak, her voice was a croak. "Have you lost your mind?"

Saying nothing, he turned his back on

her. With his sneaker, he moved aside a small black duffel bag, which must have been what she'd heard drop after he carried her inside. Walking beneath the ceiling fan, he yanked on a string hanging from it. The motor hummed, the blades began to turn, stirring the warm air and cooling it slightly.

They were in what appeared to be a cabin with a living area and kitchen combined into one room. Britt assumed that the open interior doorway led to a bedroom, but it was dark beyond the door. The furniture was old and mismatched, but the place was clean and neat. All the windows were opened. Insects batted against the screens, trying to fly into the light. Beyond the screens, the darkness was absolute, impenetrable, unrelieved by moonlight or man-made lights that she could see.

She was still wearing the camisole and boxer shorts she had gone to bed in, but she also had on a nylon windbreaker that belonged to her. The last time she'd seen it, it had been hanging in her closet. He must have put it on her while she was unconscious.

He took a bottle of water from a vintage refrigerator, uncapped it, and drank thirstily, emptying the entire bottle, which he then tossed into the trash can beneath the sink.

He glanced at her, then got another bottle of water from the fridge and uncapped it as he walked across the room. The ceiling fan fluttered his hair, causing her to notice another distinctive change in his appearance. He used to wear his hair short, almost in a military cut. Now it fell an inch past his collar and over his ears to blend into the beard. She detected a few touches of gray among the wavy, dark strands.

He extended the water bottle toward her mouth.

"You'll have to untie my hands."

"Fat chance."

"I can't—"

"You thirsty or not?" He pressed the top of the plastic bottle against her lips. She took it, gulping until the water began flooding her mouth. She tilted her head back to signal she was finished.

He stopped pouring, but not soon enough. Water dribbled over her chin and onto her chest. Some trickled from the lip of the bottle and splashed onto her bare thigh. She looked down at the spot where several drops beaded on her skin. When she looked back up, she caught him staring at that spot, too. Then his eyes connected with hers.

He moved so quickly, she jumped. "Will you relax?" he said. "I'm not going to hurt you."

"You already have."

He reached toward the back of her head again and dug his fingers into her hair, then tentatively moved them along her scalp until she winced. "You've got a goose egg."

"What did you expect?"

"I expected you to have a goose egg. Because you didn't do what I told you to do. If you'd been quiet and cooperative, I wouldn't have had to clip you."

She started to say that she would be sure to remember that the next time an intruder snatched her from her bed and carried her off in the middle of the night. But she held her tongue.

It couldn't be a coincidence that Raley Gannon had kidnapped her two days after she woke up with Jay Burgess lying dead beside her. She didn't know how the two events were connected, but she knew they must be, and all the implications were frightening.

He disappeared through the darkened doorway. A light came on in the adjacent room. She heard him rustling around, opening doors and closing them, and soon he returned with a bottle of pills. He shook out two tablets and extended them to her. "Take these."

"What are they?"

"Ibuprofen." He turned the bottle so she could read the label. "Generic."

"I'm not taking them."

"How come? Afraid that I switched them with a date rape drug?"

She looked up into his face, and it was remarkable how much he had aged since the last time she'd seen him. It was evidenced by more than just a few gray hairs. His skin was dark from sun exposure. His beard and mustache were as black as any pirate's and concealed his lips, which she imagined were firmly set and slow to smile.

But what really added years were his

eyes. Not only were there pronounced lines radiating from the corners of them but the irises themselves had become hard and cold, as if a pond that in summer was placid and green had now frozen over.

Or maybe they'd always been that way. After all, she'd seen him only a few times and from a distance as he'd dodged reporters. She'd really known him only as the blurred figure fleeing the video camera, as the subject of a hot news story.

If it was retribution he was after, she would just as soon get it over with. "Why did you bring me here?"

"Take a wild guess."

"Jay Burgess."

"Go to the head of the class."

Jay's death had prompted this . . . this whatever it was. Jay's death had brought Raley Gannon out of obscurity. He had left Charleston five years ago, never to be heard of again. At least not by her.

Possibly he and Jay had stayed in touch. Jay had never mentioned him, though, and it had never occurred to her to ask him about Raley Gannon. As soon as he was no longer news, she'd forgotten about him.

He bounced the tablets in his palm. "It's going to be a long, uncomfortable night for you. Take the pills."

She hesitated only a second, then opened her mouth.

"No way in hell am I going to let you bite me. Stick out your tongue."

She did. He set the tablets on her tongue, then pressed the water bottle against her lips again. He poured more slowly, she swallowed more easily, until she'd drained the bottle. He turned and walked into the kitchen to throw away the empty bottle.

"Did you . . ." She stumbled over the words, tried again. "Did you have anything to do with what happened to Jay and me night before last?"

"Why would you ask that?"

"Did you?"

On his way back, he dragged a chair from the small dining table and placed it no more than two feet away from the one in which she was sitting. Straddling it backward, he folded his arms over the back of it. "You tell me."

Britt Shelley, Miss Calm, Cool, and Collected when in front of a television camera, was remarkably composed facing her kidnapper, too. Oh, she was afraid, no doubt about that. But she was putting up a good front. He had to give her high marks for not going hysterical the moment she recognized him, which she'd done almost immediately. Although his appearance had changed, she'd placed him. His face anyway.

"Do you remember my name?"

She nodded.

"You should."

It was she who had hammered the last nail into the coffin of his reputation. She'd sealed his fate but good. No telling how many other reputations she had demolished since then. Should he be flattered that she remembered him out of so many? Probably not. Maybe she never forgot the faces and names of the people she destroyed.

"I remember you, Mr. Gannon."

"From five years ago. But your memory can't account for hours of time night before last. Or so you say."

"It's the truth."

"Sounds like an awfully convenient case of amnesia."

He could see that she was plotting the best way to handle him. He could almost follow her thought processes as she considered one tactic and then discarded it in favor of another.

She said, "I'll tell you anything you want to know, if you'll take the tape off my hands and feet."

So, she'd decided to try to bargain. "No deal. Tell me what happened in Jay's place that night."

"If you'll remove—"

"Tell me what happened in Jay's place that night."

"Don't you think I wish I could?"

So much for her bargaining scheme. It gave way to shouting and frustration. Fear, maybe. He saw a tear pick up light in the corner of her eye, which left him unmoved. He'd been looking for it, expecting it.

"You could have saved yourself the dramatic kidnapping, Mr. Gannon. And the gasoline to and from Charleston, and the jail time you're going to serve for this, because it's going to yield nothing. I'm blank, completely blank on what happened after Jay and I got to his town house."

She looked at him imploringly, tilting her head at an angle that looked defenseless, blinking until the tear slipped over her lower lid and rolled down her cheek. "Free my hands and feet. Please."

Bargaining to frustration to tearful appeal in under sixty seconds. The lady had talent. "No."

"I'll tell you anything I can," she said. "I promise. But I'm very uncomfortable. Please."

"No."

She nodded toward his open front door. "Where would I go? I don't even know where I am."

"Tell me what happened at Jay's place."

Her head dropped forward, sending a curtain of pale hair over each shoulder. She remained that way for several seconds, then raised her head and said emphatically, "I can't remember."

Defiance now. She must have read a how-to book. "Tell me what you do remember."

For a full minute, maybe more, they stared across the narrow space separating them. In person, with her face clean and her hair loose, she looked younger than she did on TV. Smaller, too. Her eyes were blue, her gaze steady and guileless, which he knew she must use to her advantage in front of the camera as well as away from it.

The earnestness in her gaze didn't work on him, though. He was immune. She must have sensed that, because she was the first to relent. She didn't break their stare, but she took a swift little breath. "I arrived . . . No, let me back up. I went to The Wheelhouse at Jay's invitation."

She told him that Jay had called her earlier that day, inviting her to join him for a drink, saying he needed to talk to her about something. "He didn't say what. Only that it was important."

She spoke without emotion, almost

by rote. He figured she'd been over this with the police a dozen times already.

"It wasn't like he was asking me for a date," she said. "I hadn't seen him in months. Hadn't talked to him on the telephone. This was the first contact we'd had in a long time. I said, 'Sure, that would be great.' He said seven o'clock. I arrived right on time." She paused for a breath, then asked, "Have you ever been to The Wheelhouse?"

"This evening."

"This evening? You stopped off for a drink before breaking into my house and kidnapping me? Although I suppose felony could be thirsty work."

Ignoring that, he said, "The Wheelhouse didn't open for business until after I'd left Charleston, so I'd never been there. I wanted to see the layout of the place."

"What for?"

"Which table did you sit at?"

"Far corner."

"Right-hand side as you enter? By the window?"

She shook her head. "Left-hand side."

"Okay."

While he was fixing that image in his head, she asked, "How did you know where I lived?"

"I followed you there."

"Today?"

"Five years ago."

He could tell that made her uneasy. She shifted slightly in her seat but didn't comment.

"I knew you'd have an alarm system," he went on. "I also knew that the back door going into the kitchen is probably the one you most frequently use and figured that it would have a delay on it. So I picked the lock."

"You know how to pick locks?"

"The alarm started beeping. I counted on having at least a minute and a half before the actual alarm went off. Most people set the delay for even longer, but I figured I had at least ninety seconds to get you to punch in the code. I also figured that a single woman, living alone, would have a remote-control panel within reach of her bed."

"How did you know I was single and living alone?"

"Jay never dated married women."

She left that alone, saying instead, "Ninety seconds for you to find my bedroom and force me to turn off the alarm. That's not much time. You were awfully sure of my compliance."

"I counted on you being scared."

"I was. Out of my wits."

"So my hunch was right."

"What if I hadn't been scared?" she asked. "What if I'd had a gun at my bedside instead of a remote? I could have killed you."

He glanced around his cabin for effect, then came back to her. "I don't have anything to lose."

That, too, made her uneasy. Her eyes drifted away, then back. "Can't you please release my feet? Just my feet?"

He shook his head.

"They're numb."

"According to the newspaper," he said, "The Wheelhouse was crowded that night."

After a mutinous pause, which didn't faze him, she continued, describing to him the usual happy-hour bar scene.

"The place was packed, but I spotted Jay as soon as I came in. I went—"

"Wait. Were there people at the bar? That's where I sat today. There are twenty or more barstools."

"People were standing three deep behind the stools."

"How many bartenders?"

"I didn't count."

"How many cocktail waitresses?"

"A few. Several. Four, five, half a dozen. I don't know."

"But all of them were busy."

"Extremely. There was noisy chatter, loud music, people—"

"Did you ask a hostess if Jay was there yet?"

"There wasn't anyone at the hostess stand. I told you I spotted him."

"So you didn't announce your arrival in any way?"

"No."

"Did anyone approach you?"

"No."

"Did you attract anyone's notice?"

"No."

He looked her straight in the eye, then deliberately dropped his gaze to her chest, and lower, to her bare thighs. He let his eyes linger there for a noticeable time before lifting them back to her face and silently communicating that he found it hard to believe no one had noticed her.

She squirmed under his gaze. “Look, I’ve been over this time and again with the police. Nothing unusual happened. Nothing.”

“You’re on TV every day. Nobody recognized you? You didn’t make eye contact with anyone besides Jay?”

She closed her eyes as though resetting the scene in her mind and trying to squeeze out a memory. “I think maybe . . . maybe . . .” She opened her eyes but made a small sound of frustration. “Possibly I made eye contact with a man at the bar, but I don’t know if I’m remembering or imagining.”

“Maybe when you’re not trying so hard it will come back to you.” He studied her for several moments, then said softly, “Unless this loss of memory thing is all a hoax and you remember everything.”

If her feet hadn’t been secured, he

thought she would have launched herself out of the chair and straight at him. Her face was flushed with so much anger, he thought she might try to attack him in spite of being hobbled. "Why would I fabricate a memory loss, Mr. Gannon?"

"Well, one good reason would be that you woke up next to a dead guy, and you're covering your ass."

"Nothing I did caused Jay to die."

"Let's say the sex got rowdy or kinky."

"Let's not."

"Before you knew it, your lover wasn't moving. Or you had a lovers' tiff that turned ugly."

"We weren't—"

"Maybe Jay went into cardiac arrest, which freaked you out, and you were useless to try and help him. Anything's possible. You were both drunk on scotch—that was in the newspaper, too—maybe scotch isn't your drink. It makes you wild, irrational, violent. You—"

"None of that happened!"

"How do you know if you can't remember?"

"I would remember if I'd killed a man accidentally or otherwise."

"Are you sure?"

The taunt only maddened her more. "I've had it with this. And with *you.* Get this tape off me!" she yelled.

"You can scream all you want, nobody is going to hear you, and you'll only make that golden throat of yours hoarse. You wouldn't want that to happen."

Blue eyes blazed at him. "I'm going to see you in prison for this. I can't wait to cover your trial. I'll be there with a microphone and camera the day they lock you up."

"Do you know how Jay died?"

"No!"

"Did you kill him?"

"No!"

"Did you fuck him?"

CHAPTER 6

The vulgarity shocked the anger out of her.

"What?"

"Want me to spell it?"

She looked away, then down at the floor. "I need to use the bathroom."

The crudity had been intentional, and it had served its purpose. Anger sometimes escalated into stubbornness. If she went tight-lipped on him out of sheer obstinance, then he'd gain nothing.

Now that she was subdued, he could be more lenient. A little more. He knelt down in front of her and used his pocketknife to slice through the duct tape around her ankles, then peeled it off.

"Thank you." She tried to stand but dropped back into the chair. "My feet have gone to sleep."

He cupped her elbow and steadied her as she stood up and took a tentative step. "Ouch."

"Wiggle your toes."

It was a long minute before she was able to put her full weight on her feet. He kept his hand around her elbow as they shuffled toward the bedroom, where the bathroom was.

"Have you lived here since you left Charleston?"

"Yes."

"Alone?"

"A raccoon hung around for a few months."

"You didn't get married?"

"No."

They were in the bedroom now. He reached through the open bathroom door to switch on the light. This afternoon before he left, he'd gone over the fixtures with a disinfectant solution. He'd hung a clean towel on the bar. A new roll of toilet paper was on the spool.

He'd put an unused bar of soap in a dish he pilfered from the kitchen.

All the while he was cleaning, he'd asked himself why he was bothering. It wasn't like she was going to be a guest. But now he was glad he'd gone to the effort. It made the room, and by extension him, more presentable.

"Weren't you engaged?" she asked.

"Yes." He stood aside and motioned her into the bathroom. He could read the question in her eyes, but he wasn't going to discuss his broken engagement. Not yet. "Hurry up. We've got a lot to talk about."

"You haven't freed my hands."

"You'll manage."

"I can't go with my hands bound behind my back."

"I bet you can if you have to go bad enough."

Once she'd cleared the bathroom door, she kicked it shut. He turned the knob and pushed it open. "The door stays open."

"That isn't necessary."

"It is if you want to use the bathroom."

"You're punishing me, aren't you? For . . . for before. You're humiliating me out of spite, when all I did was my job."

"If you're not going to pee, back in the chair you go."

She thought it over, then said, "Can you at least close the door halfway?"

He conceded her that much. While she was attending to her business, he moved restlessly around the bedroom. He went over to the window and looked out on a night that was black and still. He fiddled with the sash on the window shade, then batted at it angrily and moved to the bed and sat down.

Damn right he was holding a grudge against her. Giving her a taste of humiliation. *Doesn't taste good, does it, Miss Shelley?* If she felt helpless and out of control, good. Because that was how he'd felt five years ago, when she'd entertained her television audience with his personal crisis. Smugly she'd broadcast his degradation with the enticement of a carnival barker.

Thinking of it now made his hands close into fists. He wouldn't hit her, but he might hit the wall, pound at it in outrage over the injustice of what had happened to him and how Britt Shelley had contributed.

With him in this fractious frame of mind, it wasn't very smart of her to mention Hallie. *Weren't you engaged?* Not smart of her at all to reopen that wound.

He was sitting on the edge of his bed when she used her foot to open the bathroom door. "You—" The word died on her lips. His expression must have conveyed to her the bitterness roiling inside him. He certainly didn't try to conceal it.

She wavered there on the threshold between the two rooms, looking ready to duck back into the bathroom for safety. Enjoying her apprehension, he stood up slowly. "Turn around."

"What for?"

"Turn around," he repeated with emphasis.

Her face filled with distress. "Mr. Gannon, please. I know you probably think that I . . . that the news coverage I gave the . . . the fix you got yourself into was perhaps . . ."

"Exploitative?"

"I was young and green and terribly ambitious. I was trying to build an audience."

"At my expense." He began walking toward her and she started backing up.

"It was a long time ago."

"My memory of it is fresh."

"You don't want to do anything now that would get you into even more trouble." She cried out when he put his hands on her shoulders and turned her around. "Oh, God," she whimpered. "Please don't hurt me."

Putting his mouth directly above her ear, he whispered, "Relax, Ms. Shelley. I only wanted to check your hands, make sure you weren't bringing something out with you." He released her abruptly.

She turned, took several deep breaths, swallowed. He watched as her fear evolved into anger. "You deliberately frightened me into thinking—"

"What? That I'm actually the brute you painted me to be?"

"What did you think I might sneak out? A *razor*?"

He didn't respond. He hadn't brought

her here to bicker. "We're wasting time. Go sit down."

"How long must we keep this up?"

"Until I've got from you everything I need."

"Everything you need for what? What is this leading to? The kidnapping, the Gestapo-type interrogation. What do you plan to do?"

"I plan to make you sit down." He hitched his chin toward the living area. "If you don't sit down willingly, I plan to tie you to the chair."

She marched back to the chair. Once she was seated, he knelt in front of her and took a roll of duct tape from the black bag. She tucked her feet beneath the chair. "Please. I promise not to get up until you tell me I can. Please."

After a short staring contest, he relented and resumed his place in the other chair. "You never answered my question. Did you have sex with Jay?"

She studied a button on his shirt. At least her gaze landed in that vicinity of his chest and remained there. "I swear to you, I don't know. My gynecologist examined me, but all she could determine was that there hadn't been any . . . any trauma to the tissue."

Raley gnawed the inside of his cheek, ruminating on that, wondering if he believed her, wondering why he gave a damn whether she and Jay had had sex or not.

"You joined him at the table in the corner of the bar. How was he?"

She laughed softly, but there was a touch of sadness behind it. "Like Jay. Handsome and well dressed. Charming. Flirtatious."

"That's our Jay."

She looked at him curiously. "Was he always like that? Even when you were boys?"

"Always. What did you have to drink?"

She seemed about to ask more about their boyhood friendship but answered his question instead. "He was drinking vodka, maybe gin. Something clear, on the rocks. He'd had two or three. He ordered another when I ordered my wine."

"From one of the waitresses?"

"She came to our table."

"Did the same waitress deliver your drinks, or another?"

"I'm almost certain it was the same one. I remember thanking her when my wine appeared, but I was involved in my conversation with Jay, so I didn't really take much notice."

"What happened then, after your drinks came?"

"We clinked glasses."

"Do you think Jay slipped something into your wine?"

"Why would he?"

"Do you think he did?"

"No."

"Did he have an opportunity to?"

"No. We—"

Suddenly she stopped, her gaze turning inward.

"What?"

"I . . ." She looked at him, wet her lips. "I just remembered something. I took a cardigan with me. I always do. Air-conditioning."

"So?"

"The bar was crowded, warm, so I didn't need my sweater. I remember turning away to drape it over the back of the chair. The chair had a curved wood back, sort of like that one," she said, nodding toward the one he was sitting in. "My sweater slipped off onto the floor. I bent down to pick it up."

"Giving Jay enough time to drop something into your wineglass?"

"I don't know. I suppose. But he would have had to be incredibly quick and dexterous." She shook her head. "I don't believe he did. And, anyway, why would he?"

"Right. When he knew you'd go to bed with him without being drugged."

She stared back at him with teeming animosity, but she didn't address the insult. He didn't apologize, but he did say, "I don't think Jay put anything in your drink, either. Resorting to that would be demeaning to his ego. He was awfully proud of his ability to get women into his bed." He let that sink in, then said, "If not Jay, who?"

"I have no idea. Maybe someone just playing an ugly prank. But I'm convinced it happened at The Wheelhouse. I was already feeling funny when we left there. By the time we reached Jay's town house, I wasn't well at all."

"Did you tell Jay you didn't feel well?"

"I don't believe so. I was anxious to hear what he was about to tell me. I didn't want him to cut the evening short, saying it could wait for another time."

"Right. You wouldn't let anything stand in the way of getting a big story."

She fired back, "You're damn right I wouldn't!"

Raley could have said how well he knew the lengths to which she would go to nail a story, but he let it pass. "Jay lured you with—"

"He didn't *lure* me. He said he needed to talk to me. When he told me about his cancer, I thought that was the purpose of the meeting." She paused, and when she spoke again, her voice had altered, become softer. "Did you know he was sick?"

Something inside him twisted, but he kept his features schooled. "Not until I heard he'd died in bed with you."

"The two of you didn't stay in touch after you left Charleston?"

"No."

"I see."

"No you don't."

"He was your best friend."

"*Was.*"

"You hadn't seen or spoken to him in five years?"

"No."

"What caused the split? Your leaving? Or the events leading up to it?"

He wasn't yet ready to talk about that. He had to get his facts straight on how Jay had died before he could address how he'd lived. "Jay told you he was dying." She nodded. "Do you think he told you because he wanted a mercy fuck?"

She gave him a withering look. "That's such a juvenile question. Such a *man thing* to conclude. I thought so when the two detectives asked me the same."

"What did you tell them?"

"I told them no. Jay didn't have to resort to pity any more than he would resort to date rape drugs."

"That's such a woman thing to conclude."

"He didn't."

"Spoken with the voice of experience."

She was about to retort to that but

changed her mind and only stared at him, seething but silent.

"So he didn't get you there to tell you he had only a few weeks to live."

"No." She told him that Jay had dismissed her sympathy. "He said he didn't have time to talk about cancer and funerals. He said that he had something much more important to tell me, and that the story he had to tell would launch me straight into a network job."

Raley waited, his heart knocking with anticipation. After several seconds passed, he said, "So what was the career-making story?"

"I don't know."

"Bullshit!" He came out of his chair so quickly, she jumped in alarm. "I'm not a competing reporter. I'm not gonna call a network and get the jump on you. You can have your precious story, I just want to know what Jay told you."

She came out of her chair to face him squarely. "Nothing! He became—"

"What?"

"Nervous. On edge."

He barked a laugh. "Jay?"

"Jay."

"Nerves of steel, always in control, never ruffled Jay? *That* Jay Burgess?"

"Yes. I realize it sounds out of character—"

"No, it sounds ludicrous."

"I'm telling you, he got jittery and began to sweat."

He raked the fingers of both hands through his hair, holding it off his heated face for several seconds before letting it go. He propped his hands on his hips and stared at her. "You're a real piece of work, aren't you? You see an opportunity and you grab it. You've got everybody by the balls and you're loving it. The police. Me. Everyfuckin'body. You're milking this thing for all it's worth, making up this elaborate story about memory loss when what really happened is that you and Jay got drunk together and then you screwed him to death."

"I don't give a damn what you think about me," she said, one angry word tumbling after the next. *"You,* who live out here in this . . . this . . . shanty that looks like Tobacco Road, have no room to talk to anybody about ambition and what one does with one's life. Think what you want about me."

"Thank you, I will. I do."

"But for whatever else I am, I'm not a liar. If you dragged me out here to beat the truth out of me, then you've committed a crime for nothing. You could have got the same truth from the newspaper. I went on record today at that news conference with the truth. You can like it or not, accept it or not, believe it or not. I really don't give a damn."

She took another step so they were standing almost toe to toe. "Jay was on the verge of divulging something vitally important to him. But he became nervous and distracted. He began to take notice of people at nearby tables. He glanced toward the bar several times. Even when he was talking to me, he was looking past me, over my—"

She broke off and for several seconds continued to stare into Raley's face, but he thought she wasn't really seeing him anymore. She backed away and sat down hard in the chair, staring into near space.

He returned to his chair and sat down,

keeping his gaze fixed on her but remaining silent, not wanting to scare away a memory that was creeping back into her consciousness. He had hoped that prodding her, hammering at her as he'd done, would shake loose a recollection. Apparently it had. He waited.

Finally she began to speak. "I once interviewed a man who agreed to talk to me about a labor strike, but only if he could remain anonymous. My sound tech and I electronically altered his voice, and he wore a hood during the interview. And even then, all the while I was interviewing him, his eyes weren't on me. Through the holes in the hood I could see them looking past me, just beyond my shoulder, anxiously darting from side to side. I even turned my head once to see what he was looking at. I didn't see anything to be afraid of. But he did."

Her eyes pulled Raley back into focus. "That's how it was with Jay. I thought his restlessness meant he wasn't feeling well, or that he'd become too warm in the crowded bar, or that, despite his dismissal of the cancer, he'd become upset when we talked about it. But now, I think he was afraid."

"Of someone in the bar?"

"What else could it have been?"

"Did you ever turn and look behind you?"

"Actually, I was about to. Maybe Jay sensed it, because he reached for my hand and asked if we could move to his place to continue our conversation. He left money on the table, and we headed for the exit."

"Did either of you speak to anyone as you left the bar?"

"No. Except to excuse ourselves as we made our way through the crowd."

"No cross words with anyone? No hostile exchange of any kind?"

"Not even a dirty look."

"See anyone who looked suspicious?"

"Suspicious?"

"Sinister. Up to no good."

"I have only blurred images." After a moment, she shook her head. "No, I don't recall anyone with clarity."

"Anyone follow you and Jay from the bar?"

"No." Then hesitantly she said, "I don't think so."

"But you're not sure?"

"A memory flickered, but . . ."

He could tell she was trying to snag it, hold on to it, but she failed to. "I don't think anyone followed us, but I can't be positive." She brought her eyes back to his. "I explained all this to the police. Nothing, *nothing* out of the ordinary happened between the table and the exit."

"What about on your walk to Jay's town house? Did you meet anyone along the way?"

"I don't believe so, although I don't have a sharp recollection of the trip. I was well looped by then. I vaguely remember going inside his town house and immediately making my way to the sofa, wanting to sit down. *Needing* to. I wondered how I could have become so drunk over one glass of wine, and I didn't even finish the glass."

"So you went to the sofa and . . . ?"

"And, that's it. I can't remember anything else."

"Did Jay join you on the sofa?"

"I'm not sure."

"Did you start making out?"

"I've just told you I don't even remember if he sat down beside me."

"Do you remember drinking scotch?"

"No. But I must have because I threw it up the next morning."

"Jay was good at talking women into doing things they were reluctant to do. Like drinking too much, taking off their clothes. He was an expert at getting a woman out of her clothes. He boasted about his technique." He watched her closely, interested to see how she would respond.

"If he exercised his technique on me, I don't remember it. I don't know how I became undressed, or how we got into bed, or what we did there." Suddenly there was a catch in her voice. Her blue eyes filled. "Can you imagine how awful that is for me? I realize you have a low opinion of me, but no one deserves to be taken advantage of that way. I don't know what was done to me that night, but the possibilities of what could have been done without my knowledge or consent make me sick and afraid."

He didn't say anything for several moments, then asked her, "Do you think Jay took advantage of you?"

She drew in a deep breath and let it out before she raised her head. The tears were gone, but her nose was running. "I can't imagine that he would, but I don't know," she finished huskily.

He got up and went into the bathroom, pulled a length of toilet paper off the roll, and brought it back with him. He folded it into a square and pressed it against her nose. "Blow." Her eyes went wide and she shook her head. "Don't be silly. Blow."

She blew. He wiped her nose, then went into the kitchen to throw the tissue away and asked her if she wanted more water. She declined.

He returned to his chair. "Tell me about when you woke up."

She described how Jay was lying on his side, facing away from her. Her head was muzzy, she was confused. She collected her clothes, finding some of them in the living room, then went into the bathroom, where she threw up.

"It should have occurred to me then

that I'd been drugged, but this was Jay Burgess. A police officer. A man I knew and trusted. I saw the empty bottle of scotch and blamed myself for losing control and doing something stupid."

She paused and gave him a pointed look. "Which is not my m.o. I'm not in the habit of drinking myself unconscious and waking up in a man's bed with no recollection of how I got there. In fact, nothing even remotely like that has ever happened to me before. I like being in control."

"That I believe." He said it in a way that didn't flatter her, and he figured she caught the nuance because she frowned.

"Anyway," she continued, "I used the bathroom and showered, the two things you're not supposed to do if you suspect you've been given a date rape drug. Consequently, I can't prove that I was."

"When did you lose your virginity?"

The question took her aback. "What?"

"How many years have you been having sex?"

"None of your damn business."

"It's not that I care, I'm just finding it hard to believe that you can sit there and with a straight face tell me you don't know whether or not you and Jay did the nasty thing."

"A condom foil was found on the sofa."

"Ahh. So you did."

"It would appear so, but I don't know. My doctor—"

"Why would you need clinical proof? Wouldn't you *know*? Even hours later, wouldn't you just feel it?"

"Would *you*?"

"I'm not a woman! My body doesn't get penetrated."

She bit back whatever she was about to say. Looking away from him, she compressed her lips and forcibly composed herself. When she looked back at him, she said, "It didn't feel to me as though we'd been intimate. But I can't swear to it. And does it even matter? Isn't that a little beside the point?"

"I guess so. Jay still wound up dead."

He stood up and took his knife from his pants pocket, then stepped around to the back of her chair. "Thank you," she said with meaning as he cut through the tape binding her hands.

"Don't get too excited. We're not finished yet." He wrapped his hand around her biceps and headed for the bedroom, hauling her along behind him.

"What are you— Wait! You said you wouldn't hurt me."

"It won't hurt. Unless you fight me."

He gave her a light push that sent her stumbling toward the bed. She broke her fall against it but bounced up and dashed toward the door. He hooked his arm around her waist as she ran past him, lifted her against his hip, and carried her to the bed, unceremoniously dumping her onto it.

Being caught at the waist had knocked the breath from her. It took a couple of seconds for her to regain it, then she was all fight again, kicking at him with all her might, flailing her arms in her effort to connect with his head.

But it was never any real contest. He straddled her thighs to make her thrashing legs ineffectual, then plucked the roll of duct tape from his shirt pocket, where he'd temporarily stowed it. Leaning away from her slapping, scratching hands, he ripped off a strip with his teeth, caught her left hand, and pulled it up to the bedpost. In seconds, he had her wrist taped tightly to the post at the level of the mattress.

He came off her and blotted his cheek with the back of his hand. Seeing fresh blood, he said, "You scratch me again and I'll tape your hand to the top of the headboard. It won't be nearly as comfortable."

"Go to hell."

Confident that she couldn't do too much damage or go very far in the amount of time it would take him to go through the cabin turning out lights, he did so. When he reentered the bedroom, she was standing at the side of the bed, tugging frantically on her left hand as she tore at the tape with the fingernails of her right, accomplishing nothing except to pull the bed several inches away from the wall.

"You plan to drag the bed all the way back to Charleston?"

"Damn you! Let me go!"

Raley unbuttoned his jeans and pushed

them down. That shut her up. She stared at him aghast. "What are you doing?"

"Taking my clothes off, what does it look like?" He toed off his sneakers, stepped out of the jeans, and removed his socks. He unbuttoned the first two buttons of his shirt, pulled it over his head, and tossed it onto the nearest chair, then bent down and picked up the roll of tape.

"Get back on the bed."

She shook her head, then said hoarsely, "No."

He was on her before she could plan an effective defense. In seconds, she was on her back on the bed. He straddled her again while he wrapped the duct tape around their joined wrists, her right to his left. Again he bit off the end with his teeth.

"You might manage to gnaw off the tape on your left wrist," he said, "but you can't get free of me."

"Maybe not," she said between gasps of breath. "But I can make life very unpleasant for you."

He should have recognized her wicked

smile as a warning. As it was, he was almost too late to react when she raised her knee toward his crotch. She missed his balls by a margin so narrow, he caught his breath in anticipation of the pain that, fortunately, never came.

Frustrated that she'd failed, she screamed up at him, "Get off me!"

Instead, he stretched out fully, leaving himself less vulnerable by pinning her legs down with his. She was hampered but not defeated. She continued to buck like a colt, trying to throw him off. He lowered his face to within inches of hers, close enough to exchange angry breaths but far enough so they could keep each other in sharp focus.

"Stop that!" he ordered.

She didn't of course.

"You want to know why I brought you here?"

"I think I know why," she replied, panting from her exertion.

"You don't know shit. I'll clue you in. But you've got to stop fighting me first."

Instantly she became still, but if looks could kill . . .

"I brought you here because I believe

you." Her blue eyes went wide. "I'm probably the only person in the state who does."

"What?" she gasped.

"Yeah. I believe your memory was deliberately wiped clean." He pressed down on her harder, for emphasis, to make certain she was paying attention. "Because the same thing happened to me."

CHAPTER 7

Britt woke up when a shaft of sunlight struck her face. She was lying on her side, facing a window. Through the screen she could see dense green forest, the leaves of a wisteria vine fluttering against the post of an old-fashioned clothesline, and a predatory bird doing spirals against the cloudless sky.

Remembering where she was, she rolled onto her back and came up on her elbows. Daylight did little to enhance the room. It was small, accommodating only the bed, a chair, and a TV tray that served as a nightstand, on which was a gooseneck reading lamp. In the corner was a large bureau with six deep drawers.

The room had no charm except for the patterned quilt covering her legs and feet. It appeared to have been hand stitched, and the fabric remnants from which it was made were color coordinated.

The only other decorative item was a sweet potato vine growing from the tuber that had been suspended in a jar of water sitting on top of the bureau. Its roots had formed a thick nest inside the jar, while the leafy vine nearly filled the corner all the way to the ceiling, its tendrils curling around a network of string tacked to the wall.

The room was humble but tidy. His clothes were no longer on the floor or in the chair where he'd left them last night when he joined her on the bed.

Her hands were free, although she still had bands of tape around the wrists. The edges trailed fine, white threads. She pushed off the quilt and got out of bed. The door to the living area was closed, but through it she could smell fresh coffee. The aroma made her mouth water.

After using the bathroom, she hesitantly opened the bedroom door. He was standing with his shoulder propped against the front door jamb, staring through the screen as he sipped from a large mug of coffee.

The same thing happened to me.

Following that startling statement, he'd continued staring down at her for several beats, then he'd rolled off her, switched off the gooseneck lamp, and stretched out on his back beside her. They had touched nowhere except the backs of their hands that were taped together.

He hadn't moved. She hadn't dared. In minutes he'd been breathing evenly, obviously asleep. Impossible as it seemed now, she'd soon fallen asleep, too.

Sensing her presence, he turned. As they continued to look at each other, she wondered about his level of hostility this morning. He would hold a grudge forever, that much she knew. But if he'd meant to get retribution with bodily harm, he wouldn't have freed her hands. His expression was blank. At least it appeared to be. It was hard to tell what the beard concealed.

Testing the waters, she said, "The sweet potato vine is a nice, homey touch."

He looked at her for several seconds more, then nodded toward the kitchen area. "Coffee mugs are in the cabinet on the right."

The sisal rug that covered most of the floor in the living space gave way to vinyl in the kitchen. It felt cool against the soles of her feet. She took a mug from the cabinet above a stained Formica counter and poured her coffee. It tasted as strong as it looked, but it was good.

"I think there's some sweetener somewhere."

She shook her head. "I'd use milk if you have it."

"In the fridge."

Once she'd added milk to the coffee, she sat down in one of the chairs at the small, wood dining table and began peeling the sticky silver duct tape off her wrists.

Watching her, he said, "If it makes you

feel any better, I had hairs caught in mine. Hurt like hell to peel it off."

She gave him a wan smile. "It makes me feel better." When she finished the task, she wadded the tape into two tight balls. He extended his hand, and she dropped them into it. He tossed them in the trash can.

"How's your head?"

"I still have a goose egg. And the roots of my hair hurt."

"The hazards of being an uncooperative kidnap victim." She gave him a withering look. Unrepentantly, he added, "I had to make you think I meant business."

It wasn't quite an apology, but she figured it was all she could expect. "At least I paid you back," she said, motioning toward the scratch on his cheek just above the beard.

"If your knee had connected with my balls, you would have paid me back." He turned and opened the refrigerator. "I assume you're hungry."

"Last night you were my abductor and this morning you're the gracious host?"

He turned on the flame beneath a burner on the gas stove, set a skillet on it, and began lining up strips of bacon in the skillet.

"Mr. Gannon? *Raley?*" she said when he still didn't respond. He glanced at her over his shoulder. "Why did you take the tape off? Why am I free now?"

"Didn't you hear what I said last night?"

"About believing me because the same thing had happened to you?"

"That's why the tape is no longer necessary."

"You could have told me that over the telephone, or in some other civilized manner. Why did you put me through all that fear and anguish last night?"

"Meanness. Retaliation."

"You admit it?"

"That was partially it, yeah. But fear and anguish are also good motivators. I needed to satisfy myself that you were telling the truth about losing your memory."

"And did you?"

"If I hadn't, you'd still have your hands and feet taped together."

She thought about it for a minute, while the bacon sizzled in the skillet and he whipped eggs in a bowl. "If you believed me last night, why didn't you let me go then?"

"If I had, you would have been so anxious to get back to your TV station and report your story, you would have hightailed it out of here, in the dark, not knowing where to go or even where you are. You would have plunged headlong into the wilderness.

"In order to keep you from hurting yourself or getting lost, never to be seen again, I would have had to chase after you. It had been a long day, I was tired, I wanted to go to sleep. I didn't even want to argue with you about it. It seemed easier just to tie you down so you couldn't leave."

Privately she acknowledged that was precisely what she would have done if she'd been free to attempt it. "What's to keep me from doing that now?"

"You won't." He'd removed the bacon from the skillet and poured the eggs into it, then put two slices of bread into a dented, rusty toaster. His motions were economical, like this was his daily routine.

"You committed several crimes, you know."

Keeping his back to her, he shrugged.

"Think what a story that would make." She glanced through the screen door toward the pickup truck parked only steps away from the cabin. " 'Raley Gannon broke into my house and kidnapped me.' I could have it on the news by noon today. There's bound to be a main road not too far from here."

"Four point seven miles. But you won't go."

He came to the table with a handful of flatware, which he dropped onto it with a clatter. The mismatched utensils were followed by a roll of paper towels. He divided the food between two plates, one of which he slid over to her. He sat down, doused his eggs with Tabasco, then picked up a fork and began eating.

The breakfast smelled delicious, but she didn't dig in. It had just now occurred to her why he was so confident that she would stay even though she was free to leave. "I won't go now because I have only a portion of the story."

He stopped eating to rip a paper towel off the roll and wipe his mouth with it. Behind the beard, she saw a trace of a smile. "Your curiosity is much more binding than my duct tape."

"This relates to what Jay was going to tell me, doesn't it? And it must harken back to what happened five years ago. Right?" To her consternation, he continued eating. "When are you going to tell me the rest of it?"

"Your food is getting cold."

He would tell her the whole story. She was sure of that. She wouldn't have to outsmart or cajole him in order to get it, either. He wanted to tell her. Just as Jay had. Whatever it was, it was a hell of a story. Possibly a career-making scoop, as Jay had promised.

But it could wait until after breakfast.

She ate ravenously. When she was done, he cleared the table. She dried the dishes he washed. Her curiosity was killing her, but he didn't speak a single word, so neither did she.

With the chore out of the way, they returned to the table and sat down across from each other. He began fiddling with a box of toothpicks in the center of the table.

The silence stretched out until it became unbearable to her. Apparently he was waiting for her to begin. She said, "If you had told me earlier last night that the same thing had happened to you, and given me a few minutes to assimilate it, I would have seen reason, just as I have this morning."

"Maybe."

"I wouldn't have hightailed it out of here, I wouldn't have plunged headlong into the wilderness. Not until I had the whole story."

"Probably not."

He was contradicting himself. She shook her head in confusion. "Then it wasn't really necessary for you to tape our hands together and bind me to the bed, was it?"

"No."

"So you did that out of sheer meanness."

"Not entirely."

"Then why? Why did you—" But she

broke off without finishing the question because suddenly she knew why.

He kept his head down for a long time. When he finally raised it and looked at her, it felt as though he'd reached across the table and socked her lightly in the lower abdomen.

Just then footsteps landed heavily on the front steps.

"Raley! Get up, boy!"

"Oh shit," Raley muttered as he came quickly out of his chair.

The strangest-looking man Britt had ever seen came barging through the screen door, nearly tearing it off the hinges in his haste. He stumbled over three hounds, who bounded in along with him, their tongues dripping slobber onto the man's crusty bare feet. He cursed them lavishly for tripping him up.

"Get those damn dogs out of here," Raley ordered. "They've got fleas. So do you, for that matter."

The old man didn't seem to hear him. Immediately upon clearing the doorway, he'd stopped dead in his tracks and stood transfixed, gaping at Britt, who had also shot to her feet, partially to protect herself from the hounds, who were circling her, sniffing at her bare legs with more curiosity than menace.

Raley whistled sharply. "Out!" The three reluctantly withdrew, whining, tails tucked between their legs. Raley held open the screen door. They slunk through it onto the porch, where they plopped down into three panting canine heaps.

Raley returned to the table and sat down as though the disruption hadn't taken place. The old man was still rooted to the floor, staring at her. "What's *she* doing here?"

Britt didn't miss the disparaging emphasis on his reference to her. "You know who I am?"

"I ain't blind. Course I know who you are." He shot a look toward Raley. "I know all about you."

His tone indicated that what he'd heard about her from Raley wasn't complimentary.

"He kidnapped me."

"Kidnapped you?"

"He came into my home, bound and gagged me, and drove me here."

"Against your will?"

"Isn't that what *kidnapped* usually implies?"

"Don't get on your high horse with me, young lady. You're gonna need all the friends you can get."

That elicited a reaction from Raley. He looked at the old man sharply. "Why? What's happened?"

"I seen it on the TV first thing this mornin'." He looked askance at her, then spoke directly to Raley. "They done the autopsy on your late friend Jay."

Any time a police officer died of anything other than natural causes or old age, it made news.

Patrick Wickham, Jr., knew that from when his father had been killed. He'd been gut-shot and left in a dirty, rat-infested alley to bleed out. Newspapers had deemed it a heinous crime committed by a lawless assailant. The community was saddened and outraged. It had lost a hero who would be long remembered and revered for his unstinting bravery on the day of the police station fire.

Barely a year had elapsed between the fire and the night Pat Sr. was slain. The brouhaha over the fire was just beginning to die down when his murder stirred it all up again.

As a trained policeman himself, Pat Jr. knew that his father had failed to follow procedure that night. He hadn't even exercised common sense. But his costly misjudgment had been obscured by the posthumous accolades to his uncommon courage.

The other three heroes of the fire were asked to eulogize his dad. Pictures of Cobb Fordyce standing with head bowed beside the casket had made him a shoo-in for the race for the AG's office. George McGowan had wept openly at the interment. Jay Burgess had offered Pat Jr. and his mother whatever assistance they needed from him and the CPD. "Anything," Jay had said, pressing his mother's hand as he kissed her cheek.

For weeks following Pat Sr.'s funeral, Jay had phoned often, even stopped by the house a few times to see how they were faring, bringing with him flowers and small gifts. But then the calls and the visits had tapered off and finally stopped altogether.

Every once in a while, his and Jay's paths would cross at police headquarters. They always exchanged friendly hellos, but it was obvious to Pat that Jay didn't want to engage in conversation, and that was more than okay with him.

Now a photo of that handsome, guileless face filled the screen of his twelve-inch kitchen TV.

"Another officer who distinguished himself five years ago during the police station fire apparently died the victim of foul play," the announcer said, all gravity.

"Daddy?"

"Shh!"

"I wan' milk."

Each morning Pat Jr. prepared breakfast for his two children. It wasn't a chore he particularly enjoyed. In fact, he dreaded it every morning—the whining, the demands, the invariable spills. But getting breakfast was the least he could do for his wife and children. The very least.

Mechanically he poured milk into a sippy cup, secured the top, then handed it to his three-year-old son. Smelling of a wet diaper, his two-year-old daughter was in her high chair, creating a mush of waffles and syrup in the tray.

"Jay Burgess was found dead two days ago in his bed by newswoman Britt Shelley. Ms. Shelley, who placed the 911 call, contends that after meeting Burgess at a popular nightspot, she has no memory of the night she spent with him."

They cut to an exterior shot of The Wheelhouse. Pat Jr. knew it, but he'd never been there.

"Daddy?"

"Just a minute," he snapped impatiently.

"Police, who've questioned Ms. Shelley extensively, have declined to cite any wrongdoing on her part. However, they did request that the autopsy on Burgess be conducted as soon as possible. Gary, in view of this report from the medical examiner's office, do you think the authorities will be questioning Ms. Shelley further?"

The field reporter, covering the story from outside Jay Burgess's town house, now a crime scene, appeared on camera. "No doubt of that, Stan. Ms. Shelley said at the news conference she held yesterday that she was eager to learn the cause of Burgess's death. By her own admission, she was the last person to see him alive. Given the findings of this autopsy, the police will have some hard questions for her."

"Pat?" Pat Jr. turned around to see his wife, who'd just come from bed. Her eyes were still puffy with sleep, but she was looking at the television. "Is that about Jay Burgess? What are they saying?"

"That he didn't simply die in his sleep." The words seemed reluctant to be spoken. They got jammed up inside Pat Jr.'s misshapen mouth, but he was finally able to articulate them.

Astonished, she said, "No kidding?"

He shook his head, wishing with all his might that he was kidding.

"So what happened to him?"

Pat Jr. didn't have the wherewithal to reply.

George McGowan already had the front door open when his father-in-law arrived and honked the car horn loudly. Nevertheless, as George wedged himself into the seat of Les Conway's latest acquisition, a spanking new, red Corvette convertible, Les shot him a look of reproof as though he'd been kept waiting.

George ignored the look, and his tongue could turn to stone before he would apologize for being not only on time but ahead of schedule.

Les, who lived barely a mile away on a similar estate, had prearranged to pick George up at promptly seven fifteen, so they could be at the country club by seven thirty and teeing off by seven forty-five. As he ruthlessly pushed the Vette's stick through the gears, he asked, "Did you bring the plans?"

"Right here." George wondered what the son of a bitch thought he had in the briefcase he'd brought with him if not the architectural plans for the new municipal athletic complex. Today they were meeting with city planners to officially bid on the job of building it. If Conway Construction was awarded the contract, Les's pocketbook would be considerably fattened.

This wasn't the first time his father-in-law had used George's celebrity, as well as his contacts in city hall, to help him land a lucrative contract. In the four years that George and Miranda had been married, there had been many such contracts. But you would never hear Les, or Miranda, giving George credit for the company's growth. He'd stopped expecting even a nod of appreciation or gratitude from either of them.

"Let them win," Les said.

George nodded. When Les's business negotiations began with a round of golf, it was standard practice for him to let his opponents win. Otherwise, he played a cutthroat game.

George had been an athlete in high school and college, participating in nearly every sport. He didn't take up golf until he was well into his twenties, but he rarely shot above a seventy-eight. Hitting with power, accuracy, and finesse came naturally to him. It galled Les that, even when he cheated, George could always beat him.

"Just don't make it obvious that you're losing on purpose." He gave George a glance, then looked at his own reflection in the rearview mirror. Like father, like daughter. They never met a mirror they didn't like.

"I won't." George felt like a child, being driven to school and given his marching orders for the day.

"How's my girl this morning?"

"Still asleep when I left."

Les laughed. "She likes her beauty sleep."

"She certainly does."

"Did you hear?"

"Hear what?" George asked distractedly. He was staring at the scenery on his side of the car, catching a glimpse of the Ashley River now and then. The scent of salt water was in the air this morning.

"The police got the autopsy report on your late buddy Jay."

George whipped his head around.

His father-in-law smirked, then laughed out loud. "I thought that would get your attention."

"Well? What was in the report?" George hated asking, but he had to know even if he had to beg the son of a bitch for the information.

Les took his sweet time. He readjusted his sunglasses and gave the mirror another glance before answering. "It concluded that Burgess didn't die of natural causes or anything relating to his cancer."

The Vette took the turn into the country club parking lot on two wheels and screeched to a halt in the parking space Les paid monthly rent for. As soon as he yanked his keys from the ignition, he turned to George. Now that he no longer found humor in the situation, the smirk, the laugh, were gone. "I don't think I need to tell you, George, that a fuckup here would be catastrophic."

"I know what to do. Play well enough, but let them win."

Les removed his sunglasses and gave him a hard look. "I wasn't talking about the golf game."

On that ominous note, his father-in-law got out and slammed the door so hard the car rocked. George alighted and followed him into the clubhouse. Les actually held the door for him, saying as George went past, "It's important for these guys to think we're doing them a favor, not vice versa. So, just to set the tone, be a minute or two late to the tee."

George nodded, glad of that plan. He was going to need an extra minute or two at his locker, where he kept a flask. He had to have a drink or he'd never be able to grip a golf club. Not the way his hands were shaking.

CHAPTER
8

Britt practically pounced on Delno. "What about the autopsy?"

Raley braced himself. He figured Britt would probably need bracing, too, so he went to stand near her where she had squared off with Delno.

"They said—"

"Who? Who said?"

"The men on the TV." Looking beyond her at Raley, Delno said, "Have you gone plumb crazy, kidnapping her?"

"Reporters?"

"Huh?" Delno's eyes shifted back to Britt. "Yeah, reporters. Them and the cop they was talking to." Then back to Raley. "What the hell do you expect to gain by—"

"What did *he* say? The cop."

Delno was losing patience with her interruptions. "He said that, accordin' to the autopsy, Jay Burgess died of suffocation."

She fell back a step. *"Suffocation?"*

"Smothered-like. With a pillow over his face."

She stared at Delno with disbelief. "That's impossible."

"I ain't lyin', lady. That's what the fella said."

For several seconds nobody moved, then Britt flew into action as though she'd been jabbed with an electric prod. "Where's your phone?" Without waiting for Raley to answer, she went tearing around the cabin, knocking a stack of books off a table, scattering a deck of playing cards, flinging aside anything her hands landed on as she searched for a telephone.

"I don't have a phone," he said.

"A cell then. You're bound to have a cell phone."

"No. And I purposefully left yours behind."

"A TV. Radio."

"None of the above. Britt, calm down."

She rounded on him, her eyes wild, arms held rigid at her sides. "Who doesn't have a telephone?"

"I don't," he shouted back.

She gaped at him as though he'd just arrived from another planet, then she headed for the door. "I'll take your truck. Are the keys in it?"

She made it through the screen door, over the mound of dogs, and down the steep steps before he caught up with her. He grabbed at her windbreaker. That broke her stride but didn't stop her. She pulled her arms free, leaving him with nothing but a fistful of synthetic fabric.

She was rounding the truck bed when he managed to hook her elbow and jerk her to a stop. "Will you wait a damn minute?"

"Let go of me!"

"Not yet. Not until you tell me what you plan to do."

"What do you think? Go back. Deny it. Tell them I had nothing to do with Jay's dying. Tell them I don't remember what happened that night, but I would certainly remember killing him. Holding a pillow over his face? My God!" She pulled her arm from Raley's grasp and put her hands to the sides of her head, grabbing handfuls of her hair.

"You already told them you'd lost your memory. They didn't believe you."

"Still don't." This from Delno, who'd come out behind them, following the action as though they were staging it for his entertainment. "They're looking for you," he said, addressing Britt. "Said a warrant had been issued. They went to your place. Said it looked to them like you'd runned off to avoid arrest." He grinned at Raley, showing his dental stubs. "Reckon they didn't figure on her being kidnapped."

"I'll make them believe me." Britt spun away and headed for the cab of the truck.

Raley reached out and caught her arm again, bringing her around. "How? How, Britt? You were there, with Jay, all night."

"Yes, but there's no solid evidence against me."

"They got the pillow," Delno said.

That statement arrested her attempt to get free from Raley's grip. She stared at Delno, then looked up at Raley. "How could I have smothered a man and then calmly gone to sleep beside him?"

"I don't believe you could."

"Then—"

"But *they* do. They *do.* Jay was one of their own. They're looking for a scape-goat and somebody—Jay's killer—made certain they'd have one."

"Jay's *killer*?" Her eyes probed his. "You knew all along he'd been murdered?"

"I suspected. I was anxious to hear the autopsy report, same as you."

"Did you suspect me?" she asked, her rich contralto suddenly going thin.

He hesitated, then said, "Not really, no."

"Do you know who—"

"Not yet."

The faint ray of hope he'd seen momentarily in her eyes dimmed and then flickered out. "I've got to go back and clear myself."

"Listen to me," he said, taking a step closer. "You can't go back unarmed.

They'll put you through a shredder. I know. I've been there. Come back inside. Listen to everything Delno heard on the news." Lowering his voice, he said, "Listen to what I have to tell you. Then I'll drive you back myself. I swear."

She stared at him, then looked at Delno, who had lifted one of the hounds into his arms and was stroking its lolling head. She looked back at Raley. "I'll give you an hour."

Delno dropped the hound onto the porch and held the screen door open for them as they filed back inside. He helped himself to the last of the coffee. Raley offered to brew a fresh pot, but Britt declined with an absent shake of her head. She resumed her place at the dining table. Raley took his previous seat. Delno sat in the third chair.

Britt seemed to have expended all her energy. She sat with shoulders slumped, staring at the nicks in the tabletop. She traced one with her thumbnail. Finally she looked up and caught him and Delno staring at her.

She turned to Delno as though only

now registering his presence. "Who *are* you?"

"Delno Pickens," he replied, at the same time Raley said, "My neighbor. He has a place a couple miles from here."

He remembered his first exposure to Delno, what a shocking sight the old geezer had been. Britt was experiencing that mix of amazement and repugnance now. Delno never wore a shirt beneath his overalls, except on the coldest days of the year. This left his arms and upper chest exposed to the elements almost year-round. His skin was crepey, tanned to leather, overlaid with a sparse crop of white hair.

It was hard to determine the natural color of the hair beneath the hat he perpetually wore. A straggly ponytail hung long down his back. He greased it to discourage lice. At least that was what Raley had surmised.

It was a testament to Britt's basic kindness that she remained sitting that close to the man, because he was no more inclined to bathe than he was to wash his hair. Or maybe kindness didn't factor into it at all. Maybe she was simply too shell-shocked to angle away from his overripe odor.

"Raley here won't get hisself a TV," he said to Britt. "Says he hates the goddamn things. So if there's something really important in the news, it falls to me to let him know."

"They have Jay's pillow?" she asked, her voice still thready.

Delno nodded. "They took it as evidence that first morning. Said it was on the floor next to the bed. One of them hard, foam kind. It bore the imprint of his face. They suspected right off you'd smothered him, but they kept it to their selves till the coroner could prove it."

"He may have been suffocated with his pillow, but I didn't do it, Mr. . . . uh . . ."

"Pickens. And it don't matter to me none if you did or didn't."

She scraped back her chair and stood up, went to the fridge, got a bottle of water and took a long drink. Raley sensed Delno watching him curiously, a thousand unasked questions in the old man's rheumy eyes. Raley pretended not to notice.

Britt said, "They went to my house to arrest me. What did you mean when you said it looked to them like I had run away?"

"Well—"

"I can answer that," Raley said. "I left my pickup and hitched into town late yesterday afternoon. After stopping at The Wheelhouse, I walked to your house."

"That's—"

"A few miles. After I knocked you out, I—"

"You knocked her out?"

He didn't acknowledge Delno's interruption. "I looked for your car keys and found them on the hook by the back door. I left as you would, going out that door and resetting the alarm."

"How'd you do that?"

"I watched when you punched in the numbers to turn it off, so I knew the code."

"Oh."

"I made up your bed and brought along your handbag. It's still in the truck, by the way."

"But not my phone."

"No."

She assimilated what he'd told her. "You left no sign of a struggle." He nodded. "You covered your tracks but made me look like a fugitive from justice."

"Basically. That was the general idea."

"Great. Fabulous." She sighed with asperity. "How did you get me out of the house?"

"Carried you. I was trained to carry people, remember?" Without waiting for a response, he continued. "I drove your car to where I'd left my truck."

"I remember you transferring me from my car."

"I knew you were conscious at that point."

"Where is my car?"

"At an abandoned airstrip. In the middle of nowhere. A road dead-ends at it. No one goes out there."

"How did you know about it?"

"Jay's uncle had a deer lease near it. We used to do target practice out there."

Mention of Jay's name brought a pained expression to her face. "I still can't believe he's dead, and that he died in that manner. He must have put up a struggle." Lowering her head, she rubbed her temples. "I want to remember. I *do.* But I can't."

"The police said he was too far gone on whiskey to have put up much of a fight," Delno said. "Course he was sick with the cancer, too. That would have made him even weaker."

"Weak enough that a woman could have killed him," Raley said.

"That's what the cop speculated," Delno said as he scratched his armpit. "Clark, I believe his name was."

"He's one of the detectives who questioned me."

"I know him," Raley said. "He's a good cop. Dedicated to his work. And one hundred percent loyal to everyone on the police force, especially Jay. If the evidence indicates you killed him, Clark will move heaven and earth to see you tried and convicted."

She turned away to look out the window above the kitchen sink. Raley looked over at Delno, but when he saw a question forming on the tobacco-stained lips, he shook his head and Delno remained quiet.

Finally, Britt turned back. "Tell me what happened to you, Raley."

"Sit down." He nodded toward the chair opposite his. She did as he asked.

Delno got up. "Heard it already, and it ain't a story I wish to listen to again. I'll be outside with the dogs."

The screen door slammed closed behind him. The hounds whined in welcome, then stood and stretched and began weaving themselves around his legs. He disappeared, trailing the pack and a stream of muttered curses.

"Quite a character," Britt remarked.

"You don't know the half of it. He has an obsessive hatred for mankind. He tolerates me. On occasion, and only then just barely."

"Once he recovered from his shock, he was friendly enough toward me."

Raley gave her a quick once-over, then he looked away, mumbling, "You're different."

He left the table abruptly, but only long enough to get himself a bottle of water from the refrigerator. Sitting down again, he asked, "How did you know that Jay and I grew up together?"

"He told me once. He said you were best friends almost for as far back as he could remember."

"From kindergarten through college and beyond. Our parents thought we shared the same brain. We shared everything else. Bikes, toys, food, clothes."

"Girls?"

"Sometimes. In our wilder days," he said without any embarrassment that she could detect.

She could imagine them almost at every stage, but especially as college men. Equally attractive. Jay: fair, suave, and charming. Raley: dark and . . . And what? Not as suave and charming. Or maybe he'd been quite charming before his life was turned upside down. Maybe the bearded, scowling man sitting across from her now had once been more of a charmer even than Jay.

"We grew up knowing that Jay was going to be a cop, and I was going to be a fireman."

"These were childhood ambitions?"

"Always. We enrolled in college knowing what we'd study."

"What was your degree in?"

"I got dual degrees. Fire science. Environmental health and safety. Then Jay and I went through the police academy together."

She looked at him with puzzlement. "*You* went through the police academy?"

"In order to become an arson investigator, you must first be a peace officer. Otherwise, once arson is detected, a fire inspector must turn the case over to the police."

"I see. So you got the police certification first."

"Then did my fireman's training and went on to get my certification as an arson investigator."

She was impressed by the amount of education and training he had.

He continued. "Jay and I excelled in our respective fields. I was working my way up through the ranks of the CFD. Jay made detective before the deadline he'd set for himself. We remained best friends." He paused to take a sip of water.

"And then?"

"And then there was the fire at the police station. That changed everything."

He scooted aside the bottle of Tabasco and reached for the box of toothpicks he'd toyed with earlier.

She was impatient to hear what he was about to tell her, but she said nothing, giving him the time he needed to arrange his thoughts. She tried not to think of police officers with a warrant for her arrest, cruising the streets of Charleston in search of her, believing not only that she'd committed murder but that she had fled to avoid capture.

She knew what she would have done with that news story if it had been about someone else. What she *had* done with similar stories. Had the subjects of her breaking news bulletins been as frightened of their futures as she was of hers now? Not once had she put herself in the shoes of the accused. She'd never stopped to consider their desperation. All she'd thought about was how much face time on camera she would have to report their crime, their flight, their capture.

"I was off duty that day," Raley said, drawing her from her disturbing thoughts. "But I lived near downtown and heard the sirens and was already on my way to the fire station when my phone rang." He glanced at her. "I carried a cell in those days." She gave him a weak smile; he continued. "The blaze had gone to two alarms. I was told to get there as soon as possible."

She watched his expression change as he reflected on that day. "I'll never forget it. You can't imagine the heat."

"Actually I can. I covered the sofa factory fire."

Another disastrous fire in which nine firemen had died.

"Did you know any of the men who died in that blaze?" she asked.

"Three really well," he replied sadly. "The others by face and name."

Neither of them said anything for a moment, then he picked up his account of the other major fire in Charleston. "The police station fire burned just as hot. Heat like Hell must be like. Consuming and inescapable."

"You went into the building?"

"No. By the time I got there—I think it took me six minutes—it was an inferno. The roof had already collapsed. Which caused the floors to cave in one by one. Everyone who could be evacuated already had been. I got into gear, but our captain wouldn't let any more of us go in. For anyone left inside, it was hopeless.

"The best we could do at that point was try to confine the blaze to that building. The first alarm had come in at six oh two p.m. Twelve hours later, we were still putting out hot spots." He looked across at her. "Were you living in Charleston then?"

"I came about a month later. The building was still a pile of charred rubble. An investigation into the cause was ongoing."

"Yeah. *My* investigation."

"You were investigating the fire?"

"You didn't know that, did you?" His facial features hardened. Anger radiated off him in waves.

"No, I didn't," she admitted.

"All those stories you did about me, and you never mentioned that."

"I didn't know it."

"But you should have, shouldn't you? You were the reporter covering my story, you should have gathered all the facts. Instead you were busy sweeping up the dirt."

"I'm sorry."

He gave the humble interior of the cabin a scornful glance. "A little late for apologies."

"I'm sorry," she repeated, a bit huskily.

He maintained his hostile silence for several long moments, then muttered "Screw it," and continued his account in a neutral tone of voice. "Pat Wickham, George McGowan, and Cobb Fordyce. Do those names mean anything to you?"

"Of course."

"Tell me what you know."

"Those three and Jay saved dozens of lives that day. They got people out of the building. Even before the first fire trucks arrived, they risked their lives to lead people out. As catastrophic as the fire was, only seven people died. If not for those four men, there would have been many more casualties."

Frowning, he said, "The four of them did lead people out. They did save lives."

"So you don't dispute that?"

"Not at all. When I arrived, it was a chaotic scene. People suffering from burns and smoke inhalation but weeping with relief that they'd escaped. Firemen battling the blaze. Policemen trying to maintain some semblance of organization. EMTs dispensing oxygen and performing triage, dispatching the worst of the injured to the hospital. Those four refused to go, even though they were near collapse. On oxygen. Scorched. You've seen the pictures. Cameras don't lie."

The bitterness with which he'd said that caused Britt to withhold her observation for several seconds. Then she said quietly, "Your best friend Jay was hailed a hero."

"Overnight."

She had dipped her toe in, she might

just as well take the plunge. "Saving people from a fire."

He came up out of his chair. "I know what you're thinking."

"What am I thinking?"

"That I was jealous of Jay because he got famous for doing what I was supposed to do. That I resented his becoming a hero in my field of expertise."

"Were you jealous? Did you resent it?"

"No!"

"Are you human?"

CHAPTER 9

Britt held her breath, wondering how Raley would react to the sensitive question.

He rolled his shoulders defensively and took a breath. "Okay, maybe I was a little pissed. Jay teased me about it. 'I be the cop, you be the fireman, remember?' He'd say it in that way of his, with that smile, and I knew he was ribbing, but, yeah, here I had gone through the training and done the studying, and then, in typical Jay Burgess fashion, he sails in and grabs the glory. *Lots* of glory."

"Anybody would resent that, Raley."

"On the other hand, I was proud of him and damn glad he'd saved all those lives. I was also grateful that he had survived."

"That was the purpose of the party, wasn't it? To celebrate his survival?"

"That's what he said. He wanted to celebrate his rise from the ashes. I told him I couldn't make it because of work, but Jay called me on the afternoon of the party. He said . . ."

"Don't let me down, Raley. You gotta be there. How can I have a party without you?"

Raley sighed into the telephone. From second grade, when Jay had talked him into putting a cricket in their teacher's desk drawer, he'd been wheedling Raley into doing things he didn't want to do. When Jay set his mind to something, he was irrepressible, and he was determined to have Raley at his party.

"I've been working day and night, Jay."

"So have I. That's never stopped us from taking time off to party."

"This is different. This investigation—"

"Will keep. For a few hours, anyway. Stop by long enough to have a beer. I've rented a frozen margarita machine, but for nondrinkers, I'll have a keg."

Raley laughed. "Jay, beer is an alcoholic beverage."

"You're kidding. It is?"

The two friends laughed, then Jay said, "It won't be a party without you, buddy."

Raley still hedged. His days were long. His nights were spent reviewing the information he gleaned during the days. Consequently, he was working around the clock.

He'd been appointed to assist the department's senior arson investigator, a craggy middle-aged man named Teddy Brunner. Brunner was a veteran and probably knew more about fires than anyone else in the department. But it was Raley who put notices about seminars and conferences under the chief's nose. When budget was the only thing preventing him from attending these conferences, he paid his own tuition, considering the out-of-pocket expense an investment in his future.

Although Brunner was the veteran, Raley had two college degrees to his credit, and advanced, scientific knowledge on firefighting. By pooling their resources, they made a good team. Raley didn't flaunt his formal education because he respected the older fireman's decades of experience.

Brunner was occasionally cantankerous and short with him. Raley realized he probably felt threatened by him and his better understanding of new technology, but he was also gradually winning Brunner's respect. Raley tried hard to keep the working relationship on an even keel.

But any way you sliced it, being appointed Brunner's apprentice on such an important investigation was an indication that he was being groomed to be the senior investigator's successor whenever the older man chose to retire. It was an enormous opportunity. As important, it would signify a personal achievement, the culmination of years of study and hard work. Because such a critical career step was at stake, he didn't want to risk any break in his concentration.

Jay could shatter a monk's concentration. And he never took no for an answer. "Come on, Raley. Can I count on you to be there?"

Again Raley stalled by telling Jay that Hallie was out of town. "She's on a business trip and won't be back till tomorrow."

"She doesn't trust you to come stag? That's an awfully short leash she's got you on."

Jay frequently gibed Raley about his upcoming marriage, reminding him of the pleasurable benefits to be had by staying romantically footloose. The teasing didn't bother Raley. He looked forward to matrimony, monogamy, and spending the rest of his life with Hallie.

He also suspected that his friend was secretly jealous of his relationship with Hallie, the likes of which Jay had never shared with a woman, and that the taunting was a product of envy.

Jay often gazed moony-eyed at Hallie, saying, "I might consider marriage myself if I could have Hallie. You snared the last good woman, Raley, you lucky s.o.b." Hallie laughed off his foolishness, as did Raley. Both knew that Jay wouldn't trade bachelorhood for a relationship where fidelity was at least expected, if not required.

"She trusts me," Raley said. "It's just that it won't be any fun to go to a party without her."

"Bring Candy. She can be your date."

Raley guffawed. Candy Orrin had grown up with them. She was several years younger, but over one summer, when she'd talked their coach into letting her be "ball boy" for their baseball team, she'd become their shadow.

She was a tomboy who could outrun, outhit, outshoot, outcuss, and when they were older, outdrink them. She was great fun and a good friend but hardly a substitute for Hallie, and he told Jay so.

Jay chuckled. "I hear you, man. Candy hasn't got Hallie's grace, charm, and beauty. By the way, have I told you I'm secretly in love with your woman?"

"About a hundred times."

"I have? Well, just so you know. Where was I?"

"Candy hasn't got—"

"Right. She's as far from Hallie as, say, you are from me."

"Ha-ha."

"But you gotta admit that Candy's good for laughs, she's currently without a beau, and she says if she can't scare up a date for my party she might skip it, too. Now, how can I celebrate my miraculous survival if my two best friends are no-shows?"

Raley had run out of excuses. The real reason he didn't want to go was that for the last several days he'd been reviewing the autopsy reports of those who'd died in the fire. To Raley, the remains weren't just so much charred tissue and bone fragments. Those unrecognizable human bodies had been people, and they'd suffered horrific deaths. His mind wouldn't let him forget how terrifying their final minutes of life would have been. Thoughts of it kept him awake at night, and when he was able to sleep, he heard their screams in his nightmares. He wasn't in a partying mood.

But to discuss that with Jay would be to remind him that, for all his heroism, he was unable to save those seven. He figured those souls haunted Jay, the same as they did him, but Jay's way of coping was to throw a party.

Perhaps his friend's way of dealing with despondency was the better one. Jay would say that no amount of regret or sorrow could bring back those seven. Bury the dead, life was for the living. And when you got right down to it, he was right.

"I could easily have died that day, you know," he was saying now. "I suffer flashbacks to it, Raley. To the fire, to being inside that building. Can't see a thing, choking on smoke, afraid the floor is about to fall out from under me. There were times when I thought, *This is it. My time's up. I'm going to die.* If not for fate, I'd be history. This party could just as easily have been my wake instead of—"

"Oh, for godsake, bring on the fucking violins," Raley groaned. "You'll use any means of manipulation to get me there, won't you?"

"I have no shame."

"I believe it."

Jay reminded him to call Candy and offer her a ride, then said, "Wait and see.

You'll have a good time in spite of your sorry-ass self."

"One more thing," Raley said, stopping him just before he hung up. "Cleveland Jones. I still haven't received all the paperwork on him."

"Oh, shit. I forgot again, didn't I?"

"I don't see how you could. This is the third time I've asked for his arrest report."

"I know, I know, and I'm sorry. I'll get it to you on Monday, first thing."

"I'm holding you to that." He hung up, disappointed that he wouldn't have the arrest report over the weekend. He hated to keep harping on Jay about it, but that report was vital to his investigation.

Jay was distracted by his personal involvement and by the media, who continued to hound him for interviews. Not that he minded being in the spotlight, but being a celebrity was time-consuming.

With the exception of this last conversation, each time Raley phoned Jay, he seemed preoccupied and always in a rush to cut short the call. Any other time, Raley would feel like he was getting the brush-off, but Jay's splintered attention was understandable. He, like every person in the CPD, was working overtime to recover from the disastrous fire. The entire department was in shambles, operating in a state of barely controlled chaos. Personnel were working out of temporary headquarters, trying to reorganize even as they went about their routine duties.

With the entire PD in this state of upheaval, Raley couldn't really fault Jay for not responding immediately to his request to see the paperwork on Cleveland Jones, but he was becoming impatient to finish his investigation. Brunner had assigned him this aspect of it, and he wanted to come through, not just to satisfy but to impress the older man.

Mainly, he wanted the nightmares to stop.

Hallie had noticed his preoccupation more than anyone, and he knew it worried her. He could hear the relief in her voice when he called to tell her that Jay had persuaded him to attend his party. "Good," she said.

"Not really, but he wouldn't let me back out."

"Why don't you want to go?"

"Because you're not here to go with me."

"I'm flattered, but is that the only reason?"

He couldn't hide much from her. "I hate to give up a night. I'm really into this investigation and don't want to lose momentum."

In a quieter voice, she asked, "How are you?"

"Missing you."

"Besides that."

"I'm fine."

"You sound tired."

"I am. But I'm okay."

She didn't dispute him, but he could imagine her doubtful frown. She had an endearing way of pursing her lips when she was mulling something over. She'd been wearing that frown the first time he saw her, two years ago on New Year's Eve, at a party hosted by mutual friends. She was at the buffet table, considering the raw oysters lying on a mound of ice. He moved up beside her and said, "I don't think they bite." And she laughed, saying, "I don't think I will, either."

That thoughtful pout made her lips infinitely kissable. He especially liked kissing that pout away when she was wearing her glasses. She didn't believe him when he told her he preferred her glasses to contacts. But it was the truth.

Switching subjects now, he asked, "How are your meetings going?"

She was a loan officer at the local branch of a banking chain. An advancement had brought her to Charleston only weeks before that New Year's Eve when they met. Since then, she'd had VP added after her name. She'd been in Boston all week at the bank's national headquarters.

"Long, but informative."

"So the trip was worthwhile."

"Um-huh." Then, "Oh! I talked to my mother today. The church is available on Saturday the twelfth."

"Great." That was the April date they'd discussed for their wedding. Spring flowers in bloom. Not too hot or humid yet. "I'll call my mom and tell her."

"My mom already spoke to her."

"Even better."

They laughed, because he had ceded all wedding planning to the three women, telling Hallie to be sure he knew what time to show up with the ring. He felt that was all he needed to know.

"It's good to hear you laugh," she said. "And I think going to Jay's party is an excellent idea. You need a break from the investigation."

"I've been lousy company lately, haven't I?"

"You've taken the job to heart."

"I know. I'm sorry."

"Don't apologize for your commitment, Raley. The fire was a tragedy. I couldn't love you if you hadn't taken this investigation to heart."

Her soft voice and the understanding behind it made him yearn to touch her. Boston might just as well have been in another galaxy. "Why aren't you here so I can make love to you?"

"Tomorrow," she said. "Don't make plans for tomorrow night. I'm bringing back a new nightie from Victoria's Secret. I intend to distract you from work, from everything."

His imagination went into overdrive. "How about some hot phone sex right now?"

"I would," she said, "but I've got a meeting in five minutes."

"It won't take me anywhere near five minutes."

"It would the way I'd do it," she purred, then laughed at his groan. "Besides, I don't want to make you late for Jay's party."

"He promises it will be one of his orgiastic bacchanals."

"I wouldn't expect it to be anything else. Should I be worried? Or are you just trying to talk me into the hot phone sex?"

"No, you shouldn't be worried. And yes, I'm trying to talk you into the phone sex. If you help me get my rocks off now, I'll be too sated to stray."

"How can I possibly resist such a romantic lead-in?"

He laughed. "No sale?"

"Sorry."

"Okay," he sighed. "But how am I going to explain this boner to Candy?"

"Candy? Did I miss something?"

"Jay rooked me into being her date tonight."

"Who's the designated driver?"

"I am. I'll have one beer. Candy can find her own way home, or stay over at Jay's, or whatever. I'm coming home early and spending the rest of tonight and tomorrow planning all the dirty things I'm going to do to you when you get home."

"I can't wait." She gave him her flight number and time of arrival.

"See you in baggage claim. And in the meantime, I love you."

Candy paused in the open doorway to scan Jay's living room. "The usual suspects."

Raley, looking over her shoulder, took in the riotous scene. "I don't recognize half the people here."

"That's what I meant," she shouted back at him. "It's one of Jay's typical free-for-alls."

His apartment was jam-packed with

people, all trying to talk above the loud music, creating a cacophony of laughter, chatter, and Bon Jovi. Having delivered Candy as promised, Raley was tempted to make an about-face and leave. But it was too late. Jay had spotted them. Holding aloft his margarita glass, he threaded his way through the crowd until he reached them. He kissed Candy on the cheek.

"You look sensational!"

"Thanks. It's new." She held out the skirt of the halter dress and executed a curtsy. "I treated myself. I may not be able to pay the rent this month, but what the hell. Does the full skirt make my butt look big?"

Dutifully he and Jay chorused, "No."

"Liars. But thanks."

Soon after she'd passed the bar exam, a job for an ADA had come open in the district attorney's office. Candy had applied for it and had hung on with bulldog tenacity until she was hired. At first, she was little more than a gofer, but it hadn't taken her long to distinguish herself. She was ambitious and self-confident, and didn't take any crap from her male counterparts. She didn't acknowledge a glass ceiling for women in the judicial system—except to say that she planned to shatter the goddamn thing.

She wasn't a natural beauty, but when she took the time and trouble, as she obviously had tonight, she could be moderately attractive.

"Hey, buddy, I'm glad you're here." Jay reached past Candy to shake Raley's hand, then threw one arm around his shoulders and gave him a hug, thumping him on the back. Raley, who was several inches taller than Jay, awkwardly leaned into the hug.

But he found himself moved by Jay's demonstration of affection and, remembering the reason for the party, said thickly, "No, I'm glad *you're* here."

They released each other quickly but maintained eye contact and fond smiles.

Candy regarded them suspiciously. "You two aren't going to swap spit, I hope."

They laughed. Jay said, "When Hell

freezes over," then motioned with his head. "Bar's this way."

It took them ten minutes to navigate the living room. As soon as he'd thrust a plastic cup of beer at Raley, and seen to it that Candy had a margarita, Jay deserted them to welcome arriving guests, and to meet the tagalongs they'd brought with them.

Candy spotted another lawyer from the DA's office across the room. He was standing with his back against the wall, looking like he was facing a firing squad. "He's married," she told Raley, "but I understand he and the missus are separated. I don't see her, do you?" Obviously it was a rhetorical question because Candy didn't wait for an answer. "He's kinda cute, in a nerdy sort of way, don't you think?"

"Oh yeah." Much more nerdy than cute, in Raley's opinion, which he wisely kept to himself. "I'll bet you're smarter than him."

Not hearing his sarcasm, or disregarding it, she said, "Oh, no question of that." She turned to him and peeled back her lips. "Do I have anything in my teeth?"

He inspected them and shook his head. "You're good to go."

"See ya."

She headed off in the general direction of the lost-looking prosecutor. *Poor bastard,* Raley thought, mentally chuckling. He was in for a night of it.

Feeling adrift, Raley stepped out onto the patio, where the noise level was a trifle less earsplitting. The concrete pad was bordered on three sides by narrow strips of grass and enclosed with a privacy fence. Tonight the gate was open. Jay's guests were free to spill out onto the common area of the apartment complex. None of the other residents seemed to mind the party racket. Raley was sure Jay had extended a blanket invitation as a preemptive strike against complaints.

And who was a neighbor to call to complain about noise? The cops? Any police department employee who wasn't on duty tonight was here swilling beer and margaritas, noshing on chips and salsa, cheese cubes, and onion dip.

Raley looked through the open gate, planning his escape. He'd already told Candy he would leave well before she was ready to go, and she'd agreed to find her own way home. If he left through the gate, he could circle around to where he'd parked his car without having to go back through the apartment, avoiding an argument with Jay, who would urge him to stay.

He finished his beer and tossed the empty cup into a trash can, then started for the gate.

"Hi."

He turned to make certain the greeting was intended for him. It was. But he'd never seen the young woman smiling up at him. "Your name's Raley?"

"That's right."

Her smile widened. "Raley Gannon. I asked." She pointed with her thumb over her shoulder, indicating that she'd asked his name of someone in the crowd.

"Oh."

It wasn't a brilliant comeback, but it was all he could think of to say. She was a stunner, from the tousled mass of blond hair to her red toenails. In between were a pair of high-heeled sandals, a white miniskirt, and a red tank top with FCUK spelled out in rhinestones. She was carrying a frozen margarita in each hand.

"You looked thirsty." She handed one of the drinks to Raley. He took it, but she noticed him looking at the glittering letters stretched across her breasts. She laughed. "It stands for French Connection UK. Like England? It's a line of clothing."

"Oh, right."

"Eye-catching though, huh?"

"Yeah."

"Makes you do a double take. At least it did you." And she gave a little shimmy that caused all four letters to jiggle. Her breasts turned seismic.

Feeling guilty for staring, he looked into the margarita. "I was about to leave."

Her evident disappointment was flattering. "You were? How come?"

"I, uh, I have some work to do."

"On Saturday night?"

"Yeah, I—"

"I don't hear any fire trucks."

He gave a quick tilt of his head. "You know I'm a fireman? What gave me away?"

Shyly she ducked her head, peering up at him through her eyelashes. "I asked that, too. I wanted to have an ice-breaker. You know, something to talk to you about? I wasn't surprised to learn you were a fireman. I thought you must be something, you know, manly like that. With your build and all. But a fire-man. Wow."

He took a sip of his margarita. It was cold and delicious, a perfect combination of sweetness and bite. "A fireman is all I ever wanted to be."

"So do lots of little boys. But you actually grew up to become one." She licked salt from the rim of her glass and smiled at him.

He smiled back.

"Is it fun riding in the truck?"

"Well, if we're going to a fire or an emergency—"

"Oh, I know it's dangerous and all. But still, it's gotta be a kick."

Self-consciously, he grinned. "Yeah, it can be a kick."

Someone jostled her from behind and she fell against him. "Oopsy-daisy." Her breast—the one with the *F* and the *C*—mashed against his arm as she regained her balance. "Sorry."

"It's okay."

"Did I cause you to spill your drink?"

"Just a little." He sucked drops of melting margarita off his hand and took another drink. Then another.

"The house is impossible," she said, "but it's getting crowded out here, too."

"Yeah, it is."

Without his making a conscious decision to relocate, Raley fell into step behind her as she made her way through the gate and out onto the expanse of lawn that connected the units of the complex. In the center of the compound was a swimming pool with a hot tub that would hold twenty, a clubhouse for residents' use, twin tennis courts with basketball hoops at each end, and several gathering places, some enclosed with lattice walls, others open-air for sunning on chaise lounges.

She placed her hand on his arm and bent down to remove her sandals, sighing as her bare feet settled into the grass. "Ooh, that's better."

"I'll bet. Those heels look lethal."

She laughed. "They're killers, all right, but they make your legs look good."

Her legs looked good without them, too. He forced his eyes back up to her face. Had she told him her name? If so, he couldn't recall it. He was about to ask when she posed a question to him. "Do you wear those wide, red suspenders?"

"They're part of our gear."

"They're such a turn-on." Again her tongue flicked salt off her glass. Her lips were very red, her tongue pointed and pink.

He glanced past her, back toward Jay's patio. He didn't realize they'd walked that far. At this distance, Bon Jovi was little more than thudding bass. His pulse seemed to be keeping time with "Wanted Dead or Alive." "Uh, as I said, I was about to leave."

"Oh. I didn't mean to keep you."

"No, it's okay, I—"

"I thought it would be nice to finish our drinks out by the pool. Where it's cooler."

He hesitated, but at that moment, cooler sounded very good. "Okay. Sure."

He walked with her toward the pool, along the way taking several missteps. "The margaritas are strong," he remarked.

"I was about to say the same thing. Want to go swimming? It would clear your head."

A question about swimsuits wafted through his brain, but it was too elusive to grasp. "No. I think I just want to sit a minute."

"Me, too. Let's go over here."

She led him toward one of the areas enclosed by vine-covered lattice. There was seating enough for a small group, but when he sat down on a chaise, she sat down on it, too. "Lean back. I'll switch on the fan."

He lay back onto the angled cushion and watched as she walked to a support post where there was a switch plate. A flick of her fingers and the overhead fan began to turn, creating a welcome breeze. His eyes closed, but he didn't realize they had until she rejoined him on the chaise and he pried them open to see her smiling down at him.

She leaned over him and ran her cold glass across his forehead. "Better?"

He mumbled something but wasn't sure that what he'd said were actual words. Her breasts were sort of in the way of his lips.

"Do you have a girlfriend?"

"Fiancée."

"I figured. Men like you are always taken."

"Men like me?"

She smiled as she undid several buttons on his shirt. "Strong, handsome firemen with hair on their chests." Her fingers combed through his. "So where is she?"

"Uh, Boston. Business."

He jumped when she grazed his nipple with her fingernail and was about to tell her not to do that—he really was—when she said, "I've never been to Boston. Too cold. I like hotter climates, don't you?"

Hallie was in meetings that were long

but informative. See? He wasn't so drunk that he couldn't remember.

"It's awfully hot tonight, though." She lifted her hair off her neck with both hands, held it up, then dropped it. When she did, her hands skimmed over her breasts, and she seemed to like the feel of them, because her right hand stayed. It cupped her right breast, and her thumb began to idly stroke her nipple beneath the shiny *F.* The circular movement of her thumb was hypnotizing, and so was what it was doing to her nipple.

But as seductive as it was, he had to blink hard to hold it in focus. Jesus, he was drunk. His body felt heavy. He wasn't sure he could move his legs, and didn't particularly want to, because that would have meant dislodging . . . uh . . .

Had she told him her name?

Anyway, moving would have meant dislodging her, and he was liking the feel of her hip against his thigh.

How had he got so drunk on one beer and half a margarita? He had a much higher tolerance than that. Years of college drinking had conditioned him . . .

Where was his margarita, anyway?

"Your fiancée left you all alone?"

There was something he should say to that, but damned if he could think of what it was.

"That was pretty stupid of her."

He didn't remember disposing of his margarita, but he must have because his hands were otherwise occupied. One was on . . .

Shit, what *was* her name?

One of his hands was on her leg, being guided beneath her short skirt and up the inside of her thigh, and the other was being pressed against that tight, hard nipple, which had been bared to him.

Her breath was humid against his face. "Stupid of her, but lucky for me."

That pink, pointed tongue he had noticed earlier . . . was it licking the salt off his lips? Something below his waist was feeling damn good, but wrong. Wrong.

This isn't right. This isn't right*! Why am I doing this?*

CHAPTER 10

When Raley stopped talking, the cabin was silent except for the occasional drip of the kitchen faucet. Eventually he looked across at Britt. "That's the last thing I remember. Her tongue was in my mouth and her hand inside my pants, and I was thinking, *What the hell am I doing? I need to stop this.*" He shook his head as though to clear it. "After that, nothing."

Britt drew a shuddering breath. "That sounds familiar."

"I thought it would."

"I don't remember anything beyond wanting to make it to Jay's sofa without falling down. Everything past that is completely blanked out."

"Have you had any flashbacks?"

"I wish I could say yes."

"You may," he said. "Some of it came back to me, the way you remember dreams days after you've dreamed them. An image flashes and then vanishes before your mind can fully register it. A group of words you know you've heard but which make no sense. Like that."

He reached for his water bottle and drained it, then folded his forearms on the tabletop and leaned across it toward her. "Don't you think it's awfully coincidental that we had similar experiences, and in both instances, Jay was behind it?"

"You think Jay set you up with that woman and had her drug you?"

"What do *you* think?"

The question wavered between them like smoke from a snuffed-out candle. After a time, Britt said, "I don't want to think that of Jay."

"No. Because he was a hero. And heroes don't do things like that. Especially not to their friends."

She pictured Jay, smiling and disarming. He always had a mischievous twinkle in his eye, but was he capable of treachery on the level that Raley had described? She couldn't conceive of it. Not the Jay Burgess she knew.

"Does it hurt?" he asked.

While lost in thought she'd been absently rubbing the goose egg on the back of her head. Raley had noticed. "It's caused a dull headache. Do you have a Coke or something?"

He got up, took a canned drink from the fridge, and passed it to her. She opened it and took a sip. "Jay may or may not have had a hand in what happened to you," she said. "But it doesn't make sense that he drugged me so I would be an agreeable lover, and then smothered himself by holding a pillow over his face."

"No. Somebody else came in and did that."

"Who?"

"I don't know."

"Who do you suspect?"

"We'll get to that. Let me tell you what happened that morning when I woke up in Jay's guest bedroom."

"He didn't live in the same town house as he does—*did*—now."

"No. His old apartment had two bedrooms, each with an attached bathroom, separated by a kitchen and living area."

"Right. The bedrooms were on opposite sides of the apartment."

Immediately after the words cleared her mouth, she realized she'd given herself away. She looked at him quickly to see if he'd realized the implication of what she'd said.

Of course he had. He said, "No surprise there."

Her expression wasn't contrite or apologetic. If anything, it was challenging. "So what? Jay and I dated when neither of us was attached, the affair was over soon. In fact, it was so short-lived it could hardly be called an affair. It was harmless."

"Harmless, huh? When you're now suspected of murdering him?"

A long silence stretched taut between them, then she said, "Tell me about the morning following the party."

He pressed the tips of his fingers into

his eye sockets, then dragged his hands down his face, over his bearded cheeks and chin. "I have no memory beyond what I've told you. But till the day I die, I won't forget the absolute horror I experienced when I woke up."

He came awake but didn't open his eyes. He lay still, sorting through the days of the week in his mind, trying to determine which day it was. What was on his agenda for today? Was he on duty or off? When would he see Hallie?

Right, he thought, as though his mind had snapped its fingers. This was Sunday. She was coming home.

With that happy thought, he opened his eyes. He was facing a wall, but it wasn't his wall. It was too close to the bed to be the wall of his bedroom, and besides, it was the wrong color.

Where was he?

He took in more of the wall, the window, and realized he was in Jay's apartment. Guest bedroom. He recognized it because he'd slept here a few times, when poker games went into the wee hours, when his own place was being painted and the fumes had driven him out. Jay had offered his guest room for as long as it took for the painting to be finished. Once, after a long dinner party, Jay had persuaded him and Hallie to sleep in this bed.

Those occasions he remembered clearly.

But he had no idea in hell how he'd got here last night. It was fairly late in the morning, judging by the light coming through the blinds. They were drawn, but bright sunlight rimmed the edge of each slat.

He rolled onto his back, and the motion caused him to moan. His head hurt like a son of a bitch and felt as heavy as an anvil. He wasn't sure he could raise it off the pillow, but he was absolutely positive that he didn't want to try. A motion that extreme would cause his eyeballs to explode. He had the mother of all hangovers, but he didn't even remember—

He gave a cry of shock when he saw the hand.

It was lying palm up, inches from his

thigh, as though seconds before it had been touching him.

That hand, lying supine and still, belonged to a woman.

He bolted from the bed. Or tried. The sheet was tangled up around his legs, causing him to stumble when his feet hit the floor. He landed on one kneecap, so hard it made a knocking sound against the hardwood floor. But in his shock, he barely felt it.

His heart was drumming, and when he heard his own gasping breaths, he willed his mouth shut in order to stopper them. He stood transfixed, but his brain was scrambling, seeking an explanation for the inexplicable.

The woman was dead.

The tanned skin had taken on the ashen hue of death. Her lips were the color of putty. Her eyes, partially open, were beginning to film.

His stupefaction lasted for maybe ten seconds. Perhaps even less. Then his training kicked in, and so did his innate compulsion to act. It wasn't so much compassion, which denoted forethought and a choice to be valiant. With

Raley, it was more like energy, spontaneity, instinct that propelled him to rescue something or someone without his even having to consider it.

He was beside her in a nanosecond, feeling for a pulse. He felt none. Her skin was as cool as marble. Nevertheless, he began giving her CPR.

"Jay!" he shouted. "God dammit, where are you? Jay!" His shouts went unheeded. He could hear no noise in the house except his own labored breathing and his muttered urging for her to move, breathe, revive.

But both his efforts and his prayers were useless. He'd known they would be, but he'd had to try. He continued until his chest was bathed in sweat, until sweat was streaming down his face. Or were those tears of anguish stinging his eyes and rolling down his cheeks?

Finally, weakened by his own exertion, he gave up. He sat back on his heels and stared at her, still trying to grasp how this horror show could possibly be playing out, with him as the lead character.

He reached for the phone on the

nightstand. It was an extension to Jay's landline. He dialed 911. The operator answered.

"There's been a death. Send an ambulance." He hung up before the dispatcher could begin asking questions.

His heels made loud thudding noises against the floor as he ran from the room and down the hallway. Jay was in the kitchen, sitting on a barstool, a mug of coffee in his hand, the Sunday newspaper spread out on the counter in front of him. Earphones bridged his head, and his bare foot was tapping out the beat of the music being piped into his ears.

"Jay!"

Raley didn't think he heard him, but he must have noticed the motion out the corner of his eye. He turned his head and immediately started laughing, which under the circumstances, was obscene. It didn't occur to Raley until much later what a bizarre sight he must have been. Naked and bug-eyed, flapping his arms to get his friend's attention.

As soon as Jay removed his earphones, he said, "The girl—"

"You look like the Wild Man of Borneo," Jay chortled.

"There's a girl—"

"I know, but I promise not to tell."

"She's dead."

Jay bit back a laugh. His smile collapsed. "What?"

Raley turned and retraced his steps to the bedroom, trusting that Jay would follow him. He did. He stopped in the open doorway, stared at the body with dismay, covered his mouth with one hand. "Fuck me."

"I tried to revive her, but . . ." Raley ran his hand over his head. "Jesus Christ." Thinking he might faint, he bent at the waist, placed his hands on his knees, and sucked in several deep breaths.

By the time he straightened up, Jay was standing beside the bed, studying the still form. "Looks like she's been dead for a while."

"I woke up. Found her. Like that."

Jay wiped his mouth again. "Shit, man."

"I know. I've called 911."

Jay nodded absently. "Get some

pants on." Raley stared at him, not quite comprehending. "Get some pants on," Jay repeated.

Staying in one spot, Raley pivoted until he spied his trousers in a heap of clothing belonging to him and the girl. FCUK spelled out in rhinestones, mocking him. He stepped into his pants, pulled them on, did up his fly, but each motion was mechanical.

"What happened?" Jay asked.

Raley looked at him blankly. "What?"

"What happened? Christ, Raley. I've got a dead woman in my house. In bed with you. What the fuck happened?"

"I don't know!"

"What do you mean you don't know?"

"I don't know. I don't remember." He motioned toward the corpse. "I don't even know her name."

Jay placed his hands on his hips and looked at him with consternation, then, hearing the distant whine of a siren, dropped the pose and went into action. His eyes skittered around the room until they lighted on a woman's handbag.

He got it and began rifling through it, coming up with a wallet. He flipped it open. "Suzi with an *i.* Monroe." He shot Raley an inquiring glance.

Raley shook his head. "If she told me her name, I don't remember."

"I never saw her before last night, either," Jay said. "I looked around for you, and saw you out on the patio making chummy with her."

Raley ran his hand down his clammy face. "Yeah, I vaguely remember that. She came up to me and started talking. She gave me a margarita. We walked out . . . out by the swimming pool, I think."

Jay was looking at him with incredulity. "I had no idea you were that far gone."

"What are you talking about?"

"Raley, you and this chick—" He broke off, shook his head impatiently. "We don't have time for this now." The siren's wail had got louder. It was close now. Jay continued to plow through her handbag.

"What are you looking for?"

"She shows up at a party uninvited, a gate-crasher. What does that tell you? She's a party girl, right?"

Raley was too befuddled to reason through whatever it was Jay was trying to communicate.

"Ah!" He withdrew a small folded square of aluminum foil from her bag. Barely pinching the corner of it between his fingernails, he held it up where Raley could see it, then dropped it back into the purse. He went down on one knee and examined the surface of the night-stand. "Un-huh." When he came to his feet, he bent down close to the girl's still face, examining it as a cop would. "She's a cokehead," he said, straightening up and turning to Raley. "Did you snort last night?"

Raley just stared at him, flabbergasted by the question. He and Jay had experimented with marijuana in college but found they got a better buzz from alcohol. Besides it was cheaper, and legal. Jay knew damn well he wasn't a drug user.

Jay said, "I'll take your whey-faced expression as a no."

The siren reached its loudest, then stopped. Jay moved Raley aside as he headed for the door. "I'll let them in. I've got to call the PD. I'll take care of it, okay? Don't say anything to the EMTs. You're too shaken to speak, all right?"

"I *am* too shaken to speak."

"Good." Jay gave him a thumbs-up, then left to let the emergency responders in.

Raley knew them. They gaped at him when they entered the bedroom and saw their cohort standing beside the bed with the naked corpse on it. But they did their job without pausing to ask questions of him.

The next half hour passed in a blur. Later, when Raley tried to recall the sequence of events, they overlapped until they became a mishmash of memories, some indistinct, others sharp. Of the night before, he couldn't remember anything except arriving at Jay's party with Candy and planning a quick getaway seconds before the girl came up to him.

The EMTs summoned the county coroner, who arrived shortly and confirmed that the body in the bed was definitely dead.

At some point Jay handed Raley a cup of coffee. "I called Pat and George, told them briefly what the situation was. Lucky for us, they agreed to come over, even though it's Sunday and neither is on duty."

Pat Wickham and George McGowan, friends of Jay's in the police department. Both were detectives who solved crimes against persons. Assault, rape, murder.

The thought panicked Raley. "I didn't do anything."

"Of course not. Nothing criminal anyway. You got shitfaced with a woman you didn't know. Turns out she was a junkie. How were you supposed to know that? You didn't know she was going to snort after swilling all those margaritas."

"I only had one, and I don't think I finished it."

"More than one, friend." Jay laid his arm across Raley's shoulders. "I've seen you wasted, but not in years, and *never* as wasted as you were last night."

Raley shrugged off Jay's arm. "I'm telling you, I had one beer. Maybe half of a margarita. I couldn't have got that drunk," he insisted.

It was then that Wickham and McGowan arrived. Raley had seen them the previous night, living it up at the party with everyone else. Wickham had been with his wife. McGowan had had an anorexic-looking girl draped on his arm. This morning, they looked hungover, unwashed, and unhappy to be back at Jay's apartment, especially to examine the body of a dead girl.

"In the guest room," Jay said, nodding them down the hallway. He and Raley followed.

The somber quartet took up most of the floor space in the compact room. The detectives looked the body over while Jay and Raley stood by, watching.

"Did you touch her?" Wickham asked.

"CPR" was all he managed to say.

Plastic bags had been placed on the girl's hands. The two detectives turned her onto her side, looking for injuries or wounds on her back. At least that was what Raley surmised.

Jay said, "There's residue on the nightstand. I think it's cocaine. There's a foil packet in her handbag. Dig deeper and we'll probably find a razor and straw, too. My guess is that she's a habitual user. She and Raley tied one on. He passed out. She snorted and died in her sleep."

McGowan said, "Autopsy will tell for sure."

Raley wasn't squeamish. In his line of work, he couldn't be. But hearing the word *autopsy* in this context made the coffee he'd drunk roil in his stomach. As though sensing his discomfort, Jay scooped his clothes from the floor, took him by the arm, and propelled him out of the room.

"Go get yourself straight." He passed the bundle of clothing and shoes to him. "Use my bathroom. Shower if you want. They'll be a while, then we'll talk."

Raley moved like an automaton, down the hallway, through Jay's bedroom, into the bathroom. He threw up. He peed gallons. He splashed his face with cold water, and when that didn't help relieve his grogginess, he showered, alternating the water from scalding to ice cold.

Feeling a bit restored, he joined the

others where they had gathered in Jay's living area, which was still littered with party debris. Wickham opened the discussion. "Hell of a thing, Raley."

After that concise assessment of the situation, anything Raley said would be superfluous, so he merely nodded.

"We, uh, found a coupla condoms under the bed, the side you slept on. They've been used. We'll send them to the lab."

Wickham didn't pose the question outright, but Raley knew what he was asking. "I don't know if we had sex or not," he said. "I don't remember."

"She was a babe," McGowan remarked. "How could you not remember?"

"I don't remember," he repeated. The retching had made his voice husky. He cleared his throat. "I'll tell you what I do remember."

McGowan made a motion with his hand. Raley began. "I came with Candy Orrin." His account lasted through reaching the pool area with the girl—Suzi with an *i*. "But that's where things get hazy. I remember thinking that the margaritas were damn strong. I was dizzy, wanting to sit down."

Jay's phone rang. He excused himself to answer it, turning his back to the room and speaking low into the receiver.

"You were lying down on the chaise," Wickham said, drawing Raley's attention back to him. "My wife and I saw the two of you. Embarrassed her no end. We beat it back to the patio, left you going at it."

Raley's cheeks grew hot. "I remember kissing her, or rather her kissing me."

"Kissing?" Wickham snorted. "Yeah, you probably kissed, too."

Jay rejoined them. "That was Hallie," he reported softly. "She was worried because she hadn't been able to reach you this morning. I told her you crashed here last night and were still asleep."

Raley had to swallow another surge of nausea. He placed his head in his hands and set his elbows on his knees.

Jay patted him on the back. "It'll be okay. It could've happened to anybody. Especially somebody who's been working as hard as you have. You didn't realize you could be slam-dunked by a few margaritas."

"I had less than one," he said, sitting up. *"One,* Jay. And one beer."

Motion drew his attention toward the hallway. The EMTs were wheeling a gurney with a body bag on it toward the front door. Raley was unable to suppress the nausea this time. As he was rushing toward Jay's bathroom, he heard McGowan suggest that Jay bring him down to the temporary PD headquarters for further questioning. Jay promised to have him there by one o'clock. In exchange, he got McGowan's promise to treat this like an accidental death.

"No need to alert the media, is there?" Jay said.

Raley was glad to hear McGowan agree. "No need I can see."

He threw up again, retching with such violence he was surprised his esophagus didn't bleed. Finally, feeling that he'd been wrung inside out, he came shakily out of the bathroom.

The apartment was deserted except for him and Jay, who told him what to do and when to do it, because he seemed incapable of making even the smallest decision.

"Want some toast?"

"No."

"You should get something in your stomach."

"Okay."

"Orange juice?"

"Sure."

"You want to borrow a shirt? Yours has lipstick on it."

"Thanks."

It went like that until they left for the police station, arriving promptly at one o'clock. Wickham and McGowan—now showered and shaved—were waiting for them in an interrogation room. "Is this necessary, guys?" Jay asked as he and Raley were ushered in.

"It is if we want privacy," McGowan said. "We're doing what we can to keep a lid on this."

He offered Raley something to drink. He declined. Jay had medicated his headache with analgesics and had forced gallons of water on him for hydration. The toast had helped settle his stomach. He felt a little more like himself, more confident and clearheaded when, for the second time, he talked them through the events of the night before.

When he finished, Jay looked at his two colleagues with an expression that said, *Satisfied?* They didn't look ready to lynch Raley, but they didn't look convinced beyond a reasonable doubt, either.

Raley knew the time had come for him to take the first proactive step toward defending himself. "I've been thinking about it. I know I was tired. The margaritas were unusually strong. Chalk it up to abnormal metabolism, whatever. One drink could *possibly* have knocked me on my ass. It could *possibly* have prompted me to have sex with that girl. She was a looker, and she came on to me.

"But the amount of alcohol I drank last night couldn't have completely erased my memory. I just don't believe that." He drew a deep breath, let it out slowly. "I think I was drugged."

The three other men just looked at him blankly, their expressions revealing no reaction to his statement. Finally Jay spoke. "Drugged? By the girl?"

"She's the one who brought me the drink. She's the drug user."

"Alleged," Wickham said.

"Alleged," Raley conceded.

"She was," Jay said. "The stash was in her handbag, and I've already tracked down the friend she came with. They were doing coke before they got to the party."

Raley was surprised that Jay had learned all that in such a short amount of time. He was impressed, both by Jay's investigative skills and by his friendship. If he doubted one word of Raley's story, he hadn't shown it.

McGowan was notified of a phone call and left the room to take it.

Jay glanced at his watch. "When Hallie called, she gave me her ETA. If the plane's on time, she's less than an hour out."

Hallie, Jesus. The pilots would be announcing their initial approach into Charleston. She would be anticipating their reunion at baggage claim. She was probably dabbing some powder on her nose, applying fresh lip gloss, checking her hair, using breath spray, innocently expecting to walk into the arms of her faithful fiancé. It broke his heart to think of the disillusionment she would suffer when confronted with his betrayal.

Neither was overly jealous. Hallie didn't come unglued if he had a conversation with another woman, and he didn't think twice about her traveling to Boston with two men from the bank with whom she worked. They trusted each other implicitly.

So how in hell was he going to explain last night to her when he couldn't even explain it to himself? He tried to imagine facing her and saying what he must. How would he even find the words? What words could he use to make this ugliness any prettier? There weren't any words to do that. The woman he loved was going to be devastated by what he'd done, and there was no way to avoid it.

Jay pressed his shoulder. "Why don't you let me pick her up? I'll give her an overview of what's happened. If I soften the blow, she'll be better prepared to hear the details from you."

McGowan, who had returned, said, "That's a good plan. At least as far as picking up Hallie is concerned. We need Raley to stay here."

"What for?" Jay asked.

"Cobb Fordyce. He heard what happened. He wants details."

Cobb Fordyce was the county's ambitious DA. It was said he had a sixth sense when it came to which cases were sound enough to take to trial and which to let go. His critics said this sixth sense was based more on ambition than on seeing justice done, but his critics were in the minority. The voting public held him in high esteem. He had always liked headlines, and since the fire and the heroism he had exhibited that day, he had cultivated them at every opportunity.

Angrily, Jay asked, "Who called him?"

"Doesn't matter, Jay. You're a cop who had a naked dead girl in bed with your houseguest. Those EMTs know Raley. Sooner or later the DA's office had to get wind of it."

"She died of a drug overdose," Jay exclaimed.

"Then neither you nor Raley has anything to worry about, do you?" McGowan said. "The DA's involvement is . . . what do you call it? Routine?"

"Pro forma," Raley said dully.

"Right," McGowan said. "Pro forma. Let Jay go pick up your lady at the airport and break it to her gently that your dick got you in a heap of trouble last night. You stay and talk to Fordyce."

Before he left, Jay pulled Raley aside. "One thing. For godsake don't say anything more about being drugged."

"But—"

"Listen, dammit!" Jay said, taking him by the arm and shaking him slightly. "You go talking about drugs in any context, the logical conclusion will be that you and dead Suzi there did them together, and did so much of them that you blacked out and lost your memory and she died."

Raley covered his head with both hands. "Jesus."

"Yeah." Jay sighed. He left for the airport.

Half an hour later, it wasn't Cobb Fordyce who showed up. Raley was alone in the interrogation room when Candy walked in. She looked worse for wear, her face bloated from a night of too much drink and too little sleep. Smeared mascara had given her raccoon eyes. She was still wearing her party dress. It was wrinkled. He figured she'd slept in it. He wondered where.

She stood in the open doorway, staring at him for several moments before slamming the door shut and advancing into the room. "I didn't believe them. It's true?"

"Unfortunately."

She tossed her briefcase on the small table and released a deep breath. "Holy Christ, Raley."

"I know."

She gathered her hair into a messy ponytail and secured it with an elastic band that had been around her wrist. "Officially I'm here representing District Attorney Cobb Fordyce. He called and asked me could I see to this 'cause he's in the middle of his son's birthday party.

Grandparents, balloons, a wife who'd be pissed if he left."

"Does he know we're friends?"

"I wouldn't be here if he did. And he would fire me if he ever found out. Where's your lawyer?"

"Lawyer?"

"Your lawyer, Raley, your lawyer," she said impatiently. "What's the matter with you? Are you still drunk?"

"I, uh . . ."

"Don't tell me you talked to the police without a lawyer."

"Not the *police,"* he said, raising his voice to match hers. "Jay."

"Oh, Jay," she scoffed. "And McGowan. And Wickham." She looked at him with a mix of bewilderment and irritation. "My boss, the DA, would shit if he knew I had said as much as hello to you without a lawyer present."

"Talk to me, Candy."

She shook her head sternly. "Not a good idea."

"Please." His voice cracked on the word, and that seemed to get to her more than the plea itself.

Her shoulders slumped. She threw a

cautious glance toward the door. "Okay. You've got three minutes before I turn back into an ADA, so be quick. Friend to friend, tell me what happened."

To the best of his ability, he did.

"So you admit sleeping with her," Candy said.

"I woke up beside her."

"She was already dead."

"Of course. Yes. I gave her CPR, but I knew right off she'd been dead for hours."

"You didn't witness her death?"

He gave her a look. She waved her hands in front of her face. "Forget I asked that. Of course you didn't. Did you have sex?"

"Maybe. Probably. They found used condoms."

"Terrific," she muttered. "And by the way, you're a cheating asshole, and I wouldn't blame Hallie if she never spoke to you again."

"I didn't do it consciously."

"Oh, I see. You contend you were *un*-conscious when you fucked her."

"I contend I was . . ." Recalling Jay's advice, he hesitated.

"Was . . . ? What?"

But the caution not to mention drugs couldn't apply to Candy. Lowering his voice he said, "I think I was drugged."

"I heard she was in possession of cocaine. You experimented?"

"No, hell no. I think she slipped me some kind of . . . I don't know. A date rape drug." After a moment, he said, "Stop looking at me like that."

"Sorry," she said angrily. "This is just the way I look whenever a good friend tells me a story that strains credulity."

"I think that's what happened."

She studied him a moment, then pulled a chair from beneath the small table and sat down. "Talk. Hurry. I'm still listening."

He told her his theory, that the drink Suzi Monroe had given him had been spiked with a mind-altering drug. "They give people temporary amnesia, exactly like I experienced."

"Right."

"Well?"

"So does cocaine."

"Jay said I shouldn't mention it."

"Jay was right." When she saw that

he was about to protest, she said, "But okay, I'll tell Fordyce you're convinced you were slipped a Mickey. I'm not sure I can convince him. It's pretty thin, Raley. As a defense, 'I don't remember' is for shit."

"You don't believe me?"

"*I* believe you because I know you. But . . ." She gestured toward the closed door. "The DA, even these detectives, will be skeptical at best. It's an awfully convenient memory loss. Get a lawyer. Now. Before you say another word to anyone. And get a urinalysis ASAP." She gave his hand a reassuring squeeze, but her smile was as thin as his defense.

CHAPTER 11

Bumblebees were buzzing around the blooming jasmine outside the kitchen window. When Raley stopped talking, Britt could hear them as well as she might have heard an airplane flying low above the roof. Their busy drone seemed that loud.

"When I first saw her there in the bed," he said in a distant voice, "I realized the effect it would have on my life. It was like . . . like . . ." He searched for a simile. "Like when you see a Christmas ornament fall off the tree and shatter into a million splinters of glass?" Britt acknowledged the description with a nod.

"Well, an instant before it does, you know there's nothing you can do to reverse the law of gravity or change the consequences of the inevitable. The damage will be done and it will be irreparable.

"When I saw her lying there dead, I knew this event would be like that to my life. I couldn't halt the certain destruction. My life was about to shatter. Trying to put it back to the way it had been before would be hopeless."

Britt covered her lips to keep them from trembling. She knew that feeling. "What you're describing is exactly how I felt when I woke up and found Jay dead beside me."

He studied her Coke can, watching a rivulet of condensation roll down its surface and puddle at the base. "To think I'd been sleeping there beside her most of the night, while she was dying." He stopped and dropped his chin onto his chest, massaging his forehead. "I was all about saving people, for crissake."

She almost reached across the table to touch his hand in consolation but caught herself before she did. "You weren't *sleeping,* Raley. You were knocked out. And *you* didn't kill her. You were innocent."

He raised his head and looked at her with green eyes gone hard and cold again. "That's not what you told your television audience."

"I never said you were guilty of a crime."

"Not in so many words, but that was the implication."

"I've said I was sorry."

"And I've said it's a little late for apologies. What happened that morning ruined my life. It cost me everything. *Everything,"* he repeated, banging the table with his fist for emphasis and making the half-empty Coke can jump. "And your slanted reporting made certain I couldn't salvage any of it."

"So what do you want me to do?" She flung her arms out to her sides. "Beyond believing you and accepting what you're telling me now as truth, what can I do to make it up to you?"

He became very still, and the look he gave her made her want to pull her windbreaker closed. But because she was no longer wearing it, all she could do was retract her arms, fold them over her chest, and endure the intensity of his gaze and what it suggested. Refusing to simper and look away, she stared back.

The legs of his chair made an irritating screech on the vinyl as he got up suddenly. He moved to the center of the room and yanked the string to turn on the ceiling fan. He returned to the kitchen but not to his chair at the table. He began to pace the narrow space between the counter and the table.

"Candy was right. My defense was thin. But I had a couple of things on the plus side. The head bartender, rented for the party, admitted that the margaritas had enough tequila in them to knock a mule on its ass as well as some Everclear just to give them an extra kick.

"And Suzi Monroe's autopsy showed enough cocaine in her system to stop her heart. But, like you, Britt, by the time I was tested for cocaine, and any of the common date rape drugs, they had already left my system."

"So you didn't take Jay's advice?"

"No, I did. When the urinalysis came

back negative, it made his appeal even stronger. I'd been cleared of any drug usage. Better to keep it that way, he said."

"What about Wickham and McGowan? They heard you say that you'd been drugged."

"Jay told me not to worry about them. He said he'd taken care of it. I guess he did. They never brought it up again."

"The DA never knew?"

"Oh, yeah. Candy believed me and decided Fordyce must know. She and I had a closed-door meeting with him."

"Just the three of you?"

"And this lawyer I retained."

"What was his name? Started with a *B,* didn't it?"

"You don't remember with good reason. I got him out of the phone book. Turns out he didn't know his elbow from his asshole. Anyway, we met with Fordyce."

"And?"

"He listened, but I got nowhere with him. The semen in the condoms was mine. From Fordyce's viewpoint, it stood to reason that, if I'd had sex with

Suzi Monroe, I could also have encouraged her to use the cocaine. Even though my urinalysis came back negative, that didn't prove I hadn't tried to get my date hopped up."

"Fordyce said that?"

"Basically. He kept calling my memory loss an 'alleged' blackout. If he believed in it at all, he reasoned it was alcohol induced. Nevertheless, he promised to carefully consider the case from every angle, which is politician-speak for 'get out of here and quit wasting my time.'

"Candy berated herself for misjudgment. She had thought my earnest testimony to Fordyce would help my position. When what it actually amounted to was a confession from me that I'd been out of my head that night and capable of doing just about anything."

"During this time, you were furloughed from the fire department."

"The chief had no choice, really." He sat down at the table again. "I never blamed him. He was only doing what he thought was right for the department. I was embroiled in a scandal involving drunkenness, sex, and death by cocaine OD. Not a good image for a fireman.

"Brunner used the incident to get me taken off the investigation. He made noises about hating having to do it, but secretly I think he was glad for the excuse to be rid of me.

"But the chief didn't fire me right away. He was waiting, just as I was, to see what Fordyce would do. Would I be charged with reckless endangerment, manslaughter, or let off the hook with nothing more than a stern reprimand and a warning to be more careful next time?"

He stopped there, and she knew what was coming next. "That's when I came onto the scene," she said softly. Although she knew it was useless, she tried again to defend herself. "It was a juicy story for all the reasons you just stated, Raley. One of the city's finest caught in bed with a dead girl."

"Drugs, sex, and rock and roll."

"Absolutely. It was a plum that got dropped into my lap. I jumped at it."

"You sure as hell did. I had cameras,

microphones, and lights trained on me day and night. You even had your damn news vans parked outside—"

When he broke off, Britt finished the sentence for him. "Outside Hallie's house."

She hoped he would continue on that subject, but he didn't. He flipped open the lid to the toothpick box, closed it, flipped it open again, then closed it with finality. She imagined he closed the subject of his fiancée just as purposefully.

He took up the story again. "I was put through extensive questioning, but in the end Fordyce didn't have enough evidence for a criminal case, so I wasn't indicted. On the record books, Suzi Monroe's death went down as an accidental overdose."

He met Britt's gaze with angry eyes. "That probably would have been the end of it. I would never have got over it—never will—but at least if it had stopped there, the burden would have been mine alone to carry. It would have remained a private matter. But then you went on TV and made Suzi Monroe out as a victim."

"She was."

"She wasn't *my* victim!" he said, digging his index finger into his chest. "She was a victim of the lifestyle she'd chosen. She was a chronic drug user. A party girl who swapped blow jobs for drugs. Jay had lined up dozens of her acquaintances who would corroborate that."

He left his chair angrily, rounded it, and then braced his hands on the back of it, leaning forward as he continued to berate her. "But you didn't show recent pictures of her wearing stiletto heels and skimpy tops with suggestive phrases spelled out in rhinestones. You showed your viewers high school graduation pictures of her." His volume increased. "In her cap and gown. She looked like a cross between the girl next door and a Rhodes scholar."

"I asked her mother for a photograph—"

"Her *mother,* who didn't want her daughter to be remembered as a coked-out whore, who would much rather Suzi with an *i* be immortalized as the victim of a brute who got her drunk, fucked her, and then did nothing to stop her from overdosing on blow."

Britt took the harsh criticism because it was warranted. Never in a million years would she admit to manipulating the story to that extent in order to impress her new employer and further her career. But in good conscience she couldn't deny that her reporting had been biased, against Raley Gannon.

"I've said—"

"Spare me," he said shortly.

He made a tight circle in the kitchen, holding his hair back off his face, a gesture that was now familiar to her. She'd seen him do it whenever he reached the limit of his frustration. It was his way of getting a grip on his temper. Whatever it took to do that she was grateful for. Angry, he frightened her.

He resumed his seat. "After Suzi was portrayed as a saint and I her despoiler, the chief had no choice but to fire me. Fordyce didn't prosecute me for a crime, but he didn't need to. I'd been tried and convicted by public opinion." His eyes said, *By you.*

After a tense silence, she asked tentatively, "Is that when you moved out here?"

He gave a curt nod. "I rented the place for several months, then decided to buy it because I knew I'd never go back. For living a life that's not worth shit, this is as good a place as any."

"Where are we exactly?"

"Inland between Beaufort and Charleston." He told her the general area, locating it for her by naming several towns.

"I never heard of them," she said.

"That's the point."

"Does anyone . . . Do you see anyone?"

"Like who? My attorney? I paid his invoice, fired him, then never saw or heard from him again. All my friends who stuck by me?" He made a scornful sound.

"Parents?"

He looked pained and said softly, "They left Charleston, too."

"Did they believe you?"

"Without question. I'm an only child. We've always had a close relationship. They would have stood by me, no matter what."

"Would have?"

"Would have and did. But because they did, they became outcasts by association. Even their oldest friends started avoiding them. They got tired of being ostracized. Dad took early retirement from a medical supply company he helped build, and they moved to Augusta, where Mom has a sister. I hate like hell what they went through on account of me. I'll never be able to make it up to them. Their whole lives had been spent in Charleston. They tell me they've made new friends, that they like it there, but . . ." He shrugged.

It was on the tip of her tongue to ask about his fiancée, but instead she said, "How do you stand it? The isolation. Having no contact with anyone. Well, except for Delno. What do you do with your time?"

He stared at her for several moments. "I plot my revenge." He spoke quietly, with menace, in a voice that raised gooseflesh on her arms.

She welcomed the noise from outside that signaled Delno's return. As he stepped onto the porch, he hung a limp carcass on a hook attached to the overhang, told the hounds to lie down, pulled open the screen door, and poked his head inside. "Okay if I come in?"

"No," Raley said.

Delno stepped inside anyway, rubbing his hands together. "Did I miss anything important?"

"Nothing you haven't heard."

His bare feet sounded like hooves on the vinyl when he reached the kitchen. "I'm hungry. You got anything to eat?" He checked the contents of the fridge and, with disappointment, said, "Lunch meat. You rather me fry up that rabbit?"

"I'd rather you go home, and take your stinking, flea-infested dogs with you." Suddenly Raley got up from his chair and stalked out of the cabin.

Britt looked at Delno, who apparently had decided the lunch meat wasn't such a bad choice after all. He folded several slices of pink processed meat into his mouth. It was such an unappetizing sight, she glanced at the screen door that had slammed shut behind Raley's abrupt exit. "He's still mad at me."

"Ah, he's just horny, is all."

Her head came around quickly. "I beg your pardon?"

"Horny." He closed the refrigerator door and wiped his mouth with the back of his hand. "I seen it right off." He dug into his ear with his little finger and extracted a wad of wax that he wiped on the bib of his overalls. "Can't say as I'm surprised. The way you've been fannin' around here in that getup."

Attorney General Cobb Fordyce had a hard time keeping his mind on the heated discussion. The long, oval conference table had become a battlefield, opposing sides facing off across its polished surface like armies camped on either side of a DMZ. He held the neutral position at the head of the table.

Before the meeting commenced, he'd considered calling the parties involved and begging for a postponement. But it had been postponed once already. To ask for another delay would antagonize both sides. There would be speculation that his avoidance was politically motivated.

The issue was vitally important and

polarizing. The legislators present were operating under a deadline. For those reasons, he'd let them assemble as scheduled even though his concentration was focused not on this topic but on another one.

After hearing the result of Jay Burgess's autopsy this morning, that was all he could think about.

"Mr. Fordyce, the new bill on gun control needs your endorsement to get passed," a constituent said when he could work the words in edgewise.

"It won't matter whether you endorse it or not, Mr. Attorney General," one of his opponents said with confidence, which to Fordyce seemed feigned. "As this bill now reads, this legislature will not vote it into law."

"Then why are you trying so earnestly to persuade him not to endorse it?" one from the other side fired back.

Cobb stood up. "Gentlemen, let's take a break before blood is shed over a gun-control bill. Wouldn't that be ironic?" He flashed his vote-winning smile and received the expected chuckles. "Help yourselves to water, coffee.

Those chocolate chip cookies are worth the calories. I'll be back in a minute."

He hoped none of them would follow him into the men's restroom, and none did. He used the urinal, feeling obliged to after having interrupted the meeting under that pretext. At the washbasin, he held his hands under the cold-water tap, making certain that his starched cuffs, with the state seal cuff links, didn't get wet.

So, he thought.

News that Jay Burgess had been murdered would blanket the state today. It would be blared from every newspaper headline and media broadcast. No one could avoid hearing about it, even if they wanted to.

When he'd arrived at his office this morning, his secretary had told him, with inappropriate excitement, that she'd heard it on CNN.

"You were mentioned, sir," she'd said. "They showed that famous picture of the four of you with the fire blazing in the background."

That fucking photograph. That fucking fire.

Since that day, there had been many times that Cobb wished he could roll back the clock, that he had an opportunity to opt against going to the meeting that had placed him at the police station that particular day at that particular time. On any other day, he would have been in his office at the courthouse, or on his way home. That day had been an exception, and he had rued it ever since.

But there had been just as many times—possibly even more—that he was grateful for the instant fame he'd received as a consequence of the fire. His political career would eventually have been launched, probably with success. But not with the velocity with which it had been. And he'd been awfully impatient to experience that soar to the AG's office, hadn't he?

He'd benefited from the fire, and consequently from the deaths of the seven people who'd perished in it. And, in the depths of his soul, where one must be brutally honest, he wasn't all that sorry about it. What kind of man did that make him?

But thinking in those terms was an exercise in futility. Fate was fate, and there was no cheating it. When it was a person's time to go, it was his time to go. He and his ambition were of infinitesimal significance when gauged against cosmic forces or, if one were religious, predestination.

That was what he told himself. That was the credo that allowed him to sleep nights. He'd made his peace with it. He could live with it, if everybody else could, if everybody else could just forget about the fire and move on.

It seemed, however, that it would never be extinguished. If Jay Burgess had gone out quietly, dying gracefully of cancer . . .

But, no, that wasn't Jay's style, was it?

Now an investigation was under way, the same excitement surrounding it as when Patrick Wickham was killed. Wickham's assailant had never been identified, or caught. Eventually his murder ceased to be the lead story and then faded until it was no longer a story at all.

After honoring his fellow hero at his funeral, as was only proper, Cobb had let Wickham's murder gradually fade from the voting public's attention. As a candidate to become the chief law enforcement officer of the state, he could have spoon-fed the voters daily reminders of the policeman's bloody slaying and used it to strengthen his campaign. He could have encouraged a full-fledged investigation until the cop killer was caught and brought to justice.

But he hadn't. He couldn't.

Staring at himself in the mirror above the basin where the cold water continued to splash over his hands, he saw reflected back at him a reasonably handsome face, graying temples, a physique kept trim with daily workouts. A face that bespoke clean living and integrity. Faithful husband, good father, churchgoer. That was what the public saw, too. A man who looked his role and inspired confidence in the judicial system, freedom and justice for all. But then people saw only what was exposed to them, didn't they?

He doubted anyone hearing the circumstances surrounding Jay Burgess's death would look beyond what appeared to be obvious: his philandering had caught up with him and he'd been smothered with his own pillow by a scorned woman.

Would anyone, he wondered, recall a man named Raley Gannon and the accusations made against him five years ago?

Avoiding his own eyes in the mirror, Attorney General Cobb Fordyce bent over the sink and splashed cold water onto his face.

Pat Wickham, Jr., worked up his courage and punched in the telephone number.

"Conway Construction."

"Is, uh, is George there?"

"I'm sorry. He's out until later this afternoon."

"Oh." Pat's forehead broke out in sweat. He blotted it with his folded pocket handkerchief.

"Is there a message I can give him?"

"Uh, no. I'll try back later."

Pat hung up quickly and peered over the wall of his cubicle, on the lookout for other officers, desk jockeys like him. His beat was a computer. He was a glorified file clerk. Guns scared him. Criminals revolted him. He carried a badge, but he wasn't cut out to be a policeman. He'd never wanted to be, and he looked upon the next twenty-two years before he could retire as a sentence he must serve.

The coast being clear, Pat dialed a cell phone number. The phone rang three times before it was answered with a brusque hello.

"George? Pat Wickham."

He could sense George McGowan's displeasure, and for a moment he thought the other man would hang up on him. But then he grumbled, "Hold on."

Pat heard a muffled conversation where George excused himself, followed by several seconds of silence while he sought privacy. Then, "How'd you get this number?"

"I'm a cop."

A sound of derision, then, "I'm in the middle of an important meeting. My father-in-law is about to wrap up a contract to build the new athletic complex. You couldn't have called at a worse time."

"We need to talk about Jay."

"Fuck we do," George said under his breath.

"They know how he was murdered."

"I heard."

"That newswoman is saying she was given a date rape drug."

"Heard that, too."

"Well?"

"Well *what*?"

Pat estimated that George McGowan outweighed him by seventy-five pounds. But at that moment, he wished for the physical strength to match his anger. He'd bash the other man's beefy head into the wall for being so obtuse.

"Aren't you worried?"

"Yeah, I'm worried. I had to play eighteen holes of golf and lose, then suffer through a two-hour lunch followed by a ninety-minute sales pitch. After all that, if this contract negotiation goes south, Les is going to blame me for interrupting his closing sales pitch to take this call."

Pat saw through the other man's bluster. George was just as concerned over their situation as he was. "Now Britt Shelley has gone missing."

"Missing? What do you mean, missing?"

"Just what I said," Pat replied irritably. "She wasn't at home when Clark and Javier went to serve the warrant. She's not at the TV station. She hasn't been seen since yesterday afternoon. There's an APB out on her car."

George silently digested all that, then asked, "What do you expect me to do about it? Go beating the bushes looking for her?"

"What do you think it means, her vanishing like that?"

"How the hell should I know, Pat? First thing that springs to mind is that she didn't want to be arrested."

There was an implied *duh* at the end of that, which Pat ignored. "How much do you think Jay told her?"

In a different tone, one rife with uncertainty, George said, "I don't know."

The other man's anxiety increased Pat's own. "Oh, Jesus."

"For crissake, will you get a grip? Don't fall apart."

"What are we going to do?"

"Nothing. We're going to do nothing

except act as though everything is normal. Do *nothing,* Pat, you understand me?"

Pat resented the other man's bullying tone. Who did he think he was, talking down to him like that? He, who everybody knew was his father-in-law's whipping boy. He, who had a wife with a leg problem—she couldn't keep them closed.

George had been one of Pat Sr.'s best friends when they were fellow police officers. By extension, he became a family friend and was often a guest at their house for dinner. Pat could remember George socking him playfully on the arm, teasing him about girls, talking to him about baseball, and playing video games with him. He was loud and rambunctious and fun.

That was before he married Miranda Conway. Before he and Pat Sr. became heroes. Before the fire.

After that, they didn't see much of George McGowan around the Wickham household.

"I gotta go now," George said. "And

don't call me again. The less contact we have, the better. You got that?"

He hung up before Pat could counter. Pat's palm was damp as he replaced the telephone receiver in its cradle. He pretended to be studying the file on his computer screen in case another officer happened by.

The call to George hadn't allayed his nervousness, as hoped, but escalated it. The big man's bravado was phony. Pat would bet that if you scratched the surface of George McGowan's brawny body, you'd find a coward as fearful as he was.

Like him, George was afraid that someone would trace Jay Burgess's murder back to the police station fire. Would anyone make that connection? Was there any suspicion that the two events were related?

Was anyone watching *him*?

Pat Wickham, Jr., often wished he had eyes in the back of his head.

And not just at work.

CHAPTER 12

Sitting on the tree stump at the edge of the woods, Raley watched Delno take the dead rabbit and his trio of hounds and tromp off in the direction of his cabin. The dense foliage seemed to swallow him whole and left nothing to indicate his passage except a cantankerous, territorial blue jay.

Around Raley's cabin, hardwoods fraternized with evergreens. In the spring, blooming trees and wild bushes created splashes of white and pastel. Even in the dead of winter, the palmettos and live oaks stayed green, giving the illusion of eternal summer.

The place could be really pretty, if one had a mind to spruce up the cabin, modernize the kitchen and bathroom, furnish it properly, add some amenities, some homeyness, some more sweet potato vines.

Impatient with himself, Raley pushed aside the daydream and the pleasing images it conjured.

He'd used his irritation with Delno as an excuse to get out of the cabin for a while. But even if Delno hadn't interrupted, Raley would have fabricated a reason to go outside. He was used to living without air-conditioning. The summer heat and humidity no longer bothered him. Except today. Today the air within the four walls of the cabin had been stifling.

But the atmosphere couldn't be blamed for his claustrophobia any more than Delno could. It was talking about the fire, and Suzi Monroe's death, and all the crap that followed that had caused anger and resentment to build inside his chest until it became so constricted he could no longer breathe.

And then there was Britt Shelley.

He'd had to take a breather from her, too. When she'd asked what she could do to make up for all the ills she'd imposed on him, several possibilities had sprung immediately to mind. All of them tantalizing. All of them prohibited.

Last night, when he forced her to sleep beside him, he'd done it to make her uncertain and uncomfortable. Call it payback for all the grief she'd caused him.

But in all honesty, he'd also done it because he couldn't resist lying down with a woman with whom he'd had a conversation—even a hostile one—that went beyond "How much?" or "I'll be gone in the morning. This is just for tonight." And usually he left long before morning.

Now, he thought sleeping beside Britt had probably been a gross strategic error. While the tactic had served its original purpose, it had also inflamed his imagination.

But skulking outside was taking a coward's way out to avoid her, wasn't it? He forced himself off the stump, across his yard, and up the steps. He went inside.

She was standing in the dead center

of the room, arms at her sides, as though she'd been ordered to wait there for his return. She was backlighted by the western sun coming through the kitchen window. The ceiling fan caused strands of hair to lift and fall around her face in an airy dance.

She said, "It's getting late. I should go back now."

"Right." He'd talked through all the morning hours and into the afternoon. Only now did he realize that most of the day was gone.

Self-consciously she tugged on the hem of the chambray shirt. It fell to midthigh on her. The sleeves had been rolled to her elbows. She'd buttoned all but the collar button. "I hope you don't mind that I borrowed this. I couldn't find my windbreaker."

It was hotter inside than out, so she hadn't put on his shirt because she'd caught a chill. More likely she'd finally realized how abbreviated her sleeping attire was. It wasn't a slinky see-through negligee, all the critical parts were covered, but by lightweight fabric that clung and looked like it would dissolve if touched. Last night, he'd done the gentlemanly thing by putting the windbreaker on her before carrying her from her house.

"Your windbreaker is on the ground out by the truck," he said. "I think one of the hounds used it for a pallet."

"It's okay."

"Are you ready?"

She nodded.

"Need the bathroom before we head out?"

"I'm fine."

"I'll be right with you."

In the bedroom, he changed out of yesterday's shirt and put on a fresh one, realizing as he reached into his tiny closet that she must have recently rifled through it to get the shirt. He wondered why she'd chosen the chambray. It was old and soft from being washed so many times. Maybe it looked comfortable. Maybe she thought it would fit her better than the others. Maybe she thought the rest of his shirts were ugly.

He used the toilet, washed his hands, and was about to leave the bathroom when he decided to brush his teeth. He noted that the cap on the tube of toothpaste had been replaced since he'd used it that morning. Her doing, because he had a bad habit of leaving it uncapped.

She had cleaned her mouth, too. For some reason, knowing that stirred him.

He turned off the fan and locked the cabin door. She had already climbed into the cab of his truck by the time he got outside. He picked up her windbreaker, shook off the dirt before tossing it into the bed of the truck, then got in.

She'd found her purse on the floorboard. Taking a small hairbrush from it, she ran it through her hair, checked her reflection in the mirror of a compact, and sighed over what she saw. However, she didn't bother to make repairs. After returning the compact and hairbrush to the handbag, she replaced it on the floorboard between her feet.

They rode in silence for as long as it took them to cover the four point seven miles to the main road. As he turned onto it, he said, "I'll drop you at your car."

She looked at her bare feet and pulled

on the stringy hem of his shirt. "If I'm arrested before I get home, I'll be taken to the police station like this."

He glanced at her legs. "That would cause a sensation."

"The last thing I want is to cause a sensation."

"What? It's not a ratings period?"

She shot him a dirty look. The snide remark had been as low as her sarcastic mention of a razor last night. But it got them safely off the subject of her shapely bare legs.

They rode in silence for another mile or so. When he finally looked over at her again, he saw that she'd laid her head back. Her eyes were closed. She was still except for her breathing. For a few seconds he watched the steady rise and fall of his old chambray shirt. It had never looked so good.

He cleared his throat. "There will be police officers staked out at your house. What are you going to tell them?"

"That I promise to go peacefully if they'll let me change clothes."

"I mean about why you weren't at home when they came to arrest you."

"I'm wondering that myself. Do I tell them I was kidnapped? Would they believe me?"

"Doubtful. Especially not after the date-rape-drug, memory-loss account of your night with Jay."

"One story sounds as implausible as the other, doesn't it?" Without moving her head, she opened her eyes and cut them toward him. "I don't suppose you would come forward and admit that you'd taken me forcibly from my home in the middle of the night?"

He shook his head.

She closed her eyes again. "I didn't think so, but thought I'd ask anyway."

"I had my time in the spotlight. I didn't like it. I'm working deep in the background now."

"So I'll have to face the music alone."

"Just like I did."

"Here we go again. Poor Raley."

That sparked his temper. "I didn't ask for your pity."

She sat up straight and turned toward him. "Didn't you?"

"No!"

"Well, you sure made certain I knew

about everything you'd lost. Your reputation, your job, your—"

"My what? Finish."

"Your fiancée."

He fixed his eyes on the road ahead. "You're just itching to know, aren't you?"

"I asked Delno."

"What he'd tell you?"

"He asked me what you'd told me about her, and when I said you hadn't told me anything, he said it looked to him like you didn't want me to know." She waited; he remained stubbornly silent. "Why don't you want me to know?"

"There's nothing to know."

"Bullshit."

He gave a short laugh. "That's a word your viewers have never heard from your sweet lips."

"What happened with her, Raley?"

"God, don't you ever give it a rest?"

"Not until I have the whole story. All I know is that her name was Hallie."

"It still is."

"Lovely woman. Smart, successful, pretty."

"All of the above."

"How long were you engaged?"

"A little over a year."

"You planned to get married on April twelfth."

"But we didn't. End of story." He almost expected another *bullshit,* but she didn't respond right away. Although his eyes remained on the road, he could feel her staring at his profile.

After several moments, she said softly, "Raley, it was a lot for her, for any woman, to . . ."

"Forgive?"

"Absorb. Before she could even begin to forgive you, she had to absorb the fact that you went without her to a party that promised to be wild. A recipe for trouble."

"She urged me to go, remember? She was glad I was taking a break from the investigation."

"She was terribly naïve."

"Say again?"

Knowing he'd heard her, she said with asperity, "Either Hallie was naïve or you were incredibly trustworthy."

"Maybe a bit of both."

"Maybe. I only know I would never have said 'excellent idea' to my fiancé going without me to a party hosted by Jay Burgess."

"That makes you possessive."

"Sensible."

"Jealous."

"Let's move past this, okay?"

"No, let's stick with it. What are you like, Britt? In a relationship, I mean. Are you a clinger? Insecure and grasping? Or do you do your own thing and let the guy hang on until he gets tired and lets go?"

His attempt to redirect the conversation from his personal life to hers didn't work. She asked, "What happened after Jay picked up Hallie at the airport?"

He rolled his shoulders as though trying to throw off a heavy mantle.

"It would help you to talk about it."

He gave her a look. "No, it would help *you.*"

"I deserve that, I guess. But this is off the record."

"Why are you so curious? Voyeurism?"

"I *didn't* deserve that."

He looked at her again, then swore

under his breath. "Okay. But you're going to be disappointed. There was no big scene, no fireworks, nothing you can dramatize on TV."

She just looked at him expectantly.

Where to start? Taking a breath, he began. "I was still at the police station when Jay got back. He'd taken Hallie directly to her place from the airport. He told me she was upset. Very. Then he patted me on the back. 'But she's strong. She'll be okay.'

"Wickham and McGowan said they had nothing further at that time; I was free to go. I left the police station and went straight to Hallie's condo. I rang the bell, but she didn't answer. I used my key and went inside. She was curled up in the corner of the living room sofa, hugging a pillow to her chest, crying."

He hesitated on the threshold, but when she didn't scream for him to get out and leave her alone, he went in and gently closed the door. Mail that had been dropped through the slot in the door during her absence still lay scattered on the floor. He stepped over it. All the shades were drawn. She hadn't turned on any lights, so the living room was dim.

They looked at each other across the space separating them, and his heart cracked in two when he saw the misery in her streaming eyes.

This was so different from the homecoming they'd planned. He projected onto his mind's eyes a corny reunion, like a scene from a commercial or a romantic movie, where the background goes gauzy when the lovers make eye contact. They move toward each other with breathless anticipation, and when they meet, they share a protracted kiss. Or maybe they embrace and spin together, giddy and in love.

He and Hallie had had moments like that, where they'd laughed for no other reason than the pure joy of knowing that they'd found in each other the perfect partner, or quiet times when they exchanged a look and a smile, content in a cocoon of shared silence.

He wondered if it were possible for them ever to have moments like that again. God, he hoped so. Perhaps this experience would strengthen their relationship. But first they must survive it.

He walked to the sofa and sat down. He didn't touch her, nor she him. She continued to sob quietly. He wanted to take her in his arms, tell her how sorry he was, how much he loved her, how everything was going to be all right. He would *make* it all right. But he allowed her to cry, hoping this was the first step in the healing and forgiving process.

Easily half an hour elapsed, although time had no relevance. He would have sat there forever, waiting for a signal from her that it was okay to speak. Finally, she blotted her eyes and wiped her nose and looked at him. In a gravelly voice she said, "Raley?"

The question mark placed at the end of his name conveyed her profound disbelief that they must even engage in this conversation. She was waiting for an explanation. He laid his arm along the back of the sofa and looked into her face. He said the only thing he could think to say, but it came from the bottom of his soul. "Hallie, I am sorry."

Somehow, they came together then,

clutching each other, crying together. It was the first time since waking up that morning that he'd been able to let go of his own emotions. He wept for the girl who had died, for the crisis his life was in, for the terrible heartache he was causing this woman he loved.

Finally, he pulled himself together, wiped his face, clasped her hand between his. "I'm going to tell you everything. Exactly as it happened. Then if you want to hit me, or order me to leave, or—"

"Just tell me, Raley."

So he did. He didn't spare a single detail, even when it was difficult to speak the self-incriminating words. She deserved the absolute truth.

"I should have excused myself the moment she approached me. I should have said no thanks to the drink and left as I'd planned to. I didn't see her and think, *Hallie's out of town. I'll cheat. She'll never know. Jay will keep my secret.* I swear to you, Hallie, it wasn't like that. I have no excuse except that she was hot looking, and she was being friendly, and I guess I needed the flattery."

"My loving you isn't flattery enough?"

"Yes. Of course. But—"

"But your buddy did your job for you. He saved lives and became a hero. That's what's been eating at you, isn't it?"

"A bit, yeah."

The confession saddened her. "You don't have anything to prove to me, Raley. Or to yourself. No one questions your work ethic, your knowledge and skill, certainly not your valor."

"I know," he said a bit testily, which he instantly regretted. "But, ever since the fire, I can't help being just a little ticked off that Jay had done what I was supposed to do. So when this chick picked me out of the crowd, yeah, I admit it, it did my ego good. Anyway, I didn't walk away. I ask your forgiveness for that. But for the rest of it . . ." He moved closer to her. "Hallie, I know—I can't prove it, but I *know*—the margarita she gave me must've been spiked."

"Jay told me that."

"You know my tolerance level. Several

sips of a margarita, no matter how strong, wouldn't have made me stupid to the point that I'd jeopardize my relationship with you. I wouldn't risk losing you for a night with another woman, any woman. It wouldn't happen. The only explanation is that I wasn't myself. I wasn't in control."

As best he could, he tried to explain how his body had responded as any man's would to the sexual stimulation, but that *he,* his heart and soul and mind, hadn't even been present. "Do you believe that? If you don't, I might as well stop here."

Her eyes searched his. "I believe you, Raley. I do. I just can't get past how you could let yourself get into a situation like that at all."

"You wanted me to go to the party, Hallie." He said that in a tone that wasn't contentious. He wasn't trying to shift blame, and he certainly didn't want to start an argument.

"I know, I know." She closed her eyes for a moment.

When she opened them, he could tell she had fortified herself to hear more.

He talked her through the harrowing experience of waking up and finding Suzi Monroe dead beside him. He told her about his series of conversations with the detectives.

"Do they believe you?" she asked.

"They seem to. Jay did, and you know how persuasive he can be. He didn't mention drugs again, but he blamed the alcohol. Combined with my fatigue, it hit me hard. He impressed upon Wickham and McGowan that I wasn't entirely responsible for my sexual escapade. I for damn sure wasn't responsible for the way Suzi died."

He told her about Candy coming to his rescue even though she was technically representing the other side. "She called me names and said if she was you, she'd never speak to me again."

Hallie gave a weak smile. "Sounds like her." Then she sighed and asked him if he'd like a Coke. They went into the kitchen and sat on barstools, knees touching as he explained what Jay had told him to expect in the days to come.

"I gave them a urine specimen, which will be tested. The semen in the condoms is on its way to the lab." He pretended not to see her wince. "There will be an autopsy. Jay says a lot will hinge on that. They're going to keep the incident under wraps, treat it like an accidental overdose, which I'm positive it was."

Hallie remained silent for a while, studying the top of her Coke can. "Why would she drug you, Raley?" Lifting her gaze to his, she repeated, "Why?"

"I guess to make sure she got laid."

"You've described her as hot looking. There are always men on the prowl at Jay's parties, looking for wild and willing girls just like you've described Suzi Monroe. Why would she single you out and drug you if all she wanted was to get laid?"

"I don't have an answer to that."

She stared at him for several seconds more, then looked away. "Do your parents know?"

"I called them from the police station and laid out the whole story. They were at a loss for words. A girl died while in my company, in bed with me. Naturally they were stunned. At first. Then they wanted to rush right down, lend support, find me an attorney. I told them not to come, that for the time being I was doing okay."

"But they believed you."

"Unequivocally."

He was hoping she would say she believed him unequivocally, too, but what she said was, "My folks will have to be told."

"Let me tell them. It was my mistake."

"They'll be . . . God, I can't even imagine." She covered her face with both hands. "Shocked."

"I think shock is a fair reaction to news this bad."

"When all their friends hear, they'll be so embarrassed."

"I hope it doesn't come to that. Jay is keeping it out of the news."

Fresh tears spilled down her cheeks. She looked at him mournfully. "Why did this happen to us?"

"Because I was stupid. Goddamn stupid." He cupped her face with his hands. "But you can't for one instant doubt that I love you, and that I would give anything, anything, to erase the last twenty-four hours."

Unable to speak, she nodded.

He drew her to him then and kissed her lips, softly, keeping the contact tender. "We'll get through this, Hallie."

"Yes."

"It's painful right now, I know, but I'll make it right."

They hugged each other tightly. Burying her face in his neck, she whispered, "I just hate it so much."

"I hate it more."

"I'm sorry, so sorry."

He thought she meant sorry for the situation, sorry that it had happened to him. Maybe at the time, she had meant that. But later, he wondered if she'd been telling him what she knew then: She was sorry, but there was no possibility of the relationship surviving.

One day melded into the next. Hallie shared his disappointment when he was drawn off Brunner's investigation and put on temporary suspension. He couldn't prove that he had been a victim, too, but he felt that Hallie believed him and was ready to defend him wholeheartedly.

Initially.

But then the heat was turned up. Unhappily, Candy informed him that Fordyce was considering an indictment, and the possibility of that got leaked to the media. Jay and the others had kept the investigation quiet up to that point, but once the story was leaked, it spread through the community like an oil slick.

Some blond reporter, new to Channel 7, seemed to have made his situation her pet project. Her reports portrayed Suzi Monroe like a novice in a convent. The autopsy confirmed that she'd died of drug-induced heart failure, but the question of who had encouraged her to snort that much cocaine was raised. He was the likely suspect.

Tests confirmed that the semen in the condoms was his.

He called Hallie immediately upon receiving this news and told her he'd be at the bank when she got off work. He wanted to intercept her before she could get home, turn on her television, and hear a discourse about her fiancé's semen from the smiling blondie who seemed to take particular delight in his misfortune.

He picked up Hallie at the bank, drove to White Point, parked, and climbed the steps onto The Battery. Looking out over the choppy water of Charleston harbor, he told her about the result of the lab tests. "I don't know what she and I did. But we had some form of sex."

Hallie didn't say anything for the longest time, just stared into the shifting patterns of sunlight and cloud moving across the water. When she did speak, she said, "I'd like you to take me back to my car, Raley."

"Hallie—"

"Please, Raley. I can't talk about it any more right now."

Maybe she'd been clinging to the hope that the semen wouldn't be his, that it was all a hoax, or a terrible mix-up. But that afternoon seemed to change her. After that, even when they were together, he felt her distancing herself in small but noticeable increments. Her kisses became dry and chaste, her hugs listless. Conversations were strained. They talked around the subject, but it was always there.

The scandal overshadowed their lives and sucked all the happiness from them. Even when they tried to ignore it, it was slowly consuming them.

Finally, when they were only going through the motions of being a couple, he asked her point-blank if she wanted to call off the wedding.

"Do you?" she said.

"You know I don't. But I don't want to keep you attached to me if you don't want to be."

"I do. But . . ."

She didn't share with him whatever that major qualifier was, the reason why she was rethinking their engagement. He supposed he could take his pick. Was it that he was still under suspicion for criminal wrongdoing? Or that she was being publicly humiliated because her fiancé's name was being bandied about on TV every night? Everyone in Charleston knew that he'd had some kind of sexual congress with Suzi Monroe, which was reason enough to break an engagement even if he was innocent of the other allegations.

Taking her hand, he said, "Hallie, I love you. I want to marry you. My feelings for you haven't changed. But I don't want you to remain tethered to me out of a sense of obligation."

"It's not like that, Raley. I swear it's not." She paused, then said, "We're both under a lot of stress. In this kind of emotional climate, neither of us can or should make a life-affecting decision. It's hard to think of marriage when we're dealing with this. We must get past this before we can take a giant step forward. I think we should give ourselves some time and space to sort things out." Her expression was one of appeal and earnestness. "Don't you?"

He leaned forward and cranked up the air conditioner. Resettling in the driver's seat, he glanced at his passenger, who asked, "Did she return your ring?"

"Not then. And I didn't ask for it. What I did was agree to her terms." He gave a bitter laugh. "I guess I was a little generous on the time and space I gave her."

"What happened?"

"I rented the cabin and started spending days at a time there. Jay seized the opportunity." He cut another glance at Britt, whose lips parted with surprise. "It wasn't enough that he had any woman he wanted eating out of his hand, eating *him,"* he added crudely. "He had to have Hallie, too.

"He had bemoaned the fact that she was the only woman in Charleston he wanted but couldn't have. She thought he was teasing. Like a sap, so did I. He wasn't. He took advantage of my distance and her vulnerability, and she . . ."

Raley had been humiliated by the speed and ease with which Jay had replaced him, in Hallie's bed, in her heart. Even after all this time, it hurt and infuriated him. "Maybe she'd wanted him all along, too. Anyway, she mailed the engagement ring to my folks. I told them to throw it away, sell it, give it to the next homeless person they saw. I didn't care."

For a time, the only sounds in the cab were the swish of the tires against the pavement and the ticking of the analog clock in the dash. He didn't know if Britt was afraid of saying the wrong thing, of speaking a trigger word that would send him over the edge, or if she was pondering what he'd told her.

Maybe she was working out the time line, wondering if Jay had been romancing her at the same time he'd been sleeping with Hallie. In any case, she didn't say anything for the next several miles.

Finally he said, "We're about five minutes from the airstrip. You'd better be thinking of what you're going to tell the police, but before you say anything to them, you should notify your lawyer."

She nodded, absently. "Was that why Jay set you up to take a fall? If he did, that is. Was Hallie the reason he made certain you got into bed with Suzi at his party? Did it then go terribly wrong?"

Ruminating out loud, she continued. "Jay didn't count on Suzi overdosing and dying in his guest room. All he planned was to catch you with your pants down while Hallie was out of town, and then make certain she found out about it so he could make his move on her."

"Jay wouldn't go to all that trouble just to get a woman. Even Hallie."

"But you believe he arranged for you to wake up in bed with Suzi."

"With *dead* Suzi." She looked at him with patent incredulity. He turned his head and nodded. "Yes, Britt. Jay planned it all. He coached Suzi on what to say to me, things like red suspenders being a turn-on, and my occupation being manly. Jay put words in her mouth that he knew would stroke my bruised ego. He knew it was going to take more than big tits and good legs to get me into bed with her."

"She came on to you with a drugged drink in hand."

"Provided by Jay. I'm sure of it. Once I was compromised and he had the condoms to prove it, he saw to it that she snorted enough cocaine to kill her."

"Raley . . ." She shook her head with disbelief. "You're accusing your oldest friend of murder."

"Yes."

"Why would Jay do that? *Why?*"

"Because my getting drunk and fucking Suzi Monroe wasn't catastrophic enough. That would have caused me personal problems, probably cost me my relationship with Hallie, but it wouldn't have affected other areas of my life.

"But Suzi dying of a cocaine overdose while in bed with me, now *that* took on the scope of total ruination. An incident like that, indefensible because of a temporary memory loss, could destroy a man's life. It would shut him down completely. Along with anything he was doing."

He stopped at the intersection of two country roads and looked at her. After several seconds, he saw understanding crystallize in her eyes. In a low, barely audible voice, she said, "Your arson investigation."

He said nothing, merely took his foot off the brake and accelerated through the intersection. Just beyond it, he turned onto an unmarked, unpaved road. The next mile and a half was riddled with potholes. The ride was rough.

"I remember this," Britt said. "Last night I was hanging on for dear life."

"You were playing possum." She had feigned sleep while his hand was under her, groping for the seat belt. She probably thought he had copped a free feel or two while fumbling around, but he really couldn't find the damn latch. It had been stuck between the seats. He considered explaining that now, then thought it was best not to mention it at all. He didn't want her to know how well he remembered it.

Her car was parked against the rusted, corrugated tin wall of the dilapidated hangar where he'd left it. He pulled up beside it, but neither made a move to get out of the truck. He left the motor running long enough to lower their windows, then turned off the ignition.

It would be dark before she got back to the city. The sun had already set. A few stars had appeared. Not nearly as many as were visible above his cabin. The breathtaking night sky was one of the benefits of living so far from a large city.

That, and the pervasive quiet, and the absolute privacy.

Although the price one paid for absolute privacy was loneliness.

Britt was taking in the scenery through the windshield. "Pretty."

"About seventy yards that way is the river," he said, pointing with his chin. "The Edisto," he said, reading her perplexity. "It forms the eastern edge of the ACE Basin. The Combahee, the western side. The Ashepoo sorta splits the difference."

"I've never really gotten out and explored the area."

"You should."

She smiled apologetically over her indifference to the topography. Then, "What happened between Jay and Hallie?"

He looked in the direction of the river. "He broke her heart. She expected faithfulness, which wasn't in Jay's character. Not even in his vocabulary. He got what he wanted, which was a hard-won notch on his belt. Maybe two since Hallie was my fiancée. In effect, she and I both got fucked by Jay Burgess."

He realized he had clenched his hands into fists and was feeling the rage he'd felt when he learned how his best friend had betrayed him with Hallie, then discarded her. To Jay, she'd been just another conquest. "She caught him cheating, scooped up the pieces of her broken heart, and left Charleston."

Feeling Britt's inquiring gaze on him, he said, "I waited a couple of years and then decided to try and contact her. I used a pay phone at the general store and called her folks, the only way I knew of reaching her.

"Soon as I identified myself, I got an obscene tongue-lashing from her dad. See, they believed what your news stories had implied about me. But before he hung up, he told me—no, he *crowed* it, proudly, triumphantly—that Hallie had married an extremely successful orthopedic surgeon in Denver and they were expecting their first child."

Even insects had abandoned the airstrip. Without their night music, there was nothing to break the heavy stillness. The clock in the dashboard ticked. That was all.

Raley heard the rustle of fabric as Britt shifted, turning toward him. She bent her left knee and tucked that foot beneath her right leg.

"Before I go back and throw myself on the mercy of Clark and Javier, I think you should tell me about your investigation into the police station fire."

CHAPTER 13

"First, I have a question for you," Raley said. "Who was your source? Who tipped you about me and the events of that Sunday morning?"

Britt took a deep breath and released it slowly. "Jay Burgess."

He didn't slam a fist into the dashboard or start cursing a blue streak. Nothing like that, nothing that she might have expected. But she saw his jaw clench so tightly that even his beard couldn't hide it. "I figured. How did that come about?"

"I met him on my first news assignment in Charleston. I was sent to report on a fatal stabbing in a seedy bar in a seedy part of town. After I'd finished doing my stand-up, Jay, who was investigating the crime scene, came over and introduced himself. He said something corny like 'Do you come here often?' "

"You thought that was cute."

"It *was* cute. We introduced ourselves, made small talk, then he asked me if I had a significant other. He said if so, he was going to throw himself off a bridge. If not, would I meet him later for a drink, in a better bar."

"And you went."

"He was good looking and charming. A policeman, which I considered safe. So, yes, I went and I liked him."

He arched his eyebrow.

"No, Raley, I didn't sleep with him that night."

"Second date?"

She refused to be provoked. "A few days after that initial meeting, Jay called me at the TV station."

She answered her newsroom extension with a bright and chipper, "Britt Shelley."

"This is your lucky day."

"I've been chosen to enjoy a weekend

in the Ozarks to look at time-share property?"

"Better."

"I've won the lottery?"

"Journalistically speaking."

"I'm all ears."

"I'd rather you not say my name."

Of course she'd recognized his voice instantly, but it no longer had a smile behind it. "Okay."

"Ever."

That tone couldn't be mistaken for anything except dead serious. "Are we talking about a story?" She reached for her notepad and a pen.

"A dilly. And it can't be divulged that I'm your source."

"Understood."

"I can't talk now, and not over the phone."

They set the time for eleven forty-five that night, after the late news broadcast and giving other personnel time to leave the building and clear the parking lot.

She wasn't surprised that Jay Burgess had called her again. She'd expected it. They'd had a good time over the first round of drinks—well, he'd had a second, but he hadn't become intoxicated. It had been an easy, comfortable, getting-to-know-you date. Where did you grow up, attend school? Do you like sports, movies, books, spicy foods? Ever been married? Favorite vacation destination? Fantasy vacation destination?

They'd closed out the pleasant evening with his promise that he'd be in touch soon, and she'd believed him.

She had assumed that his follow-up call would be to ask her out again, not tip her to a "dilly" of a story. But she wasn't disappointed. She was far more interested in building a faithful following of viewers than in entering into what she knew would be nothing more than a compatible fling. For both her and Jay, hormones might have become agreeably involved, but never hearts. She had determined that within half an hour of meeting him.

Over time, she'd realized that, among many young professionals on their way up, there was an unspoken understanding that any kind of romance was a frivolity. She had come to recognize men who were of a similar mind as she, those who weren't looking for a permanent partner, those to whom dates were occasions for relaxing and unwinding, or sometimes, by mutual consent, for assuaging sexual impulses. Nothing more.

Among this unspecified group of upwardly mobile people, rarely did anyone enter into a relationship that was expected to withstand the demands of two careers and the ambitions of the individuals driving them. Lasting relationships required time and attention that was, instead, channeled into professional pursuits, which took precedence over *amore.*

She liked men. She enjoyed their company. Periodically she enjoyed sleeping with one. But she had moved frequently, sometimes staying at a station for no longer than a year before sending out her résumé to see if there was an opportunity for her to advance to the next level.

There had been neither the time nor the desire to develop anything more meaningful than a handful of friendships, most of which had, by her design, remained platonic and, most important, uncomplicated. She was able to give notice, pack, and leave a town without a backward glance, without regret, without a broken heart, either hers or an abandoned admirer's.

On the horizon of her mind she would occasionally glimpse herself meeting someone irresistible, someone who would become as important to her as her work. Commitment and marriage, a sense of belonging to someone else would be nice, especially since she'd spent almost half of her life alone.

Yes, certainly, she would like to have that kind of intimacy with a man, one who would anticipate her needs, know her feelings, appreciate her ambition, receive and reciprocate her love. She would love to have children, more than one, because she wouldn't want to leave a child of hers without a family, as she'd been left without one when her parents died.

But for now, all that could stay on the distant horizon. That life belonged to "someday." Today, she was happy to be unencumbered.

She immediately recognized that Jay Burgess subscribed to the same policy. He was an unconscionable flirt, obviously a man who liked women but who probably would never settle for one. He was fun to be with, but woe be to the woman who fell in love with him.

But as she sat inside her car in the darkened parking lot of the television station, waiting for him to arrive, she was squiggly with the excitement of a spinster waiting on her first beau to call.

He pulled his car into the empty slot next to hers, got out, and after taking a cautious look around at the deserted lot, opened the passenger door and got in.

"Hi." He leaned across the console and pecked her on the lips.

"I never kiss my sources, Jay."

"Really?" His expression was one of actual surprise. "I kiss everybody. Girls, I mean."

"I'll bet you do," she said, laughing. "This isn't a scheme to get me alone and in the dark, is it?"

"That scenario has distinct possibilities," he said, giving her a wolfish grin. "I'd definitely like to pursue it sometime." He paused, his smile faltered. "But not tonight."

"Then you really do have a story."

"I'm afraid so."

" 'Afraid so'?"

"I'm part of the story, Britt. It's not a nice story, and before I say anything else, you've got to give me your word that you won't use me as a source."

"I already have."

"This meeting never happened."

"I get it, Jay. You can trust me."

He nodded and began by asking if she'd heard anything about the recent death of a local young woman named Suzi Monroe. Britt recalled reading a story about it inside the newspaper.

"Cocaine overdose, wasn't it? I'm vague on the details."

"There's a reason for that," he explained. "The PD didn't release any details to the media. Her death was passed off as a routine drug overdose. But there's more to the story, much more, that we kept under wraps."

"Who are 'we'?"

"The detectives who were called to the scene of her death. And me."

"Why was the information withheld?"

"Because she died in my apartment."

The implications of that weren't lost on Britt. She began to envision a spike in her ratings.

Jay talked nonstop for ten minutes, telling how the girl had died while in bed with one of the city's firemen, who happened to be his lifelong friend, a man named Raley Gannon.

By now her journalistic radar was blipping like crazy. If this were fiction, the plot had just thickened.

"This is a guy who should have made every attempt to save her," Jay said, sounding almost angry. "Except that he was so intoxicated he was unconscious."

He went on to admit how wild the party had been, how much alcohol had been consumed. "I'm famous for my . . . hospitality," he said sheepishly. "Live here long enough and you'll learn that. But . . ." He hung his head, shaking it sorrowfully.

"This party got completely out of

hand. I was having a whale of a time, celebrating being alive." Here he paused and glanced at her. "You know about the police station fire?"

She nodded. "You were one of the heroes of the day."

He appeared flattered that she knew that but continued without further comment. "I wanted this to be the best party in history. But, I should have stayed sober. I should have kept tabs on how much my guests were drinking, how drunk they were getting. I'm a cop, for crissake. Protecting people is part of my sworn duty."

She said nothing as he castigated himself. At one of the stations where she had previously worked, an old pro had advised her that when someone had something to tell, and he was telling it without any prompting, it was better not to prompt.

"I should have especially been keeping an eye on my best friend," Jay said. "I didn't realize how wasted Raley was getting. I shouldn't have let him drink that much. He's been working too hard, taking on extra responsibility, and it's a bad habit of his to take responsibility for every damn thing that goes wrong in the world. Planets collide, he's at fault. It's his nature. He's too hard on himself.

"So here he's got one night where his main squeeze is out of town, he can let off some steam, get a little wild and crazy for once, and . . ." He exhaled a gust of air. "Shit. I even goaded him into it." He rubbed his eye sockets tiredly. "We're both to blame. I'm as guilty as he is."

"For Suzi Monroe's death?" She couldn't help herself. The question popped out before she could stop it.

"For the way she died, yeah."

Shocked by the admission, she listened as he detailed how this Raley Gannon had got blitzed on margaritas and taken the equally drunk Suzi Monroe to Jay's guest bedroom.

"Did you supply the cocaine, Jay?"

"No! Christ, no. And knowing Raley as I do—I'm telling you, he's a freaking Boy Scout and always has been—I would swear on a stack of Bibles that Raley didn't do any drugs with her. I would come close to swearing that he wouldn't allow her to do any, either. I think what happened is exactly what he said. They had sex a couple of times, he passed out, and didn't know anything until he woke up the next morning and found her dead."

"What do the investigators think?" Britt asked quietly.

"The same."

He told her that the district attorney himself was carefully reviewing the case, but that he doubted it would result in Raley Gannon's being charged with a crime. The autopsy revealed no evidence of foul play except for a lethal ingestion of cocaine, which in all likelihood was self-administered.

"We didn't supply the drugs, and we didn't push that stuff up her nose. What's eating at me is keeping our involvement hush-hush. It feels furtive. It smacks of a cover-up, and I can't, in good conscience, participate in it anymore."

He was right, it was a great story, the kind that an investigative reporter usually had to dig for, Woodward and Bernstein style. Amazingly, it was being served to her on a silver platter. She, the rookie. She, the one trying to earn her spurs in a TV market of respectable size and reputation.

She wondered if she was dreaming. But, no. When she reached out to give Jay Burgess's arm a consoling squeeze, it was tangible. "What happened wasn't your fault, Jay. The individuals who stumbled into your guest bedroom were adults. They were responsible for their own actions."

"I know that, but—"

"Actually it's a credit to your character that you're shouldering some of the responsibility, much less coming forward and telling me about it."

He glanced at her and gave a weak smile. "So what's it to be? Forty lashes, or a hundred Hail Marys?"

She smiled but was all seriousness when she said, "The story needs to be told."

He sighed and leaned back against the seat. "That's why I'm here. Meeting you the other night was like providence or something. Like you were sent so I'd do what my conscience was dictating."

"The story will have explosive impact. You realize that, right? Especially for your friend. As you said, he's supposed to save people."

"That's why I and the other detectives kept it quiet in the first place. It's going to create a shitstorm for Raley, and he's a hell of a guy. Truly," he said, detecting the skepticism behind her frown.

"Everybody likes Raley. He's a stand-up guy. This is going to damage him, and he's taken it so hard already. I mean, this girl was in bed with him, and she fucking *died."* Looking at her directly, he said, "I don't want him ever to know that it was me who blew the whistle. It would destroy our friendship."

"I understand, Jay. But you also have to understand that once the story of his complicity becomes public knowledge, it can't be recalled like a bad batch of canned beans. It can be denied, or refuted, or debated, even retracted, but it'll still be hanging out here, forever."

"I know what you're saying. Hell, I know there will be fallout, for me, too. But I'm at the point where I say, bring it on. My conscience won't let me live with this subterfuge any longer."

Britt stopped talking and took a deep breath, then looked over at Raley. Throughout the telling, he hadn't moved. She leaned toward him now, much as she had that night in her car with Jay, and laid her hand on his arm.

"His contrition, his willingness to assume some of the blame for Suzi Monroe, placed me in his camp immediately. It made him a sympathetic and totally credible source, Raley. I didn't question him because he was implicating himself as well as you. Why would he put his neck on the line, expose himself to public censure, if what he was telling me wasn't the absolute truth and a matter of conscience?"

"Because he knew it was my head that would be chopped off. Not his. His timing was no accident, either. No doubt he wanted to get in your pants as soon as possible—"

She angrily yanked her hand away from his arm.

"—but that wasn't his primary reason

for contacting you at that particular time. The scandal hadn't yet produced the desired result. I was on suspension, but not fired. Hallie was upset and hurt, but accepting of my explanation. Our relationship still had a fighting chance of surviving. Cobb Fordyce was reluctant to charge me with a crime.

"If things had been left alone, I would soon have been able to salvage my reputation and start rebuilding my life. I'd be damaged, but not destroyed. But that wasn't good enough," he continued angrily. "I had to be *eradicated.* In order to do that, Jay had to go the distance and expose the ugly truth, even if it meant admitting to being a careless host." He made a scoffing sound to underscore his sarcasm.

"I didn't realize I was being manipulated," she said.

"No, you just took his story and ran with it. Minutes of airtime were devoted to how drunk I was, how irresponsible I'd been not to realize that 'my date' was snorting huge quantities of cocaine in combination with drinking alcohol. And who was the supplier of the cocaine? You made sure to raise that question in the minds of your viewers, without flat-out accusing me of giving it to her.

"You interviewed people who were at the party and said they saw me leading her out to the pool. A lie, by the way. It was said we swam naked. Maybe we did. I didn't remember. I think if I'd tried to swim, I would have drowned, but . . ."

He shrugged. "I couldn't swear to anything. My defense was that my memory had been wiped clean by a substance secretly put into my drink. But Jay, my bosom buddy, had advised me not to use that defense because if I did I'd look like a drug user as well as a heavy drinker."

"You could have called me, told me your side."

He scoffed at that, too. "And of course you would have believed me."

No, she wouldn't have. She knew she wouldn't have.

As though reading her mind, he laughed with scorn, but she refused to apologize again. She'd admitted that her reporting had been slanted. She'd said she was sorry; he had rejected her apology. Time to move on.

But before proceeding, she let a few moments pass to clear the air. Then she said, "Jay wanted to halt your investigation."

He gave a curt nod. "He knew I'd trained as a cop first. I think he always resented that, but who knows. Maybe not. Anyway, I was getting close to discovering something he didn't want discovered."

"Like what? The cause of the fire?"

"I knew the cause. No question. Somebody set fire to papers in a trash can."

"As simple as that?"

"No, not quite so simple." He hesitated, as though he would go into more detail, then changed his mind. "My investigation was incomplete and inconclusive. At the time of Jay's party, there were outstanding questions I never received answers for. After I was ousted, Brunner went with the explanation given him, made the official ruling. People accepted it and embraced the heroes."

"The heroes." She ticked them off her

fingers. "Pat Wickham and George McGowan."

"Who were the two hungover but Johnny-on-the-spot detectives called to investigate Suzi Monroe's death."

"Cobb Fordyce."

"The DA, who didn't press criminal charges but publicly commended the fire chief the day my dismissal from the department was announced."

"And Jay."

"Who was the best person I ever knew at covering his ass."

The picture that began to form in her mind wasn't very pretty. "Are you saying the four of them orchestrated the thing with Suzi, even going so far as to make sure she snorted a lethal amount of cocaine, in order to stop your investigation?"

"You're the hotshot reporter, what do you say?"

"Are you disputing that they were heroes?"

"There's no disputing that," he said. "Hundreds of witnesses saw them carrying people from the burning building, reentering it several times to bring people out."

"Then why were they threatened by your investigation? Why would they go to such lengths to stop it? They wouldn't. Unless . . ."

When she didn't speak for several seconds, he prodded her. "Unless?"

Her mind was now speeding along a track. "Unless your investigation was about to expose something that happened *before* the fire."

He sat silently, giving her time to sort it out.

"That's it, isn't it? You were about to discover something that wouldn't just take the glint off their heroism but cancel it." Talking fast now, trying to keep up with her thoughts, she said, "That would make sense. They went to all that trouble, risked incriminating themselves in Suzi Monroe's death, to keep you from finding out something very, very bad that only the four of them knew."

"One for all, all for one," he said bitterly.

"Jay was about to tell me their shared secret. That night at The Wheelhouse.

Wasn't he? He was about to unburden himself, for real this time."

"Good guess," he said, again with that bitter tone. "He'd been given only a few weeks to live. Before he met his Maker, he wanted to clear his conscience. And who better for him to tell? You, his personal herald, who'd done such a good job for him before. Although, this time, he probably would have made you promise to withhold the story until after he died."

"So what was it?"

"What?"

"The *secret*? What had those four done, or not done, that they didn't want exposed? You were on the brink of finding out, right? What was it? Do you know? What do you suspect?"

He merely stared back at her, saying nothing.

"Ra-ley?" she exclaimed with exasperation. "What questions were you asking that were never answered? What was bothering you? Something about an arrest report, right? In your conversation with Jay, when he called you about the party, you told him you needed paper-

work on one of the casualties, right? You were missing something. What was it? Where was your investigation going?"

He shook his head. "Un-huh."

"Un-huh?"

"Un-huh. I've told you what you need to know, and that's all I'm going to say about it."

"What? Why?"

"Because I still don't have all the answers myself, and I don't want to hear myself quoted on the news tomorrow morning."

"I won't be on the news tomorrow. I'll be in jail, defending myself against a murder charge."

"Oh, I have every confidence in you, Miss Prime Time. You'll find a way to get on camera with a microphone. Even from jail."

"Insult aside, I wouldn't quote you. If I was able to get before a camera, I'd say my information came from an unnamed source."

"You won't say anything, because I'm not telling you any more than I've already told. It's all speculation anyway, and you should have corroboration.

Isn't that the golden rule of sound, reliable journalism? Always have the corroboration of at least two sources?"

She heard the taunt behind the words. "You're still pissed at me," she said accusingly. "That's why you're withholding information, isn't it?"

"It's as good a reason as any. Don't forget your purse." He opened the driver's door and stepped out.

For several seconds she remained looking at the vacant space behind the steering wheel, then she picked up her handbag and clambered out. When she dropped to the ground, the soles of her feet were pricked by stalks of dry weeds.

She didn't realize how dark it had become until she picked her way around the hood of the truck, trying to avoid stepping on anything hurtful. Raley had the beam of an industrial-strength flashlight aimed into the toolbox attached to the back of the cab and was digging through wrenches and pliers and such.

"What are you doing?"

"Looking for your car keys. I dropped them in here last night."

"Your behavior is childish. And criminal."

"Criminal? How's that?" Metal clattered against metal as he continued to search amid the tools.

"Jay was silenced, wasn't he? Just like you were silenced five years ago. Someone drugged me, like they did you, then killed Jay, like they did Suzi, and left a scapegoat that can't remember. That's your theory."

"Right."

"Then by keeping what you know or suspect to yourself, you're impeding the investigation into Jay's murder. That's obstruction of justice."

"Wrong. I've assisted the investigation. Why do you think I kidnapped you? I did it so you could use what I've told you to steer Detectives Clark and Javier toward the surviving heroes, George McGowan and Cobb Fordyce. One of them snuffed Jay."

"George McGowan is a former cop and Fordyce is the attorney general of the state."

"I didn't say it would be easy."

"Those detectives won't listen to anything bad about Jay. He's their idol. Without proof, they'll never believe that Jay was involved in a conspiracy and cover-up, especially not with those other two men."

"That'll be a tough sell all right, but I'm betting you can convince them."

"You could help me convince them."

"I could."

"But you won't."

"No. I won't." When he pulled his hand from the toolbox, her key ring was dangling from his index finger. He extended it to her; she snatched the ring. He said, "I'd like my shirt back."

She hesitated, then dropped her handbag to the ground, rapidly undid the shirt buttons, and shrugged the garment off. He took it from her and tossed it through the open driver's door into the cab, then reached for her windbreaker in the bed of the truck and passed it to her. "You probably should sterilize that before you wear it again. Delno's hounds—"

She yanked it from him and threw it back where it had been. "Raley!" Her voice cracked with impatience. "Why didn't you expose Jay and the others five years ago?"

"It took me months to figure out that I'd been duped. I think I began to see the light about the time he started fucking my fiancée. Then when I thought it all through, what could I prove? Not a goddamn thing, and moments ago you yourself cited what a commodity proof is when it comes to a criminal investigation.

"My reputation and credibility had been shot to hell. Who would believe that I'd been drugged to produce a total memory loss? All Fordyce—the legal eagle of the bunch—had to say was that he'd already heard that lame defense and dismissed it out of hand. I had nothing to work with, Britt. And besides . . ."

"Besides, what?"

He gnawed the inside of his cheek, then said, "I didn't want to believe my friend would do that to me. I'm still reluctant to believe it. In my gut, I knew it, but my mind wouldn't accept it. And every once in a while, I would almost convince myself that I was delusional. I would try and talk myself into believing that bitterness and professional jealousy had caused me to turn heroes into monsters. For five years I've been second-guessing myself." His eyes refocused on her face. "Then, yesterday morning, I saw your press conference. I knew I'd been right all along."

"Absolutely," she said vehemently. "What happened to me is confirmation of what happened to you. The similarity of our stories can't be denied or ignored. We'll go to the police together."

"Sorry. You're on your own." He dug into his shirt pocket, pulled out a folded piece of paper, and handed it to her.

"What's this?"

"Directions home. It's a little tricky driving these back roads after dark, but if you follow these directions you won't get lost. Eventually you'll get to Highway Seventeen. Hook a left. That'll take you straight into Charleston. Drive carefully." He turned away.

"You're a coward."

His right foot was already in the cab of the truck, but he turned his head and looked at her over his shoulder. She almost withered in the heat of his fierce expression, but held her ground. "With very little resistance from you, Jay stole your reputation, your career, and Hallie. Why didn't you fight for her at least? Maybe that's what she wanted you to do. For that matter, when you were being bashed in the media, why didn't you come to me and insist on being given equal time?

"Instead you slunk away into the woods, grew a beard, and became a hermit whose only confederate is an old man with fleas and body odor. True, you had no solid proof of what these men had done to you. But I think that's a flimsy rationalization. Shutting yourself off from the rest of the world is hardly an act of courage, Fireman Gannon. It's giving up. It's surrender.

"I don't think you spend your time out there in that remote cabin plotting your revenge. Not at all. I think you spend your time licking your wounds and feeling sorry for yourself. You'll never be vindicated because you haven't got the nerve to try. It's safer to stay in your lair than it is to come out and fight for the justice you deserve."

By the time she finished, she was breathing hard with righteous indignation. Raley hadn't moved a muscle during the diatribe. Now he withdrew his foot from the truck's cab and slowly advanced toward her. "You think you know me?"

She set her chin defiantly. "I think I've got you pegged perfectly. You say you want revenge on everyone who brought about your undeserved downfall. Well, this is your chance to get it."

He narrowed his eyes and studied her for a moment. "You know, you're right." Moving suddenly, he placed his hands on her shoulders, backed her into the side of the pickup, and moved in close. "Your clever mouth helped bring about my *undeserved downfall.*" He fixed his gaze on her lips, which had parted in surprise when he grabbed her. She closed them now. He smiled, revealing teeth, but it wasn't a pleasant expression.

"Believe me, Britt Shelley, star of Channel Seven live-coverage news, in the past twenty-four hours, I've fantasized taking liberties with your mouth, the way it took liberties with my life five years ago. Revenge? Oh yeah. I've thought of a dozen ways to hush you up, and all of them were dirty."

He leaned in, pressing her between him and the side of the truck, his mouth coming within a hairbreadth of hers. "But I wouldn't touch you. Never. Not because I'm too much of a coward, and not because it wouldn't give me pleasure, but because I don't like you. Mainly though . . ." He paused, the green eyes shifting back up to hers. "Mainly because Jay had you first."

CHAPTER 14

Releasing her as suddenly as he'd grabbed her, he turned abruptly and climbed into his truck. He cranked the engine and left it to Britt to leap out of the truck's path as he wheeled it around and headed for the road. She choked on the dust cloud that rose behind him.

Tears of outrage made red blurs of his taillights. Once they had disappeared, she was left in total darkness. Quickly, she retrieved her handbag from the ground and got into her car. The driver's seat had been moved back as far as it would go to accommodate Raley Gannon's long legs, and all the mirrors had been adjusted. Having to reset everything made her even angrier than she already was, and she was bristling.

The condition of the road didn't improve her state of mind. It allowed for only one speed—slow. She never caught sight of Raley's taillights again, although she continued to eat his dust all the way to the main road. It was nothing to brag about, but at least at some point in time the road had been tarred. Maybe during the Truman administration.

She consulted the directions he'd written out for her—she supposed she should be grateful for that much consideration—and turned as indicated. She kept her car at a moderate speed, not only because the road cut through dense forest, making it dark and winding, but because she needed time to reflect on her experience with Raley and prepare herself for what lay ahead. Before things could get better, they would get worse, and she dreaded that interim.

She had been on her own since her parents had died less than a year apart—her father of lung cancer when she was a senior in high school, her mother of a stroke a few months later.

As a college freshman, she hadn't had the luxury of mourning her mother. Not wanting to skip a whole semester, she'd taken only a week off from classes to handle the funeral and deal with all the paperwork left in the wake of a sudden passing. Then she'd dusted herself off emotionally and returned to her studies, accepting that she was an orphan now and that what she made of her life was strictly up to her.

She was the beneficiary of her parents' modest life insurance policies, which she used to finance her education. Upon graduation, she sold the family home. That had been a painful decision, as it represented a definitive severance from the only family life she'd had, but she'd needed the proceeds from that sale to subsidize the menial wages she earned at various cable stations. These jobs amounted to little more than internships, but she used them to gain experience with video cameras and editing equipment, in addition to writing and producing her reports.

At one station, in exchange for access to the editing room, she had to empty the wastepaper baskets and sweep up each night after everyone else had gone home. She didn't like it, but she did it, telling herself that it was character building. It also earned her an extra thirty-five dollars a week.

Eventually she moved to a station with a wider viewership where she didn't have to pull janitorial duties to augment her salary. Over the course of the next few years, she went from station to station, always moving up, learning, gaining experience, and developing her on-camera technique.

By the time the job in Charleston became available, she had acquired industry know-how along with an engaging TV persona—salable assets. Being hired as a feature reporter represented a quantum leap in her career. The job wasn't going to make her rich, but she could afford her mortgage and good designer knockoffs.

Although she would always lament

the premature deaths of both parents, she was suited to living independently. Or maybe she had embraced her solitary state only because she knew she had no choice. Either way, she was accustomed to earning her own keep and standing on her own two feet. She was reliant on no one. She was free to make decisions without interference from anyone.

Tonight, however, she wished to be not quite so free. She didn't feel so much independent as alone, friendless, and vulnerable. These were rare and unwelcome sentiments for her, so she wasn't sure how to cope with them. Why, after living totally on her own, was she wishing for someone on whom she could lean, from whom she could seek counsel, receive reassurance?

But there was no one, was there? Just as there had been no one when at age eighteen she'd been left parentless. Now, as then, she must accept and deal with the circumstances with as much determination and dignity as possible. She had survived so far. She would survive this.

But how could she help but be apprehensive over what the next few hours would bring? Would the policemen staked out at her house treat her kindly, or would they swarm her as she alighted from her car? Would she be handcuffed, read her rights, and hustled into a squad car before being given a chance to offer any explanation for her disappearance?

However it played out, it would be unpleasant and humiliating. She was a suspect now. The detectives wouldn't extend her any more courtesies just because she was a television personality. Clark would be less polite, Javier more cynical. The interrogations would be more grueling.

Even if Bill Alexander acted with dispatch, he couldn't get her released on bail until her arraignment hearing, and that wouldn't take place until tomorrow at the earliest, requiring her to spend at least this night in police custody.

Jail. The very thought of it, even for one night, made her physically ill.

And then something even worse occurred to her. She was accused of murdering a police officer. As if that weren't bad enough, to the court's eye, it would appear that she had fled to avoid arrest. *Thank you, Raley Gannon.*

While his kidnapping stunt had given her ammunition for a more solid defense than the feeble "I don't remember," it also had greatly reduced her chances of being released on bail. Prospects were good that she'd be kept in jail until her trial, and God knew how long that would be.

One second she was grateful for Raley's intrusion, because his information would be invaluable to her defense. The next second she wanted to throttle him. For a number of reasons.

When he'd grabbed her like that, why hadn't she pushed him away or put up some kind of resistance? She hadn't been afraid that he would hurt her. If he hadn't harmed her in the last twenty-four hours, he wasn't going to.

Still, she shouldn't have just stood there and let him manhandle her like that.

Calling him a coward had been a calculated attempt to keep him talking. As much as he'd told her, there was more he had omitted. She'd deliberately goaded him, hoping to make him lose his temper and blurt out something that would help exonerate them both.

The taunt had sparked more of a reaction than she'd bargained for. And a different kind of reaction than she'd anticipated. Her ill-chosen words had given him an opening, and he'd taken it. He—

The thought was interrupted by her cell phone's musical ring.

Automatically she reached for her handbag, then thought: *My cell phone?*

The two men were bored.

They were extraordinarily patient men who could sit for hours without moving, or even blinking, if the job required them to do so, but they'd rather be out and about, active, doing something instead of sitting in a room waiting for their next assignment.

They were presently playing an unambitious game of gin rummy and monitoring a telephone line on which they'd planted an illegal bug earlier today. Of all the boring aspects of their work, monitoring a telephone line was perhaps the biggest snore.

They were currently operating under the aliases of Johnson and Smith, and like the false names, the two men were practically interchangeable, having matching skills and personalities. They had no ties to anyone on the planet and had loyalty only to whoever was paying them at the time. In cash.

Their names weren't on any rolls for taxes, driver's licenses, Social Security, nothing. They'd left the country a decade and a half ago to fight a secret war against various factions in an African nation that few Americans had even heard of, much less could point to on a globe. There, the individuals they had been vanished. When they reentered the United States, they had different names, fingerprints, identities, and even those records had soon been destroyed.

Their employment was always temporary, but they sometimes worked for a client more than once, and they had a long list of satisfied customers—nations, cadres, individuals. They always worked as a team and were exceptionally good at what they did because they had absolutely no compunction about doing whatever was necessary to get the job done. Neither possessed a conscience. Their souls had been sacrificed in a wasteland of unimaginable violence.

Most remarkable, however, was that they weren't at all remarkable. The violence they were capable of was belied by ordinary looks. They didn't wear paramilitary camouflage. The weapons they carried were well concealed even to people trained to look for such, and their weapons of choice were their hands. Their strength came from conditioning, not bulk. They could pass for accountants, junior professors, or something equally benign. In a crowd, they could blend in so well as to become invisible.

They had blind obedience to whomever was paying them for their services. They never suggested an alternate plan, never expressed their opinions unless asked for them. They were incurious to the point of indifference about their orders. They didn't care a whit about the whys and wherefores of a job. They were apolitical and nonreligious. They did what they were told to do without question or discussion.

Those attributes made them ideal for their current retainer's needs. They'd been hired to disable Britt Shelley and kill Jay Burgess.

They'd been shown Britt Shelley's photograph and had seen her on television. They'd picked her out the minute she came into the bar. The Wheelhouse itself had served their purpose because it was crowded and busy, and the waitresses were so rushed that trays of drinks were kept on the bar long enough for a sleight of hand to take place without anyone noticing.

They'd been given explicit instructions and had carried them out to the letter. They'd been told to neutralize the woman and leave it to look like she had killed Burgess, and that was what they'd done.

It had helped that Burgess was careless about setting his security alarm. Getting inside the town house had been a matter of opening a terrace door and strolling in. The drug had hit Britt Shelley hard, and when Johnson and Smith had ambled into Burgess's living room, Burgess was anxiously asking her if she was all right. Clearly she wasn't.

Taken by surprise, weakened by his illness, and more than a little intoxicated himself, Burgess had been easily overpowered. The two pros had then forced the couple to drink the bottle of scotch. Burgess had protested, but he'd complied. The woman was too far gone to care what was being done to her, so they'd funneled the scotch down her throat with no difficulty.

When both were incapacitated, Johnson and Smith had stripped them of their clothing, put them in the guy's bed, then smothered the guy. They'd planted the empty condom packet on the sofa, all the while being careful not to leave any traces of themselves for a clever crime scene investigator to find.

The stage had been set precisely as they'd been told to leave it. Everything had gone as planned . . . until this morning, when it was discovered that Britt Shelley had up and disappeared.

This had really pissed off their retainer, who hadn't anticipated that development. Initial efforts to track her had rendered nothing.

So they'd been ordered to keep tabs on Bill Alexander, attorney at law. At first their client had considered having them torture the lawyer until he gave up the whereabouts of his client. But it was soon determined that his frantic nervousness was genuine and that, when he was seen in news reports averring to police that he had no idea where Britt Shelley had gone, he was telling the truth.

However, the assumption had been that he would be the first person she'd contact when she resurfaced—if she wasn't found by the police and arrested first—so Johnson and Smith had been ordered to bug the lawyer's phone.

Duck soup. He was a bachelor who lived alone and was too penurious to hire a maid. During the day, while he was at his law office, his house stood empty. The two-man team had been in and out in a matter of minutes and had spent the rest of the day monitoring their equipment, waiting for something to happen.

Finally it did. Their ears perked up when they heard the dial tone and the beeps of Alexander punching in a number. Johnson dropped his cards and made note of the time. Smith started the recorder.

Three rings, then a hello. Female voice, sounding hesitant and puzzled, then exasperated.

"Ms. Shelley! Thank God you answered!"

"Mr. Alexander?"

"Where have you been? Haven't you heard the news? The police have issued a warrant for your arrest."

"Yes, I know."

"Where did you go?"

"I didn't exactly . . . go. It's a long story. I'll explain everything when I get home. I suppose the police are watching my house."

"Yes, you'll have quite a reception committee. I must warn you, Ms. Shelley, that they obtained a search warrant this afternoon. Prepare yourself for a mess."

"A search warrant? Why?"

"Because you're a fugitive!"

"No, I'm not."

"What would you call yourself then? When a person flees to avoid arrest—"

"I didn't."

"Well, that's how it looks to the police. To everyone."

"I know, but I can explain. I—"

"As you said, save the explanation until you arrive. And the sooner the better. Where are you now?"

"I'm not sure."

"Not sure?"

"I'm an hour away, at least. I'll be there as soon as I can get there."

"If you're not captured first. Both Twenty-six and Ninety-five are crawling with—"

"I'm not on an interstate. I'm in the boondocks, and the roads aren't great. Do you know where Ye . . . Ye . . ."

"Yemassee?"

"Yes, this says I'll go through there."

"What says?"

"Long story. From there I take . . . uh, River Road to Highway Seventeen."

"Okay, okay, get here as soon as you

can. I'll go to your house and wait for you there. When you arrive, do not say a word unless you've cleared it with me. Do you understand, Ms. Shelley? Not a single word."

"I understand, but I have a lot to tell. Primarily, that Jay's murder is linked to the fire."

"The fire?"

"The police station fire five years ago."

"He was one of the heroes. Everybody knows that."

"Yes, but there's much more to it. Jay was—"

The call ended abruptly.

Johnson looked at Smith, who shrugged and said, "Sounds like her cell went dead."

They heard Alexander redial twice, but both calls went automatically to voice mail. With a muttered "Damn," he hung up.

Smith reached for his cell and punched in a number that no one knew except him and Johnson. As soon as it was answered he said, "Her lawyer just called her. We've got a recording."

Without further ado, Johnson started playing back the recording.

Their employer listened to it straight through, then when it ended, said, "She remembers that Jay told her something about the fire. Her memory wasn't totally wiped clean."

A bit defensively, Smith said, "Sometimes the amnesia is temporary. Each person reacts differently to the drug."

"In hindsight, I should have had you kill her, too. You could have made it appear like a murder-suicide. But it's too late for seconding-guessing, isn't it? However . . ."

Apparently their boss's mental gears were cranking.

"She ran, and that's actually to our advantage. It makes her appear criminal, capable of killing her ex-lover. Also desperate and liable to say just about anything to save her own skin. If she starts casting aspersions on Jay Burgess and his heroism, who will listen? Or, better yet . . ."

Johnson and Smith could see it coming: Better yet was that Britt Shelley never have an opportunity to say anything to anyone, sparing their retainer more worry and trouble.

They left the hand of gin rummy unfinished, happy to have something more stimulating to do.

Raley noticed that his truck was almost out of gas. It would be an annoyance to stop and fill up but even more of an inconvenience for the tank to run dry between here and his cabin.

He wheeled into the first service station he came to, got out, and walked up to a small structure to prepay. The cashier conducted the transaction through a window with metal bars. Signs were posted saying that security cameras were in place, but Raley seriously doubted that. One thing he didn't doubt was that a loaded shotgun was underneath the counter, out of sight but handy.

He returned to the pump and fit the nozzle into his gas tank. As he did so, he noticed Britt's windbreaker lying in the bed of his pickup, where she'd angrily pitched it. Seeing it gave him a twinge of remorse, although it shouldn't have. Admittedly, he'd acted like a bastard most of the time they'd been together, but she deserved no better from him.

As soon as she got back to Charleston, she would be in the limelight, and that was where she thrived, wasn't it? Perhaps not immediately, but soon enough, she would be cleared of all suspicion regarding Jay's murder. She would have her career-making story. He had filled in the critical elements that had been missing from it, and had added a touch of melodrama as well. So while she might not feel too kindly toward him at this moment, she would soon be thanking him.

As the tank continued to fill, he gazed in the direction of the city. He was homesick for it, for movie theaters, for restaurants that served shrimp and grits and crab cakes, for ball games, for long Sunday jogs along the harbor.

Mostly, though, he missed his work, which he'd loved.

Maybe he'd loved it even more than he'd loved Hallie. That was a tough confession, but in all honesty, he regretted being robbed of his career more than he regretted losing her.

He'd come to realize that, if she had loved him as much as she claimed, she wouldn't have doubted him. Once he'd admitted to responding to Suzi Monroe's initial flirtation, Hallie should have accepted as absolute truth everything else he told her, just as his parents had. She should have believed him without hesitation or qualification.

But she hadn't. If she had, she wouldn't have let him go so easily. And if he'd loved her as much as he'd thought he did, he wouldn't have retreated, leaving her free for Jay to grab.

You're a coward.

He could see where Britt might think him a coward. But it wasn't courage he'd lacked, it was backup. A smart man didn't barge ahead, slinging accusations against people in authority, unless he had proof. If you didn't have solid proof, the next best thing was a witness who could corroborate your allegations.

Now, after waiting for five long years, he finally had one.

To Britt it might appear that he had armed her, then sent her to the front to fight his battle for him, not knowing that he planned to wage his own war from behind the lines. That was the only way this conflict could be won, because at this point he wasn't even sure which of the two surviving heroes had conspired to have Jay killed.

Both McGowan and Fordyce had been in on the plot to stop his arson investigation. Had one acted singly to have Jay silenced, or were they in cahoots? One thing was certain: Neither was the hero he pretended to be.

Raley would happily let Britt receive all the credit for exposing them, their deceit, and their crimes. All he wanted was exoneration. He wanted his life back.

Of course, he didn't delude himself. It wasn't going to be a cakewalk. Each of these men had much to lose, and neither would go down without a struggle. Each also had the resources to fight long and fight dirty.

Whoever was responsible for Jay's murder was accustomed to subterfuge, and was good at it. He must have been keeping a close eye on Jay, afraid that, in light of his recent diagnosis, he might feel compelled to confess before dying. Britt had said that Jay called her earlier that same day to make their date. Which meant a plan to kill him and leave her the only viable suspect had been quickly plotted and implemented. One or the pair of them had moved with swiftness and surety.

As soon as Britt began raising questions about the fire, the so-called heroes of it would come under scrutiny by the public as well as by the police. One or both would begin to squirm, and Raley planned to be watching to see who squirmed the most, who was the most desperate to defend himself against nasty allegations, and who was most willing to give up the answers that Raley didn't yet have about the fire.

He intended to get them. He'd thought of little else these past five years. Now, because of Jay's death and Britt's involvement, he could finish the job without the fear of being disbelieved or discredited. He supposed he had Jay to thank for that.

That was all he had to thank Jay for. Jay, Pat Wickham, Cobb Fordyce, and George McGowan. The first two were out of it. The other two were about to experience the kind of public scourging Raley had received.

They would become the focus of local media. Britt would see to that. Everything they said and did would be reported. The louder they protested, the more pressure she would apply. She would be in her element.

The gas nozzle shut off. Raley replaced it on the pump and screwed the cap back onto his tank. He waved a thanks to the watchful, taciturn man in the barred window. Then, lifting the windbreaker out of the bed of the pickup, he took it into the cab with him and tossed it on the passenger seat along with his chambray shirt.

He pulled away from the station, but as he was about to turn onto the road that would take him home, he braked instead and let the engine idle while he wiped beads of sweat off his forehead and stared at the windbreaker. It didn't smell like hound dog. He'd only told her one had slept on it to rile her. It smelled like her.

She would probably be arrested and booked for Jay's murder immediately. But it wouldn't be long before she would play the card he'd given her. When she did, she'd make instant enemies of two powerful men.

She would be all right, though. Neither Fordyce nor McGowan was crazy enough to hurt her, not while she was standing in the glare of television lights and the attention of every person in South Carolina was on her. Her celebrity would protect her. Besides, she would be in police custody.

But, God, that woman was reckless when it came to getting a good story. In her determination to nail it, would she throw caution to the wind, lose all perspective and good common sense?

Looking back in the direction from which he'd come, he wondered if he'd been clear on the directions he'd given her. Had he told her not to turn left until she crossed the double railroad tracks?

If she turned left after crossing only the single track, she could drive for miles before realizing her mistake.

Hell, had he made that clear? When writing down the directions this morning, he'd been distracted by thoughts of her sleeping in his bed, curled up on her side, knees pulled to her chest, so the directions might not have been as detailed as they should have been.

He shot a glance down at the windbreaker, then with a heartfelt expletive, turned the pickup onto the narrow road in the direction from which he'd come and practically stood on the accelerator.

"Damn him!"

Her cell phone had been in her possession all along.

Fifteen minutes after her phone battery ran out, abruptly ending her conversation with Bill Alexander, she was still seething. She'd discovered her ringing cell phone in a zippered compartment of her handbag that she never used. Gullibly, she'd believed Raley Gannon when he'd told her he left her phone behind.

She wondered how many other fibs he'd told her, how many half-truths.

If they came so easily to him, and he was able to tell them so convincingly, could she believe his story about Suzi Monroe's death? He'd heard her say during her press conference that she'd been given a date rape drug that had wiped clean her memory of her night with Jay. Was it even remotely possible that Raley had concocted a similar scenario for his own vindication?

A tale like that would also implicate Jay Burgess in all sorts of misdeeds, and it was clear that Raley bore a grudge toward his former best friend. In one fell swoop, he could clear himself and destroy Jay Burgess's heroic legacy.

Was she being taken in?

If so, Raley was a great liar, because she believed everything he'd told her. She also gave credence to his story because he had withheld some of it. Based on experience, she knew that people with the most valuable information were often the ones most reluctant to impart it. He knew more about the fire, its origin, or *something* that he was withholding.

Sooner or later, he would have to give up everything he knew or speculated, because she had no intention of letting him sulk out there in the woods while she took on the CPD, Fordyce, and McGowan all by herself.

After she shared the story with Detectives Clark and Javier, someone would be dispatched to find Raley Gannon and bring him in for serious questioning. The fire chief would be clamoring to talk to him, too. Raley would be forced to divulge what he knew, and Britt Shelley would be on the scene to cover the story as it unfolded.

Jay had promised her a groundbreaking story, and he'd been true to his word. It troubled her, though, that the charmer she'd known and the deceiver Raley had described were the same man. If everything Raley had told her was the truth, and she believed it was, then Jay had sacrificed a girl's life, his lifelong friendship with Raley, and even his own honor as a police officer. He'd forfeited all that to protect whatever it was that Raley had been about to discover, something so terrible that Jay felt he must confess it in order to die in peace.

Unfortunately, his killer hadn't allowed him to unburden his conscience.

Britt was so deep in thought, she didn't realize she was lost until her headlights shone on the city limits sign of a wide-spot-in-the-road town she'd never heard of that wasn't in Raley's directions. Pulling onto the shoulder, she consulted his handwritten notes.

"Double railroad tracks?" The railroad tracks where she'd taken a left turn were fifteen miles behind her. "Would have been nice if you'd emphasized that, Gannon," she muttered as she made a U-turn. Of course he *had* written "double railroad tracks," she just hadn't read the directions carefully enough. But still . . . This had cost her a lot of time. Bill Alexander would be having a fit.

Her windshield was spattered with dead bugs. Twice she'd caught the glowing topaz eyes of deer in her headlights. Fortunately they'd stayed in the underbrush at the side of the road and hadn't dashed out in front of her car. But she'd slowed down anyway.

The backtracking cost her almost half an hour. As her car bumped over the all-important double railroad tracks, she cursed Raley Gannon once again and made the correct turn.

"Go a quarter mile, then watch for a sharp right," she read aloud from the paper she now held against the steering wheel in her line of sight to avoid making another mistake. "Okeydokey. Here we are," she said as she found the turn.

The road was dark. The branches of trees on both sides spanned it to form a canopy. It meandered through the woods, crossing swampy areas and creeks, tributaries of the major rivers, she supposed. She really should explore this area of wild beauty. She would do that.

If she didn't go to prison, she thought grimly.

Yes, definitely. Getting back to nature would be on her things-to-do list. But she wouldn't venture into this low country wilderness without a guide. Not without someone who knew their way around.

Raley, maybe.

Or maybe not. He didn't like her. He'd said so.

She jumped when an owl—or some nocturnal bird with a wide wingspan—swooped across the road directly in front of her grille. Then, feeling foolish over her jumpiness, she laughed with self-deprecation. But who wouldn't be a little nervous driving alone at night on a dark country road?

A few minutes later, she was actually happy to notice a pair of headlights up ahead. The vehicle was on a side road, waiting for her to pass so it could pull out. She was relieved that it turned onto the road behind her. She welcomed the company.

But then the headlights loomed up in her rearview mirror.

For one irrational moment, she thought, *Raley!* He was coming back to Charleston with her.

But immediately reason asserted itself. He wouldn't be coming from that direction, the headlights were too low to belong to a pickup, and Raley certainly wouldn't zoom up behind her, practically riding her rear bumper. He wouldn't flash his headlights onto bright and leave them on, as this driver had. Raley wouldn't drive that dangerously close to another car, not even to get her attention and announce his presence behind her.

"Jerk," she muttered as she gave her car some gas. The other driver did the same and stayed directly on her bumper for the next half mile. If he was impatient with her for driving the speed limit, why didn't he just go around? There wasn't a double yellow stripe prohibiting passing, but even if there was, anyone who didn't have qualms against tailgating wouldn't have qualms about breaking the no-passing law. There was no oncoming traffic to prevent him from passing her.

Raising one hand against the glare reflected in her rearview and side mirrors, she could make out two silhouettes in the other car. They appeared to be male, but she couldn't tell with any degree of certainty, and now she was going too fast not to keep both hands on the wheel.

They were probably kids, making mischief, too foolish to realize they were playing a life-threatening game. She should do a story on it, posing the question: Should the legal driving age be raised to eighteen?

After another mile, she was frazzled. Her hands seemed grafted to the steering wheel from gripping it so tightly. Her shoulders ached with tension.

"You win." She eased her car closer to the shoulder, which was nearly nonexistent. But the driver didn't use the extra space to go around. Instead he pulled up so that his right front bumper was slightly overlapping her left rear one. She moved over more, until her right tires slid into soft mud. The other driver compensated, keeping their bumpers only inches apart. "What is wrong with you, you moron?"

But her irritation was steadily turning into panic. This was more sinister than teenagers playing a prank. Should she speed up, slow down, stop? All of the options posed risks, especially the last one. She was barely dressed. Her cell phone was dead. She had no weapon. She hadn't seen another car for half an hour. Occasionally she had noticed lights from homes tucked into the woods, but not for the last few miles.

No, stopping wasn't an option. Slowing down hadn't discouraged him; he'd simply pulled his vehicle closer to hers. That left her only one thing to do, keep her speed up and hope that they wouldn't crash before they reached the heavily traveled Highway 17, or that these two would tire of their game and leave her to go her way.

But instinctually she knew that wasn't going to happen. This was menacing, not playful. The two in the other car meant to hurt her.

The driver seemed to have an uncanny knack for keeping his headlights shining directly into her mirrors. They were blinding her. Going on the offensive, she pressed her accelerator to the floorboard and at the same time jerked her wheel sharply to the left. She missed clipping his right front bumper by a hair.

Now back on the hardtop surface, her car surged ahead.

But the advantage was short-lived. The other vehicle roared up behind hers, then whipped around the rear of it and overlapped bumpers again. “Dammit!” she shouted in fear. “Why are you doing this? What do you want?”

Again, she was blinded by his headlights, but up ahead she could make out the signpost for the river. Just beyond the sign, the shoulder tapered to nothing and the road narrowed to form a bridge.

Britt’s anxiety increased. She thought of the blackwater river she and Raley had crossed several times on their way from his cabin to the airstrip. Even with her limited knowledge, she knew that several great rivers converged and emptied into St. Helena Sound and from there into the Atlantic, their direction of flow shifting four times a day, depending on the ocean tide.

A lot of water. People died in it. Recently she’d reported on the recovery of a man’s body. He was an experienced swimmer, but he’d drowned when his fishing boat capsized. Two kayakers had been lost for days before their bodies were recovered miles downstream from where they'd put in to take advantage of a river swollen by heavy spring rains.

She'd feel safer once she was across that bridge. But when she sped up with that purpose in mind, the driver matched her speed and inched closer to her car.

In desperation, she flattened the gas pedal onto the floorboard again. Even then her speed wasn't enough to pull ahead of the other vehicle. Just as she reached the signpost, the other driver outmaneuvered her. He edged his car to the right, forcing her off the road and onto the soft shoulder that soon gave way to nothingness.

She was probably going close to a hundred miles an hour when her car hit the water. It slammed into the surface of the river with such impact that her air bag deployed. That saved her life but wasn't really a blessing. Because she was still conscious when her car was swallowed by the greedy, swirling water.

CHAPTER 15

Raley was speeding toward Charleston, his truck eating up the miles, when he spotted dual sets of taillights ahead of him. They flickered through the trees, often disappearing for minutes at a time before he caught sight of them again.

But even being as far behind them as he was, he could tell the second driver was tailgating the first. "Idiot." It was just plain stupid to drive that aggressively, especially on a highway like this. If the driver was that impatient to get where he was going, why didn't he just go around the other car?

In the back of his mind, he was hoping the first driver wouldn't be a prick, a road hog who refused to let anyone pass him. He was in a hurry to reach Charleston and warn Britt to tread carefully. He wasn't sure how he was going to make contact with her. She would be surrounded by police and—

"What the hell?"

The first car had moved onto the shoulder, but the second car didn't pass. In fact, it looked like the tailgating guy was trying to nudge the other driver off the road.

He was gripped by a terrible intuition. *Britt.* And as suddenly as he thought it, the cars disappeared.

Had he had time to catch up with her? Not unless she was a slow driver. Not unless she'd got lost.

"Shit!"

It seemed to take forever for him to come out of the curve that had temporarily blocked the other two cars from sight, but once he did, he squinted for sharper focus. Unfortunately, he was too far away to make out the shapes of the taillights and determine the models of the cars involved in the dangerous cat-and-mouse chase. He pushed the pickup as fast as it would go, but the other cars were lighter, faster, and he couldn't close the distance.

Again they disappeared.

He counted the seconds. Twenty maybe? Thirty?

And then he had another flickering view of one set of winking taillights disappearing from sight altogether, and those of the tailgater speeding across the bridge.

Raley uttered a sharp cry as he crammed his gas pedal against the floorboard. It seemed to take a thousand years to cover the distance to the bridge. He pounded the steering wheel as though whipping the truck to go faster.

It skidded to a jarring stop just inches away from the brink of the eroding earth embankment that supported the bridge. He was out of the truck before inertia settled it. He opened the toolbox and took out the heavy-duty flashlight he'd used earlier, then grabbed the first weighty metal object he touched. A wrench. It would have to do.

He scrambled down the embankment, half sliding, half hopping as he pulled off his sneakers. By the time he reached the water, he was barefoot and huffing deep breaths to fill his lungs, then without a second thought, he dived in.

His flashlight had a powerful beam, but he might as well have been shining it through blackstrap molasses. He knew the river, knew how impenetrably dark the water could be even where it was most shallow, and this wasn't one of those places. Here, the channel was deep.

Frantically he swept the light from side to side and was becoming panicked when he spotted the car, settling heavily on the riverbed, surrounded by a nimbus of swirling silt. He shone the light in the direction of the driver's window. The beam picked up a pale palm, flattened against the glass, a strand of blond hair floating eerily in the feeble shaft of light.

Britt.

The flashlight blinked once and went out. The darkness was absolute.

He dropped the light, but gave a hard kick and within seconds reached the passenger side of the car. Feeling his way, he found the windshield and hammered the wrench against it as hard as he could. It didn't give. He pounded it several more times. Nothing.

His lungs were beginning to burn.

He continued banging the wrench against the windshield until finally he felt the safety glass break but not shatter. He kicked at it again and again until his foot pushed through. He widened the hole by continuing to kick, then wedged his shoulders through it. Broken glass scraped against his head and arms, but he ignored the pain.

Blindly he groped for Britt and found her right arm. When he touched it, she didn't react, and his mind screamed, *God, no!*

He groped for her seat belt. It was unfastened. She'd managed to do that. He hooked his hands under her arms and guided her through the hole in the windshield, carefully but quickly. Neither had much time left. He was out of air, and she was completely still.

Once he had her clear of the windshield, he executed a hard scissor kick and used his free arm to claw toward the surface. His lungs were screaming for oxygen. He kicked as hard as he could, but his limbs were becoming heavier by the second, rubbery and uncoordinated. It had been five years since he'd done any rescue training; he was out of condition.

He looked toward the surface, but it was only a lighter shade of black. Still, he struggled toward it. Up. Up. And finally, his head broke the surface and he gulped a mouthful of air.

But Britt wasn't breathing.

He made sure her face was clear of the water, then began to swim to the bank. His body was still hungry for oxygen, and he was exhausted, but he swam as fast as he could against the current. When his feet touched bottom, he waded the rest of the way, then crawled up onto the bank, dragging Britt along with him.

He flipped her onto her back and straddled her. She had a weak pulse but wasn't breathing. Placing his hands in the center of her chest, he began CPR.

"Come on, Britt," he said as he rhythmically pumped her chest. "Do not die on me. You're not finished yet. Come on, come on."

River water trickled over his face and into his eyes, but he didn't stop the compressions or the litany of encouragement that eventually took on the inflection of a dare. "You called me a coward, but you're the one giving up here. Are you going to let some other TV dolly grab your story? You'd never forgive yourself if you let that happen. Now breathe, goddammit!"

River water spewed from her mouth onto him. He dropped his head against his chest, weak with relief. "I thought that might bring you around." He turned her head to one side. She coughed and gasped, coughed some more. "Get it out, that's the way, that's good," he murmured, holding her wet hair away from her face as she vomited up the water she'd swallowed.

When she was breathing more easily, she turned her head and looked up at him. Her eyes were streaming tears. Her voice was hoarse, and she strangled when she tried to speak. She spat out more water, then finally managed to say, “They tried to kill me.”

He nodded. A thousand questions were demanding answers, but they would have to wait. He needed to assess her physical condition. But he also thought they needed to get the hell away from here. He couldn’t be sure that his headlights had gone unnoticed by whoever was intent on pushing her off the road. The asshole might return to make sure she hadn’t been rescued or by some miracle survived. If the would-be killer came back, they were sitting ducks.

“We need to get to the truck. I’ll have to carry you.”

“I can walk.”

He didn’t think so, but he didn’t argue. He stood up and extended his hand to her. She took it and pulled herself up. But as soon as she was on her feet, her knees buckled. He caught her, then giving her no choice or opportunity to argue, lifted her into a fireman’s carry across his shoulders and started up the embankment.

In the darkness he searched for toe-holds he could use for leverage. His own knees almost gave way several times. He stumbled over rocks, dodged wild shrubs and spiky palmettos, and once barked his shin on the branch of a fallen tree. His bare feet got stuck in the mud several times.

When they finally reached the truck, he lowered Britt to the ground and propped her against the fender long enough for him to open the passenger door, then boosted her in.

Reaching across her, he picked up the windbreaker and put it on her, guiding her arms into the sleeves. He pinched her chin between his fingers and searched her face. Her lips were no longer blue. He picked up her hand and studied her fingertips. Color seemed to be returning to them, too, although the dome light wasn't that bright, so it was difficult to tell.

"Rub your hands and feet. I'll be right back."

She gripped his hand in panic. "Where are you going?"

"To get my shoes." He pulled his hand free and closed the door of the truck.

He tramped around on the riverbank until he found both sneakers, not wanting to leave them behind. So far, whoever had forced Britt into the river was unaware that she'd been rescued. He certainly couldn't be identified as her rescuer. For the time being, he thought it best to keep their alliance unknown. There was nothing he could do about his footprints in the mud or his tire tracks. He hoped if anyone returned to check, he would be looking for traces of her submerged car. Satisfied that it had sunk from sight, he wouldn't give the area a detailed search.

He explained this to Britt when he climbed into the cab and dropped his sneakers into the foot well beside her bare feet. Then he started the truck and pulled back onto the road. He headed in the direction from which he'd come, away from Charleston. His destination was anywhere but here. He wanted to leave the scene. "Who was it, Britt?"

"Two men."

He reached for her left hand and laid it, palm up, between them on the seat.

He pressed his fingers firmly against her pulse. "You couldn't see their faces?"

She shook her head.

"What kind of car?"

She shrugged.

"License plate?"

She shook her head again.

He counted her pulse. It was a little higher than normal but seemed strong and steady. "Open the glove box. Get the first aid kit. There's a thermometer in it. Take your temperature."

"I'm okay."

"Will you just get the fucking thermometer and take your temperature without an argument?" His tone was harsh, but not from irritation so much as fear. If he'd been a few minutes longer at the gas pump, if he hadn't heeded his instinct to go after her, if he'd been unable to break the windshield, Britt would have drowned. The what-ifs made his hands tremble.

Subdued, she did as she was told. They rode in silence until she removed the thermometer from her mouth and read it. "Ninety-seven point five."

"Close enough."

"I'm rarely ninety-eight point six."

"Okay. Good. Now here's the thing. You probably should be checked out at the hospital. There's one in Walterboro. Your body temp is okay, and your circulation has returned. Before my flashlight went out, I saw your hand pressed against the window. You were conscious then, so you couldn't have been out long. Maybe two minutes total, which means there's probably no brain damage.

"But your oxygen level should be checked anyway. You've got some bleeding cuts and scrapes from when I pulled you through the windshield, possibly a concussion. There may be sediment in your lungs, although you'd probably be coughing if there was any significant amount. CPR keeps your blood circulating until you can breathe on your own, but when there's a near drowning victim, there are emergency treatment protocols that—"

"Raley?"

"What?"

"Why don't you want to take me to the hospital?"

In spite of all the reasons he was listing that he should, she'd been able to tell he was discouraging it. "Because I'm afraid if I do, you won't live long." He saw no merit in sugarcoating it. She needed the truth and needed it told to her without any buffering bullshit. "Somebody killed Jay. Somebody tried to kill you. I think you'll be safer if they think you're dead."

"Cobb Fordyce was behind this?"

"Or George McGowan. Or maybe both."

"One for all," she said softly, repeating what he'd said earlier.

"After we separated, I got to thinking about how vulnerable you are. I was coming to warn you to be careful, to remain in police custody if you could. After this, it's no longer a matter of speculation. Whoever killed Jay believes you pose a threat."

"Why didn't they kill me when they killed Jay?"

"I'm sure they're asking themselves the same question, regretting that they didn't."

Out of the corner of his eye, he saw

her hug her elbows and rub her upper arms. Despite the outside temperature, he switched the truck's AC over to heat and aimed the vents at her.

"Did you see the other car?" she asked.

"Couldn't make it out. Too far away and too dark. What I can't figure is how they knew where you were. Unless they put a transponder on your car. But if they'd done that, why weren't they waiting for us at the airstrip? Or why didn't they intercept us when I took you from your home last night?"

"My telephone," she said dully. "I found it."

"Oh."

"It rang shortly after I left the airstrip. My lawyer was calling. We had a two- or three-minute conversation before the battery went dead. Could they track it by satellite?"

"I guess. If they had the equipment and were set up for it. Did you tell Alexander where you were?"

She nodded. "Which road I was going to take and how far out I was."

"Anyone hearing that could have

been waiting on a side road. When you passed, they pulled out behind you."

"That's exactly what they did. At first I was glad to see another car."

"Did you mention me to Alexander?"

"No."

"Did you say anything about what I'd told you?"

"Only that Jay's murder and the police station fire were connected. That there was more to the story."

Raley expelled his breath. "How well do you know this lawyer?"

"I met him yesterday morning." She flung back her head and released a mirthless laugh. "Was that only yesterday?"

"Seems he double-crossed you, Britt."

"I guess."

"Or his phone was bugged."

They came upon a tackle shop that, along with live bait, sold cold beer, hot coffee, fireworks, and the best burgers in Dixie. Or so boasted the handwritten sign in the window.

Raley parked in front and opened his door. "I'll be right back." When she didn't argue or pepper him with questions, he knew she was still in shock. He preferred the questions.

A bell above the screen door jangled when he went in. A man wearing a stained white wife-beater and khaki pants was leaning on the counter, eating a bag of onion-flavored potato chips and thumbing through a hunting and fishing magazine. Above and behind him on the wall was the mounted head of a snarling razorback.

As Raley approached the counter, the man wiped his salty fingers on his pants legs and looked Raley over, starting at his muddy bare feet and moving up his clinging, wet clothes to his dirty, bearded face and matted hair. "Out for a swim?"

"Hot tea, please. One."

"Hot *tea*?" He chortled. "Want fries with that?"

Raley just stared at him.

The man's silly grin slowly evaporated. "Coffee machine's over there. Hot water spout's on the side of it."

Raley went to the self-serve area and scrounged around until he found a crushed box of Lipton tea bags. He filled a foam cup with hot water—which was barely tepid—dropped the tea bag in, and put a lid on it. He returned to the counter. "How much?"

"Is it for the lady?"

The man peered past Raley, who turned to see what he was looking at: Britt with her head leaned against the passenger window, wet hair obscuring most of her face, except for her eyes, which were staring blankly through the windshield. "That's right," Raley said, coming back around.

"Rough night?"

"You could say."

"On the house," the man said, sliding the cup of tea toward Raley.

"Thanks."

"Don't forget the sugar."

Raley picked up two packets of Domino, nodded his thanks to the man, and returned to the truck. He handed the tea and sugar to Britt, then started the truck and pulled it back onto the road.

"I don't want this." She had removed the cap and was looking into the cup of tea, which had brewed barely to the color of apple juice.

"Drink it anyway."

Obediently she placed the cup between her knees, emptied both packets of sugar into it, and bravely took a sip.

He said, "I have an oxygen tank at my place." She didn't say anything, but in his peripheral vision, he could see that she was looking at him quizzically. He kept his head forward. "I got it thinking that I might need it for an emergency, that Delno might go into cardiac arrest from eating too much fatty food like possum. He fries everything in lard and thinks bacon grease is a beverage."

She took another sip of the tea, still looking at him over the rim of the cup. "You want me to go back to your cabin with you?"

He turned his head. "Not really, no. But I've got something to show you."

"In addition to your oxygen tank?"

"My files. Everything I have on my investigation into the fire."

"Official documentation?"

"In anticipation of being fired, I sneaked into Brunner's office and made a copy of everything. I'd be willing to let you read through it, but first I must have your word that you won't make me a news story until I give you the go-ahead." He paused to let that sink in.

"Or?"

"Or I can drop you off at an emergency room, where you can get proper treatment. Or I can drive you to your house and you can surrender to the police. In all fairness, I have to tell you that either of those options would be wiser than sticking with me."

She ran her finger around the rim of the cup several times. "My own lawyer may not be trustworthy."

"Whether or not he betrayed you to the bad guys, he's compromised."

"You said yourself that the detectives on my case idolized Jay and wouldn't want to hear anything negative about him."

"I'm confident you would get them past that. They'd have to accept the truth about him sooner or later."

"But later. Because right now my credibility is nil."

"In the meantime, you're exposed and in danger."

"There's no disputing that. Someone tried to . . . tried to . . ."

"Kill you."

Too emotional to speak, she nodded.

Raley considered that answer enough.

Thank Jesus the last of the guests were straggling toward the front door to say their thank-yous and good-byes. George had had about all of this party he could stand. Les's idea of a good time was to gather his toadies and their wives around him, ply them with rich food and strong drink, and let them know how fucking great he was and weren't they lucky to be paid to kiss his ass.

Ostensibly the party had been a last-minute thing to celebrate the deal with the city that had been consummated this afternoon after a slow eighteen holes of golf and an endless lunch. George doubted its spontaneity.

By the time he got home from the country club, catering trucks and hired bartenders and waiters were already there, setting up. Guests began arriving at six thirty, continued until seven, and the attendance rate had been one hundred percent of those invited. He figured Les had had this soiree planned for weeks.

The son of a bitch had never entertained the thought that he might be unsuccessful in securing that athletic complex contract.

"Mr. McGowan, there's a call for you."

George turned toward their housekeeper, who had touched him on the arm to get his attention. "Take a message."

"I tried, sir. He was most insistent on speaking with you."

"George?" Miranda, looking stunning in a black, body-hugging, strapless dress, approached. Her pink martini matched the diamond drop nestled in her cleavage. The five-carat stone was spectacular but couldn't hold a candle to the lush breasts. "The Madisons are waiting to say good-bye to you."

Madison was further up Les's ass

than the rest of them. "I've got to take a phone call. Say good night for me."

She looked perturbed but said nothing, only turned her back on him and rejoined Les, who was glad-handing Madison and insincerely complimenting his plump, mousy wife on her drab dress.

George drained his highball and handed the empty glass to the housekeeper. "Thanks. I'll take the call in the study."

It was a pretentious room. The bookshelves were filled with books he'd never read, written by authors he'd never heard of. Adorning the paneled walls were the stuffed heads of deer and elk he hadn't shot. There was a glittering display case full of trophies for golf tournaments and tennis matches he didn't remember playing. One of his racehorses had won several silver cups, too, but George had had nothing to do with that beyond paying the exorbitant bills that came with owning, stabling, and training a high-strung, ill-tempered Thoroughbred.

And there was that famous photo of

him and the others at the scene of the fire. Miranda had blown it up to an embarrassing size and hung it on the wall in a frame that the Queen of England might have used for her state portrait.

He avoided looking at it as he sat down at the desk and picked up the phone. “Yeah? Who’s this?”

“Cobb Fordyce.”

Despite his determination not to look at the photo, his eyes went straight to it. “It’s after office hours for you, isn’t it?”

“I felt I should call.”

“We’re having a party, Cobb. I have guests.”

Ignoring that, the attorney general said, “I had an interesting call a few minutes ago.”

“Oh?”

“Bill Alexander.”

George swallowed. Or tried. Actually, his mouth had gone dry. He wished he’d poured another drink before picking up the phone. “The lawyer?”

Sounding vexed, Cobb said, “Come on, George.”

“Okay, why did he call you at this time of night?”

"Because I'm the state AG. Therefore, he thought I should know that Britt Shelley had told him there was a connection between Jay Burgess's murder and the police station fire."

George propped his elbow on the desk and dropped his head into his palm.

Fordyce went on. "I asked Mr. Alexander why his client, Ms. Shelley, would link the two tragedies. Was she merely surmising, or had Jay told her something before he died? Mr. Alexander explained that he didn't have time to ask her these questions before their cellphone conversation was cut off.

"I'm not sure how well you know Bill Alexander, George, but he is an excitable individual on his best day. When he called me tonight, he was near panic. He had promised Detective Clark that Ms. Shelley was due to arrive at her house within an hour of their conversation to turn herself in. She never showed. Once again, her whereabouts are unknown."

"Huh. Why did Alexander call you with this news flash?"

"He's wondering if he should give any credence to Ms. Shelley's allegation that there's a relationship between the fire and the murder of Jay Burgess. He asked my opinion on the matter. Did I think it warranted further investigation? Should it be made public? Or kept quiet? In short, he's got a rattlesnake by the neck and doesn't know where to pitch it."

George wanted badly to throw up. "When Alexander called Detective Clark, told him that Britt Shelley was on her way home to surrender, do you know if he mentioned this business about the fire?"

"No, he didn't. He thought he should consult me first."

Well, George thought with relief, that was something. Not much. But something. Sensing movement, he looked up to see his father-in-law and Miranda standing side by side just inside the study door.

Cobb was saying, "I don't like this harkening back to the fire, George. It could become very uncomfortable for all of us."

"Yeah, I'm aware of that." He took a quick breath. "Look, I've got to go. I'll call you tomorrow."

"We must talk, George."

"Right. I'll call you early." He hung up before the AG could say anything further.

Miranda walked to a leather sofa and draped herself over the arm of it, stretching languorously, expanding those creamy breasts above the low neckline of her dress. "Who was that, darling?"

"Cobb Fordyce."

Her eyebrows arched eloquently, but it was Les who asked, "What did our attorney general have to say for himself at this hour of the night?"

George divided a look between them. "He said we have a problem."

CHAPTER 16

Britt objected to the oxygen. "I'm okay. Honestly."

"Breathe it for five minutes. Long enough for me to shower." She relented and positioned the cannula. "Just breathe normally." She gave Raley a thumbs-up, but it was a feeble gesture.

Exhausted and emotionally shaken, they had exchanged only a few words on the long drive back to the cabin. There was much to discuss, but they had tacitly agreed that all of it could wait until they were physically restored.

Fearing bacteria that may have latched on to him in the Combahee, Raley showered vigorously. None of the cuts and scratches on his arms and hands looked serious, but he dabbed them with antiseptic before putting on a clean T-shirt and a pair of old jeans he'd cut off at the knees.

Britt was sitting exactly as he'd left her in one of the chairs at the dining table, her bare feet resting on the dowel between the front legs, toes curled under. He switched off the oxygen, and she removed the tubing from her nostrils. "Can I shower now?"

He motioned her toward the bedroom. "I left a fresh towel and some clothes in the bathroom."

"Thank you."

"Are you hungry?"

She shook her head as she disappeared into the bedroom, moving like a sleepwalker.

He'd thought he was ravenous, but when he opened the refrigerator, nothing looked appetizing. Forgoing food, he returned to the bedroom. The shower was still running. His gaze drifted around the room, lighting on the sweet potato vine.

It *was* a nice, homey touch.

The shower went off. He stepped

back into the living area and waited until he heard the bathroom door open, then went as far as the bedroom door. She had put on the T-shirt and boxer shorts he'd left out for her. They were huge on her, of course. The shorts rode low on her hips, and the shirtsleeves drooped past her elbows, but she was decent.

Her hair was still wet. Her eye sockets were dark, and her eyes themselves looked extraordinarily wide and vacant. He doubted anyone from her television audience would recognize this bedraggled waif as the with-it woman who brought them the latest news.

"Sit down on the bed," he said. "I'll put some stuff on those cuts. It stings, but that means it works."

Without argument she went to the bed and sat down. He returned from the bathroom with a bottle of antiseptic and a roll of toilet paper. He didn't have cotton balls.

He hunkered down in front of her and ripped off a wad of the tissue, dousing it with the strong-smelling liquid fire. He swabbed a scrape on her arm. Breath hissed through her clenched teeth. "Warned you," he said.

"It's okay."

"I'll be quick." He moved to another cut, this one on her knee. "I had to pull you through the windshield."

"I couldn't break it."

"I took a wrench down with me, hammered on it until it broke. You don't remember that part?" She shook her head. "Probably just as well," he said.

"I remember the car hitting the water. Hard. My air bag opened, then deflated. The car tipped down. My seat belt held me in. I remember thinking how sudden it all was. But it also seemed that everything went into slow motion, you know?"

He nodded as he ripped off several more sheets of tissue and dribbled the liquid onto them.

"The headlights and all those on the dash went out. It was dark. So dark."

"You don't have to talk about it, Britt."

"The car filled with water." She continued as though she hadn't heard him. He didn't think she had. "It closed over my head. I undid my seat belt and started banging on the window, but . . ." She turned her head from side to side. Tears filled her eyes. She was shivering. "I kept trying to break the glass, but I couldn't. And I couldn't hold my breath any longer."

"Britt, are you cold?"

"No."

But her teeth were chattering. He stood up and yanked the quilt off the bed, then pulled it around her. She clutched at the fabric, crossing her arms over her chest, huddling inside the quilt.

He knelt in front of her again and assessed a cut on her temple. "Bad enough, but not so deep that you need stitches. You might have a faint scar, at least for a while. With makeup on, you probably won't be able to see it at all. Especially on camera."

He was talking to keep her calm. Or maybe he was talking to keep himself calm. One of them had to hold it together, and she was the one who'd been the most traumatized and who now looked extremely fragile.

What she was experiencing was typical. Now that the imminent danger was over, the realization had set in—she'd had a near miss with death. He'd seen it happen dozens of times with people who'd been rescued from a burning building or some other perilous situation. When the adrenaline rush ebbed, and they fully grasped the mortal danger they had been in, they often became hysterical.

He heard a little hitch in her breathing, and it alarmed him. "Are you having trouble breathing?"

"No."

He poured antiseptic onto a fresh pad of toilet paper and applied it to the jagged cut on her forehead. She made another hiccuping sound. The tears standing in her eyes spilled onto her cheeks. "I'm sorry. I know this medicine stings," he said. "But only for a little while. I promise."

"It's all right."

"I'm almost finished. You don't want to host a parasite." He dabbed the cut several more times, then set the roll of tissue and the bottle of antiseptic on his TV tray night table. "There. See?" He came to his feet, dusting his hands. "All done."

She looked up at him, her eyes so large and watery they dominated her face. She was making sobbing sounds and her lips were trembling. A tear slid into her mouth, at the corner of it, where her lips met. She seemed unaware of it.

"I was so . . . so scared."

He dropped his phony cheerful manner and said solemnly, "I know."

"There was nothing I could d-do."

"No."

"I tried to get away from them, but the road—"

"You did your best."

"When the water rushed in, I panicked."

"Who wouldn't?"

"I've always thought . . . thought I'd be brave. But I wasn't."

"You were—"

"I knew I was going to die."

"But you *didn't.*"

"It wasn't . . . you know how people say their life flashes in front of them?"

"Yeah."

She shook her head furiously. "Mine

didn't. There was nothing. Nothing but the water and . . . and terror. I just wanted to escape. I was so af-afraid. Raley?"

"Hmm?"

She reached for his hand, but when he extended it, she grasped his forearm instead. Then her other hand hooked his waistband, pulling at him. Dropping the quilt, she practically climbed him, using parts of his upper body as handholds to help her stand up, and when she was on her feet, she wrapped her arms tightly around his neck and clung fast.

"I didn't want to die, I didn't want to die."

"You didn't. You're okay. You're safe."

"Oh, God." Coming up on tiptoe, she burrowed her face in his neck. "I thought I was going to die."

"It's over. You're safe." Awkwardly, he patted her back. "You're gonna be fine."

Then her hands were on his cheeks, tilting his face down toward hers, her lips frantically seeking his. She threaded her fingers up through his hair and formed tight fists that nearly ripped his hair out by the roots. She kissed him and continued to kiss him between words that were choppy and unintelligible but had the ring of desperation.

The feel of her body, much smaller, softer, than his. Her bare legs rubbing against his. Her hands, clutching. Her lips, moist and yearning. It was all too much. He was consumed by raw desire.

His arms closed around her. His hand on her ass, he drew her up and into him. He angled his lips against hers. When he did, hers parted. Tongues touched, then his was filling her mouth, and, Jesus, he was lost.

Inside his head a bell of warning was clanging louder than any fire alarm, but he didn't heed it. She smelled good, she tasted good, her mouth was silky and hot and hungry, and it had been a long time since a woman had wanted him. With desperation.

She continued to clutch handfuls of his hair, then his T-shirt, until her hands slid beneath it onto his back. Her nails dug into his skin. He broke the kiss long enough to pull his shirt over his head and fling it away, then went back to kissing her. They separated again only long enough for her to take off the T-shirt he'd given her to wear. When they came together this time, her breasts were pressed against his chest, and he heard himself growl with pleasure.

She took hold of his waistband again and tugged him forward as she fell back onto the bed. He followed her down. She undid his fly, or rather they undid it together, clumsy fingers battling over the metal buttons until her fingers, no longer clumsy, closed around him. He groaned an incoherent string of swearwords as he shoved off his cutoffs and then worked the baggy boxers down her legs. She kicked them away even as he thrust into her.

It was hard and fast and graceless, and in under a minute they both came, hugging each other tightly, moaning, gasping for breath.

Then for several minutes, they lay locked together, completely spent. She didn't move, so neither did he, although the consequences of what had just happened fell on him like a ton of bricks.

Jay was here first.

Despite how goddamn good she felt, that was what he was thinking when her leg slid off his hip and her arms relaxed their embrace, then let go.

He rolled off her onto his back and closed his eyes. Minutes passed in ponderous silence, so many minutes that the situation became even more awkward than it already was. Somebody had to say something sometime, but it wasn't going to be him.

Finally, he felt her sit up. He opened his eyes as she reached for the boxers that had been kicked to the foot of the bed. He couldn't resist glancing at her in profile. Remarkable ass. Lovely, smooth back. Lovelier front. The curve of her breast full but natural. A pink nipple that looked delectable.

Bothered by another twinge of arousal, he swung his feet to the floor and sat up. He retrieved the T-shirt she'd been wearing from the floor and without turning around passed it back to her. She took it without a word. He gathered his two articles of clothing, then got up and went into the bathroom, closing the door behind him.

He stood at the sink, turned on the water, and used a cloth to wash himself, thinking, *Christ, Christ, Christ.*

He buttoned his cutoffs—remembering, with chagrin, the hackneyed adage about closing the barn door—then turned out the light before opening the door. She was lying on her side, facing the opposite direction. She had put on the T-shirt and pulled the quilt up to her waist. He lay down and turned onto his side so that they were back to back.

Huskily she said, "They say . . ." She hesitated, cleared her throat, tried again. "They say that when you . . . when you experience something like I did tonight, or when you go to a funeral, when you have an encounter with the reality and finality of death, it's normal for you to . . . to want sex. They say that what happened just now . . . between us . . . What I mean is, they say it's a natural reaction to the kind of trauma we went through tonight. Because sex is the ultimate . . . It's the . . . It's life affirming."

Raley lay still for several moments, then reached for the gooseneck lamp and switched it off. "Is that what they say?"

He was gone when she woke up. There was a note on the dining table. White lined paper ripped from a spiral notebook, a bold, familiar script written in black ink. "Back soon." A man of few words.

According to the time he'd jotted down beneath the brief message, he'd been away over two hours. She made toast and coffee, and was finishing her second cup when she heard his pickup coming up the lane.

She scampered back into the bedroom and closed the door, not wanting it to appear that she had been anxiously awaiting his return. While she was hiding there, it occurred to her that, when it came to sex, grown-ups could certainly behave childishly. Even so, she didn't come out.

She heard the screen door squeak open, then slap shut, heard his footfalls going toward the kitchen area. When she worked up enough courage to open the bedroom door, his back was to her.

He was piling several plastic sacks on the dining table. They bore the familiar Target logo.

"I wondered where you—"

She broke off when he turned around. He'd got a haircut. It wasn't short like he used to wear it, but it had been clipped and moderately tamed. But the most startling change was his beardless face. She'd forgotten the angular bone structure of his jaw, the jut of cheekbones. And without the beard detracting from his eyes, they seemed greener, more arresting.

She wondered if she should comment on this sudden and drastic change, but before she could, he turned back around and began unloading his purchases. "Did you eat something?" he asked.

"Toast."

"I brought some fruit."

She approached the table and saw a plastic basket of strawberries and a cantaloupe. She picked up the berries and carried them to the sink. "These look delicious." She turned on the faucet and rinsed the berries.

"I got you some clothes," he said. "I don't know if they'll fit." She set the basket of berries on the counter to drain. He extended her several of the sacks. "Don't expect too much."

Curious, she peered into one of the bags. "Thank you. I'll go change into something now."

She had almost reached the bedroom when he said, "Are you on the pill?"

She came back around. "What?"

He frowned as though to say *You heard me. Are you going to make me repeat it?*

She made a noncommittal rolling motion of her shoulders.

He propped his hands on his hips. "Is that a yes or a no?"

Britt liked neither his stance nor his tone. "It's a *none of your damn business.*"

"Unfortunately, as of last night it is."

A tide of anger surged through her. "Listen to me, Mr. Gannon. Of the men I've slept with, most were flattered, some were grateful, all were satisfied, but none felt *unfortunate.*"

"How nice for you. Are you protected or not?"

"Either way, it's no concern of yours. It won't be. Ever. You've got nothing to worry about, okay?"

Then she turned on her heel and stalked into the bedroom, soundly closing the door behind her. Still feeling the simmer of anger in her cheeks, she unceremoniously dumped the contents of the sacks onto the bed, prepared to hate everything.

Actually, the selections were pretty good.

Everything was white, black, or denim. Mixable basics. The kinds of garments you'd pack for a casual weekend trip. She wondered if Hallie had taught him that fashion sense.

She ripped the tags off a set of underwear and put on the panties and bra, then dressed in a pair of white jeans and a black T-shirt, white sneakers with silver leather trim. Not bad at all. The sizes were either spot on or not too far off, even the undies. It made her flush hotly to think that, if he'd bought these items yesterday, he might not have been as accurate.

Along with the clothes were some basic toiletries, including body lotion, a lip gloss, a compact of blusher, and a tube of mascara. For added confidence, she applied them before returning to the kitchen, where he was gutting the cantaloupe. He glanced at her over his shoulder but didn't remark on the new clothing.

"I feel more like myself now," she said. "Thank you."

"You're welcome." He reached around her to take a bowl from the cabinet, but he wouldn't look her in the eye.

"Is it going to be the purple elephant in the room?"

He hacked into the hapless melon with a butcher knife, slicing it quickly and efficiently. "What?"

"Don't play dumb, Raley. Are we going to act like adults and talk about what happened last night, or are we going to ignore it?"

"We already talked about it. Last night."

"That was talking about it? You

grunted a few syllables and turned out the light."

He shrugged. "You didn't leave me much to say. All that mumbo jumbo you spouted was—"

"You thought it was mumbo jumbo?"

He set down the knife and turned to her. "Well, what we did was either that, what you said, or it was two people just wanting to hump each other. You pick."

"You don't have to be so crude."

"You don't have to be so analytical." He picked up the knife and went back to slicing the cantaloupe.

"I thought you would rather it be analyzed," she said. "You're the one who vowed he'd never touch me, remember? Then a few hours later you were—"

"Fucking you like there was no tomorrow. But there is a tomorrow. Today is tomorrow," he said, making stabbing motions toward the floor with the knife. "And I don't want to talk about it."

"Except to reassure yourself that there won't be any consequences to you nine months from now."

"Aren't you worried? I could have an STD."

"You? Careful, paranoid-about-protection Raley Gannon? Not a chance. I think I'm safe." He turned away, but she caught his elbow and brought him back around. "My *analysis* is as much for your benefit as for mine. It relieves us of responsibility. It lets you off the hook for having a woman that Jay had first, that Jay had only a few nights ago."

His jaw turned to iron. "You said he didn't."

"I said I didn't think so."

"You were emotionally hopped up the night he died, same as last night. How do you know you didn't climb all over him the way you did me?"

"What if I did? What do you care? Why are you so hung up on that? Because of Hallie?"

He pushed the bowl of melon toward her. "Do you want any of this? If you do, eat up. We've got work to do."

She stared up into his newly shaven face and saw in his expression a steely resolve not to take this conversation any further. Fine. She didn't want to talk about it, either. He could believe what he wanted. She knew why she'd thrown herself at him.

Remembering it now made her burn with embarrassment. But that outpouring of lust was excusable because of her experience in the river. That was the only reason she'd behaved as she had. She hoped he understood that.

She hoped *she* did.

She bit into a slice of the melon, talking as she chewed. "Are you going to tell me about the fire now?"

"Later. First I'm going over to Delno's and see what's on the news this morning. See if they've found your car."

"Do you think they have?"

"Doubtful. The guys who pushed you off the road surely didn't report it. While I'm gone you can—"

"I'm not staying here by myself."

"Why not?"

"Somebody tried to kill me last night!"

"So they think you're dead. And even if they don't, they don't know you're with me."

"They might."

"They couldn't."

"I'm going with you."

"It's a long walk. It's hot. You'll get your new sneakers dirty. And Delno's place isn't exactly a garden spot."

"If there's news about me, I want to hear it firsthand."

He stared at her with vexation, then shrugged. "Suit yourself."

He took two bottles of water from the fridge and handed one to her, then tramped out, she behind him. They thrashed through the woods, where there were bugs and nettles. Her new sneakers did get dirty, but she didn't utter a word of complaint.

If there was a trail, it was undetectable to her, but Raley knew where the worst of the briars grew. He gave wide berth to a dead tree where yellow jackets had made a nest and said, "Mind the gator," when they walked along the edge of a swamp where there was a thick grove of cypress trees. Their knobby knees poked up out of the cloudy water like stalagmites. The alligator was completely submerged except for his malevolent eyes.

By the time Raley announced, "We're

here," she had sweated through her new T-shirt.

He'd warned her that Delno's place was no garden spot, but he hadn't told her it was a dump ground surrounding an odd-looking structure balanced on stilts but bolstered by all the stuff crammed into the crawl space.

Raley led her through an obstacle course of junk—some of the rusted objects she couldn't even identify—and up a set of rickety wood steps. Animal pelts and reptile skins were tacked to the exterior walls. For decoration? she wondered. Or were they patches?

The three hounds were dozing on the small porch. They must have recognized her and Raley's smells because they didn't bark, or even move, when they approached, although one whined when Raley nudged him away from the door.

"Delno?" he called through the screen.

"Comin'!" The shouted reply came from the far side of the clearing. Delno appeared out of the underbrush, pulling up one strap of his overalls. "I's in the john." He halted abruptly when he saw

Raley's shaven face. "Well, I'll be double-dog damned."

Without a word, Raley opened the screen door and went inside. "Hi, Delno," Britt said, then followed Raley into the stifling cabin, saying in a whisper, "He uses an *outhouse*?"

"I warned you." He made straight for a television with a rabbit-ear antenna and turned it on. He glanced back at Delno as he came in. "Did you see any news this morning?"

"She's still missin'," he said, nodding at Britt but never taking his eyes off Raley.

Raley, annoyed by his gaping stare, said, *"What?"*

"Nothin'. Nothin' a'tall." He ran his hand over his own scratchy face, then motioned toward a stove, where a pot was simmering. "Y'all want some of that stew?"

"Thank you, no. We just had breakfast," Britt said politely, not even wanting to speculate on what was stewing in the pot.

There was a game show on TV, although if not for the sound track, Britt wouldn't have known that. She could make nothing of the snowy picture. Raley switched through the limited number of channels, but regular programming was on each station. He switched off the set. "Was anything else said about her, other than she's still missing?"

"They interviewed this guy, said he was her lawyer." Before continuing, Delno spat tobacco juice into an empty green bean can. "He said he'd talked to her last night by phone, said she was going to surrender. But the cop said she never showed up, so she's still at large and they're still lookin'. Cop said that when she's caught she'll have a lot to answer for." He stopped and looked at Britt expectantly, but she didn't elaborate on what he already knew.

Raley asked, "Any mention of an accident on River Road?"

"Naw. Not that I heard."

"Any mention of me?"

"You? Naw."

Raley looked down at her. "That's good."

"I guess. It still makes me a fugitive

instead of the victim of an attempted murder."

"You tried to *murder* her?"

They turned to Delno, who'd asked the question of Raley. Britt laughed, but Raley frowned and said, "No, I didn't try to murder her. Thanks for the use of the TV. If you hear anything about either of us, will you come tell us?"

Delno moved the wad of chaw from one cheek to the other. "I might. If I'm not otherwise occupied. I ain't Walter Cronkite, you know."

Raley gave a snort of derision. "I don't think anyone would mistake you for Walter Cronkite." He headed for the door. Britt thanked Delno for the information, then followed Raley out.

They were halfway across the yard when Delno called after them, "She make you shave?"

Raley didn't stop or turn around.

The old man cackled. "I thought maybe on account of whisker burns on parts o' her where they oughtn't to be."

Britt pretended not to hear that. So did Raley.

"She tell you no shave, no more—"

Raley stopped and spun around. “She had nothing to do with it. All right?”

“Then how come—”

“I’m going to a funeral.” Raley turned again and stepped into the cover of the forest.

He was walking faster now than he had on the trek over, and she had difficulty keeping up. Once, when she lagged far behind, he had to stop and wait for her. When she caught up, she was breathing hard. “Sorry. I caught my foot on a vine. My sneaker got stuck.”

“Where’s your water?”

“I finished it at Delno’s.” He passed her his bottle, but she declined it. “You’ll need it.”

“I’m okay.”

She drank from the bottle but left some for him. He finished the rest and recapped the empty bottle. “Not much farther.”

He was about to continue on their way when she said, “Jay’s funeral?”

He gave a brusque nod. “It was on the radio when I went into town this morning. His body was released to relatives yesterday after the autopsy. Funeral is at three o'clock this afternoon."

He had got a haircut and shave to make himself more presentable, she supposed. "They'll be there. Cobb Fordyce. George McGowan."

"Probably."

"They'll recognize you."

"So? Jay was my boyhood friend. Why wouldn't I attend his funeral?"

"Because of what he and they did to you."

"But they don't know that *I* know. They think they accomplished what they set out to. They ruined me and got away with it. For five years, I've been out of the picture. No longer a threat to them."

"Then why are you going to the funeral?"

He grinned. "To make them wonder if maybe they're wrong."

She found herself responding to his grin. "Seeing you will make them nervous."

"That's the plan and my heart's desire. Plus, I hope to see Candy."

He set out again, and she fell into step behind him, staying as close on his heels as possible. "When are you going to tell me about the fire, your investigation?"

"This evening. When I get back from Charleston."

"That'll be hours. I don't want to stay out here by myself."

"You can't go with me, Britt. You can't be seen. Whoever tried to kill you will try again if they know you're alive."

"I'd be defenseless out here."

"I'll circle by Delno's on my way, ask if he'll come over and stay with you."

"That isn't funny."

"Wasn't meant to be. If anyone tried—"

He stopped so suddenly Britt ran into him. Before she could even ask what had caused him to stop, he spun around, hooked his arm around her waist, and drew her into some brush.

"What—"

"Shh," he hissed close to her ear. "Someone's inside the cabin."

CHAPTER 17

"Who is it?" Britt whispered.

"I don't know. I just caught a glimpse through the window above the kitchen sink of someone moving around."

Peering through a tangle of wild shrubbery, he watched the window for a full minute but no longer saw the moving shadow. However, he knew he hadn't been mistaken. His first impulse was to charge into the cabin and confront the intruder. But he hadn't been able to determine if the person was male or female, large or small, a potential threat or someone who was lost and seeking the help of a stranger.

Given the event of last night, he feared the worst.

Apparently Britt's thoughts were moving along the same track, because she looked at him with apprehension.

"Stay put," he said.

But when he tried to move, she grabbed his arm. She seemed about to beg him not to leave her alone. Instead she nodded. "Be careful."

Raley took a deep breath and stepped from behind the concealing shrubbery. If the intruder happened to look out a window, he would see him running in a crouch toward the north exterior wall of the cabin. The distance could be covered in seconds, but during those seconds Raley was exposed and virtually defenseless.

When he reached the cabin, he hunkered down beside a brick pier. He expected a shout, a challenge, something. Nothing. He'd made it across the clearing unseen. He assumed.

He looked back toward Britt's hiding place. He couldn't see her. If he couldn't, probably no one looking out a cabin window could, either, which gave him some relief as he crept along the wall toward the front of the cabin, where he hoped to catch the intruder when he or she came out.

He was moving along the outside wall of his bedroom. Hearing movement inside the room, he halted and cursed under his breath. It sounded like someone was searching the room. Opening drawers, closing them. He heard the familiar squeak of his closet door, hangers being moved along the metal rod, someone knocking against the wall.

Then there was a crash and the sound of breaking glass and he figured that casualty was his reading lamp on the TV tray. If you backed too far away from the closet without looking, you'd bump into his makeshift nightstand.

Then for several minutes there was no sound from inside. Just when Raley was about to go and investigate, he detected footsteps through the wall, the volume of them fading as they went from bedroom to living area.

Keeping against the wall, he crept to the corner of the cabin and remained crouched there as the screen door was pushed open and a man stepped onto the porch. "Anything?"

Until then, Raley hadn't realized there was a second man. He was seated in the passenger side of the pickup, apparently searching the glove box.

Raley ducked out of sight and held his breath. If he was seen, he would have to face these guys without a weapon. He was convinced that this was no ordinary burglary, and that it was no coincidence the pair of them had shown up the morning after two men had tried to kill Britt.

He heard the glove box being snapped shut, then the passenger door of his truck. "There's drying mud on both sides of the floorboard. He's had a recent passenger. What about inside?"

"I'll tell you on the way back." The man on the porch leaped over the three steps and started across the yard. "But I think my hunch was right."

Raley didn't want them to leave without his getting a look, so he risked peeking around the corner of the cabin. The one who'd been in his truck had already got in on the passenger side of a maroon sedan. He was in shadow, but Raley could make out his profile. Sloping jaw, sunglasses, receding hairline. Nothing noteworthy that Raley could detect from this distance.

He got a better look at the one who'd been inside the cabin. He was of average height, slender and fit, mid-forties. A no-nonsense haircut. Conservative dark slacks and a light blue knit golf shirt.

There was nothing noteworthy about him, either—except for the pistol he returned to the holster clipped to his belt at the small of his back before he climbed into the driver's seat, started the car, and backed away. He executed a precise and economic three-point turn, then drove off down the lane toward the highway.

Raley made note of the make and model of the car and memorized the license plate number. He didn't move until he could no longer hear the car's motor. Then he slowly came to his feet, wiping sweat off his forehead with the back of his hand and shaking his legs to return circulation.

Staring down the empty lane, he

thought, *This changes everything.* Then, out loud and with heat, "Son of a *bitch.*"

Galvanized, he took a more direct route back to where he'd left Britt. When he was still a ways off, he called to her. "It's okay. They're gone." There was no movement of leaves, no sign of her white pants and black shirt. "Britt?" Still nothing. His heart hitched. He ran the remainder of the distance to the clump of shrubbery and pushed aside the branches. *"Britt?"*

She was where he'd left her, but her back was to the cabin. She was sitting on her bottom, her knees hugged to her chest, and when she raised her head and looked up at him, she looked like she'd just seen a ghost. And in a way she had.

"He was there. At The Wheelhouse. That night."

Raley hustled her into the cabin. "Gather up that stuff I bought you this morning, whatever you want to take. We've got to get out of here, and we may not come back for a while. Hurry."

While going through the living area,

he surveyed it with a keen eye. After Britt's rampage the day before, when she'd launched a reckless hunt for a telephone, he had put everything back in its place. On the surface it seemed as though nothing had been disturbed. It took someone who lived here, lived here alone, someone trained to store fire-fighting gear to exact specifications and keep everything spotless and ready for use, to notice that things had been moved, even a fraction of an inch.

Whoever had searched had been meticulous about replacing things, but not so well that Raley couldn't tell that drawers and cabinets had been opened, cushions squeezed, rugs lifted, pieces of furniture scooted aside, then re-placed.

It was the same in the bedroom. Even the TV tray had been placed upright. The lightbulb was missing from his gooseneck lamp. He remembered the long minutes of silence following the crash. Had the tidy intruder been sweeping up the shattered bulb? Obvi-ously. Also obvious was that he'd taken the broken glass with him, because Raley didn't see even a sliver of it.

He registered all this within a second of entering the room, because he looked immediately toward the bureau. One drawer, which he knew he hadn't left open, was slightly ajar, but he expelled a light laugh of relief and said, "He didn't find it."

Aware that Britt was watching him as she stuffed her new clothes back into the plastic sacks, he lifted the jar containing the sweet potato vine off the top of the bureau and set it on the floor. He pulled tendrils of the vine away from their anchors tacked to the wall and coiled them around the jar.

"You said it was a nice touch. I didn't think anyone would disturb it." Then he put his knee and shoulder to the heavy bureau and pushed it away from the wall. "There's a hammer in a toolbox on the floor of the closet. Bring it to me, please."

Britt found the hammer in seconds and carried it to him. He used the claw at the end of it to pry away several nails, then pulled a section of the cheap paneling away from the wall. Behind it was a hollow space. He reached in and withdrew several folders. They were banded together with a thick rubber band and wrapped in protective plastic.

"Your files," Britt said.

"Yeah."

"Did you see the guy?"

"Both of them."

"There were two?"

"One searched the truck while his buddy was in here."

"What did the other one look like?"

"Like the one you saw. Like guys who just walked off the eighteenth tee, except with guns."

Reaching beneath the bed, he pulled out a duffel bag and placed the package inside it, then grabbed handfuls of underwear, socks, and T-shirts from the bureau drawers. From the closet he got several pairs of jeans and crammed them into the duffel. He gave her a look, then reached into the closet again, took a ball cap from the top shelf, and handed it to her. "Put your hair up under this and pull the bill down low."

Then he took his one pair of dress shoes and a dark suit from the closet.

"You still plan to go to the funeral?" she asked.

"Yes."

She opened her mouth, but he cut her off before she could say anything.

"We'll talk about it on the way."

"On the way to where?"

"That's part of what we'll talk about."

"Raley." She caught his arm as he moved past her, carrying the hastily packed duffel bag and his suit. "Were these the men who pushed me off the road last night?"

"I wouldn't bet against it."

"Who are they?"

They had no time to lose, but he took a moment, holding her gaze. "I don't know who they are, Britt. But I can guess who sent them. And I know they aren't fucking around."

Raley had heard one of the intruders say "on the way back." "I assume that means they're returning to Charleston," he told her as they sped away from the cabin. "If that's the case, we're probably okay for the immediate present.

"On the other hand," he said grimly, "these two assholes seem to enjoy vehicular homicide. They could be waiting at the intersection with the main road, knowing this road is a cul-de-sac, the only way in to my place, the only way out. Sooner or later, we'd have to pass this way, and these guys strike me as men who wouldn't mind the wait, even indefinitely."

He reached beneath his seat and, to her startlement, produced a pistol. "I'm surprised the guy searching the truck didn't find this. Or maybe he did, and just didn't want me to know he did."

It was a revolver. A big, evil-looking thing with a long barrel. He released the cylinder and checked it. From where Britt was sitting, she could see that each chamber was loaded. He snapped the cylinder back into place.

"They're under the assumption that we don't know about their visit," he continued. "That we're unsuspecting. They could be waiting at the main road planning to pull out behind us, follow us until we reach a convenient spot, and do another hit-and-run that would look like an accident. We'd be found dead, end of story. No one would suspect murder."

They were fast approaching the intersection he was concerned about. Raley told her to lie down on the seat. "I want you to keep your head down. Understand?"

She nodded, but apparently he didn't trust her to do as instructed. His hand was firmly planted on the top of her head when he barely slowed to check for oncoming traffic, then shot out onto the road and jerked the truck into a turn so sharp, the tires squealed and smelled of burning rubber.

He kept his hand on her head for several more minutes, until he was convinced that no one was following them. Then he told her she could sit up, but he still drove fast, his whole aspect alert and tense, his eyes shifting often to the mirrors. She was relieved when he replaced the pistol under the seat.

"Would you have shot at them?"

"If they'd tried something like they did last night? You bet your ass, I would've." His tone left her with no doubt.

"Then I'm glad they weren't waiting to follow us."

"Now I'm thinking that maybe they didn't need to," he said. "The guy searching the truck could have put a tracking device on it. They'll take us out when they get the go-ahead from their boss, and it's convenient." He ruminated for a moment, then looked over at her. "Is there anybody you can go to?"

"Go to?"

"Stay with. Till it's safe for you to come out of hiding."

"No."

"Family?"

"No."

He looked at her dubiously.

"No, Raley. No one," she said. "My parents are dead. Both of them were an only child, and so was I. No siblings, no aunts, uncles, nobody. Okay?" Realizing she sounded defensive, she changed tones. "Even if I had a clan of kinfolk, I wouldn't involve anyone else in this. I'm a fugitive. Besides—"

When she broke off, he looked over at her. "What?"

"Nothing."

"What?"

"I'm onto a huge story. I'm not just reporting it, I'm living it."

"Living it," he said with scorn. "Yeah. *For the time being.*" Then, angrily, "Jesus, Britt, this isn't a game. Five minutes from now you could be dead."

"I realize that. I was the one in the flooded car last night, remember?"

"I remember. Do *you*?"

"Your life is on the line, too. Would you give up your investigation?" she demanded. "Well?" she prodded when he didn't respond. After several more seconds of stubborn silence, she continued. "I'm not giving up my story, either. And I'm not going into hiding. That's that."

A mile whizzed past. Maybe two. Finally he said, "You could surrender to the police. You'd be safe in police custody."

"No I wouldn't. If Fordyce and/or McGowan can't kill me, they'll make dead certain I'll be convicted of killing Jay.

You said so yourself. They'll make sure I look so guilty that no one would believe anything I told them about Jay, the fire, nothing.

"You should know. They stopped just short of having you charged with Suzi Monroe's death. If it hadn't been for your friend Candy's influence on Fordyce, he probably would have seen you tried and convicted of something. Not premeditated murder, but something where you would have been muzzled and put away for a long time."

When he muttered a heartfelt *goddammit,* Britt knew she'd won the argument. To seal it, she added, "Unfortunately, I don't have a Candy running interference for me."

"I hate to call and ask a favor. It's been five years since I've talked to her. Besides, she's busy with this Senate confirmation thing."

Britt's jaw went slack with disbelief. "Are you . . . Is . . . Your Candy . . . Candy Orrin . . . is Judge Cassandra Mellors?"

"Yeah. I thought you knew that."

"No!"

"Oh." He shrugged an apology of

sorts. "I always think of her as Candy. She hated Cassandra when we were kids. Wouldn't answer to it. Said it made her sound stuck-up. Now, I guess it sounds more professional."

"Judge Mellors is your friend," Britt said, trying to wrap her mind around this startling revelation.

"A friend I haven't talked to in years. I started to contact her when her husband died but figured she didn't need me crawling out of the woodwork when she was trying to cope with her personal tragedy."

Britt knew from the background research she'd done for her feature story on the judge that she had been married less than a year when her husband, some kind of software developer, had been killed in a ferry accident in New York harbor. He'd gone there on business and was calling on clients on Staten Island. His ferry had been struck by another vessel and sunk rapidly. He'd perished along with twenty-four others.

"I know her," Britt told him. "I did a piece on her, and we got along well. I tried to contact her . . . actually it was the day you kidnapped me. I was trying to line up support from influential people. Anyway, I called her office, but she wasn't available to take my call. But she might now, especially if she knew I was with you."

"I hope I can get her to myself for a minute or two at the funeral. Gauge her thoughts on Jay without coming right out and asking for her help. She put her career on the line for me once before. I don't think she'd want to do so again, not before the Senate vote anyway."

Britt understood his reasoning, but having Judge Mellors in their corner certainly couldn't hurt. Lost in that thought, she gazed out the passenger window. Nothing looked familiar. It wasn't the route he'd mapped out for her last night. "Are we headed toward Charleston?"

"Ultimately. But we've got to have new wheels first. Just in case the truck's got a transponder on it. Even if it doesn't, we can't drive around in this. They know it now."

Noting the severity of his expression,

she said, "They really and truly are after us."

"They really and truly are."

"Then why didn't they do something at the cabin?"

He frowned. "I can't figure that. Maybe, as I said, they get off killing people in their cars. Or maybe their contract was just to locate me and now they're waiting for further instructions. Maybe they want an advance on their fee before committing a double murder. Maybe what the guy found in my cabin threw him for a loop."

"He didn't find your files."

"But he found *you,* and he thought you were dead." She opened her mouth to speak, but before she could, he asked, "How'd you recognize the guy? Did you get a clear look at him?"

"Through the window in the bathroom. He looked out. His face was perfectly framed. He was there fifteen, twenty seconds, searching the area at the back of the cabin."

"He didn't see you?"

"I'm sure he didn't, or he would have reacted. I didn't move. I couldn't. I was frozen with shock because I recognized him instantly."

"You're sure? You're positive you saw him at The Wheelhouse?"

"It was like one of those flashbacks you described, except it stayed fixed in my mind. I remember seeing him the moment I arrived. He was seated at the bar, near the door. When I walked in we made eye contact."

"Did you speak?"

"No. Just looked at each other the way strangers do. No smiles were exchanged, just pleasant-like. You know. Then I spotted Jay and . . . Wait." She stopped and squeezed her eyes shut. "I may have seen him when Jay and I left the bar. There was a man sitting in a car, parked across the street from the bar's entrance."

"Ordinary sedan? That's what they were in today. Maroonish?"

"Maybe. You know what the traffic is like on East Bay during the dinner hour. In between passing cars, I saw . . ." She strained to remember clearly, but the image remained cloudy. "There was a man sitting in the driver's seat, but I don't know for sure that it was the same man as the one at the bar."

"But you're sure the man at the bar and the one in the cabin today were the same?"

"Positive."

"Okay." He gnawed the inside of his cheek, thinking.

"What?"

He tapped the steering wheel with his fist several times. "Couple of things I can't figure out. First, why did they come snooping around my cabin? What were they looking for?"

"How did they find you?"

"It wouldn't be hard. I have a driver's license. I pay property taxes. It would be easy enough to find out where I live. But why did they come looking?"

"They could've put two and two together."

"What do you mean?"

"I mentioned Yemassee to Bill Alexander. If they located your address—"

"And saw it wasn't far from there." He nodded. "Yeah. I see where you're going. They would have thought that was a weird coincidence."

"Maybe McGowan and Fordyce are thinking you're a loose end they can no longer afford to leave loose."

"That's what I'm thinking," he mumbled. Giving her an uneasy glance, he said, "And so are you, Britt. A loose end they thought they didn't have to worry about anymore. Bet it came as a shock to discover that you're still alive and in my company. That would make them real nervous."

To stave off her rising fear, she insisted again that the man in the cabin hadn't seen her. "If he had, he would have done something."

"But the Target bags were on the bed in plain sight. He would have looked inside them, checked the date on the receipt, seen the clothes, seen the new makeup in the bathroom. I doubt they'd mistake me for a cross-dresser."

"You could have bought all that for another woman."

"What other woman?"

"Any other woman. A living woman. They think I'm fish food at the bottom of the Combahee."

"I hope that's what they think. But if I

were them, and I hadn't seen your corpse for myself, and I saw new clothes in your approximate size in the home of a man with whom you have something in common, like being screwed over by Jay Burgess and friends, I'd be thinking that maybe you hadn't drowned. I'd have a *hunch,* just like this guy said. So until proven wrong, I'm going to assume this is a fight, and it's us against them. For reasons known only to them, they didn't take us out at the cabin, but that doesn't make me any less paranoid."

He left the pickup's motor running while he went into a bank to "cash out," as he put it. When he returned, he brought with him a zippered bag, which Britt figured contained currency.

"I'll owe you half of our expenses," she said. Her wallet was in her handbag, in her car, in the river. She didn't like being completely without means, but she had no ATM card or ID with which to withdraw anything from her bank. Not that she would anyway. A bank withdrawal would be the first thing Clark and Javier would watch for.

"Don't worry about it," Raley said. "Money's the least of our problems."

"What have you lived on for the past five years? If you don't mind my asking."

"I sold my house. The cabin cost a fraction of the equity I got from that sale. I had another car. Sold it, sold my fishing boat and trailer. Liquidated everything. Bowling ball, skis, bicycle, scuba gear, everything. I don't have as many toys now, but I don't have as many expenses, either."

"Are you okay with that?"

"I'm fine with that." He looked over at her and added, tongue in cheek, "About as fine as you are with having no family."

He slowed down to survey the inventory of a place on the highway that advertised used cars, boats, trailers, generators, and propane tanks. Easy terms. Priced to sell.

About fifty yards past that was an AME church. Raley turned in to the church parking lot and pulled the pickup into the shade of a live oak draped in

Spanish moss. He counted out several thousand dollars from the money bag and pocketed the hundred-dollar bills. He told her to stay in the truck. "If anyone comes close, honk the horn, and I mean sit down on it."

He walked back to the car lot. She watched as he moved along the row of cars and pickups. Soon a short, potbellied man, whose shirt showed sweat rings under his arms, came out of the sales office and approached Raley. They shook hands, had a brief exchange, then the salesman began pointing out various models for Raley's consideration. He dismissed some straightaway, inspected a few, deciding against them until he was directed to a sedan with a generic body style and drab color.

While the salesman gave his pitch, Raley walked around the car kicking the tires, then got behind the wheel. He turned on the ignition, popped the hood, checked the engine, looked underneath the body to check for oil drips—or so Britt assumed—then seemed to make up his mind. He followed the happy salesman into the office and emerged a few minutes later with a handful of yellow papers and a set of keys.

He drove the car to the church, parked it behind the pickup, then came to the passenger side and opened the door for her, handing her the new set of keys as she alighted.

"You drive that car. They won't know to look for it. I'll take the truck. If something happens—"

"Like what?"

"Anything. You keep going. Drive straight to Charleston and throw yourself on Detective Clark's mercy. Got it?"

"I thought you would trade the truck in," she said as she followed him over to the new purchase.

He stuffed the paperwork, including the title and a short-term insurance policy, into the glove compartment. "A trade-in is a transaction too easy to trace. Besides, I like my truck."

"Where are you going to leave it?"

"The airstrip. I thought about taking it to Delno's, but I don't want to involve him. I don't think they know about the airstrip, so it's best to leave it there, even though it means doubling back several miles." He saw her settled behind the wheel of the sedan. "All right?"

She adjusted the seat and the mirrors. "The upholstery stinks."

"Can't have everything. Follow me, but stay close. Don't let a car get between us. Okay?"

"You don't have to worry about that."

He closed the door but left his hands in the open window. "Remember what I told you, Britt. If something happens to me, you keep going."

But nothing untoward happened. They arrived at the airstrip without incident. They took their belongings, including the pistol, from the pickup, then got into the sedan together, although he took over the driving. She noticed him giving his pickup a wistful glance as they pulled away from the old hangar. He was abandoning his one remaining toy.

"Now where to?" she asked.

"Home sweet home."

"Where's that?"

"I'll know it when I see it."

• • •

It was quaintly called a motor court. Twelve cabins were tucked into a grove of trees set back off Highway 17, west of the Ashley River, which they would cross to get into Charleston proper. The motel had little to recommend it. There was a swimming pool, but it had been drained; the bottom of it was littered with debris both natural and man-made. Enclosed in a chain-link fence was a rusty swing set that had a yellow plastic seat hanging by only one chain. The rest of it was missing.

Again Britt was left alone while Raley went into the office. He returned. "Number nine."

"Presidential suite?"

"Yes, but there's no room service after ten p.m."

The appointed cabin had two double beds with a nightstand and lamp between them. There were a small table with two chairs, a bureau with a cracked mirror above it, a TV, and an air conditioner in the window just under the ceiling. Raley flipped a switch, and it came on with a reassuring hum and a waft of cool air.

Britt lifted the bedspread and inspected the sheets. She didn't see any unsightly or suspicious-looking stains, and the percale smelled of strong detergent and bleach. There was a paper band across the bowl of the toilet, which was also reassuring.

"Not too bad," she said as she emerged after washing her hands in the minuscule sink.

Raley had taken off his shirt. Seeing his bare chest was a reminder of the night before, which caused her to stub her toe on the doorjamb. "Mind if I take a turn?" He motioned with his head toward the bathroom behind her, but her mind was still snagged on the erotic memory and she failed to answer. "I'm gonna be late," he said.

Snapping out of it, she stepped aside, and he squeezed through the narrow doorway, carrying his suit and dress shoes in with him. Since his hands were full, Britt reached for the door knob and closed the door for him.

She sat on the bed she'd claimed as hers, looked up at the acoustic tile ceiling, down at the orange shag carpet.

The commode was flushed. Water ran in the sink. She heard a thump, as though a bony body part had bumped against the tile wall, followed by a muffled curse.

She'd never lived with a man and wondered if this was what it sounded like. Hearing a shoe drop, she smiled.

He came out five minutes after going in, but the change he'd brought about in that period of time was remarkable. He was dressed in the suit slacks and an ivory shirt. His hair had been finger-combed. He'd put on the dress shoes but was carrying the suit jacket.

"You look nice," she said. Actually, he looked *great.*

"Thanks. I'll put on the jacket when I get there."

"Tie?"

"Forgot it because I didn't see it in my closet. Maybe I threw them all away. Anyway, when Fordyce and McGowan see me, they won't be thinking about neckwear."

"So you're going to make yourself seen?"

"Oh, yeah." He glanced at the bank

bag he'd set on the table, along with the plastic-wrapped files and the pistol. "In case of emergency, take those and run."

"Do I have your permission to look through the files?"

He hesitated, then said, "After you do, don't rush out and call your cameraman."

"I won't." He looked at her with patent mistrust. "I *won't.* I promise."

He gave a curt nod. "Keep the door locked. Don't even look through the peephole without having that pistol in your hand. Don't open the door for anybody except me. Remember, not even a cop could possibly know you're here, so don't be deceived by a uniform. I'll stop on my way back and pick up some food. Any requests?"

Come back soon. Come back safe. Don't go at all. "Lysol spray."

"For?"

"The car upholstery. And Diet Coke. Now go. Being late to a funeral is the height of disrespect."

CHAPTER 18

He wasn't late, but he was among the last to slip into the funeral home chapel before the service began. The entire left side had been reserved for policemen, and every seat was occupied. The other side was filled to capacity with civilians.

Raley stood against the back wall, along with dozens of others who'd arrived too late to get a seat. Hymns were piped through invisible speakers, but the service was more secular than religious. Indeed, if Jay had had a spiritual conviction of any kind, Raley was unaware of it. Raley had been required by his parents to attend church with them regularly. Jay had always ribbed him about it.

Familiar scriptures were read from both the Old and New Testaments, and the Protestant chaplain of the police department said a prayer. But most of the service was given over to eulogies that extolled Jay's virtues and wit, his commitment to law enforcement, and of course, his heroism on the day of the police station fire.

The overriding theme of each speech was that the police department and the community as a whole had been robbed of one of their finest members and that the world was severely diminished by Jay Burgess's departure from it.

One of the last and most touching eulogies was written by Judge Cassandra Mellors. It was read by the funeral director in her absence. Pressing matters and professional obligations prevented her from attending the service, he explained, and she deeply regretted not being there to express, in person, her affection for Jay Burgess and sorrow over his passing and the unfortunate circumstances surrounding it.

Ever since his arrival, Raley had been scanning the sea of heads looking for

Candy. It was sorely disappointing to learn that she wasn't there and that he wouldn't have an opportunity to reestablish contact with her face-to-face.

Naturally he wouldn't have broached the subject of the fire. Nor would he have mentioned Britt. Candy would be under the misconception that Britt was a fugitive from justice. But if it became necessary later on to seek Candy's help, a prior personal meeting would have made it less awkward to contact her after such a long absence.

At the conclusion of the service, everyone stood. A bagpiper played "Amazing Grace" as the casket was carried up the center aisle and out the wide doors to the waiting hearse. Burial was to be private, with only Jay's surviving kin—a smattering of cousins and one uncle—in attendance. Once the coffin had cleared the door, the congregation was ushered out by funeral home staff, a row at a time, starting with the first rows and working backward.

Among the first up the aisle was Cobb Fordyce, walking arm in arm with an attractive woman whom Raley assumed was his wife. Both wore stoic, solemn expressions, the standard visage of dignitaries at funerals. If the attorney general picked Raley out in the crowd, he gave no sign of it.

But George McGowan did. He wasn't far behind Fordyce, and when he saw Raley, he did a double take and came to a dead stop, causing Miranda to look at him with consternation. His father-in-law, coming up behind him, gave him a slight push.

George averted his head and continued up the aisle and out the doors. Not wanting George to get away, Raley flouted protocol, maneuvered his way through the crowd along the back wall, and fell in with those who were exiting.

It was a hot, airless afternoon, heavy with humidity. Men not dressed in police uniform were discarding their suit jackets as they stood in groups, talking. A few were lighting up cigarettes. No one was really looking toward the hearse, but everyone was respectfully mindful of it and seemed reluctant to leave before it did.

Raley scanned the crowd that had

spread out onto the chapel lawn. Fordyce and his missus were already being assisted into a limousine. But George McGowan was standing with his wife, father-in-law, and several people Raley didn't know.

He made a beeline for the group.

George, seeing him, separated himself from the others and met him halfway. His smile was broad and guileless, his voice as big as his barrel chest. "Raley Gannon. I thought I spotted you in there. Christ, how long has it been?"

"Five years. Hello, George." He played along with George's blatant bullshit and pumped the hand extended to him.

George clapped him on the back as he looked him over. "Lookin' good, Raley. Still fit. A few gray hairs, but hell."

"Thanks."

"Me?" he said, slapping his gut. "I've put on a few."

There was nothing to say to that. He had. More than a few.

"I got married."

"I heard."

"I left the PD and went to work for my father-in-law."

Raley acknowledged that this wasn't news, either.

"You know my daddy worked for Les up till the day he keeled over," George said. "I thought marrying the boss's daughter would give me privileges. Don't you believe it." He socked Raley's shoulder and laughed, but his laughter sounded hollow and forced.

Underneath the affected bonhomie, George was nervous. He kept wetting his lips; his eyes darted about. He wasn't glad to see Raley, making Raley all the more convinced that George had good reason to be jittery. Had it already been reported to him that it appeared Britt Shelley was camped out at Raley's cabin in the woods, not at the bottom of the river as believed?

"Enough about me," he said, "what are you doing these days?"

"Well, today, I'm attending a funeral."

George's affability deflated like a punctured balloon. Without the balancing smile of large, white teeth, his facial features looked heavier. The flesh sagged, forming crevasses of dissipation and unhappiness.

He glanced toward the hearse still parked in front of the chapel. "Hell of a thing, wasn't it?"

"Um-huh."

"A total shock. Like the cancer. Did you know about that?"

"Not until after he was murdered."

George took a handkerchief from his pants pocket and blotted his sweating upper lip. "First the big c, then . . . that."

He was regarding Raley closely, as though gauging his reaction. Raley kept his features carefully schooled.

"You and Jay had been friends for a long time."

"All our lives. Until five years ago."

George shifted his big feet, rolled his shoulders, cleared his throat. Obvious signs of general discomfort, which an ex-cop should know how to conceal.

"Aw, Raley, you know how Jay was about women," he said, deliberately skipping over any reference to Suzi Monroe. "He could have slept with a thousand and it wouldn't have been enough. Always on the scent of fresh meat, and he'd had a lech for your lady for a long time. Besides, by the time they hooked up, you'd sorta moved on, hadn't you?"

"No, I'd got kicked out. Disgraced, discredited, and fired."

George was about to respond when he was interrupted. "George?"

He turned, looking grateful for the interruption. "Honey, come here." He took his wife's arm and pulled her forward. Miranda was wearing a snug black dress and high heels, a wide-brimmed, black straw hat, and dark sunglasses. Funeral attire gone glam. "Do you remember Raley Gannon? He was an old pal of Jay's. From when they were kids."

"The fireman. Of course I remember." She removed her sunglasses and gave Raley a smile that suggested he was the only man on the planet and he had a twelve-inch dick she was just dying to treat like a lollipop.

"Hello, Miranda."

"Where've you been keeping yourself all this time?"

"Here and there. Nowhere."

Her laugh was throaty and sexy. "That sounds like an ideal place to be." She paused, then said, "It's good to see you. Shame about the circumstances, though."

He nodded.

"But Jay wouldn't want us to grieve, would he? And it's so mother-lovin' hot out here." She dragged her finger down her throat as though to call attention to the dewy skin above the neckline of her black dress. Not that she needed to. If you were a man, and breathing, you'd have already noticed.

Keeping her gaze on Raley, she addressed her husband. "Daddy suggested we go to the club and have a drink."

"Great idea," George said, mopping his face with the handkerchief.

"Please join us, Raley. You can ride with George. He and I came in separate cars." She put one earpiece of her sunglasses between her lips and sucked on it. "You will come, won't you?"

He wondered if the double meaning of her phrasing was intentional, but he didn't have to wonder much. "Sorry, I can't. I have plans."

"Oh, shoot." Her lips formed a pout. "That's too bad."

"But I would like to talk to George for a minute."

"Well then . . ." She reached out and laid her hand on his arm. "So nice seeing you. Don't be a stranger. Bye." She dropped her hand and said to George, "See you there, sweetheart."

George and Raley watched as she rejoined her father, who was bidding good-bye to the group he'd been chatting with. Together she and Les walked down the incline toward a shiny red Corvette convertible. George came back around to Raley. "What do you think?"

"I think you did very well for yourself."

The other man laughed, ducking his head and looking abashed. "You could say that, yeah." Then he looked up at Raley from beneath his eyebrows. "Did you ever fuck her?"

Raley was taken aback. "Jesus, George. That's your *wife.*"

"Did you?"

"No."

"Did Jay?"

"I don't know."

"Doesn't matter if you tell me now. He's dead."

"I don't know," Raley repeated.

George held his stare for several seconds, then muttered, "I never got a straight answer from him about it, either." He looked away, but when he did, something caught his eye that caused him to wince. Raley turned to see what had caused the facial tic.

Clusters of people were still standing around talking, fanning themselves with their service programs, waiting for the hearse to leave before they did. The circumstances were somber, but Raley didn't detect anything sinister about the scene, nothing to make George any jumpier than he was.

But then he noted one couple among the crowd, his attention drawn to them because the man's gaze was fixed on George and Raley while the woman with him was involved in conversation with other people.

When Raley caught the stranger staring, he quickly turned away. Raley looked back at George, sensing the other man's increased agitation. He asked, "Who's that?"

"Who?"

"The guy, George. The one who had a bead on us."

"You mean Pat?"

Raley didn't buy George's dumb act, especially when he identified the man. "That's Pat Wickham?"

"Junior."

Raley wouldn't have recognized him. Of course he was older now than when Raley had last seen him—and he couldn't remember how long that had been. But the drastic change in Wickham's appearance hadn't been caused by aging. "What happened to his face?"

"It got fucked up in an accident. Long time ago."

"Who's that with him?"

"His wife."

"He's married?"

"Got a coupla kids. He joined the department, but he's a desk jockey. Computers and shit. Not a real cop like his old man was."

Raley gave Pat Wickham, Jr., a long, considering look, then came back around to George. "Do you two stay in close touch?"

"Not at all."

"Huh. You and Pat Senior were best friends."

"True. But after he died, you know how it is." George looked around as though searching for rescue. "Look, Raley, it's been great seeing you. But Miranda and Les will be—"

"Has it struck you as odd, George?"

George's wandering eyes snapped him into focus. "What?"

"Come on. Cut the crap. You know what I'm talking about. The similarity between the night Jay died and the night Suzi Monroe overdosed."

"Jay didn't overdose. He was smothered by that newswoman."

"Was he?"

"Yeah. I mean, that's the allegation. That's what I hear."

"Did you also hear her say that she was drugged? Weird, don't you think? Britt Shelley echoed exactly what I said the morning I woke up in bed with a naked dead girl and couldn't remember how I got there."

George was getting increasingly hot under the collar. He assumed a belligerent stance. "I didn't mention that 'cause

I figured you'd just as soon not talk about it."

Raley smiled and said softly, "No, George, *you'd* just as soon not talk about it. See, I don't think you'd want anybody to know that I told you, Jay, Pat Wickham, and Cobb Fordyce that I'd been given a drug in my drink to wipe clean my memory of that night. Because it might strike them as strange that Britt Shelley has said the same thing about the night Jay died."

"Date rape drug, my ass," George said, bringing his florid face closer to Raley's. "That's a real convenient defense that can't be proven."

"Something I know all too well."

"Look, she and Jay had a lovers' quarrel. End of story."

"She claimed they weren't lovers."

George guffawed. Or tried. It sounded more like choking.

"Besides," Raley continued, "Jay didn't quarrel with women. Never. He spared himself such scenes. When he wanted to end a fling with a woman, he just stopped calling her. No fuss, no muss."

"Maybe this gal didn't know that. Maybe—"

"Jay had only weeks to live. I wonder what it was he wanted to tell a celebrated newswoman that night. Have you thought about that?"

George fumed for several seconds, then said, "He might have wanted to tell her how easy it was for him to get in your fiancée's pants."

Raley didn't flinch. "I think he wanted to give Britt Shelley a big news story with his deathbed confession built in."

George took another aggressive half step forward. "What would Jay have to confess?"

"You tell me."

"You're full of shit, Gannon. You're holding a grudge against Jay for taking Hallie away from you. If I was still a cop, you know what I'd be thinking? I'd be thinking that maybe *you* sneaked into his place that night and held a pillow over his face."

"If I was going to kill him, it wouldn't have taken me five years to do it. This isn't about him and Hallie."

"No?" George sneered. "You know, a

few months after you left town, I went by Jay's place one day. Middle of the day. Broad daylight."

"Somebody's going to connect the dots, George. You, Fordyce, Pat Wickham, Jay, Suzi Monroe, me, Britt Shelley."

"I was about to ring Jay's doorbell when I saw them through the window."

"Somebody's going to make that connection, George, and the common thread is the fire."

"Your girl's legs were draped over the arms of a chair, and Jay was on his knees, his face buried in her pussy, and she was loving it."

"This cast of characters originated with the *fire.*"

Raley said it loud enough to draw attention to them and halt the conversations taking place nearby. George, his face suffused with heat, looked around, smiling, but his worry of being overheard was apparent.

In that moment of suspended animation, the hearse pulled away. Raley and George, like the others, solemnly watched its slow progress down the hill.

No one moved or said anything until it turned at the end of the lane and disappeared behind a dense hedge of evergreens, then a collective sigh of relief could be heard among the last of the mourners.

George mumbled, "Well, that's that."

"You wish." Raley turned back to George and thumped him softly in the chest. "You'd better go have that drink, George. Have two. I think you need them." Then he smiled. "See you around."

"But if he's any judge of smiles at all," Raley told Britt an hour later, "he'll know mine wasn't for grins."

"I've seen that smile." She dunked a French fry into a puddle of ketchup. "It's wicked."

"Wicked?"

"Villainous. Hungry. Wolfish."

Raley scoffed. "I don't think any of those descriptions fit me. Especially now that I've shaved off my beard."

"They fit you *more* without the beard. The jaw, the eyes. Definitely lupine."

He had returned to the motor court,

bringing with him, along with a six-pack of Diet Coke and a can of Lysol spray, a sack of cheeseburgers and fries with a side order of fried shrimp, and two milk shakes. In the amount of time it had taken him to pull his shirttail from the waistband of his trousers and toe off his shoes, Britt had had the food unwrapped and on the table. They'd dug in.

While they ate, he recounted his conversation with George McGowan, trying to be as precise as possible. Britt didn't allow anything to be glossed over or summarized. She demanded elaboration and details.

"Is she gorgeous?" she asked now.

"Miranda?"

She smiled wryly. "I see you didn't have to pause and think about who I meant."

"Yes. Gorgeous."

"I've only seen pictures of her. Did Jay . . . you know?"

He raised one shoulder. "Maybe. Probably. Everybody else has."

Britt stopped chewing, the unasked question evident in her expression.

He wiped his hands on a paper napkin. "The first time Miranda caught my eye, she was a high school cheerleader in a short skirt, doing high kicks on the sidelines. Jailbait. By the time she was old enough, I was away at school, and after that I was with Hallie."

"I see. Lousy timing and lack of opportunity."

He thought, *Let her wonder,* and reached for his milk shake. He took a long pull on the straw, then for the next several minutes they ate in silence.

"Raley?" When he looked across at her, her gaze was soft, earnest. "How did you feel? During the service, I mean. How was it for you, coming to grips with Jay's death?"

"You're not going to say the word *closure,* are you?"

She frowned at that. "Despite what he'd done to you, he was your oldest friend. Did you feel a loss? Were you able to mourn?"

He popped a shrimp into his mouth. "Always the interviewer, aren't you?"

She yanked her head back as though he'd slapped her. Then she tossed down her last French fry and began gathering up the trash, stuffing it into the sack. "Forget it. I thought you might be feeling some conflicting emotions and would appreciate a sounding board to help you sort them out. My mistake."

She moved back her chair and stood up. Raley caught her arm. "Okay, sorry."

She pulled her arm from his grasp. "You're still looking for an ulterior motive in everything I say and do. I thought we were past that."

"I may never be past that."

Angrily, she held his gaze for several moments, then expelled a long breath, her shoulders relaxing. "I deserve your mistrust, I guess. But I honestly thought you might want to talk about you and Jay."

He hesitated, then with a small motion of his head, invited her to sit back down, which she did. He leaned back in the chair, which was much too small for his tall frame, and stretched his legs out in front of him. "You're not a reporter for nothing, and I mean that as a compliment. Your instincts are excellent. Your questions about the funeral struck a nerve. That's why I said what I did."

He shot her a quick glance but found it difficult to look her in the eye while he verbalized these particular thoughts, so he focused on the happy face printed on the cup of his milk shake. “Jay was one of those people you make excuses for. Excuses to yourself.”

“How do you mean?”

“We’d make plans. To go to a ball game. To water-ski. Whatever. He’d arrive an hour late. I’d be furious. He’d be apologetic and penitent. ‘You have every right to be sore,’ he’d say. And even though I did have every right to be mad as hell, I’d let it go. I’d excuse him.

“He’d borrow my car and return it with an empty gas tank. I’d be steamed, but I’d never say anything. We’d be out to dinner. He’d let me pick up the check, saying he would get it the next time, but ‘next time’ never came. It wasn’t a matter of money. That’s not what I resented. It was his taking for granted that I’d pay and never make an issue of it.

“He treated all his friends like that. With a casual disregard that would piss people off if it was anybody else besides Jay.” He sliced the air with the back of his hand. "No matter what the offense, people excused him, saying, 'That's just Jay.'

"But—and that's a big word here—he also had a talent for cheering you up when you were having a crummy day. He could get you to laugh when you felt like crushing something. He was the life of the party. He was never in a bad mood. He was affectionate and fun. That's why people were drawn to him. Everybody wanted to be near Jay, inside his energy field. Because it was electric and exciting. The air around him crackled. From the outside looking in, it seemed like he had a thousand friends."

He paused and thoughtfully uncrossed his ankles, pulling his legs in and setting his elbows on his thighs, leaning forward. "But I wonder. Did he have friends, or just acquaintances he could manipulate and get away with it? Was he a friend, or a man who could use you with such finesse you didn't even realize you were being used?"

He paused a moment, then said, "Looking at his casket today, I had to wonder if *anything* he had ever said to me, in our entire lives, was honest and real. When I was down or in doubt and he doled out encouragement, was it just so much rhetoric? When I shared my ambitions and dreams, was he bored? Secretly laughing up his sleeve? I think maybe his special gift was just knowing the right thing to say and when to say it, to make you think he was your friend."

He sighed. "Did I feel a loss? Yeah, I did. I thought my friendship with Jay ended five years ago. Today I realized that it had never existed. We'd never had a true friendship. That's what I mourned." Feeling slightly embarrassed over the sentimentality, he slapped his thighs lightly and stood up. "Finished?"

She cleared her throat. "Yes. Thank you. It was delicious."

He slipped on his sneakers and carried the debris to a trash can outside so as not to stink up their small quarters. As he headed back toward the cottage, he questioned whether or not to tell Britt about what had happened after he parted company with George McGowan. She deserved to know, but did she need to be any more frightened than she already was?

He scanned the parking lot, but there was only one other car parked outside a cabin, and it had been there when they checked in. He went back inside, making certain the door was locked and the dead bolt secured.

He turned to find Britt facing him squarely, hands on her hips. "When are you going to tell me?"

"Tell you what?"

"Why you're walking around with that cannon tucked into your waistband." She lifted his shirttail and pointed at the pistol grip. "Tell me why you got up to look out the window twice while we were eating. Why—"

"They were at the funeral."

"Who?"

"Butch and Sundance. The two men who came to the cabin."

She backed up until her knees hit the edge of the bed, then plopped down on it. "Did they see you?"

"Yes, but I pretended not to recognize them."

"What happened?"

He'd left George looking ready to implode. Going down the incline toward his car, he'd spotted the maroon sedan out of the corner of his eye. He tried not to give any indication that he recognized the car or the man sitting behind the wheel, although he was sure it was the same man who'd searched his cabin. He was still wearing the pale blue shirt. There was another man in the passenger seat, and although Raley had never got a good look at him, he saw that he was wearing a pair of aviator sunglasses and had to assume it was the man who'd gone through his truck.

He had no choice but to drive away in the sedan he'd recently purchased for the express purpose of getting rid of an identifiable vehicle. "A wasted thirty-five hundred dollars, asshole." Covertly he shot the finger at the driver of the maroon sedan.

He nosed his way into the line of cars leaving the funeral and was glad to see that the maroon sedan had to wait for another opening in the stream, which didn't come until six more cars had passed. When Raley reached the exit, he turned onto the thoroughfare, going in the direction opposite from the motor court where he and Britt were registered. He drove as fast as he dared without risking getting stopped for speeding.

Nevertheless, the maroon sedan caught up with him at the second traffic light. It remained in his rearview mirror for the next few blocks, keeping several cars between them but matching Raley's speed and shifting lanes whenever he did.

It took him five miles in heavy traffic to finally shake the other vehicle, but he couldn't be certain that Butch didn't have someone else bird-dogging him. He continued to weave through traffic on the boulevards, got on and off the expressway several times, and doubled back on his route so many times he didn't think he could possibly have been followed.

That was what he told Britt now, and wished his voice held more conviction. "I think I evaded them, but I can't be sure."

"We won't know until someone

comes barging through the door, guns blazing."

"I've got a gun, too."

That didn't seem to console her all that much. "You're not always here, Raley. And now that they've seen the new car, they know what we're driving."

"I drove into a parking garage at the hospital and switched license plates with a minivan, then I got a felt marker and made an eight out of a three. And I chose this car because there are a lot of boxy gray sedans similar to it. So it'll be hard for them to track us."

"They've done okay so far."

She was right, so he didn't insult her with a lame contradiction. "You could still turn yourself in."

"Not until I'm better equipped, ready to fight fire with fire. So to speak." Reaching behind her, she took several copied documents off the bed, where she had obviously been reading them during his absence.

"You took pains to hide all this stuff. Why?"

"I wanted to be sure a copy of the original records existed. I was afraid that, after I left the department, they would be doctored or accidentally-on-purpose misplaced, never to be found."

"When you were stonewalled by Jay, what specifically were you investigating?"

"The seven victims."

"According to these reports, one was a file clerk."

"Her body was found in a stairwell. She was trapped there when the ceiling collapsed. Cause of death, she was crushed, but she probably would have died of smoke inhalation anyway."

"The jailer."

"Was rescued but died two days later of burns and smoke inhalation. It wasn't a merciful death," Raley said grimly.

"Five prisoners died in the holding cell."

"Four died in the holding cell. But there was a fifth detainee who also died."

She glanced down at the sheets of paper in her hand. "You've circled a name in red."

"Cleveland Jones."

CHAPTER 19

"Cleveland Jones was in a small, enclosed office with no window, not even in the door. It was being used that day as an interrogation room," Raley said.

"Why that day?"

"Curious, isn't it? Especially when there were two other bona fide interrogation rooms. Anyway, it's believed that he set the fire."

"By igniting the contents of a wastebasket. You said it wasn't that simple."

"It wasn't. As a seasoned inspector, Brunner knew that, too. Ordinarily, the trash can fire would have burned itself out in a matter of minutes, when all the combustibles were consumed. But this trash can was placed near an intake air vent. The grille was missing and no telling for how long."

"I only saw the building as a pile of charred rubble," she said. "But I understand that it was old. The department was mere months away from moving into new headquarters."

"That's right. The building was overcrowded, outdated, and in need of extensive repair. The insulation was old. There were holes in the ductwork. Old wood beams formed the infrastructure, and many were rotted. The wiring was faulty. It had a sprinkler system, but it was an antique, insufficient and unreliable on its best day. The day of the fire, it failed completely.

"But no one wanted to spend money on extensive repairs when the department would soon be vacating the place for the new facility. Repairs that were absolutely necessary were done hastily and sloppily. Band-Aids put on a massive hemorrhage. Unfortunately, all this was discovered during our inspection after the fire, not before. Even dust is flammable, and it had been accumulating in the structure since the turn of the last century. It was a disaster waiting to happen."

"When the small trash can flame was sucked into the wall through the intake vent . . ."

Raley made a motion with his hands, indicating ignition. "It had a draft pulling it upward. It had more than enough flammable material and virtually nothing to impede its path through the walls. From the first spark, it was deadly."

"Seven people," she said, shaking her head sadly.

"Six."

She gave him a sharp look. "What?"

"Six. Cleveland Jones didn't die in the fire. He was dead before it started."

Her lips parted in surprise. "How do you know?"

"Did you come across Jones's autopsy report?"

"I did, yes. It's here somewhere." She shuffled through the documents scattered across the bed until she found that report and handed it to him. "It says his body was found on the floor of that locked room, curled inward, hands under the chin."

"Which is typical. As a burning body dehydrates, the muscles contract and pull it into a fetal-like position. That doesn't mean the victim burned to death. Cleveland Jones didn't. His cause of death was blunt trauma to the head."

He flipped over a few pages of the autopsy report to a page on which there was a diagram of a human male body. He pointed to the head, where the coroner had made markings. "Skull fractures. Both significant."

Britt read out loud what the coroner had written. "Fatal." She looked up at Raley. "A falling beam? Collapsing ceiling?"

He shook his head. "If that was the case, the fire would have been raging for some time. Jones's lungs would have shown significant soot and smoke inhalation. There would have been a high level of carbon monoxide." He held up the report. "That's not what the ME found. As soon as he made these determinations, he called Brunner and told him that one of the victims was dead before the fire started. Brunner asked me to inform detectives that they had a possible homicide. I was to work with them on the investigation. That's what I was doing when Jay called to invite me to his party."

She exhaled deeply, readily seeing the import of that.

"As soon as I started asking questions about Jones and his arrest, I began to get the runaround. Jay claimed not to remember the details of Jones's arrest. It wasn't his case, he said, but he promised to find out what he could.

"Keep in mind that the PD was in chaos. Construction on the new building was still months away from completion, so they were working out of temporary headquarters. Jay's procrastination made sense. Now, I see it as avoidance. He didn't want me to know anything about Cleveland Jones, other than that he was the firebug. And that's another thing. Jones had committed a wide range of crimes, but arson wasn't one of them. I learned that from his rap sheet, which I had to obtain from the state."

Tiredly, he rolled his shoulders. He

was tempted to save some of this until tomorrow, but he knew Britt wouldn't let him stop until she had the whole story, so he continued. "After repeated calls, Jay finally sent me a message through a PD secretary, telling me that Jones's blows to the head had been sustained *prior* to his arrest. The arresting officers—never identified—didn't realize how serious the injuries were until Jones began behaving irrationally while under interrogation.

"He was left alone while arrangements were being made to transfer him to the hospital. Apparently that's when he started the fire. Jay's message went on to say that he was sorry, that was all he knew, but he was checking into it and when he had further details he would get back to me. He didn't, of course."

"What about Brunner? After you were ousted, didn't he pursue the matter of Jones's death?"

"In the final report, he went with Jay's explanation. The paperwork regarding Cleveland Jones's arrest had been destroyed in the flames, so there was no documentation, but Jay was a hero, so Brunner didn't doubt his word. You and the other media were so swept up in my story, so busy extolling the heroes, that the small footnote about Jones faded into obscurity. And anyway, he was the arsonist who'd caused death and destruction. Who cared how he'd died?"

"Brunner might now. If you went to him—"

"Can't. He died. About six months after the fire. Cardiac arrest."

"Oh."

"In a way I'm glad he won't be here to experience the shakedown. Whatever form it ultimately takes, a lot of blame would fall on him. I don't think he was corrupt. A bit tired and lazy, maybe. Or just unwilling to rock the boat."

She thought this over for several seconds, then said, "What about Cleveland Jones's family?"

"A father. I called him, hoping to get some background information. The guy was hostile, said he didn't want to talk about his wayward son. I stayed after him and finally wore him down. He agreed to meet with me. But when I got to his place, he wasn't there. I went back several times. Called. Never could contact him again."

"You know no more details than you did the night you went to the party."

"No."

"Did you ever learn why Jones was arrested?"

"Assault. Conveniently, no one could remember the nature of his crime, or where it was committed, or what time of day he was brought into the station. Amid all this hazy information, there was one fact of which everyone was absolutely certain: Jones's fatal head injuries hadn't been inflicted by anyone within the CPD."

"Hmm. Just a tad suspicious."

"You think?"

"Jay promised he'd have the arrest report to you by Monday."

"It was an easy promise for him to make. He knew that by Sunday morning I'd have a dead girl in bed with me."

He went to the window and parted the faded orange curtains, which matched the ugly carpet. Satisfied that no one was about to ambush them, he turned back into the room. “There was another unanswered question, and it was a dilly. How did Jones start the fire? With what? When he was arrested, his pockets would have been emptied, right?”

She shrugged. “He sneaked something past.”

“I’d buy that, except that no accelerants were found in that room.”

“They would have burned up.”

“Gasoline, kerosene leak into cracks and corners. It would have been detected even in that devastation. Anyway, Jones couldn’t have carted a gas can in there.”

“Matchbook?” she suggested. “Something that small would have been easy for him to conceal. In his sock or something. He could have lit one match, then thrown the book of them into the trash can, maybe saving some to light debris inside the air vent.”

Long before she finished, he was shaking his head. “No silica. It’s a compound found on match heads. It can withstand a fire. There was none.”

“So it was never determined exactly

what was used to ignite the matter in the wastebasket?"

Facetiously he replied, "I suppose Jones could have rubbed two sticks together. Besides that, how did he light the fire, and see to it that it spread into the building, without inhaling any smoke? But for the sake of argument, let's say he did. What did he hope to accomplish?"

"Escape?"

"Okay. That's reasonable. But he'd been through this process dozens of times. He was only twenty-one, but he was a veteran criminal. He would have known that he would be locked inside that room. Seems really stupid, doesn't it, to set a fire in a room where he'd be trapped?"

"If he was suffering from a skull fracture and behaving irrationally—"

"Assuming that much is true."

"He could have been trying to commit suicide."

"A tough guy like that?" He shook his head. "I don't think so. And who, even someone with a bone fragment short-circuiting his brain, would condemn himself to such a horrible death?"

"Maybe he only wanted to scare people," she said. "He didn't realize that, once the fire was inside the walls, it could spread that quickly. It was a prank, or the desperate act of an irrational man, that went haywire."

"That still doesn't explain the absence of smoke in his airways," he argued. "But the biggest mystery of this whole thing is Jay's stonewalling. He loved being in the spotlight, Britt. You know that. He was ambitious, and he had high goals. He freely admitted that he wanted to work his way up to chief of police. So why wouldn't he want to be in the thick of the investigation, especially when the ME determined that one of the casualties was a possible murder?"

He began to pace. "Jay was a homicide detective. He should have been all over that unexpected development. The investigation would have kept him in the news, made his celebrity star shine even brighter. Instead, he distanced himself from it and avoided involvement. Very unlike Jay."

"Very."

"I think he stayed at arm's length of the investigation because he feared the outcome. He was afraid it would be ruinous to either him or one of his buddies."

"You were his buddy, too, Raley."

"But I wasn't in on the crime." He stopped pacing and looked directly at her. "My gut tells me that our four heroes were covering up something having to do with Cleveland Jones, specifically the way he died. The fire was set so no one would ever know what took place in that room. That's what Jay was going to confess to you at The Wheelhouse."

She didn't rush to either dispute him or agree, but held his stare, her brow furrowed with contemplation. After several long moments, she looked away, releasing a long breath. "You think someone killed him in that room."

"Yes, I do. Do you believe I'm right?"

Her eyes moved back to him. "More than I believe you're wrong. Everything points to it. Why would they go to such lengths to cover up anything less? But how do we prove it? How do we prove it and remain alive?"

"I'm not sure we can."

She was still sitting on the edge of the bed, her face turned up to him. He could tell that the candid statement had taken her aback. He'd outlined the problem; she'd expected him to have ideas on how to solve it.

He had an intense but misplaced urge to reach down and touch her cheek, but he restrained it. After holding her gaze for a long moment, he said, "Britt, listen to me now, and listen good. You saw how I live. I've got nothing to lose. No career, no possessions or relationship . . . no nothing. But you've got everything going for you. You're on the brink of a career breakthrough."

"What are you saying?"

"Turn yourself in."

"To Clark and Javier?"

"To the FBI."

Her reaction wasn't what he expected. She actually smiled. "I'll admit, I've considered it. But murder is a state offense. The FBI would be reluctant to touch it. They don't like interfering with local and state agencies unless they're invited to, and the chances of that happening in this case are slim to none. Within hours, I'd be right back with Clark and Javier, and would look even more desperate than I already do. Not to mention how chapped they'd be that I'd gone over their heads."

"You could tell them where to find your car."

"But could I prove I was forced off the road?"

"Did the guys ram your bumper?"

"No."

"Bump against your fender enough to scrape paint?"

"I don't think so. Near misses, but—"

"No metal-to-metal contact?"

She shook her head. "Clark and Javier, probably even the FBI, would think I'd staged it to appear innocent."

"Shit. That only goes to show how good Butch and Sundance are." He plowed his fingers through his hair and, after a litany of curses, said stubbornly, "You can't be convicted of murdering Jay. Not without more solid evidence than they've got."

"Maybe not, but the circumstantial evidence is compelling. Besides, what do you think a murder trial would do to my career? Not to mention my checking account. Retaining a good defense attorney would deplete my savings in about a week and a half. After the trial, I'd have an enormous debt. Even if I was acquitted, I would have lost a year of my life defending myself, and who would hire me with that taint on my record?

"Just like you, Raley, the moment I woke up with Jay, the life I had lived to that point was over. They used me, just like they used Suzi Monroe to get to you. I'm lucky they kept me alive, a decision which they obviously regret now. I had a good thing going, and they robbed me of it. So, not only do I want the story, and want to see justice done, but I want my payback from these bastards."

Secretly he admired the fire he saw in her eyes, but he was still afraid for her. Afraid for them both. "Sleep on it."

"I don't need to."

"Sleep on it."

To put an end to the discussion, he

went around the room switching out lights, then dragged one of the chairs over to the window, sat down in it, and opened the curtains a crack.

He heard papers rustling and knew she was moving aside the open folders so she could lie down. Fifteen minutes of silence elapsed, then she said, "Butch and Sundance?"

"The only pair of crooks that sprang to mind. We could refer to them as Assassin A and Assassin B, I guess."

"No, I like Butch and Sundance."

Another five minutes ticked past, then she asked, "Are you going to sit there all night?"

"For a while longer."

He waited another forty-five minutes before he felt comfortable enough to give up the vigil. If someone had been out there watching, they likely would have made a move once the lights went out, especially since they were unaware that he and Britt knew they were being hunted.

Still dressed, he felt his way to the second bed and stretched out on it. He set the pistol on the nightstand, then thought better of it and placed it on the bed beside him.

Britt was long asleep. The room was silent except for her soft breathing and the hum of the mercury-vapor light outside in the parking lot. Lying on his back, his head barely denting the hard pillow, he stared up through the darkness. He tried not to think about how narrow the space separating them was, tried not to think about last night.

But he thought about it anyway. Remembered every detail with stark clarity. Insisted to himself that it wasn't those recollections that gave him an uncompromising erection he couldn't do a damn thing about.

He closed his eyes and tried to sleep, but his mind wouldn't shut down. It obstinately seesawed between their predicament and last night's sexual peccadillo, until finally thoughts of the former were obscured by thoughts of the latter. He surrendered and let his mind drift on a current of erotic recollections.

She must have hollow bones, he thought. He hadn't realized how dainty she was, how unsubstantial, until she'd been under him and he was too far gone to be gentle. Andre the Giant ravaging Tinker Bell.

On the other hand, the depth of her passion had surprised him. Yeah, she'd been upset, scared out of her wits, in the grip of hysteria, her emotions off the charts, but still . . . Who would've guessed that the cool lady on TV was one and the same with the woman who fucked like—

"Raley?"

Her soft voice stopped his breath. He swallowed, managed to say, "Hmm?"

"I'm staying."

George air-kissed the teenybopper cocktail waitress good-bye and let himself out of her apartment. He'd given her quite a workout tonight. Or, more truthfully, she'd given him one; as he made his way to his car, he realized how dog tired he was.

It had been one hell of a day. He'd spent all morning at the office, finishing up a contract Les had reminded him was already late. He'd barely had time to scarf down a sandwich lunch before leaving for the funeral. The ceremony would have been bad enough, but added to it was the encounter with Raley Gannon, who had appeared like some chain-rattling ghost.

Jay's death had resurrected Raley Gannon. There was an irony in there somewhere, but George was too tired to think it through.

He turned his car toward home, hoping to God Miranda would be asleep when he got there. He might even forgo their comfortable bed for the sofa in the study, just to avoid her shit. Their cocktail hour at the country club had been too short, the dinner in the club dining room too long. All through it Les had badgered him about this and that, while Miranda sat there sighing with boredom when she wasn't gazing at her reflection in the mirror behind their table.

When the meal finally concluded, George asked Les if he would drive Miranda home, saying he needed to return to the office to check his e-mails. He did make a quick stop at the office, but only to pick up condoms, which he kept in his desk drawer, then he spent the next hour with the cocktail waitress who wasn't only good looking but also one hell of a contortionist.

Their acrobatics in bed had left him sated, almost too weary to drive home. But while his body was languishing, his brain was acting like an overloaded circuit board, sizzling and sparking with a fresh worry every few seconds.

Les and Miranda had dismissed his concern over Raley's unexpected appearance at the funeral. "He taunted you. So what?" Les had said as he stirred cream into his after-dinner coffee. "If that guy had anything to back up his beef, he would have used it five years ago. He's history. Forget him."

But worry continued to gnaw at George, and apparently Pat Wickham was also feeling its bite. He wasn't as good at hiding his uneasiness as George was. George could choke the little turd for letting Raley catch him staring at them. He'd looked bug-eyed and scared enough to wet himself, and Raley had picked up on it.

George's cell phone rang. Probably Miranda, checking up on him, although she must have had a good idea where he'd been. He flipped open his phone. "I'm on my way."

"George?"

"Yeah?"

"This is Candy."

"Oh, hell, Candy, I thought you were Miranda."

"I get that a lot," she said with drollness and good-natured self-deprecation. "Don't I wish." Then in a lower, sadder tone, she asked, "Is this a bad time?"

"No. I'm in my car on my way home."

"Sorry it's so late, but I wanted to call before the day was over. I hated like hell having to miss the funeral. George, you know that if it weren't for this—"

"You don't need to explain, Candy. We all know and understand why you couldn't make it."

"I appreciate your understanding. But that doesn't make me regret it any less. How did it go?"

"I think Jay would have liked it. Except for the organ music. He would have preferred a jazz quartet."

She laughed.

"The thing you wrote was a highlight. If Jay's in heaven, he's blushing."

"I meant everything I said. He was a good friend. I'm going to miss him."

"Yeah." George waited a beat, shifting uncomfortably in his seat. "Guess who showed up?"

"Half the city, I expect."

"Nearly."

"Cobb Fordyce, I'm sure."

"He even brought the wife."

"He's a politician," she said, but without rancor. "He's got an image to uphold."

"And Raley Gannon."

"Seriously?"

"I shit you not. In the flesh."

"Did you talk to him?"

"We had an . . . uh . . . exchange."

"Exchange? That word sort of qualifies what would normally be referred to as a conversation."

"Yeah."

"So, what kind of qualification, George?"

He began by describing Raley's appearance and general demeanor. "He looked basically the same, except he's wearing his hair longer. Some gray in it now. Friendly enough, but he never was as outgoing as Jay. He didn't say what he was doing or where he was living these days. But he, uh . . ." He hesitated, then said, "He did bring up the business with Suzi Monroe."

"That surprises me," Candy said thoughtfully. "You would think he'd want to keep that well buried in his past. What was the context?"

"He remarked on the similarity between the night Jay died and the night the Monroe girl overdosed."

"Jay didn't overdose."

By now George had arrived at his house. He parked in front but kept the engine running so the air conditioner would stay on. "I was quick to point that out to him. He said the similarity was that Britt Shelley claimed she was drugged the night she was with Jay, same as he was the night he was with Suzi Monroe."

"Suzi Monroe was a habitual drug user. Jay never used drugs. So did he venture to guess who'd slipped Britt Shelley a Mickey?"

"We didn't get that far, but Raley is of

the opinion—" He broke off when Miranda opened the front door and stepped onto the porch. Light from the doorway outlined her body through the sheer nightgown she was wearing.

"Raley is of the opinion . . . ?" Candy prompted.

Holding his wife's gaze through the car window, George said, "He's of the opinion that Jay made the date with Britt Shelley to give her a big news story. One with a deathbed confession built in."

She groaned. "Poor Raley. He just won't give up."

"I called his bluff, told him he was full of shit, said he was still pissed at Jay over him snatching Hallie out from under his nose."

Candy sighed. "I guess you can't blame him. Even after all this time, even now that Jay's dead, Hallie's rejection is bound to hurt. But Raley refuses to accept responsibility for his misfortune, which came about because of his own stupidity."

"And his dick."

"Redundant."

George snuffled a laugh. "You have a point, Judge."

"Do you know how to get in touch with Raley?"

"No. Why?"

"It might help if I talked to him."

George waited several beats, then said, "I wonder . . ."

"What?"

"Could Raley's grudge against Jay have driven him to commit murder?" He let the question reverberate. The judge didn't respond immediately, but he knew he had her attention. "I halfway accused him of it. He said if he'd wanted to kill Jay, it wouldn't have taken him five years. But it smacks of poetic justice, doesn't it? Using a date rape drug? It's something to think about." Another short pause, then, "What do you hear about Britt Shelley?"

"Nothing."

"I thought maybe you'd picked up some scuttlebutt going around the courthouse."

"Only what's been in the news. Apparently Bill Alexander was the last person she talked to. He's an idiot. That's off the record and just between us, of course."

George laughed. "Gotcha."

"Listen, George, I need to get to bed. Again, I apologize for calling so late, but this is the first private moment I've had all day. Until the Senate vote, my time's not my own."

"Good luck with that. Not that you need it."

"Thanks." A short silence followed, then she said, "At least Jay is at peace now."

"One hopes."

After their good-byes, George closed the phone, then stared at it thoughtfully before turning off the car and getting out.

As he trudged up the steps, Miranda asked, "Who was that?"

"Judge Cassandra Mellors."

Miranda's eyebrow arched eloquently. "My, my. You're awfully popular this week, George. First the state attorney general calls. Now a district court appointee. Doesn't she have anything better to do than place late-night phone calls to old chums?"

"She wanted to hear about the funeral. I told her about Raley."

"Oh? And what did she say?"

He recounted their conversation. "Candy ended by saying that at least Jay was at peace."

Miranda stepped closer to him. "In between conversations with people in high places, you had time to screw your little cocktail waitress. I can smell her on you."

"Can you?" He pushed his hand between Miranda's thighs and squeezed her sex. "Jealous?"

"Why would I be?" she said, deliberately rubbing herself against his hand. "When I know that every time you're with her, or any other woman, you'd much rather be having me."

It was the truth, and George hated her for knowing it. "But I can't really *have* you, Miranda, can I? No matter how many times I fuck you, I'll never have you."

She didn't even pretend not to understand. Nor did she refute him. She merely stared back at him with that knowing smile that tormented him.

Frustrated, he withdrew his hand and stepped around her, moving toward the door.

She caught his arm and stopped him. "I don't like it."

"You'll have to be more specific."

"Jay dies, and all your old cronies start showing up. They're like buzzards drawn to a carcass."

He chuckled a mirthless laugh. "You may not like it, but you can't be surprised. Did you think Jay's murder was going to go unnoticed? It was bound to have a ripple effect. Like Raley said today, we're all connected." Bending toward her, he said in a stage whisper, "To the fire."

Miranda released her hold on him and backed away, separating them in more ways than just linear distance. "That may be, George, but I'm not part of that dysfunctional little family." Her eyes shone with an even colder glint. "If you go down, sugar pie, don't expect me to be dragged along with you."

CHAPTER 20

"I see Mr. Jones hasn't made any home improvements since I was last here," Raley said as he brought the car to a stop.

The mobile home squatted on a barren lot and had an aura of general neglect. A short-haired, heavily muscled dog bared his teeth and strained against the chain securing him to a metal stake.

"How do you know he still lives here?" Britt had to speak loudly in order to make herself heard above the dog's ferocious barking.

"I looked up his name in the phone book while you were showering."

"Do you think he's home?"

"Truck's here."

Parked only a few feet from the door of the mobile home was a pickup with a camouflage paint job and mud-caked tires almost as tall as Britt. The Stars and Bars flag of the Confederacy hung from the radio antenna. "He should live in the pickup and scrap the trailer," she remarked. Of the two, the truck was in far better condition.

She had insisted on coming along, and Raley had put up only a token argument. For one thing, if the men looking for them tracked her to the motor court, she had no way to protect herself. Even if he left the pistol, he doubted she would use it. She flinched each time she looked at it.

And if the pistol had stayed behind with her, he would have had no way of protecting himself in case of attack, except with brute force, and he didn't trust himself to be as ruthless as men who would smother a terminally ill man with a pillow and force a woman's car into a river, leaving her to drown.

The only solution had been to bring both the weapon and Britt with him when he came to call on the late Cleveland Jones's next of kin, his father.

He opened his car door and put his left foot on the ground. The dog went berserk. "I hope that stake holds."

"Do you think a doughnut would appease him?" Britt picked up the Krispy Kreme bag containing the leftovers of the doughnuts they'd eaten for breakfast.

"I doubt it. He looks pure carnivore."

Raley got out and gave the dog a wide berth as he approached the rusty mobile home. He'd left his shirttail out to cover the pistol in his waistband and checked now to make sure it was still concealed. Mr. Jones hadn't been at all cordial five years ago. He would be even less so now if he saw Raley coming to his door armed with a .357.

When Britt joined him at the steps leading up to the door, he gave her a critical once-over. She was supposed to be incognito, but he didn't think she would pass for anything other than a babe who happened to be wearing a baseball cap, maybe because of a bad hair day.

She wasn't made up and camera ready, but the facial bone structure that made her photogenic was hard to disguise. Today she'd dressed in a pair of jeans and a white T-shirt. Raley thought maybe he should have gone up a size on both. The white cotton hugged her torso, and the denim molded to her ass. They looked great on her but weren't the best choice of clothing when the goal was to make her inconspicuous and forgettable.

"Remember," he said, "if he recognizes you, we're outta here immediately. No ifs, ands, or buts. Don't say anything that would give away where we're staying. Don't—"

"We already went over this, Raley."

"Yeah, but this is still a bad idea."

"I'm not an idiot. I won't give anything away."

"You should stay in the car."

"I have better interviewing skills than you."

She'd taken that position during their argument about whether or not she would be present when he talked to Jones. He'd said no, definitely not. She would stay in the car and not risk exposure.

"I interview people for a living," she argued. "I get information out of them, often when they're reluctant to give it up."

"I got information out of you."

"By tying me to a chair!" There was nothing he could say to that. "Besides," she persisted, "you tend to get impatient. Chances are good you'd rile Jones and shut him up before we learned anything useful."

He knew firsthand that she did have a talent for getting someone to tell more than he intended. She would know the questions to ask and how to ask them in a way that required more than a yes or no answer. One earnest look from her, a blink of those oh-so-interested baby blues, and a person heard himself babbling.

Also, and this was the biggie, he was afraid that, if he let her out of his sight, she would vanish and never be seen again. He had flashbacks of her engulfed in river water, her palm futilely pressed against the window of her car.

So, here she was.

They started up the steps, but before they reached the door of the mobile home, it was pushed open with a strong *whoosh* of air and a bellowing voice. "Shut up, you goddamn mutt. That barking's driving me crazy!"

The man hurled a chunk of something that looked like the fatty meat from a can of pork 'n' beans. Barely missing Raley's ear, it landed on the bare dirt of the yard with a wet *splat.* The dog fell on it like he hadn't eaten in days.

Bracing the door open with his shoulder, the large man pointed toward a No Trespassing sign nailed to the utility pole at the corner of his trailer. "Can't you read?"

"Lewis Jones?"

"That ain't what it says."

Britt had been right. Three sentences into the conversation and already Raley was impatient with this asshole. "Lewis Jones?" he repeated.

"Who're you? What do you want?" He was asking Raley, but his beady, close-set eyes were fixed on Britt.

"My name is Raley Gannon. Remember me?"

The flinty gaze cut back to Raley. "Why would I?"

"I was investigating the police station fire. We never actually met, but I spoke to you on the phone about Cleveland."

His eyes narrowed, and he divided a suspicious look between them, ending on Raley. "I remember your name. Vaguely. Told you then, telling you now, I don't want to talk about Cleveland. He's dead. End of story. Now beat it."

He backed into the trailer, pulling the door closed as he went.

Britt lunged across two steps and grabbed the edge of the metal door before it shut. "We apologize for coming without calling first, and promise not to take up too much of your time. Please, Mr. Jones? Can't we talk to you for just a few minutes?"

Jones didn't close the door, but he was still regarding them warily. "What for? It happened a long time ago. Anyway, what's it to you, lady?"

"Britt Shelley."

Raley couldn't believe she'd told

Jones her name, especially since he'd emphasized to her that she should remain anonymous. Then, to his greater dismay, she extended her right hand. Raley curbed an impulse to push it away before Jones could touch it, but he didn't. She apparently knew what she was doing, because her straightforwardness totally disarmed the man.

He looked at her hand and seemed to be as taken aback by the friendly gesture as Raley was, then he wiped his hand on the seat of his pants before giving hers a brisk shake. "Guess I can spare y'all a minute or two," he mumbled grudgingly.

He turned his back on them, and they followed him into the mobile home. Britt shot Raley a cheeky grin over her shoulder. He scowled.

The interior of the trailer was even more oppressive than the outside. The floor was uneven, causing them to walk uphill to reach the sofa that Jones motioned them toward. It was filthy, but Britt sat down without hesitation. Raley was more reluctant as he took a seat beside her.

In addition to the sofa, which was essentially the width of the trailer, there was a round end table with a gaudy Hawaiian print cloth draped over it and, separating the living area from the kitchen, a dining table pushed against one wall with two chairs beneath it.

No TV, Raley noted. No newspapers evident. Which explained why Jones hadn't reacted with recognition to Britt's name.

In fact, the man seemed to have entirely shut himself off from the rest of the world. Every window had been covered with black poster board. The sheets were taped to the walls so securely, they prevented any natural light from getting in. There was one ceiling light fixture, with a naked yellow bulb that made them all look jaundiced. It shone onto the top of Jones's head, which had been shaved but was dusted with several days' stubble.

He had on a pair of camo pants that had been cut off just above his knees so that the pockets hung down beneath the ragged legs. His black combat boots were shined, but the laces were untied and he wasn't wearing socks. Completing the outfit was an olive drab tank top that showed off his muscled arms and chest, as well as an array of elaborate tattoos.

Most depicted either a lethal weapon or a symbol of death. The most detailed tattoo covered his biceps and shoulder. It was a rendition of the grim reaper with a jeering skeleton's face, waving a frayed Confederate flag in one hand and a saber dripping blood in the other.

He hooked the toe of one combat boot around the chrome leg of a dining chair, dragged it across the buckled linoleum floor until it was directly in front of the sofa, and sat down in it. He crossed his arms over his chest, rattling the dog tags that hung from his neck on a silver bead chain, and stared at them.

Britt opened the conversation by asking politely, "Did you serve in the military, Mr. Jones?"

"Not the official one."

"I see."

It was readily apparent that Jones was affiliated with a paramilitary group. Photographs covered nearly every inch of wall space not taken up by the black poster board. There were pictures of men in camouflage fatigues, men in black balaclavas, men holding the leashes of vicious-looking dogs wearing spiked collars, men standing over the eviscerated carcasses of deer, men armed to the teeth.

Weaponry catalogs were scattered about and stacked on the floor, their pages curled and dog-eared. The only oasis of neatness amid the clutter was a three-level shelf constructed of concrete blocks and plywood planks. The planks were lined with felt. Laid out on them like a museum display was an extensive collection of handguns, rifles with scopes, one sawed-off shotgun, knives, bayonets, tripods, a fully loaded bandolier, and most disturbingly, grenades. All the firearms were highly polished so they gleamed in the yellow light. In fact, the smell of gun oil permeated the trailer.

"I'm sorry about your son, Mr. Jones," Britt said, trying again to start a conversation.

Jones looked her over, his expression doubtful. "You knew Cleveland?"

"No," she admitted.

"Then what's your stake in this?"

"I'm just a friend and associate of Mr. Gannon." He seemed about to pose another question when she said, "Losing a child is a cruel tragedy."

He shrugged. "Cleveland wasn't a child. He was old enough to take care of hisself. We hadn't seen each other in . . . hmm . . . maybe a year before he died. The last time I saw him, I told him I's done, I was washing my hands of him and wasn't going to bail him out no more. Guess he took me at my word, 'cause next I heard of him, they called to say he'd died down at the police station during that fire."

"It must have come as an awful shock."

Misinterpreting her meaning, he said, "Not really. I couldn't keep up with all the times that boy was in and out of jail."

Britt looked past his shoulder toward the end table on which was an eight-by-ten framed photograph. The quality was poor, the color resolution too vivid, but the costume couldn't be mistaken, and neither could the hatred channeled through the gleaming eyes of the man wearing the pointed hood.

Jones followed Britt's gaze to the photo, and when he brought his head back around, he was smiling proudly. "My daddy."

Raley asked, "Are you Klan?"

"You a fed?"

"No, a firefighter."

"Maybe I am, and maybe I ain't. What difference would it make to you?"

"None."

Britt said, "Mr. Jones, on that day, Cleveland was apprehended for assault, correct?"

"Yeah. I mean, I guess."

"Do you know the circumstances of his arrest?"

"Circumstances?"

"The nature of the crime, why he was arrested."

"No, all I was told was assault," Jones said. "Later, you know. After Cleveland was dead. Didn't seem to make much difference what he'd done. Anyway, he never said—"

"He?" Interrupting, Raley sat forward, leaning toward Jones.

"Some guy." Jones's expression became belligerent, obviously disliking Raley's encroachment. He didn't say anything more until Raley returned to his original position. "A cop. Came by to tell me none of Cleveland's effects were salvaged after the fire."

"Do you remember the cop's name?" Raley asked. "Was it Burgess?"

"I don't remember."

"McGowan?"

"I said I don't remember."

Britt nudged Raley's thigh with her knee, her way of saying to let her ask the questions since his, as predicted, seemed to rub Jones the wrong way.

"You never knew what Cleveland had done that caused him to be in the police station that particular day?" she asked.

Jones snorted a sound that could have been generated by either humor or disgust. "No telling. He'd just about done it all. His mother run off, you know, leaving me with him. He was wild from the get-go. Always skipping school and causing trouble when he went. Getting expelled, stuff like that. Busted his gym teacher's nose once when he made him run extra laps. He quit after tenth grade."

He made a dismissive gesture. "I didn't make him go back. I'm not that big on public education myself. Schools only teach you what the government wants you to know. Not the truth. Not the real history of this country."

He paused as though waiting for them to take issue with his stance on education and government interference, but when they didn't, he continued. "I tried to discipline the boy, knock some sense into him, but . . ." He made another gesture of indifference. "He was just one of those kids born bad. Stole, lied, fought with anybody who looked at him crosswise.

"He killed a neighbor lady's cat once for keeping him up all night. It got romantic outside his window. Next day Cleveland went over to her trailer and wrung the cat's neck while this old lady carried on something awful. She threatened to call the police, but she didn't, or else they didn't care about her dead cat because they didn't come for him that time."

Suddenly he sat forward in his chair and shook his index finger at them. "But that business with the girl? Now that? Un-huh," he said, shaking his head adamantly. "That was a bad rap, was what that was."

"The business with the girl?" Britt asked, her voice going thin.

Jones sat back in his chair and folded his arms across his chest again. "She looked more twenty-two than twelve," he said scornfully. "You ask me, I think she was a little tart that got scared after her cherry got popped and blamed it all on Cleveland. But I don't think he had to force her into doing *nothing.*"

Raley's gut tightened with repugnance, and he sensed Britt was experiencing much the same. Cleveland Jones hadn't been any great loss to the world. By his own father's admission he was a thief, a violent thug, and a rapist.

But was his character really the point? He'd been in police custody when he died. The sworn duty of law enforcement officials was to protect every member of society, no matter how loathsome that individual might be or how heinous his crime. Until society changed the rule, that was the prevailing one, and it had been broken.

But it was unlikely that Lewis Jones would be able to help him prove it. He seemed to know no more about his son's arrest than Raley did.

"The policeman who came to see you," he said, "did he mention that Cleveland's autopsy revealed that he actually died of an acute skull fracture, not smoke inhalation or burns?"

"Yep. Said he'd had his head busted in a fight just before his arrest. Said the officers who brought him in didn't know the injuries were serious till he started acting funny. They were going to take him to the hospital and get his head X-rayed, but then he started the fire. If the brain injury hadn't killed him, he'd have died anyway." He rubbed his jaw. "Actually, I was glad to know he just blinked out and didn't suffer. And he didn't have to answer to that arson business and all those folks dying. That's some serious shit."

After several moments of silence, Raley asked, "Where is Cleveland buried?"

Jones got up and reached past Britt's head toward a shelf affixed to the wall. On the shelf was a small statue of Jesus with bleeding palms and side, a metal swastika soldered onto an upright pipe, and a cardboard canister that might have contained a half gallon of ice cream.

"Cleveland."

Raley and Britt stared at the cylinder Jones held out for their inspection. Raley said, "You had his remains cremated."

"Not me. That cop told me there wasn't much of him left, especially after the autopsy, and the PD felt bad on account of him dying while he was incarcerated, so unless I had already made other plans for burial, they'd take care of the arrangements and pay for everything. I said sure. I signed the paper saying it was all right for them to burn the rest of him. A few days later that cop brought me this."

Raley looked at Britt; she looked at him. Each had things to say about this information, but their discussion would keep until they were alone.

Lewis Jones returned Cleveland to his final resting place and sat back down. Raley said, "I never got to complete my investigation into your son's death, Mr. Jones."

"Why's that?"

"Circumstances suspended my involvement. But now, new evidence has come out."

"Like what?"

"I'm not prepared to disclose that yet, and won't be until I've gathered all the facts."

"That's why we've imposed on you," Britt said. "Will you help Mr. Gannon by answering some more questions, particularly questions relating to Cleveland's arrest?"

"Already told you, I don't know nothing. Have you asked the cops? Wouldn't they have records?"

Dodging that for the moment, Raley asked, "Do you know the names of any of Cleveland's friends?"

"No."

"Enemies?"

Jones snorted. “He was sure to have plenty of them, but I didn’t know them.”

“You don’t know who he fought with that day, or who may have struck him hard enough to fracture his skull?”

“No.”

“You weren’t told?”

He shifted impatiently in his chair. “Ain’t that what I said?”

Raley pressed on. “Was he employed?”

“Ain’t likely.”

“Was he involved with a woman?”

“Prob’ly ever’ night and twice on Sundays,” Jones said with a proud grin. “But not one woman in particular. Not one I knew of.”

“Do you know where he was living?”

“No.”

Dead ends. They sat through another silence. Finally Britt said, “You mentioned that none of Cleveland’s effects were salvaged.”

“Nothing. The stuff they’d emptied out of his pockets when they hauled him in got burned up. So did the list they’d filled out, but this cop remembered what Cleveland had on him.”

"Did he mention anything in particular? A weapon?"

"Nope. Just the usual stuff. Some money. Sixty dollars and thirty-seven cents. That cop paid it back to me. He said Cleveland had a key, but it never turned up, and I wouldn't have known what it belonged to anyway. A pack of cigarettes. That's all."

Raley sat forward again. "Cleveland was a smoker?"

"Since he was a kid. Used to steal cigs from me and my old man, and wasn't long before he was up to three, four packs a day. Never without one." He hitched his thumb toward the photo of the Klansman. "Once, when we all went to this carnival that came to town, Daddy bought Cleveland a lighter. Not the cheap disposable kind, but the real thing. Had a naked girl on it. A whachacallit. A hologram. When you turned it a certain way, her legs opened." He slid a sly glance toward Britt.

"The old man thought it was funny. Cleveland felt all grown-up. He loved that thing. Even when he wasn't lighting up, he played with it. Always was fiddling with it, like a nervous habit, you know?"

"You'd think the policeman would remember an unusual lighter like that," Raley said. "He didn't mention it?"

"No. And I even asked. He said he didn't recall Cleveland having a lighter."

"A heavy smoker without a lighter? That didn't strike the cop as unusual?"

"I'm just tellin' you what he said." Jones stared into near space for a moment, then said ruefully, "I'd have liked to have that lighter back. As a keepsake, you know, of Cleveland and my old man. But I guess Cleveland lost it, had it stole, something. He shit away everything else of value in his life, I guess he did that lighter, too."

Raley and Britt looked at each other again, then Raley turned back to Jones. "Can you think of anything else that could be useful to my investigation? Was there a special place Cleveland liked to go? A favorite hangout?"

"Like I said, we hadn't stayed in touch."

"Was Cleveland a member of a gang?" Raley cast a glance toward the photos tacked to the wall. "A member of any group?"

"Not that I know of," Jones replied. "I tried to get him to join up with me and some guys. He was good with weapons and enjoyed being out in the woods. But he didn't have the patience to be a good hunter. Too fidgety, you know. And a true soldier needs discipline. Cleveland didn't want nobody telling him what to do."

Raley was disappointed that the interview hadn't yielded more, but he could think of nothing else to ask. When he silently consulted Britt, she shook her head. Seeing no reason to continue, they thanked Jones for his time. Britt preceded Raley out. Jones ordered the dog to be quiet, but it growled deep in its throat, hackles raised while its slitted eyes followed Britt as she walked to the car.

His owner was watching her just as hungrily. In a confidential voice he said, "You got yourself a sweet and juicy peach there, Gannon."

"Thanks," Raley said tightly.

"She's that TV gal gone missing, ain't she?"

Raley vaulted the last of the cracked concrete steps and whipped back around.

"Relax," Jones said as he sauntered down the steps. "I ain't going to rat her out. I got all the respect in the world for a high-toned piece of tail like that." His gaze shifted to Raley, and he winked. "Y'all are thinking there was something fishy about that fire and the way my boy died. Right? You're trying to sniff out some bad cops and expose the corruption within the P fucking D."

"Something like that."

Jones grinned, showing gold caps on most of his molars. "More power to you." He extended his fist, palm side down.

Raley stared at the tattoos on the man's knuckles, then bumped his fist against Jones's.

The grim reaper twitched as every muscle in the hard body contracted. "Gig 'em good, brother. I fuckin' hate those commie government sons o' bitches."

CHAPTER 21

Britt gave Raley a sidelong glance and tapped her fists together. "You two are buddies now?"

"Brothers actually. Because I'm trying to expose the corruption in the police department."

"Ah." As they drove away, she gave the trailer one last glance and shuddered with revulsion. "He gave me the creeps."

Tongue in cheek, Raley said, "He spoke highly of you."

"He said something about me? What?"

"You don't want to know. But he also recognized you as the TV gal gone missing." Her surprise must have shown. Raley added, “I didn’t think he knew you, either, but we don’t have to worry about him blowing the whistle. He made it clear he hates cops.”

“And everybody else. I found myself feeling sorry for Cleveland Jones.”

“He raped a twelve-year-old.”

“I know, I know, but . . . He was baptized in hatred. It sounds like he never knew a single day of love or nurturing, not in his whole short life.”

“His granddaddy gave him a cigarette lighter, don’t forget.”

“With a naked girl on it.”

Her disgust made him smile. “Granted, it wasn’t a standard keepsake from a grandfather, like, say, a pocket watch, but it shows there was some affection there. Obviously it meant a lot to Cleveland.”

“Yet it was conspicuously missing from the things the unidentified policeman said Cleveland had on him the day of his arrest.”

“Um-huh. Funny that a lewd cigarette lighter would slip his mind when he could remember the exact amount of money Jones had, down to thirty-seven cents."

"They had him cremated so his remains could never be exhumed and reexamined."

"Very tidy." He thought a moment, then said grimly, angrily, "They covered this thing, Britt, and they did it right. We are exactly nowhere."

"I can't continue playing Nancy Drew forever. I can't stay in hiding the rest of my life."

"If you come out of hiding, your life may not last all that long."

"That much we have determined. So, what next? Any ideas?"

"If I made another run at George McGowan, he would only bow his back and tell me to fuck off. Or worse, if he's the one having me tailed. I don't want to risk leading them to you."

"That leaves Cobb Fordyce."

"Who's in his ivory tower at the state capitol, protected by guards and his lofty office. I couldn't get near him without being arrested, and even if I could, he isn't going to raise his hands in surrender and confess."

"Jay and Pat Wickham are dead."

"Right. They're not talking."

She suddenly remembered something Raley had told her the night before. "What about Pat Junior?"

"What about him?"

"You said you caught him staring at you and George McGowan after the funeral, and that his attention seemed to make George nervous."

"Nervous or angry, I couldn't tell. But Pat Junior was definitely flustered."

"Flustered? He's a police officer," Britt argued.

"Yeah, but he wasn't looking at us like a cop would. His staring was covert, but in a jittery way, not a surveillance sort of way."

"Two men who hadn't seen each other in years, chatting at the funeral of a mutual friend. What about that would give a police officer the jitters?" she asked, surmising out loud. "Why would seeing you and George McGowan talking together bother him? But since it did, why didn't he mosey over and check it out? Better yet, why didn't he speak to you at all?"

Raley stopped at a red light and looked over at her. "Maybe we should ask him."

"Maybe we should."

"I wonder what his shift is."

"Eleven to seven," she replied. "A.m. to p.m. Unless that's changed since I interviewed him."

Raley turned his head toward her so quickly, his neck popped. "You interviewed Pat Junior?"

"When his father was killed." Feeling the familiar stirring of excitement that came with being on the trail of a hot story, she checked her watch. "He'll be on his lunch hour. We can catch him there."

"You know where he's having lunch?"

She nodded happily. "Same place every day."

He looked at her for a moment longer, then said, "You're full of surprises today. Where to?"

"That's it," Britt said, pointing. It was a basic house in a basic middle-class neighborhood.

"He eats lunch at home?"

"Every day," she replied. "He told me he likes to take a power nap, so he comes home, eats a sandwich, then sleeps for twenty minutes before going back to work."

"A creature of habit."

"Apparently."

"And kinda squirrelly."

She shrugged. "Different strokes."

"You got to know him pretty well."

"Not really. I interviewed him three times, and the focus was Pat Senior. But I remember the bit about his lunch hour."

Raley parked at the curb in front of the house. It was a white frame structure with dark green storm shutters and a well-maintained yard. "You're a fugitive from the law," he observed as he turned off the car's ignition. "He's a police officer. You're about to come calling at his house."

"I've done crazier things lately," she said, pushing open the passenger-side door. "Ever since you kidnapped me, the rules of standard and sane behavior have ceased to apply."

They went up to the front door, and

Britt rang the bell. They waited, but a minute passed and no one came to answer. “Sound sleeper,” Raley said. “Or else he’s inside with his service revolver trained on us while he’s calling in backup. But somehow that image doesn’t jibe with the man I saw yesterday. He’s no Dirty Harry.”

Britt tilted her head to one side as though listening. “Do you hear that? Water running?”

She followed the sound to the corner of the house, then along the side of it toward the back. Walking behind her, Raley glanced over his shoulder to see if anyone on this placid, tree-lined street had a bead on his broad back. If there was a sniper, he didn’t see him. But then he wouldn’t, would he?

He wondered what Butch and Sundance were doing right now. Searching his cabin again for something they might have missed yesterday? Had they been dispatched first thing this morning to return and eliminate the dual problem of Raley Gannon and Britt Shelley? Finding the cabin abandoned, were they now scouring the city, checking hotels and motels for recent check-ins that fit his and Britt's descriptions? Or were they just laying low, waiting for him and Britt to pop up again? Whatever, he felt certain the pair hadn't been pulled off the job, and they wouldn't be until it was finished.

So his paranoia wasn't an overreaction. It wasn't silly. He would continue to watch his back.

Pat Jr. kept a neat backyard. There was a sandbox and a swing set, but also a lawn of lush Saint Augustine grass and pretty flower beds. Using a hose and nozzle, Pat Jr. was watering a bed of red flowers with waxy green foliage. His back was to them, and he didn't hear their approach.

To announce them, Britt said, "Those are beautiful begonias. They must be the hybrid that likes sun."

Pat Jr. was so shocked to see them, he dropped the nozzle. The water pressure caused it to flip and roll, spraying wildly until he recovered his wits enough to rush to the faucet at the foundation of the house and turn it off. He was dressed in civilian clothes. A badge was clipped to his belt, but Raley noted that he wasn't armed.

His eyes darted back and forth between him and Britt. To her he said, "You're wanted for murder."

"I didn't kill Jay Burgess."

"Clark and Javier think you did."

"They're wrong."

He looked at Raley. "What are you doing with her?"

"We want to ask you some questions."

"About what?"

The suburban backyard was as peaceful and benign a setting as could be, but Raley still felt exposed. "Inside."

Pat Jr., who should have been reading Britt her rights, looked ready to bolt and run, or wet himself, or be sick on the begonias, but after a long hesitation, he nodded and led them toward a screened back porch. He went in ahead of them, something no savvy cop would do.

The porch was casually furnished. Britt chose a wicker chair, Raley took the matching settee, and Pat Jr. remained standing. "I can't let you leave here. You know that."

Under other circumstances, his aggressive posturing would have been comical. Raley certainly didn't quail from it. "Is anybody else here?"

Pat Jr. shook his head. "My wife volunteers two days a week at the hospital. She drops the kids off at her mother's. Did you plan to hold us hostage?"

It was such a ludicrous notion, Britt didn't even honor it with a reply. "The last time I saw you, your wife was expecting."

"With our son. We've had a girl since then. They came close together. Just a little over a year apart."

"Belated congratulations," she said.

The man seemed to mistrust her politeness. Nervously, he licked his misshapen lips, calling attention to them. His mouth and jaw were out of kilter. His mouth stretched toward the left side of his face, his jaw stretched toward the right. His nose, too, was off center and crooked. Raley wondered about the nature of the accident that had rearranged his face and couldn't help but compare the young man with his late father.

Pat Sr. had been average looking, tall and slender, not brawny, but certainly beefier than his son. Until the morning that he'd woken up with Suzi Monroe beside him, Raley had known Pat Sr. only through Jay. Their paths had crossed a few times, always in Jay's company, and always socially. He'd seemed a nice enough guy. He wasn't gregarious, but no one was when around Jay, who was always the center of attention. In his company, no one else was allowed to shine. But Pat Sr. wouldn't have shone anyway. He came across as reserved, serious, a man who could intimidate with his stoicism.

Raley saw nothing resembling Pat Sr. in his son, and the differences between them went beyond the physical. Pat Jr. possessed none of his father's stolidness. He was unsettled. Sweat beaded on his upper lip, and he couldn't keep his eyes focused on any one spot for too long.

Despite these giveaways to his nervousness, he made another futile stab at seeming courageous. Addressing Raley, he blurted, "You left town in disgrace. Why'd you come back?"

"So you did recognize me yesterday at Jay's funeral."

"Of course."

"Why didn't you come over, say hi? Was it because you remember the circumstances of my getting fired and leaving town?"

Pat Jr. wet his lips again. "I remember my dad talking about it."

"Oh, yeah? What did he say about it?"

"I . . . I don't remember details. Just that you were involved in some sort of sex scandal and a girl wound up dead." He looked at Britt. "Are you in cahoots with him now? I could have the whole police department here in under two minutes, you know."

Britt didn't even blink. Raley actually smiled. Rather than following through with what was so obviously an idle threat, Pat Jr. looked nearer to crying. "Whatever it is the two of you are doing, you're going to get caught."

"What do *you* think we're doing?" Raley asked calmly.

"Evading capture."

"I'm not wanted."

"She is!" he said, his voice cracking. "You're aiding and—"

"Abetting. I know. Sit down." Raley put menace behind the order and the other man crumpled. He dropped into the chair behind him, again looking like he might throw up. Raley was afraid he would have a heart attack before he could ask him the important questions, so he started with something easy. "I didn't see your mother yesterday at the funeral."

"She's in a . . . a facility. Alzheimer's."

"I'm sorry to hear that," Britt said.

"Me, too," Raley said.

"At first I thought her symptoms were part of the grieving process, you know, after Dad was killed, but she just kept getting worse. Couldn't trust her to be alone anymore. She's been there two years."

"It must have been a terrible blow to her."

Pat Jr. looked over at Britt. "What?"

"Your father's death."

"Oh. It was. Terrible for all of us."

"Refresh my memory of how it happened," Raley said.

"It's painful. I don't like to talk about it."

Raley just stared back at him unsympathetically.

Reluctantly, Pat Jr. complied. "Dad was off duty. He'd gone to the supermarket for Mom. On his way back, he saw some guys fighting in an alley. He used his cell phone and called it in, said the officers on that beat should come check it out." He raised his narrow shoulders and released a sigh through his twisted mouth.

"We can only speculate what happened after that. The best guess is that the fight turned violent quickly and Dad was afraid somebody was going to get hurt before the patrol officers could get there. In any case, he left his car and went into the alley."

He paused for a moment, released another sigh. "When the officers arrived, Dad was lying in the alley. He'd been shot in the stomach. He was in shock. He bled out before the ambulance could get there." He looked at Raley, at Britt, then back at Raley. "That was it."

"The crime remains unsolved, correct?" Raley asked.

"There weren't many leads," Pat Jr. said. "No weapon, no eyewitnesses, nothing really to go on."

"His killer has gone unpunished. That must be frustrating."

Britt's observation caused Pat Jr. to lower his head. "You have no idea."

After a short silence, Raley asked, "Who investigated the homicide?"

Pat Jr. raised his head and looked at him. "Well, several detectives. The whole department was gung ho to catch the killer, or killers. You know how it is when a cop is killed," he added, glancing at Britt, a none too subtle reference to the murder of Jay Burgess.

Raley said, "Was Jay on the case? George McGowan?"

"Along with others." At the mention of their names, he became visibly more nervous. "Why do you ask?"

"Their names, along with Cobb Fordyce's, are always linked to your dad's because of their heroism the day of the fire."

"Did your father ever talk about that?" Britt asked.

"The fire? No," he said, answering hastily. "Not really. Not often."

"Why not?"

"He hated all that hero b.s."

"Why?"

"What Dad did that day, he saw as his duty. Nothing else."

Raley said, "That fire was a defining moment in his career, in his life, and he didn't talk about it?"

"No."

"Not even privately? Not even to you and your mom?"

Pat Jr. glanced in Britt's direction before answering. "The news media wouldn't leave it alone. Dad didn't like all the publicity. He didn't want a big to-do made over it."

"Jay and the others made a big to-do over it," Raley said.

"Dad didn't want to capitalize off a tragedy."

"Did that affect his friendship with the other three who did?"

"No."

"Really?"

"No."

"Okay." Raley paused for several beats, then asked, "When did you last see Jay Burgess?"

"To talk to? At Dad's funeral."

"Not since then?" Raley asked in surprise. "That's a long time, Pat."

"Well, I saw him occasionally at headquarters," he said. "But not . . . not socially or anything. Why's that important?"

"Because hours before Jay was smothered, he told Ms. Shelley that he had a story to tell that would boost her ratings, probably get her on a network. She was drugged and Jay was killed before he could give her that exclusive. Do you know what that story might have been?"

Pat Jr. came to his feet jerkily, like a puppet whose master was uncoordinated. "I have no idea. Like I said, I hadn't had a private conversation with Jay in years." Then he turned to Britt and pointed a shaking finger at her. "I'm placing you under arrest."

"Not today." Raley stood up. Britt, taking her cue from him, did likewise.

Raley walked toward Pat Jr., essentially trapping him against the chair in which he'd been sitting. "What do you know about the night Jay died?"

"Nothing."

Raley gave him a hard look. Pat Jr. squirmed like an insect about to be pinned to a corkboard. "Nothing except that she killed him," he stammered. "I don't work homicide, but I've heard word around the department. Everybody has. It's a big case. Clark, Javier, they've got solid evidence that proves she killed him."

"Wrong," Raley said. "Either you're lying now or the detectives are feeding bullshit to the grapevine. They don't have any such evidence, because there is none. She didn't do it. And when you see Clark and Javier, you tell them I said so." For emphasis, he poked the policeman in the chest.

"Now Ms. Shelley and I are walking out of here, Pat."

"I can't let you do that."

"We're leaving and you're not going to do anything to try and stop us." Raley held him with a warning stare, then motioned Britt toward the door. He went out after her. As expected, Pat Jr. did nothing to impede or halt them.

Raley kept their pace calm and easy, but when they rounded the corner of the house, he dropped the pretense. Taking Britt's elbow, he hustled her toward the parked car, scanning the peaceful neighborhood street for signs of the men in the maroon sedan and listening for the wail of police car sirens.

Pat Jr. wasted no time. Using his cell phone, he punched in a number committed to memory. It wasn't 911, and it wasn't the number of the police department.

He was hoping he'd get voice mail and not have to talk directly to the person on the other end, but it was answered on the third ring. "It's Pat Junior."

"What?"

"Guess who paid a surprise visit to my house."

"I don't want to guess, I want to know."

"Britt Shelley."

A moment of stunned silence, then, "You don't say. That is a surprise."

"She was bold as brass."

"What did she want with you?"

"To ask what I knew about a big story Jay wanted to tell her before he was killed."

"Fuck!"

Pat Jr. wiped his sweaty palm on the leg of his trousers. "It gets worse. Guess who was with her."

"Raley Gannon."

Well, he thought with relief, at least he hadn't had to be the bearer of that bad news.

"What did you tell them about Jay?"

"Nothing! Nothing, I swear. I tried to arrest her, but couldn't get to my service weapon. Gannon, uh, overpowered me, wrestled me to the floor, stunned me. While I was down they ran."

"In the gray sedan?"

"Yes, same car he was driving yesterday at the funeral."

"License plate number?"

"I . . . I thought you had it."

"He's no fool. He would have switched."

Pat hadn't thought of that. "B-by the time I got to the window, they were too far away, and it had mud—"

"Did you get it or not?"

"Not."

Another expletive was hissed in his ear. "Did they say where they were going?"

"No."

"Give you any hints?"

"No."

"Did you think to ask?"

He hadn't. Why hadn't he? "They wouldn't have told me."

"Why didn't you notify me while they were there?"

"I couldn't. Gannon had a pistol."

"He threatened you at gunpoint?"

To tell the truth, no. The pistol had remained securely tucked in Gannon's waistband. "It was an implied threat. He made sure I saw it." Which wasn't exactly true, either, but it made his situation sound more life threatening than it had actually been.

"What will you do now, Pat? Call your fellow officers and tell them the fugitive they seek was in your house?"

The question was a ploy. Actually, he was being instructed not to do any such thing. “Gannon threatened my family with harm if I told anybody.”

“You must protect your family.” That was said with a trace of amusement. “If you see Gannon or Britt Shelley again—”

“I’ll let you know immediately.”

“Do, Pat. Because this big story of Jay’s could ruin all of us. Including you.”

On that ominous note the call ended.

CHAPTER 22

Raley switched license plates with a jungle-ready Jeep with an aggressive-looking brush guard.

"You're getting good at this," Britt remarked as he rejoined her in their gray sedan.

"Not that good. I should trade this in for another car, but I'm afraid they've laid groundwork for that."

"Butch and his sidekick?"

"Hmm. All they'd have to do is work their way down the dealerships listed in the yellow pages. As soon as we drove a car off a lot, the bribed salesman would be on the phone with the news flash. We don't have time to track down individuals with cars for sale. Not to mention the expense of buying another car."

"I meant what I said about paying back half of everything you spend."

He actually laughed. "You keep track of the accounting, and I'll try to keep those hired guns off our asses."

"You think they're hired guns?"

"Neither Fordyce nor McGowan would do his own dirty work. The guys after us have got to be pros."

"I thought that only happened in the movies."

"So did I, until I saw you being forced off the road and into the river."

He pulled out of the parking garage where he'd made the license-plate swap and turned onto the busy boulevard, where to everyone else in Charleston it was business as usual. They passed a group of tourists on an escorted walking tour of the historic district. For the most part the sightseers were in sensible shoes and sun visors, weighted down with cameras and guidebooks, but Raley eyed them suspiciously, looking for anyone who didn't fit the stereotype.

"Butch and Sundance are the ones we've spotted. There may be more," he said.

"Not a comforting thought." Britt looked askance at the motorcyclist revving his Harley in the lane next to them.

"These guys aren't going to give up and go home, Britt. Meanwhile, we're spinning our wheels, making no headway. Lewis Jones was a bust. His hatred for cops, the government in general, was sincere. You agree?"

"I agree."

"If he knew anything about Cleveland's death that would expose criminal activity within the police department, he would gladly have shared it. So, while he's one hundred percent in support of our goal, he's useless."

Britt winced. "I don't want him on our team."

"I'm not fond of the idea, either."

"Were those real hand grenades?"

"I wouldn't want to pull the pins and find out."

They rode in silence for a moment, then Britt said, "Pat Wickham—"

"Yeah?"

"Is lying."

"Through his crooked teeth."

"You thought so, too?"

"I know so. But how do we persuade him to give up whatever it is he's hiding? Accusing him of lying didn't work. We can't beat the truth out of him. I'm open to suggestions."

"Besides being a liar," she said, "he strikes me as sad."

"Because of his face?"

"The disfigurement, yes, but I sense something beyond that, a deep-seated torment."

"He's a desk cop, and gutless to boot. His dad was a detective, a tough guy who would go alone into an alley in a bad neighborhood to break up a gang fight."

"Maybe Pat Senior wasn't so tough as he was reckless," she said. "Why didn't he wait for backup? Isn't that standard operating procedure?"

"It was a misjudgment that cost him his life. In any case, Pat Senior's hero status is a hard legacy for Junior to live up to. Especially—"

He broke off without finishing. Britt looked across at him. "What?"

He shook his head absently. "I had a thought, but it escaped me. Maybe it will come back."

During their conversation, he'd been weaving in and out of traffic, shifting lanes and taking corners quickly, keeping his eye on the rearview mirror to try to spot anyone who might be following. He was traveling in the general direction of the motor court but taking a circuitous route.

"Raley, what if I called Detective Clark and told him everything? Laid it all out. About your kidnapping me, and why you did it. About the men forcing me off the road."

"Can't be proved, remember?"

"Well, the car would be something. They couldn't prove I *wasn't* forced off the road."

"No, but here's what Clark would think. One, you're accused of murder. Two, your alibi is that you were given a date rape drug. Not only is it unlikely but it's impossible to prove. Three, you flew the coop to avoid arrest."

"But I didn't."

"Doesn't matter. I'm telling you how Clark would think." He paused and glanced at her. She motioned for him to continue. "You're claiming to have been run off the road into the river, perhaps by the men who actually killed Jay. But your car isn't damaged, except for a busted windshield, which you could have shattered yourself. You drove your car into the river, jumping free just in time. That's how Clark would see it."

"Point made," she said despondently.

"Besides, he and Javier probably anticipate that you'll call sooner or later. They'll have a trace set up for when you do."

"You learned a lot when you trained at the police academy."

"I learned the basics. Enough to guess that if you turned yourself in, or you were arrested now, the true story of the fire and Cleveland Jones—none of it would ever be made public."

"I'm sure you're right, but—" Suddenly she sat up straight. "But what if it *was* made public?"

"How? What do you mean?"

She bent her knee and turned toward him. "There's a young man at the station. A video photographer. He's good. We work together well. He likes me. Not like *that,*" she said when he gave her a look.

"Ten to one, it's like *that.*"

"He's married."

"I stand by my bet."

"Anyway, what if he met us at a remote location and we recorded a video? He could take it back to the station and put it on the news."

"What kind of video?"

"You tell your story, and I tell mine."

"Would they air it?"

"After my news conference, I was given a leave of absence with pay. My station manager was all gooey, promising help and support but backing away in spite of what he was saying. I figure my days of employment there are over. But if Channel Seven declined to air this video, competing stations damn sure would jump at the chance."

"There would be consequences to the photographer."

"Short-term maybe."

"A jail term, Britt. The cops would be all over him to tell where we were, and if he didn't, they'd toss him in jail."

"Which would bring out every First Amendment advocate in a thousand-mile radius. With all that publicity, he'd probably advance his career."

Raley examined the idea from several angles but eventually gave a negative shake of his head. "Say the photographer is willing to spend some time in jail if it makes him a star, and one or all of the TV stations broadcast the video. What about liability?"

"They'd air it with a disclaimer."

"What about *our* liability? Fordyce, McGowan, maybe even Jay's family and the Wickhams, could sue us for slander, and they'd win. We can tell all, but we can prove nothing."

"Dammit," she said, thumping her knee with her fist. "It always comes back to that."

"It always comes back to that," he echoed grimly. "In addition to trying to pay off the lawsuits, you'd be looking over your shoulder for the rest of your life. They killed Jay to keep the secret intact, and he was one of them."

"They didn't kill you."

"They didn't think they had to. Banishment was sufficient. Now that I've talked to George, they know I'm onto them. I practically waved a red cape at him."

"Why *did* you tip your hand to him?"

"Are you asking as an ally or as a reporter?"

"Both."

He thought about it, then said, "To bring it to a head, I guess. For five years, it's festered inside me. I want it resolved, over, finished, one way or another."

His last phrase was sobering enough to silence them for several minutes. Then Britt said, "You're going to like this suggestion even less than the previous two."

"Try me."

"Call Judge Mellors."

"No."

"Listen, Raley, I know you're reluctant to bring her into this, particularly at this time, but she's a valuable contact. If you don't want to call her, I will, although that would really compromise her. I'm a fugitive. To help me would be not only unethical but also illegal. But you're an old friend, seeking answers to a—"

"I know it's the commonsense thing to do," he said, interrupting. "It's just that I hate putting Candy in a no-win situation. If she agrees to help, she's jeopardizing her appointment. If she doesn't help, she's letting down a friend. She's damned either way."

"Unless she could help you without anyone knowing."

He thought on that for a moment. "And unless I asked her for only one small favor."

"What one small favor do you have in mind?"

"A phone call."

"To?"

"Cobb Fordyce." Seeing Britt's surprise, he said, "I'd like to resume that one face-to-face meeting I had with him, the one where he dismissed my claim that I had been drugged."

"Why didn't he investigate that further? At least make a show of investigating it?"

"Damn good questions," he said. "Fordyce didn't do squat beyond going through the motions. He kept himself at arm's length from the whole nasty business of Suzi Monroe. A *safe* arm's length."

"Odd behavior for a man who prides himself on being an advocate for victims of crime. He also courts the media."

"My thoughts exactly. He detached himself from the Suzi Monroe case the same way Jay avoided having anything to do with my arson investigation."

"Fordyce must have been involved."

"You'll get no argument from me on that point."

Making a sudden decision, Raley turned sharply in to the parking lot of a convenience store and drove to the side of the building where a pay telephone was mounted on the exterior wall. It was out of sight of the busy storefront, where there were security cameras and a steady flow of customers going in and out.

"Since the advent of cell phones, are

those things still in service?" Britt asked.

"Let's hope BellSouth hasn't got to this one yet."

The lady with the mellifluous voice didn't recognize his name and refused to put him through to Judge Mellors, not even when he identified himself as an old friend. "I'm sorry, Mr. Gannon. A crew from *60 Minutes* is due here momentarily, and the judge is preparing—"

"Ask her if she's found any unusual prizes in her Cracker Jacks lately."

"I beg your pardon?"

"Ask her that. She'll talk to me."

She released a long-suffering sigh, put him on hold, and the next voice he heard was Candy's. "Eat shit and die, asshole."

He laughed. "I figured that would get you to the phone."

"I hadn't thought about that for years. I could still sue you for sexual harassment, I'll bet. What's the statute of limitations on that?"

"You're asking me? You're the legal whiz kid."

He and Jay had been seniors in high school, Candy a freshman. She'd developed a crush on one of their friends. They'd told her the guy loved Cracker Jacks, ate them all the time. If she wanted to win his heart, she would share a box of Cracker Jacks with him. Which she did, only to discover, to her mortification, that Raley and Jay had replaced the prize inside with a gold foil–wrapped condom.

"How did you manage that?" she asked. "Did you go through the bottom of the box?"

"I don't give away my trade secrets."

When their laughter subsided, she said, "Gosh, it's good to hear your voice. I called George McGowan last night to ask about the funeral. He told me you were there. I wish I could have been, if only to see you. How are you, Raley?"

"I'm good."

"Really?" she said, doubt in her tone. "I know you and Hallie broke it off for good after you left Charleston. I'm sorry about . . . well, how that turned out."

He was certain she'd heard about

their breakup through Jay, probably in the form of a boast. "It turned out okay for Hallie. She's married with children." After a beat, he said, "I was sorry to hear about your husband."

"Was that the pits, or what? I finally got a guy to marry me, and then he goes and drowns." Despite her joking, Raley could tell the loss had caused her pain. Speaking more seriously, she said, "He was a great guy. You would have liked him. I was devastated when it happened, but . . ." She paused and took a deep breath. "Life goes on."

"It does."

"Thank God for my work."

"Oh, congratulations."

"Congratulations are premature until after Friday's vote, but thanks."

The conversation ran out. Pleasantries were over. He could imagine her consulting her wristwatch, reading hand signals from her assistant alerting her to the arrival of the television crew.

"Raley, did you call to talk about Jay?"

"Easy guess."

"I'm glad you did. You've got to come

to terms with what happened between him and Hallie. George said you were still holding a grudge, and it's futile to hold a grudge against a dead man. You can never be reconciled."

He could think of no appropriate response, because she was right. Jay's betrayal of their friendship was a lost cause. So was the issue of Hallie. He was past seeking vengeance for what had been done to him. After this played out, if he was vindicated for the Suzi Monroe incident, that would be a bonus, but exoneration was no longer his main goal.

What he sought now was justice for the casualties of that day.

Seven lives. Seven homicides. Seven people who shouldn't have died. That sounded rather high-minded, so he hadn't given it as his reason when Britt asked why he'd waved that red cape at George. But that was the truth of it. He wanted justice for those who couldn't get it for themselves. Even Cleveland Jones. Even Suzi with an *i.*

"I want to talk to you about all that," Candy was saying. "But today, in a few minutes actually, I'm doing an on-camera interview. In fact, no matter how the Senate vote goes, until it's over, my schedule is nuts.

"But next week I have a couple of evenings free," she continued. "Let's have dinner at my house. I still don't cook, but we could order out. Something fattening. For you I wouldn't have to wear a power suit and control-top panty hose. We'd have an entire evening, uninterrupted, to eat, drink too much, get maudlin, catch up. I'd love that."

"I'd love that, too," he said. "Let's definitely do it. But in the meantime, I have a favor to ask."

"Anything for you, you know that."

"Get me an appointment with Cobb Fordyce."

She gave an abrupt laugh. "What? Are you serious?"

"As a heart attack," he said, using a phrase they'd used when they were teenagers.

"What for?"

"I told you five years ago that the business with Suzi Monroe was a setup. I haven't changed my mind, Candy. In fact, I'm more convinced than ever. I want to look the attorney general in the eye and ask him what he knows about it."

He could hear her inhaling deeply, and could envision the vertical frown line between the eyebrows that she'd often cursed as the bane of her existence. She had to pluck them weekly.

She said, "If you *were* set up, why do you think Cobb would know anything about it?"

"Because he was one of the fabulous four."

"You mean one of the four heroes of the fire?"

Tired of skirting the issue, he was ready to lay it on the line. "Those four plotted to discredit me and stop my investigation. Suzi Monroe's death was part of their cover-up."

"Cover-up for what?"

"Cleveland Jones and how he died."

"Cleveland Jones? The detainee who set the fire?"

"Allegedly. It's too long a story to go into now, but basically my investigation was getting close to the truth, and the truth was that Jones was murdered in that quasi interrogation room, and the fire was a smoke screen, literally. Suzi Monroe was killed to sabotage me."

She took several moments to absorb that. He could sense her shock. Finally she said softly, "Holy *merde.*"

"Not so holy. Definitely *merde.*"

"Do you have any proof?"

"I'm working on it."

"Working on it," she repeated dismally. Several more seconds elapsed, then she said, "Raley, you're the most levelheaded person I know. You wouldn't accuse men of something this serious if you weren't convinced they were guilty."

"I am and they are."

"But . . . This is . . ." He'd left her at a loss for words, possibly for the first time in her life. Trying again, she said, "This is preposterous. Cobb Fordyce is the top law officer in the state. You're about to accuse him of conspiracy and murder. Think about the repercussions."

"I have. For five years I've thought of

little else. He's an elected official, but if he committed a crime—"

"I wasn't talking about the repercussions to him but to *you.*"

"I haven't got anything to lose."

That silenced her for half a minute. "You're saying Jay, your *friend,* was part of it, too?"

"They all were."

"When I talked to George McGowan last night, he sounded a little shaken," she admitted. "I thought it was because of the funeral."

"It was seeing me that shook him."

"He told me you believed Jay was about to confess something to Britt Shelley."

"I think Jay was going to come clean about what really happened in the police station that afternoon, about Suzi Monroe, all of it. He was silenced before he could, and I think he had an intuition that he was in danger. That's why he took her to his town house."

"He took her to his town house because Jay, being Jay, wanted nooky. Even cancer wouldn't prevent him from getting it when he could. True, she said in her press conference that he told her he had a big story, but that could have been a smooth come-on."

"It wasn't."

"How do you know? You're speculating. You're—" Then she stopped. "Oh, shit. You've been in contact with her, haven't you? Jesus, Raley. If you have, you could be charged with aiding and abetting."

He didn't address that because he didn't want Candy to be compromised. "Can you get me an appointment with Cobb Fordyce?"

"No."

"Candy."

"Okay, highly unlikely."

"Persuade him."

"With what?"

"He and his cronies stole my life," he said with heat. "For that alone don't I deserve fifteen minutes of his time?"

She pondered it for a full minute, during which Raley kept quiet and fed coins into the phone, which he'd steadily been doing during the entire conversation.

He'd just about given up all hope that she would grant his request when she said, "I'll put in a call to his office. That's all I'll do, but I'll do that. When would you like to see him?"

"Tomorrow."

"Tomorrow. Are you insane?"

"Call him today, set up an appointment for tomorrow."

"Raley, be realistic. He's the attorney general."

"He's a public servant," he said, raising his voice again. "I pay his fucking salary."

"But you can't just waltz in—"

"Which is why I'm calling you."

"Hold . . . Dammit! Raley, hold on." She covered the mouthpiece. He could hear her impatiently apologizing and requesting that she be given a few more minutes to conclude this phone call. When she came back on the line, she said, "They're waiting on me. I've got to go."

"I'm running out of coins anyway. Will you call him?"

"If he agrees to see you, which I seriously doubt, what are you going to say to him?"

"I'm more interested to hear what he

has to say to me." He could still sense her uncertainty. "I promise not to outright accuse him of murder."

"Not in so many words, but if you say to him what you've told me, it's a damn strong implication."

He had one shot at closing the sale; he took it now. "Look, Candy, more than anyone I know, you're the standard-bearer for truth and justice. Fordyce may be pure as the driven snow, the shining example of integrity he appears to be. If so, he'll be receptive to my questions about Jones, the fire, and Suzi Monroe. He'll order an immediate and thorough investigation.

"*But* if he was a conspirator in a criminal cover-up, he doesn't deserve the office he holds and should be made to answer for his crime, or crimes." He let that sink in, then added, "Either way, whether he's true-blue or guilty as hell, justice will be served."

He waited, practically holding his breath and fingering his last quarter, while she considered it. Then she said, "Christ, you're tenacious. You're also right, goddamn you."

"You'll get him to talk to me?"

"I don't know if I can. He'll ask why you want to see him. What should I tell him?"

Searching for an answer to that, he glanced over his shoulder and made eye contact with Britt, who was still in the passenger seat of the car, anxiously watching him through the windshield. "Tell him I want to nominate a poster child for victims of date rape drugs."

She drew a deep breath and released it on a sigh. "The timing of this sucks for me."

"I'm aware of that. And I'm sorry as hell about it."

"What's the urgency? You've lived with this for five years. It can't keep until next week?"

He thought of the men in the maroon sedan, of Britt's car sailing off the embankment into the river. "No. It can't keep."

"I'll do what I can."

"Thank you."

"Don't thank me yet. I don't promise a thing. I may not be able to reach him. Even if I do, he'll probably refuse, and he'll think I've lost my marbles for asking."

"I understand that. But try and convince him."

Once again sighing with reluctance, she said, "Okay. Where can I reach you?"

Miranda, George, and Les were sipping cocktails on the terrace when George excused himself to answer a call on his cell phone. The caller was Candy Mellors, sounding harried and unhappy over the necessity of calling him. She was brusque, and the conversation didn't last very long. When it ended, George reluctantly returned to the terrace, dreading the news he must impart to his wife and father-in-law.

"Who was that?" Miranda asked.

He considered lying, but that would only prolong the inevitable. "Judge Mellors."

"Two nights in a row? Are the two of you dating, or what?" Miranda asked snidely. She took a dainty sip of her Cosmopolitan. "No, that can't be it. She's a dyke."

George retrieved his drink. "She's not a dyke."

"She looks like a dyke."

"She was married."

"Oh please, George. You are so naïve." She looked across at Les with an expression that said, *Can you believe he's such an idiot?*

"Well, whether she is or isn't," he said, "she had some disturbing news."

That got Miranda's attention. A Botox-defying frown appeared on her forehead. Les didn't have Botox to ameliorate his frown. "Well?" he barked. "Are you hoping this news will improve with age? Let's hear it."

"She heard from Raley Gannon this afternoon. He called her office. Since she wasn't at the funeral and hasn't seen him since he left town years ago, she wanted to know if I thought he was stable."

"Stable?" Les said.

"What did he say to make her think he was unstable?" Miranda asked.

"He asked her to set up an appointment for him." He paused deliberately, knowing it would irk them. "With Cobb

Fordyce." No one moved for several seconds, then George shook the small ice cubes from the bottom of his empty glass into his mouth and crunched them noisily. "Cat got your tongues?"

"This isn't funny," Miranda snapped.

"Did I say it was funny?"

"What does Gannon want to talk to the AG about?"

"Three guesses, Les, and the first two don't count."

His father-in-law looked past him and addressed Miranda as though he weren't there. "Your husband does like to crack unfunny jokes, doesn't he?"

George's blood came to an instant boil. "No, Les, I don't. I just don't know how to handle this situation, so mocking the absurdity of it is the best I can do."

"With that kind of chickenshit attitude, no wonder you're a failure."

"Boys," Miranda said, *tsk*ing. "There's no call to take potshots at each other. We'll figure this out if everybody just stays calm. Although I must agree with Daddy, George."

"Shocker." He went to the portable bar and poured himself another scotch.

"This *is* serious," she said.

"Right. It is. And urgent. She said Raley wants to set the appointment for tomorrow. He plans to confront Cobb about several issues. The judge said he was making noises about Cleveland Jones and Suzi Monroe. He's also convinced that Jay was going to make a full confession to all his sins, but that someone bumped him off before he could." He looked at them in turn and snuffled a mirthless laugh. "Got to hand it to ol' Raley. He may be unstable, but he's sure as hell not stupid."

Miranda said irritably, "Surely the judge wouldn't set up any such meeting between him and Cobb Fordyce."

George would have sworn he saw a flicker of apprehension in her eyes. Although he was certain it was brought on by concern for her own sweet ass, not his. "She said she would prefer not to, especially not this week, when she doesn't need any hassles. She tried stalling him. It didn't work."

"Already she's playing politics," Les grumbled. "Why didn't she just hang up on him?"

"I asked her that," George said. "She's afraid that if she doesn't get him his meeting with Cobb, he'll do something crazy."

"Like what?"

Again George shrugged. "Strap himself and a few sticks of dynamite to Cobb's desk. Something. That's why she asked my opinion on whether or not Raley is mentally and emotionally balanced."

"What did you tell her?" Les asked.

"Personally? I think Raley Gannon is the sanest of us all. The most noble, too. Jay said he was always idealistic, taking up for the underdog. Called him Saint Raley behind his back.

"But Gannon's also very pissed off. With all that righteous indignation bubbling inside him all these years, who's to say he won't blow at any moment?" Again, he gave a muffled laugh. "But then so could any of us."

"What do you think she'll do?" Miranda asked.

"Candy? Undecided."

"She's a fool even to consider it," Les snapped. "It could be disastrous for her.

Has she forgotten she's the one who convinced Fordyce not to prosecute Gannon for that dead girl? Does she want that career blip exposed? This week, in particular."

"No, I'm sure she doesn't. But she's more concerned about what Raley will do if he doesn't get face time with Cobb than with what will happen if he does. If he were to raid the capitol building, it would draw a hell of a lot more attention than a closed-door meeting."

Les was pacing the brick terrace, tugging his lower lip. "Have you talked to Fordyce since that night he called here?"

"No. He phoned the office the following day, but I never called him back. There was nothing more to say. But if he was bothered by what Bill Alexander told him, about Jay making a deathbed confession to Britt Shelley, imagine his reaction when Raley starts singing the same song. He could panic."

It made George nauseated to think about the fallout this could cause. Up till now he'd thought that today's bad news was hearing from Pat Jr. that Raley and

Britt Shelley were sleuthing together. Miranda had gone ballistic when he'd told her and had demanded to know how that was possible. Les had also wanted to know. George had been helpless to provide them an explanation.

Tiredly, he massaged his forehead. "Fucking Jay. This is all his fault. Why'd he have to go and call Britt Shelley? Of all the dumb-ass things to do."

"Stop your whining," Miranda hissed, glaring at him. "We've got to do something, George. I've told you, and I meant it. I won't get stuck holding a bag of your shit."

"You're in this as much as I am," he shouted. "And so is daddy dear."

Her face turned cold, and he could have chipped ice off her voice. "We don't know what you're talking about. Exactly what is the *this* we're supposed to be in?"

"Good try, Miranda," George said softly. "But you don't really want me to call your bluff, do you? Do *you,* Les?"

In answer, she went to stand next to her father, the two of them facing him, as they had on the day he and Miranda got married. In St. Philip's Church downtown. Everybody who was anybody in attendance. A dozen bridesmaids. Flowers by the truckload. Miranda wearing a designer gown that had cost more than most men earn in a year.

Standing together at the altar, Les had handed her over to him, her groom, her husband, her life partner. But it had been a symbolic gesture without substance. George had soon learned what his status was in the family structure. In this trio, he would always be the odd man out.

Les said, "Make this problem go away, George. Right now. For good this time."

"How in hell am I supposed to do that?"

"F.I.O.," Miranda said, tossing her hair. "Figure it out."

It had been a slow day for the two men known as Smith and Johnson. They were having an early dinner at a steak house that featured an unlimited salad bar and free apple cobbler. Two clean-cut men sharing a meal and conversation, never drawing attention to themselves, men who'd be forgotten as soon as they left the restaurant.

Yesterday they had got their asses chewed for losing Raley Gannon after he left the funeral. It was pointed out to them that they'd missed a golden opportunity, especially since he was now partnered with Britt Shelley, who twice had survived them.

"No way she could've got out of that car," Johnson had said when they learned she was alive and seemingly fine.

"Well, obviously she did," their employer had said with rancor.

Had they been sharp enough, they were told, they could have followed Raley Gannon from the funeral, back to the newswoman, and taken care of both of them, then collected their pay and disappeared.

They took the reprimand stoically, knowing they deserved it. They had enjoyed the car play on that dark country road, but it hadn't been an efficient form of assassination. In fairness to themselves, they cited that it had been their retainer's idea to intercept the woman on the road and make her death look like a suicide.

At present, no one knew where Gannon and Britt Shelley were holed up. Charleston didn't seem that large until you were trying to find someone in it, and most of the population seemed to be driving gray sedans. License plate numbers were pointless; Gannon was smart enough to switch them.

"We should have put a transponder on the car while he was inside the chapel," Smith observed now as he cut off a piece of blood-rare sirloin.

"Too many people around. Late arrivals. Chauffeurs. Grave-diggers."

The drop-in visit to Wickham's house had been reported to them.

"Do you think Gannon is carrying, or was Wickham dramatizing?" Smith asked, chewing thoughtfully.

"From what we've been told about Wickham, I'd say he was probably dramatizing."

"But is Gannon carrying?"

"I think we have to assume he is."

"Do you think he knows how to shoot?"

"Doesn't matter. We do."

Johnson was grinning confidently at his partner when his cell phone vibrated. He answered with a brusque "Here," then didn't speak another word for sixty seconds. "Got it." He slapped the phone closed and said to Smith, "Showtime."

CHAPTER 23

Raley's paranoia was contagious.

Britt didn't argue when he suggested that they move again. After his call to Judge Mellors, they returned to the motor court only long enough to gather their things. It took less than ten minutes. Raley drove into the urban area of Charleston, then beyond it, crossing the Cooper River before he found another suitable motel. Combined with an RV park, it had individual cabins lining the edge of a pretty marsh.

Raley used an alias to check them in, paid for a couple of days in cash, and parked the car behind their cabin. "I asked for this one. Easy in, easy out," he said as he ushered her into their new quarters, which were furnished similarly to the previous place but were much nicer and newer. They kept the curtains over the front window tightly drawn, although Raley peered through them at regular intervals to check for anyone encroaching on their bolted door.

"Did the judge give you a time frame?"

"She asked for several hours. Then I'll go out and find another pay phone."

"What do you think Fordyce will say?"

Killing time, Raley was lying on his back on the double bed next to the one on which she was reclined. He'd bunched up the flat pillows beneath his head. His forearm was resting on his forehead. "I don't know. But Candy was my best and last resort. I laid it on pretty thick, the obligation factor and her belief in the law. It was crass manipulation, but at least she promised to try to talk him into seeing me."

"Maybe you shouldn't have been so brutally honest."

Keeping his arm on his forehead, he looked at her across the narrow space separating the beds.

She said, "What I mean is, you told her you suspected him of several felonies. Maybe you should have fudged a little."

"Maybe I should have let you ask her. You're all about fudging."

"Some would call it diplomacy."

"Some would call it lying."

Her breath gusted out in frustration. "God, you're unbending."

"Candy called it tenacious."

"Call it by any name you like, you're unforgiving. That's probably why Hallie—" She broke off, then mumbled, "Never mind."

"Oh no," he said, turning onto his side and propping himself on his elbow. "You opened that can of worms. That's probably why Hallie *what*?"

She watched him closely, half out of curiosity to see how he would react, half out of wariness of his reaction. "Your unforgiving nature is probably why she didn't come back to you."

"After Jay, you mean. After he threw her over for the next flavor of the month."

"If she had crawled back, full of contrition, would you have resumed your relationship with her?"

"After Suzi Monroe, I couldn't very well condemn anybody on faithfulness issues, could I? I would have forgiven Hallie on a cerebral level. But, no, I wouldn't have taken her back."

"Because it was Jay she turned to."

"Because she turned to him so easily. She knew how he was, how shallow and self-serving he could be. We'd talked about his character flaws. Even laughed about how he'd made egomania an art form. And still she chose him over me."

Britt considered letting it drop there, but prodded by curiosity, she said, "But you sort of . . ."

"What?"

"Nudged her away. Didn't you? When you offered her time and space, were you testing her love and devotion?"

"Maybe." He flopped onto his back again. "If it was a test, she failed. You said I hadn't fought for her, but she didn't fight for me, either."

"Then why did you try to contact her years later?"

He gave a harsh laugh. "Good question, Ms. Shelley. I've asked it of myself a few thousand times. Self-flagellation? I wasn't quite miserable enough? Curiosity? Loneliness? Maybe a combination of all those reasons.

"Anyway, I got extremely upset when I heard that she'd married and was having a baby. But not out of jealousy. I didn't love her anymore, but I cared enough about her to be glad that she'd survived Jay."

"Then why did you get upset?"

"Because her newfound happiness underscored how crappy my life was. It made me furious. She, Jay, Fordyce, all of them were flourishing. Suzi Monroe had been nothing more hazardous than a speed bump in their lives. They were past it, moving forward and upward. I was stuck in neutral and couldn't do anything about it."

"You could have gone to another city, applied at the fire department and—"

"And been told thanks but no thanks. Soon as my previous employment was checked, I'd've been turned down on character issues."

"You could have done something else. Changed careers."

"I wanted to be a firefighter. That's what I'd spent years training for. That's what I did and wanted to do. Besides, my job here wasn't finished."

"To unforgiving, add stubborn."

She'd meant it as a gibe, but he didn't respond, so she figured he'd taken it as another criticism of his character. For several minutes, silence simmered between them. He was the first to speak. "Candy thinks this is about the Suzi Monroe thing. Hallie and Jay. All that. She said it's futile for me to hold a grudge against him because you can never come to a reconciliation with a dead man."

"Very perceptive of her. You told me you've spent the last five years plotting your revenge."

"Yes, I did, but that's not what it's about now."

"What's it about now?"

"It's about the seven people who died. Eight, if you count Suzi."

He was still staring up at the ceiling, so his profile was all she could see of his face, but the tenor of his voice had changed. "Those people were murdered, Britt. No one knows that a killer or killers went free. No one even *suspects.* There's been no accountability for those crimes. Call me unforgiving and unbending, that's okay. I won't forgive and I won't bend because even Cleveland Jones, who by all accounts was irredeemable, deserves justice."

After a moment, she said, "You're passionate about this."

He turned and looked at her, then gave a small shrug. "Passionate? Yeah, I guess. When I was a kid, I had this dream of becoming a fireman so I could save lives and property, put my life on the line to rescue others, see that arsonists were caught and punished. Very idealistic. Even arrogant. But that's how I felt."

"Most little boys want to become firemen so they can ride on the fire truck."

"Well, there was that," he admitted with a flash of a grin. "Not to mention the cool-looking, badass gear, and sliding down the pole, and getting to hang out at the firehouse. All that macho, male bonding stuff." They smiled across at each other.

"What's your most memorable experience as a fireman?"

He didn't have to think about it but said instantly, "I rescued a man who was pinned in his wrecked car."

"Tell me about it."

"When we arrived, he was screaming, hysterical, but he wasn't hurt all that badly. I calmed him down, told him we'd get him out and that he'd be all right. A half hour later he was in an ambulance on his way to the hospital, a little beat up, but fixable."

"That's a good story with a happy ending."

He looked over at her, then back at the ceiling. "Not really. After we got him into the ambulance, we had to go back and cut his four-year-old son out of the wreckage. His body was crammed up under the engine block, and when we tried to pull it out . . ." He stopped, waited, started again. "Nothing held together. He was in pieces." He paused again and cleared his throat.

"See, his dad had taken him to the

supermarket with him. When they came out, the kid set up a howl about getting back into his car seat. His dad was embarrassed because the kid was yelling, everybody in the parking lot was staring, he didn't know how to deal with a tantrum.

"So he gave in and told the kid okay, he could ride in the front seat. They weren't that far from home. And it was just for this one time that he'd be allowed to sit there. But it only took one time, one bad decision. A truck ran a red light and T-boned the car." After several seconds, he added, "That kid would be eleven or twelve now. I imagine his dad thinks about that a lot."

Britt let moments pass, then said, "Have you had many experiences like that?"

"No. Thank God. But you asked me my most memorable. That's it. By far." Turning his head, he said, "What about you?"

"Me?"

"Are you passionate for your work?"

Her reply was slow in coming. "Yes."

Her hesitancy raised his eyebrows. "I

know what passion sounds like, and that's not it." He gave her a long look, and she remembered the hungry, sexy sounds that had filled his bedroom the night before last.

She looked away and in a quiet voice asked, "Want to know a secret, Raley?"

"Hmm."

"Are you sure? If I tell you, I'll have to kill you."

He smiled.

"Shelley Britt Hagen."

He looked at her blankly. "Okay."

"That's my real name. But sometimes even I forget I wasn't born Britt Shelley, because I adopted it as my professional name even before I graduated college."

"You don't have to kill me to protect that secret."

"Well, that's not the big one."

"Oh. You have a darker one?"

"Um-huh."

"Well, whatever it is, it's safe with me."

He said it in all seriousness. Meeting his gaze full-on, she said, "I'm certain of that."

She thought that loyalty was probably one of his strongest qualities. In that regard, being muleheaded was an attribute, not a flaw. If someone told him a secret, he would take it to his grave. If he made you a promise, he would keep it. A commitment would be a commitment for life. He would be faithful to a woman.

Frankly she thought Hallie was a fool for doubting, even for an instant, that he wasn't in control of his faculties when he was with Suzi Monroe. His body had functioned as conditioned, but his brain was shut down. Certainly his heart hadn't been involved. If his fiancée truly had loved him, if she had known him at all, she would have accepted his explanation without question.

But she herself had deemed him guilty, hadn't she? She'd doubted nothing Jay told her, but had believed the worst of Raley Gannon without so much as a single meeting. When he dodged her microphones and cameras, she had concluded that his avoidance was as good as an admission, and taking it one step further, she had swayed her viewing audience into believing likewise.

For five years, his unfinished investigation had haunted him. He'd borne the weight of eight murders that had gone unaccounted for. With sadness and shame, Britt acknowledged that she was partially responsible for that.

"I'm sorry, Raley."

"For what?"

"For my partial reporting."

"You already apologized."

"Yes, but when I did, I was still working an angle. I was trying to weasel more information from you. I wanted this new, bigger story, and I wanted to stay with you until I got it. This time I mean my apology sincerely."

After a beat or two, he said, "That's your secret?"

"No." She took a deep breath as she turned onto her back. "My secret is that I've had job offers in larger TV markets. One was even a network job. A contributing reporter on weekends, but it would have been a good start. I've turned them all down."

"How come?"

"Fear of failure."

She glanced at him but quickly cast her eyes back toward the ceiling. "I called you a coward, but the truth is, I'm the coward. I'm afraid to leave my small pond here, where I'm a big fish. In a larger market, the competition would be tougher. The expectations would be greater. What if I couldn't hack it? What if I made a colossal fool of myself? So every time my agent came to me with an offer, I turned it down.

"I always had a reasonably valid excuse, but the bottom line was that I was afraid to give up my star status here. Anywhere else, I may discover I'm only average, and then what?

"I've been working without a net since I was eighteen, and it's been good for me. I'm independent and self-sufficient. When everything is going well, I tell myself I'm capable of anything. But if things were to go terribly wrong, I don't have anything or anyone to fall back on, even temporarily, even long enough for me to get back on my feet and dust myself off and try again. That frightens me.

"When I was younger, I could afford a career setback or two. I moved frequently, and the risks always worked out in my favor. But I'm not so young now. I'm no longer the fresh face. I've got more to lose and can't afford a major setback. So I don't gamble with my career. I stay well within my comfort zone." She took a deep breath and looked over at him, expecting a comment. When he didn't say anything, she said, "That's it. That's my secret."

"You're full of shit."

"What?"

"You're not giving yourself enough credit." He looked almost angry as he swung his feet to the floor and stood up. "First of all, your face is fresh enough. You could take it anywhere and become a star." Turning away, he stalked to the window and parted the curtains, looked out, drew the curtains together again, came back around.

"Second, you're alone because that's your choice. You could have a safety net if you wanted one. You may not want to leave this TV market for a larger one, but that doesn't mean you couldn't, and do it successfully."

Britt angled herself up, supporting herself on her elbows. "I appreciate the vote of confidence, but I'm not sure I can trust the opinion of a man who doesn't even own a television."

"I've seen you enough times to know you're good. I saw a replay of your press conference. You had them eating out of your hand. You convinced me of your innocence, and I was your most skeptical viewer."

"The police weren't convinced, though, were they? Clark and Javier believe I killed Jay. Pat Junior believes I did."

"Does he?" His eyes moved down to her chest, and he stared at it hard enough to make her uncomfortably aware of the snug fit of her T-shirt. Then his eyes snapped up to hers. *"Does* he believe you killed Jay? He accused you of it, but . . ." Muttering an expletive, he began to pace. "That whole scene with him was off. I don't know how, just off."

"I know what you mean. You said he was squirrelly. Maybe that's what we're picking up on."

"Maybe." Suddenly he checked his wristwatch, then, moving quickly, he worked his feet into his sneakers. "This should time out about right. Come on. Hurry. Put your shoes on. Get your cap."

"Where are we going?"

"To the police station."

"Anyone who passes this way could spot this car," Britt said. She was hunkered down in the passenger seat, her hair tucked up underneath the baseball cap.

The central police station sat atop a rise overlooking the Ashley River. Adjacent to the campus, which also housed the DMV, was a Marriott hotel. It was in the parking lot of the hotel that they were parked beneath a row of young live oak trees. From there, they could see the police department employee parking lot.

"I don't think anyone in that building knows to look for this car," Raley said.

"Except Pat Wickham."

"And I'm almost positive he kept the information to himself."

"You don't think he called the police after we left?"

He shook his head. "We would have known it. Patrol cars would have been converging on that area in a matter of minutes. Even if we hadn't seen them, we would have heard sirens. They would have formed a blockade around the vicinity. They probably would have put up a chopper, too."

"And media would have been racing to the scene."

"As you would know. No, I'm betting Pat Junior didn't tell anybody that a fugitive from the law came to visit."

"So why not?"

"That's why we're here."

Although they were a safe distance from Pat Wickham's car, which they could single out because they'd seen it in his driveway earlier that day, they had a clear view of it. His shift was almost over. He couldn't leave without their seeing him. They hoped he wouldn't notice the gray sedan. Raley doubted Pat Jr. would be looking. The last place anyone would expect to find Britt was within shouting distance of police headquarters.

"He was scared of you today," she said.

"I wasn't that scary."

"He saw the pistol and went pale."

"Yeah, but it was more than me and the pistol that had him about to pee his pants."

"He was afraid of what Jay had told me."

"Or would have told you if he had lived long enough."

"Why would Jay's deathbed confession be a threat to Pat Junior?"

"Maybe we'll have an opportunity to ask him. There he is."

Raley spotted him as he exited through a rear door. They watched him enter the parking area and weave his way through the rows of cars. To Raley his movements seemed furtive, but he admitted that could be his imagination. The man was nervous by nature.

He didn't look in their direction as he unlocked his car, tossed his jacket inside, and climbed in. "So far, so good," Britt said.

Their plan was to follow Pat Jr. and see where he went after hours. Probably he would go straight home, and this would be another dead end. But Raley felt that the man was hiding something;

Britt sensed it, too. Following him might provide them with a clue.

Besides, staying cooped up with Britt in the small cabin for hours on end was becoming an uncomfortable test of his endurance. The intimacy of sharing small spaces with her was getting to him. He was constantly aware of her nearness. Each time she moved, he knew it. He woke up every time she stirred in her sleep, even though she was in another bed.

For five years he'd had only fleeting contact with women, never being with one for more than an hour or two, certainly not long enough to start recognizing her habits and anticipating her reactions.

Now he was surrounded by Britt's femininity. Inundated by it. He was conscious of those little things that were purely female—her vexation over a chipped fingernail, the daintiness with which she sipped from her can of Diet Coke, the meticulous way she tied her shoestrings by making the ends perfectly even. He was captivated by these and a hundred other manifestations of femininity. Furthermore, he was enjoying them.

He found himself watching her when she didn't know it, in a kind of fascinated trance, his thoughts more often than not veering toward the prurient. He should never have put his hands on her. Because, try as he might, he couldn't forget how she'd felt, how she'd moved, how she'd wanted him. He couldn't look at her mouth without remembering kissing it, or her legs without remembering how tightly her thighs had hugged him.

He excused that night on the basis of him being lonely and horny. But he'd been lonely and horny before, and as soon as he said thanks and left a woman's bed, it was forgotten.

Not this time.

His resolve not to touch her again was as strong as ever, but it was becoming increasingly difficult to enforce. A car was more public than a motel room. So part of this mission was to escape the confines of their compact room before he lost his mind, his temper, or his control. The main goal, however, was to try to discover the source of Pat Jr.'s jitters.

Raley waited until the policeman had driven out of the parking lot before starting the sedan and following. He kept well back and let several cars get between them. But not too many. There was a lot of traffic. There had been a break in the weather; the humidity wasn't as high as it had been. The pleasant evening had brought people out. Luckily Pat Jr. stayed in one lane and drove the speed limit.

After ten minutes, Britt said, "Not too exciting so far."

"No, but he's not going in the direction of home."

Pat Jr. kept driving, eventually making a large loop around the city before heading into downtown and the historic district, where the streets became narrower and even more congested with motor traffic and death-defying pedestrians, who crossed against lights and often took their chances on the street rather than the crowded sidewalks.

Pat Jr. turned onto a side street off the main drag of King, then in midblock he entered a driveway that ran along the side of a nightspot. Raley and Britt looked at each other but said nothing. They didn't have to. The club was well known in the city.

Raley drove past the drive, but when he looked down it, he could see the policeman wedging his car between two others. Farther along the street, Raley spotted a car leaving a coveted parallel parking slot. He wheeled into it and cut their lights, hoping they wouldn't be noticed by Pat Jr.

They weren't. He had walked along the side of the building toward the entrance of the nightclub but had stopped short of the corner and remained in the sliver of shadow against the exterior wall. He pulled a cell phone from his pocket and made a quick call.

Seconds after he clipped his phone back onto his belt, a young man emerged from the door of the club. He walked straight to the corner of the building and turned. Pat Jr. greeted him with a smile. They had a brief exchange, then together walked quickly back to the parking lot. They got into a car—not Pat Jr.'s—and left, pulling out onto the street in front of the club and driving away, unaware that they were being closely observed.

The silence between Raley and Britt was thick with all the implications of what they'd seen. Eventually he said, "I think I knew. In the back of my mind. From the time I knew who he was. That's why I was surprised when George told me he was married. And then today, he didn't look at you."

Sensing her misapprehension, he turned toward her. "He didn't *look* at you." He looked down at her chest before meeting her gaze to make sure she'd got his point. She had. She lowered her head with apparent embarrassment.

Raley said, "Lewis Jones looked. Delno looked." I've *looked plenty.* "Pat Junior didn't. That should have tipped me off."

"He's leading a secret life."

"The wife and kids are for show."

"It must be misery." She pulled off the baseball cap and shook her hair loose. "I feel just awful, spying. Let's go."

"We can't."

"Sure we can."

"No. We can't. *Dammit!*" He rubbed his eye sockets, feeling as awful as Britt about what they were doing, feeling even worse about what he knew they had to do. "We can't go, Britt. Because I just figured out that the whole thing started with this poor bastard."

CHAPTER 24

Pat Jr. didn't see Raley until he got behind the steering wheel of his car and Raley splayed his wide hand upon the younger man's chest. He cried out in fright.

"I'm not going to hurt you. But we're going to talk, and every word out of your mouth had better be the truth. Understand?" Raley's voice, while soft and calm, was also steely. Britt imagined the other man sensed his resolve. She could practically smell Pat Jr.'s fear as he wobbled his head in agreement.

"H-how did you know I was here?"

"Do you have your service weapon?" Raley asked.

He shook his head no, then nodded

yes. “In . . . in the glove box. Were you following me?”

Raley opened the glove box to verify that the pistol was there, then closed the door of the compartment without touching it. “That’s not too smart of you, Pat, leaving your police-issue gun where anybody could break into your car and get it.”

“Why are you following me? What do you want?” By now, having realized that Britt was in the backseat, he addressed the question to her reflection in the rearview mirror.

“As Raley says, we want to talk to you.”

“About what?”

“About your face,” Raley said.

“My face?”

“What happened to it?”

“It . . . I . . . I used to do a lot of cycling. I ran into a tree on my bike. Injured myself so bad, I gave up the sport.”

Raley didn’t move, not even his eyes. He continued to hold Pat Jr. with his resolute stare. The man turned his head and looked hopefully toward Britt. She slowly shook her head. “That’s the story you told, but that's not what happened, is it, Pat?"

He swallowed, visibly and audibly.

"Tell us about Cleveland Jones."

Pat Jr. let go of the small measure of courage he'd been clinging to. His misshapen face contorted with his effort not to cry. His marred lower lip began to tremble.

Britt could hardly bear to watch his meltdown. Raley had shared with her his theory on Pat Jr.'s involvement, how the whole sordid mess began with him. It wasn't a pretty story, and what they were doing to him now was as cruel as holding a mirror up to his disfigured face. But it was also necessary. Raley had cautioned her not to let her compassion for the man's plight soften her determination to wring the truth from him.

"He's pathetic, yes. But he might also be the key that will open up everything," he'd said. "We've got to get from him as much as he knows, and it probably won't be easy. It for sure as hell won't be pleasant."

"I don't look forward to it."

"Neither do I," Raley had said.

Now, no doubt feeling as rotten as she did about this ambush, Raley said, "Along with all his other crimes, Cleveland Jones was into gay bashing."

Pat Jr. nodded.

"And you were one of his victims."

Another nod. A sniff. He wiped his nose on the back of his hand. "He and two others."

"Where?"

"Hampton Park."

"Tell us what happened."

"I . . . I'd . . . gone to the park. Actually, I was riding my bike. But I was . . . I stopped at the men's room."

"You and another guy had sex in the restroom," Raley said. "Was this a date, like the guy tonight?"

"No. I went in. He was there. Older guy. We . . ." He shrugged self-consciously. "After, I left ahead of him. When I came out of the restroom, they were there. Three of them. They jumped me. Jones—"

"Did you know him?" Britt asked. "Had he done this to you before?"

"No. But I knew the type. I'd been

warned, you know, by guys I hooked up with. Charleston is a fairly gay-friendly city now, but this was five years ago and there had been several recent attacks. More than the standard name-calling. Brutal, physical attacks. A bunch of local skinhead types had decided we weren't fit to live," he said bitterly.

"But you went out cruising anyway. In a public park, for godsake." Raley sounded angry over the other man's carelessness.

"I didn't have a choice!" Pat Jr.'s ragged cry reverberated in the car. For a moment nobody said anything, then he repeated, "I didn't have a choice. I hadn't come out. My dad was a cop. He'd worked vice. He'd arrested guys like me who met in public restrooms, parking lots, whatever.

"At the dinner table, he and George McGowan would laugh about the homos they'd caught blowing each other. I laughed with them, knowing that's what was expected."

Watching him in the rearview mirror, Britt could see tears forming in his eyes.

"Then one day Dad caught me and

one of my friends in my bedroom. I think he had suspected, but when the truth was right there . . ." He paused, shuddered. "He went berserk. He actually drew his pistol. I think he might have killed us if Mom hadn't stopped him."

Britt could only imagine this scene and the chasm it must have created between father and son, between husband and wife. The whole dynamic of the family would have changed after that. Gently she prodded him to continue. "Cleveland Jones and two others attacked you."

He stirred, drew a breath, expelled it slowly. "I never got a good look at the other two. But Jones swung a baseball bat at my shin and broke the bone. Once I was down, he and the others kicked me. One got my nose with the toe of his boot. Pulverized it. I couldn't breathe out of it for months.

"Before I passed out, Jones grabbed me by the hair and forced me to look up at him. He was grinning. 'Suck this,' he said, then used the end of the bat like a pile driver on my mouth." He looked at Raley, then at Britt and, almost apologetically, added, "The surgeons put everything back as well as they could."

"The man with you in the restroom, what happened to him?"

"While they were working me over, he ran away. I'd never seen him before, never saw him again. I lay there for almost an hour, but it seemed like ten. Some kids doing dope happened on me. They called 911, then split, too.

"The ambulance took me to the hospital. My folks were notified. I was barely conscious, about to go into surgery, but Dad leaned over me and said, 'I told you it was dangerous to ride your bike at night.' That was his way of clueing me in to the lie we'd tell. I'd had a biking accident."

Another car pulled into the parking lot, sweeping its headlights across them. Two well-dressed young men got out and walked along the alley toward the entrance of the club. "Nice place?" Raley asked.

Pat Jr., surprised by the question, replied, "I hear it is. I've never been inside. I'm still not out. Officially."

Raley picked up the story. "Pat Senior

covered your beating with a lie, but privately he wanted to catch the guys who'd done it."

"Right," Pat Jr. said. "I guess he still loved me. I was gay, but I was his son. Maybe it was more of an honor issue with him than love. Anyway, when they'd reduced the dosage of painkillers so I could think straight, Dad brought several books of mug shots to my hospital room. He promised they were going to get the guys who'd done this to me and make them sorry."

" 'They'?"

"Dad, George McGowan, and Jay Burgess."

"He admitted to his best friends and fellow detectives that you were gay?"

"I suppose. He must have. George McGowan has barely spoken to me since. His contempt is plain. Jay never paid much attention to me one way or the other. I was beneath his notice even before this happened. I saw through him, and I think he knew it. Anyhow, Dad enlisted him and George to help flush out my attackers. I could only identify Jones, and did so as soon as I saw his most recent mug shot."

"How long before they found him?" Raley asked.

"Couple of days. Dad called my hospital room and told me they had him in custody. He said Jones had copped an attitude, denied the attack, said he wouldn't go out of his way to bust a queer, but Dad was certain they'd get a confession out of him by the end of the day, and that, if they didn't, he'd get Cobb Fordyce to throw the book at this little Nazi. His exact words."

"What day was that?" Britt asked.

He looked at them in turn, then reluctantly said, "The day of the fire."

Raley leaned toward him, and Britt was struck by the difference between the two men. Raley's superior size and physicality would cause Pat Jr. to feel threatened even if that weren't Raley's intention. The younger man recoiled, leaning as far away from Raley as he could.

"Did they get a confession out of Jones?"

"I don't know."

"Did your dad mention that Jones had two skull fractures when they arrested him?"

"No."

"Did he call you with progress reports?"

"No. I didn't hear from him again. Just that once when he told me they would be interrogating Cleveland Jones until he cracked."

"What happened while they were interrogating him?"

"Nothing!" Then he repeated it with a firm shake of his head.

"But you suspect—"

"I don't suspect anything."

"That's bullshit, Pat," Raley said, with heat.

"I was in the hospital for weeks. I was on painkillers. Groggy. My recollections of the fire aren't even clear, so how would I know what took place before it started?"

"You don't want to know." Raley's accusation struck hard. The other man lowered his head to avoid Raley's piercing gaze. "You don't want to know, because then you'd have to acknowledge that seven people died because you got blown in a public men's room."

"Raley." Britt's softly spoken chastisement went unheard because of Pat Jr.'s harsh sob. His shoulders shook. The raw, choppy sounds of his weeping were heart-wrenching.

"You're right. I didn't want to know," he said miserably. "I heard that guy didn't die because of the fire, but I never asked Dad about it. I can't tell you any more because I don't know any more. If they knew I'd told you this much, they'd kill me."

Raley pounced on that. "Who? George McGowan? Was he there when your dad interrogated Cleveland Jones? He and Jay Burgess?"

"I don't know," Pat Jr. sobbed.

"Fordyce was there, too, wasn't he, Pat? He'd come over to the police station to throw the book at Jones if he didn't confess. Wasn't that the plan?"

"I told you, I don't know. I *swear*!"

Raley eased up and sat back against the passenger-side door, staring hard at the other man but giving him a moment to collect himself. When the crying had subsided into an occasional sniffle, Britt asked, "Why did you get married, Pat?"

Raley answered for him. "For the same reason he became a cop. It's part of his cover."

Pat Jr. looked over at Raley, obviously impressed that he had guessed so accurately. "I made a pact with Dad."

"After the fire?" Raley asked.

He nodded. "He made me swear that nobody would ever know about the incident in the park. My attacker was dead, and he was nobody's loss. It was over, he said. But it could never happen again.

"He told me to enroll in the police academy. He and his friends would make certain I got a spot. He told me to get married and have kids. He told me I had to stop . . . stop being a fag." He gave a caustic laugh. "As if being gay was something I could reverse or turn off."

"Why did you agree to this pact?"

"I owed him, didn't I? Even though I had disgraced him, he and his friends had come to my defense. So whatever

Dad said to do, I did. It would have been selfish of me not to."

"It was selfish to deceive a woman into marrying you," Britt said.

He looked back at her and nodded forlornly. "She was a girl from my mom's church. Brought up very strict. She was younger than me, and innocent. She didn't know exactly what to expect from a husband, so I wasn't a disappointment to her."

"The children?"

"I can do it when I have to."

"She doesn't know?"

He shook his head, looking at her imploringly. "She can't find out, either. I can't do that to her." Then to Raley, he said, "Please. She's great. Truly. I don't want to hurt her."

Britt felt that the lie he was living was more hurtful to his family than the truth would have been, but that was a conversation for another time.

Raley said, "You told us earlier today that Pat Senior didn't enjoy being a hero."

"He didn't. That fire ruined his life," Pat Jr. said with vehemence, showing more mettle than he had up to that point.

"How do you mean?" Britt asked.

"Just that. He was never the same after, and it was more than what happened to me in the park that changed him. He didn't like all the attention heaped on him. The commendations, the praise, the spotlight. Burgess and McGowan got off on all that. Fordyce used it to get himself elected AG, but Dad just wanted it all to go away. It didn't. Things really got bad after—"

He stopped and looked nervously at Raley, who asked, "After what?"

"After the business with you and that girl."

"What do you know about that?" Britt asked.

"Only what everybody else knows. What the newspapers said, what you reported on TV."

"Did your dad talk about the Suzi Monroe case?" Raley asked.

"Not in my hearing, but I knew he was investigating it. That was the last big case assigned to him. After that, he became depressed. More so every day.

Drank a lot, alone, late into the night. Most mornings I think he woke up still drunk. He started missing work. Nothing Mom said seemed to get through to him."

"Did she know about you, Jones, the park?"

Pat Jr. shook his head. "She believed the bicycle story because that's what Dad told her. But I think she always suspected there was more to it. I guess she wanted to think I'd been *cured* after being caught in bed with my friend. Don't ask, don't tell."

There had been a lot of denial going on in the Wickham household. Britt thought that was a terrible way to run a family.

"Okay, go on," Raley told him.

"Well, Mom could see that Dad was getting more depressed by the day. She begged him to get counseling, but he refused, said he could work it out by himself, but he never said exactly what 'it' was.

"George and Jay tried to boost him. Took him fishing. Stuff like that. But nothing they said or did helped. He sank lower and lower. One night I woke up to a strange sound. I found him sitting out on the back porch, crying his heart out. I'd never known him to cry before. Never. But I'll never forget the awful sound of it. I crept back to bed. He never knew I had witnessed that." He paused to wipe his nose again. "The very next night, George and Jay showed up at our door to tell Mom that he'd been fatally shot."

After a short silence, Raley said, "I knew your dad. Only slightly, but I knew he was a good and conscientious cop. Why did he place himself in such a dangerous situation that night, Pat? Why did he break the first rule of self-preservation by not waiting for backup?"

"To prove to himself that he was the hero everybody believed him to be."

It sounded like a stock answer, something he might have heard a therapist say. Raley picked up on it just as Britt did. "That's not what you really think, is it?"

Pat Jr. seemed ready to take issue, then slowly shook his head. "I've wondered if maybe he was just tired of it all and wanted it to be over. I know that feeling." He looked at his reflection in the rearview mirror. "I know how it feels to just want out of your body, out of your life."

He paused for several moments before continuing. "Maybe Dad went into that alley hoping that he wouldn't come out, but knowing that, if he didn't, Mom could still collect on his life insurance policy."

Britt had never actually heard anyone admit to suicidal feelings, and it shook her. Apparently the confession subdued Raley, too. For at least a minute no one said anything, then Raley spoke.

"I have another theory, Pat. I think maybe the crying jag you heard was your father's surrender. He'd reached his breaking point. He'd decided to unburden himself of the guilty secret he'd been keeping along with his buddies." After a significant pause, he added, "Maybe one or both of them wanted that secret protected at all costs. Your dad could have been lured into that alley and killed to make certain he wouldn't rat them out."

Pat Jr.'s nervousness returned. He wet his lips. His eyes darted to Britt, then back to Raley. "You didn't hear that from me. In fact, I don't know anything about a secret. What secret?"

Raley frowned at his attempt to play dumb. "Jay had something important he wanted to tell Britt. He was killed before he could, but I'm dead certain that it related to Cleveland Jones, that interrogation room, and the fire."

"You need to get off that track," Pat Jr. said nervously.

"And let Britt go down for a murder she didn't commit?"

"No. Of course not, but this talk . . . what you're alleging . . . is dangerous."

"I'll take my chances to get to the truth," Raley said.

"But in the meantime you're placing me and my family in danger." His face twisted with emotion again. "Look, I'm a lousy husband. I lie to my wife every hour of the day. But I do love her and my kids. They're innocents. I don't want anything bad to happen to them."

"I don't want anything bad to happen to them, either." Raley leaned closer to the other man. "So tell me who you think killed your father and Jay."

"*You* think that, not me."

"You're lying, Pat. You know I'm right."

"If you keep talking like this, you're going to get us and yourself killed." His voice was tearful, his eyes wild with fear.

"Who's going to kill me? McGowan? Fordyce? Both of them? Which one? Who?"

Pat Jr. was shaking his head.

"Who is it?" Raley pressed.

"Please don't ask."

"But you know, don't you?"

"I can't say anything more."

"Tell me why."

"Because nobody knows about me!"

His face crumpled with misery. His cry was so loud, so raw, that for a moment Raley remained quiet.

Then he nodded, as though saying he got it now. "They didn't betray your dad's trust about your homosexuality, so you can't betray theirs. Is that it?"

Pat Jr. nodded.

"Even if it kills you?"

"My life's shit anyway." He broke down into sobs again.

Raley regarded him closely, then looked at Britt. She indicated with a small shake of her head that she didn't believe the weeping man would give up any more information. He was held in a grip of fear more threatening to him than Raley.

"Pat?" Choking back sobs, he responded to Raley's softer tone and raised his head. "I think you're a creep for doing what you're doing to your family. It isn't fair to them, and it isn't even fair to you. You all deserve a happier life than the one you're leading. If it's true that you love your wife, tell her now. It will hurt, but it won't hurt as much as it will if you let this pretense continue.

"But in the meantime, I don't want to be responsible for your family's safety or yours. Talking to Britt and me could prove dangerous, you're right about that. I suggest you leave tonight."

"Leave?"

"Go home, pack up your wife and kids. Take them to the beach, to the mountains, just get lost for a while, a couple of days at least. Empty your ATM and don't use your credit cards. Throw away your cell phone. Cover your tracks."

Pat Jr. looked back at Britt as though asking, *Is he nuts?* "Take his advice, Pat," she said. "I was drugged the night Jay was murdered. But on the outside chance I might recover my memory of what happened, someone tried to kill me. My car was run off the road. It's submerged in the Combahee River. If Raley hadn't been there to rescue me, I would have drowned. Anyone who would do that wouldn't hesitate to harm your children, if only to punctuate their threat. Take your family and go tonight."

"If you notify your boss at the PD, don't tell him your destination," Raley advised him. "It might get back to George McGowan or Cobb Fordyce."

Pat Jr. looked at them, swallowing hard. "They've known me since I was a boy. I really don't think they'd do anything to me."

"That's probably what your dad thought," Raley said grimly. "Jay, too."

• • •

He and Britt walked back to the gray sedan still parked down the street, got in, and watched as Pat Wickham, Jr., drove away from the nightclub he'd never seen from the inside.

"Do you think he'll do what we advised?" Britt asked as they watched his car disappear around the corner at Meeting Street.

"Either he will or he's already on his cell phone calling in the cavalry."

"Which would mean he lied when he said he didn't know what had happened to Cleveland Jones after his arrest." She considered it a moment, then said, "I think he was telling the truth. He doesn't want to know what happened in that interrogation room because of the implications to himself. Don't ask, don't tell."

"He may not know specifically what happened, but I don't think he believes Jones had two skull fractures when he was arrested. He knows that whatever did go down was consequential. He also knows who killed Jay. And he must be scared out of his wits of him."

"Or them."

"Or them. Because if he wasn't, he'd

have exposed them when Pat Senior was shot. He let them get away with murdering his own father, which is incomprehensible. He—" Suddenly he reached out and clamped his hand over her head, shoving her down. At the same time, he slouched low in his seat.

"What?" she asked.

"Our friends just came out of the club."

"Butch and Sundance?"

"The very ones." He'd seen them in the side mirror. Glancing over his shoulder to make sure his eyes weren't deceiving him, he slid the pistol from his waistband.

Alarmed, she said, "You're not going to shoot them, are you?"

"Not unless I have to."

"Do you think Pat Junior called them?"

"Maybe, but I don't think so. If he had told them we were right outside, they'd have torn out of there. They're in no apparent hurry. See for yourself. They're going the other direction, their backs are to us."

He removed his hand from her head,

and she raised it far enough to peer over the seat. The two men had set off down the sidewalk, walking toward King Street. They weren't dawdling, they looked like they meant business, but she figured they always walked with a purposeful stride. But, as Raley had said, they didn't seem to be in a huge hurry, either.

"They don't look like a gay couple on an evening out," she said.

"Nope."

"Then funny they should show up here."

"Hmm. The same way it was funny they showed up at The Wheelhouse the night you and Jay met there. At least the one did. This is the first time you've seen the second one. Look familiar?"

"No. But I haven't seen his face yet. Do you think they were looking for Pat Junior tonight?"

"God, I hope not. He wouldn't last ten seconds against these guys."

Britt said, "It's a small triumph, but it sort of does my heart good, knowing they were in there wasting time while we were within yards of them."

The pair met three men on the sidewalk and moved aside to let them pass. Butch watched them over his shoulder until they entered the bar. He said something to his buddy, who took umbrage and gave him the finger, which caused him to chuckle. Then the two continued on their way.

"Did you get a better look at Sundance when he turned around?" Raley asked.

"Yes, but I don't think I've seen him before. I didn't have the reaction I did when I saw Butch through your cabin window."

The two reached the end of the block and turned the corner, disappearing. Raley poked the pistol back into his waistband and started the sedan. "How 'bout a little role reversal?"

"What are you going to do?"

"I'm gonna follow them."

CHAPTER 25

The maroon car had been left in a public parking lot two blocks off King Street. Because of the traffic, Raley was able to go slow and keep well back until the pair retrieved their car. He followed them out of the historic district, and then several miles along a major boulevard to an older Holiday Inn.

"Assassins on a budget," Britt said.

"No, they're charging the client three times what the rooms cost."

The hotel had two levels of rooms accessed by open-air corridors. The men parked their car steps away from rooms on the ground floor. Watching from a strip-center parking lot across the busy, divided thoroughfare, Raley and Britt saw the driver, the one they called Butch, open the trunk and remove a duffel bag.

She said, “That looks heavy.”

“Tools of their trade.”

Thoughtfully she asked, “That night on the road, why didn’t they just shoot me?”

“The risk of leaving evidence. The timing.”

“Two homicides so close together, mine and Jay’s, our being friends, that would have roused suspicion.”

“Your murder might not have passed as a random act of violence. Better that it take days, weeks maybe, for some poor fisherman to discover your car with you inside.”

“And then it would have appeared I’d killed myself.”

“Right. Then if you *had* remembered something Jay told you, and *had* passed it along to someone else, it could be discredited and dismissed.”

“The ramblings of a distraught woman about to take her own life.”

“Exactly.”

“They’re very clever, aren’t they?”

Her serious tone of voice brought his head around. “Very.”

The two men went into neighboring rooms. Butch kept the duffel bag with him. “He must be the senior partner,” Raley said. “Or maybe just the best shot.”

Britt asked, “Now what?”

After taking a glance around, he said, “Keep an eye on their rooms. Signal me if they come out.” He pushed open the car door.

“Where are you going?”

“To call Candy before it gets any later.” He pointed toward a telephone booth at the far end of the shopping center. “Since the booth is still there, I’m thinking the phone will be working.”

“Let’s drive over.”

He shook his head. “We couldn’t see their rooms as well. Stay put. Watch those rooms.”

“You’ll be exposed. They could see you.”

“They’re not looking. But just in case . . .” Holding the pistol by the barrel, he extended it to her. “You keep this.”

She recoiled. "Leave it on the seat."

He got out and carefully set the pistol on the driver's seat, then set off across the parking lot at a jog. Despite what he'd told Britt, he didn't like being so exposed. He stepped into the phone booth but didn't close the door, so the light wouldn't come on. Fortunately the telephone was still there. Even more of a break, it was in working order. He'd come up with a pocketful of change.

Candy answered his call on the first ring. "Where have you been? I was beginning to think that you'd come to your senses and weren't going to call back."

He plugged his ear with his index finger to help filter out the swishing noise of traffic. "I got tied up. Sorry I kept you up late. What have you got for me?"

"An appointment with Fordyce."

He was stunned. He hadn't admitted, even to himself, that she might manage to pull it off. "No shit?"

"Oh he shit, all right. At least I'm fairly sure he did. He was having no part of it at first, but I eventually wore him down. I told him he was lucky you hadn't accosted him at Jay's funeral like you did

George. I advised him as a former colleague that he should talk to you in private before you did something very public and probably crazy. He's expecting you to be just shy of a complete mental case, so hopefully your reasonable state of mind will come as a pleasant surprise." She hesitated, then said, "You aren't a mental case, are you?"

"No. Just a man with a mission."

"Same as," she muttered.

"What time?"

"Eleven o'clock. His office. Check in with the guard. A page will escort you."

"Candy, I don't know what to say."

"Say good night," she said querulously. "I've got back-to-back interviews all day tomorrow and need to go to bed. I'm retaining fluid because I never have time to pee, so my eyes are already puffy. Don't even get me started on my ankles."

He smiled at the picture she painted. "I owe you. Huge."

"Red *and* white."

"What?"

"When you come to dinner next week,

you have to bring both colors of wine. And no cheap stuff."

"You've got it."

"And, Raley."

"Yeah?"

"Hold his feet to the fire. Pun intended."

"What time?" Britt asked when Raley returned to the car with the good news.

"Eleven o'clock. His office."

"I'm surprised. I hoped he would agree to see you, but I doubted he would."

"Frankly, so did I. Maybe he's got bigger cojones than I give him credit for."

"It's easy to be brave when you're inside a guarded government office." She gazed thoughtfully at the maroon sedan parked outside the rooms at the Holiday Inn. "Or when you have someone fighting your battles for you."

She repeated the statement to herself and realized how accurately it applied to her. Acting on impulse and before she could change her mind, she opened her car door and stepped out.

"What are you doing?"

"I'll be right back."

"Britt?"

Ignoring him, she ran toward the busy boulevard, calling to him over her shoulder. "If something happens, drive away and call Detective Clark."

"Britt!"

"Drive away."

Her timing couldn't have been better. Just as she reached the curb, there was a break in the traffic. She sprinted across two lanes, the dividing median, and then the other two lanes, and came out on the sidewalk bordering the parking lot of the Holiday Inn.

She didn't dare look back at Raley, fearing that he would be in hot pursuit. Instead she continued moving purposefully across the parking lot toward the two rooms with the familiar car parked in front of them.

She couldn't positively identify it as the car that had forced hers off the road and into the river. But she couldn't eliminate it, either. She also knew that at least one of these men had been at The Wheelhouse, where she had been drugged. All circumstantial, but awfully suspicious.

What she knew with certainty was that they had searched Raley's cabin and truck yesterday, and that they had doggedly followed him from Jay's funeral, indicating that they were men whose purpose was shady, and possibly deadly. Nor did she believe for a moment that their being at the notable gay bar tonight was happenstance. Whether they were allies or enemies of Pat Wickham's, their intentions were contradictory to hers and Raley's.

The bastards had this coming.

Keeping her eyes trained on the windows and doors of the two rooms, she cautiously approached the car. She glanced around to make certain that no other guests or hotel employees were in sight or looking out the windows.

Seeing no one, she crouched down behind the sedan. The lights were still on inside both rooms. She didn't dare take her eyes off the windows. At any second the door of either room could have burst open. The occupants might even have been able to hear her heart pounding.

She crept to the left rear tire and ran her fingers along the rim until she located the air valve stem and hastily twisted off the cap. Clutching it in her hand, she duckwalked to the front tire.

She could hear the sound track of a TV sitcom coming from one of the rooms. Had the curtain moved, or was that her imagination? Was the air-conditioning unit beneath the window causing the curtain to flutter?

Her nervous fingers found the valve of the front tire and removed the cap. Her thighs were burning by the time she duckwalked the length of the car and around the back of it, then up to the right front tire. She twisted off that cap. The fourth and last one was more stubborn than the others. She was sweating and the pads of her fingers were rubbed raw from the effort by the time she got it off.

Then, holding all four in a tight fist, she stood up.

In the same instant, the door of one of the rooms was pulled open.

Instinctually she whipped her head around.

Sundance was framed in the open doorway. He was barefoot, still wearing his trousers, but he had replaced the dress shirt he'd worn into the nightclub with a white T-shirt. The tail of it was neatly tucked into his waistband. It was a ridiculous thing to note at a time like this, but irrationally it flashed through her mind how silly and uncomfortable that looked.

He was holding a plastic ice bucket, which he dropped the instant he spotted her, and reached for a shoulder holster that wasn't there, shouting, "Hold it!"

She did the opposite. She turned and ran for her life. She expected to see Raley waiting anxiously inside the gray sedan across the boulevard. But neither he nor the car was where she'd left them.

Behind her, she heard pounding, and figured Sundance was beating on his partner's door. He yelled, "Get out here!"

She didn't stop to look back but ran

headlong toward the street, not even knowing in which direction to go. *Where was Raley?* She had told him to drive away if anything happened, but she really hadn't expected him to desert her.

She thought she heard one of the men call her name, but she didn't need to look back to know that they were hotfooting it and closing in fast. She could hear the slaps of bare feet on pavement, their huffing breaths, cursing.

She leaped off the sidewalk directly into the path of an oncoming car and managed to jump back only a nanosecond away from being struck. The driver blasted his horn. It deafened her to the approach of the car that screeched to a stop within inches behind her, nearly shaving the jeans off her butt.

"Britt!"

She whirled around. Raley had pulled the car between her and the two men. Seeing the pistol aimed at them through the open driver's window, they skidded to a stop. *"Back up or you're dead!"* Raley shouted. They started yelling at him, but he was gunning the motor of the sedan to a roar while keeping his foot on the brake.

Britt scrambled into the passenger seat. Before she had even closed the door, Raley lifted his foot from the brake pedal and the car shot forward like a racehorse bounding out of the gate. He bumped over the curb and sped across the opposing lanes. Her teeth slammed together when he hit the median at about eighty miles an hour, then they were speeding away in the outside lane, their rear end fishtailing for several yards before Raley could bring the car under full control.

She glanced back. The men were running across the parking lot toward their now disabled car. Butch had been caught with his pants down. She got a fleeting glimpse of boxer shorts and well-toned legs before Raley took a sharp right turn that put the Holiday Inn out of sight. He turned left at the next opportunity, then another right.

He was cussing a blue streak.

Adrenaline pumped through her. His erratic driving was pitching her from one side of the seat to the other. She managed to fasten her seat belt, saying, "You can slow down. They can't come after us. Even if they try, their tires will go flat before they can catch us." She opened her fist. Her fingernails had gouged four half-moons out of her palm, but on it lay the four valve caps.

"What in the *hell* were you *thinking*?"

"I was thinking of slowing them down, preventing them from coming after us."

"They didn't know we were there! You could have got shot!"

"But I didn't!"

"Shit!" He hit the steering wheel hard.

In his present mood, arguing was futile, so she said nothing more.

For anyone who may have wanted to follow them, it would have been hopeless. Even she had lost all sense of direction by the time they crossed the Ravenel Bridge. A few miles later, they arrived at the RV park.

Raley wheeled their car behind the cabin, got out, and stormed toward the door, but he held it open for her, keeping an angry bead on her as she walked toward him. Once she had cleared the door, he slammed it shut behind her and bolted it.

Coming around, he bore down on her. "That was a dumb, reckless stunt, Britt."

"It'll slow them down."

"Granted."

"So it wasn't dumb at all, was it?"

"It wasn't worth the risk."

"I think it was. Anyway, it felt good to get back at them."

"Felt good? They could have killed you!"

He looked ready to do that himself. A vein in his forehead was pulsing. His hands were clenched at his sides. In her defense, she said, "I needed to do something for myself, Raley. I feel dependent and useless, and I hate that. I needed to *act.* I'm tired of relying on—"

"Me?"

"Yes! On anybody. I'm not used to it. I've always taken care of myself."

"Then be my guest." He unlocked the door and yanked it open.

She stared into the rectangle of darkness, broken only by the flashing red neon arrow with *Vacancy* spelled out along its shaft that hovered above the park's office. He'd called her bluff, and now she felt rather foolish. If she left, where would she go and how would she get there? She was without resources.

Her gaze moved from the flickering sign back to Raley's face. His lips were white with anger. They barely moved when he said, "Already one woman died on account of me. I'd rather avoid that happening again."

"You should have thought of that before kidnapping me."

With an expletive, he slammed the door closed, bolted it, then plowed his fingers through his hair.

"That's right," she said, "don't forget that it was you who dragged me into this mess."

He lowered his hands from his head. Looking at her hard, he said in a soft, measured tone, "Wrong. You got into this mess by falling for Jay Burgess's charm."

She held his stare for several beats, then strode past him and snatched up the plastic bag that contained the clothes he'd bought her. Which was particularly galling at the moment. She carried the package with her into the bathroom and closed the door, making sure he heard the click of the lock.

When she came out ten minutes later, showered and shampooed, he was sitting on the end of his bed, staring into the TV. The sound was muted. He looked up at her. "Finished?"

She gave him an aloof nod.

He got up and, taking his things with him, went into the bathroom and closed the door. She lay down on her bed and tried to get interested in the soundless sitcom rerun, but after a few minutes got up and turned off the set, then moved restlessly around the cabin.

They had so little with them, there was nothing to tidy up, nothing to read except for the out-of-date telephone directory, a dusty copy of the Gideon Bible, and Raley's files, and she had reviewed them so many times she had practically memorized the material. There was nothing to do except wait for morning, when they would drive to Columbia and Raley would accuse the attorney general of being a felon. And then what?

Less than a week ago, she'd had a great job, celebrity status, the respect of her peers, friends she could count on. Now she was a journalist whose credibility would forever be in doubt. She was the target of powerful men who would murder their own friend to keep their criminal secret intact. And she was a fugitive who, when caught, would face an indictment for murder. What could the future possibly hold for her? If she survived to have a future at all.

The bathroom door opened and Raley stepped out. His hair was still wet. He had on cargo shorts, no shirt. He dropped his dirty clothes and the duffel bag on the floor beside his bed. He ran his hand around the back of his neck, then propping his hands on his hips, he looked up at the ceiling and mouthed something that could have been either a curse or a prayer.

Only then did he look at her, and when their eyes connected it was with an impact that stole her breath. He reached her in two strides. Before another heartbeat, she was being crushed against him and his mouth was on hers.

Their kiss was long and lusty and left her wanting more.

When his lips skated down her neck, she threaded her fingers through his hair. "I thought you didn't like me."

"Not much, no." He breathed the words against her lips before claiming them again.

His body was hard, his skin still damp and warm from his shower. When he spread his hand over her bottom and fit her against his lower body, she made a small, yearning sound. "Raley, about Jay—"

"Never mind."

"It was a fling. Nothing more. A long time ago."

"Okay."

"And that night he died, I swear I don't know what happened between us."

"I don't care anymore."

"I can't remember."

"Doesn't matter."

"It didn't feel—"

"Hush, Britt."

"But you . . ." She rubbed herself against him. "You I remember. You I felt. I still feel you."

A gravelly sound vibrated in his throat as he lifted her against him and carried her to the bed. "Take off your top." Her mind was spinning because of what his fingers were doing inside the front of her pajamas bottoms, but she could think clearly enough to do as he asked. She pulled off her tank top and tossed it aside, then folded her arms around his head as he lowered it to her breasts. His mouth was hot and possessive.

The dual sensations of his swirling tongue against her breasts and his stroking fingers deep inside her, combined with the edginess of her emotions, rapidly brought on a shattering orgasm. But the release was momentary. When she coasted down from it, he was peeling her shorts down her legs, and once she was free from them, he kissed her softly just above her pubic hair. Gently, so that she barely felt the pressure of his thumbs, he exposed her to his tongue. The touch was feather light, but it sent an electric pulse of pleasure through her, breath-stealing in its effect, and the second orgasm, or maybe just an extraordinary aftershock of the first, radiated from it.

He didn't stop until she came at least once again and was listless and breathless, begging him softly to give her a moment.

He turned onto his back, unzipped his shorts, and took them off. Seeing his erection made her smile drowsily. Reaching for him, she traced the rigid length with her fingertips, her touch as light as a whisper. He groaned and tried to move her hand aside. But she began to stroke him, and when her thumb pressed the smooth tip, his breath hissed through his teeth. "Stop, please. I don't have anything."

"I'm aware of that." She moved onto him and slowly bent her head over his lap.

He thought the sexiest sight he'd ever seen was Britt's damp hair spread loose and shiny across his stomach and thighs. But it wasn't. Even sexier was when she gathered her hair in one hand and held it back so he could watch as her lips closed around him.

He heard his first gasped expletive when her tongue found the slit. And stayed. And kept on doing what it was doing until any sounds he made were completely involuntary and incoherent.

From that point forward, he didn't know what else he said, or if he said anything, because the sensations that assailed him rendered him mindless to anything except this, this incredibly erotic experience that was all the silky wet dreams he'd ever had concentrated into one.

Sexier still was after he climaxed, when she pulled him over onto her. He lay his head on her breasts while he caught his breath and let his fever cool. It was so good, feeling her fingernails idly scratching his back, the gentle rise and fall of her breasts beneath his head, the beat of her heart against his cheek.

Finally he lifted his head and surveyed the exquisite terrain. He grazed her nipple with his lips. "They're always slightly raised."

"It's embarrassing."

"It's maddening."

"You didn't buy the right kind of brassiere."

"That depends on your point of view."

Her soft laughter turned into a whimper of pleasure when he touched her lightly with his tongue, then sucked her into his mouth. Her legs folded across his back, hugging him close. That was sexy as hell.

But the sexiest yet was when he lowered his mouth to hers. It was a lazy kiss that went on forever, a melding of their mouths, an exchange of tongues, intensely intimate, dangerously evocative.

He got hard against her belly, and he wanted to be inside her so damn bad his heart ached for it as much as his body did. He had just enough willpower to resist burying himself again in the snug, wet heat he remembered from that one time that had been way too rushed, too brief.

He had to content himself with her nakedness beneath him, and with her matching desire, which manifested itself when she gripped his ass and pulled him tightly to her, groaning something about life not being fair.

She said, "You could—"

"I could, but I wouldn't. Once inside you, I know I wouldn't."

So they had to settle for kissing, touching, and eventually spooning, his arm across her waist, their hands clasped between her breasts.

Just before drifting off, he whispered sleepily, "I may like you a little."

CHAPTER 26

"Britt?"

"Hmm?"

Raley, already up and dressed, leaned down and rubbed the curve of her hip. "Get up. Time to go."

Squinting against the cruel glare of the overhead light, she rolled onto her back and came up on her elbows. Shaking her tousled hair off her face, she yawned. "What time is it?"

The bedcovers dropped to her waist. Her breasts were within reach and looked oh-so-touchable. But he resisted. "Just after six."

"Six? It's only a two-hour drive to the capitol."

"That's right." He grinned at her bafflement. "I'll explain in the car. Come on. Haul ass."

Fifteen minutes later, as he drove away from the motor court, he noticed her yawning again. "Did I get you up too early?"

"You kept me up too late." Then, smiling shyly, she looked across at him. Their gazes held for several seconds, but neither remarked on what had transpired between them last night. None of it. Not their fight. Not their first heated embraces. But especially not . . .

No, don't even think about that. Like her sleep-flushed breasts, it was a distraction he couldn't allow himself this morning.

She said, "I'm surprised."

"At what?"

"Your bringing me along. I intended to come, but not without an argument."

"After what you did to Butch and Sundance's car last night, they'll be breathing fire this morning. I was afraid to leave you alone."

"They couldn't have followed us."

"I wasn't willing to take even the outside chance."

"You would worry about me?"

He gave her a look, and the smile she sent back was as good as a caress.

Well, almost. Not quite. Her caresses were mind-blowing.

He turned his attention back to the road and concentrated on his driving.

"How do you plan to sneak me into the capitol?" she asked. "I'll be arrested on the spot."

"I have a plan."

"Good to know. But I have one, too."

"What's that?"

"Pull in there."

"Wal-Mart?"

It was one of the chain's superstores, open twenty-four hours. Since the sun was barely up, there were only a few other cars in the vast parking lot. He wondered what this was about but did as she asked.

She opened the glove box and rifled through the contents: the paperwork he'd got when he bought the car, the owner's manual, a folded state map, a card about air bag safety. She ripped a blank page from the back of the manual. "Do you have something to write with?"

He didn't, but a former owner had left behind a ballpoint pen. It was almost dry, and the tip had lint on it, but it was usable enough for her to scratch several words onto the paper. Passing it to him, she said, "Your shopping list. If they don't have that particular brand in stock, it's okay to buy another so long as it has the same features. I'll reimburse you, of course."

He read what she'd written, then nodded his understanding. "Keep your head down. I won't be long."

In less than ten minutes he returned with a package tucked under his arm and carryout cups of coffee in both hands. Once they were under way again, she placed her coffee in the cup holder and began unpacking the shopping bag. Raley watched out of the corner of his eye as she tore into the box containing the camcorder.

"Do you know how to use it?"

"Do I know how to use it," she muttered with scorn. Then she told him about the smaller stations where she'd got on-the-job training in every aspect of broadcast news. Some of the work had been menial.

When she finished, he said teasingly, "If this TV thing doesn't work out for you, you can always go back to sweeping floors."

"Ha-ha." She plugged an adapter cord into the car's cigarette lighter so the camcorder battery could charge. She adjusted the small video screen that served as a viewfinder, fiddled with the zoom, and tested the built-in microphone. "I've operated cameras more sophisticated. This one is a no-brainer. I'm no Spielberg, you understand, but I'll get an image and audio. Besides, I've got hours to practice."

"You've got less than two," he said.

"But the appointment isn't until eleven."

"That's when the appointment is, but that's not when we're meeting with the attorney general."

"How did you know where he lives?" Britt asked when Raley pointed out the stately, red-brick Colonial. They cruised past it slowly, then continued down the street and turned at the next corner.

"After he was elected, I followed him home from the capitol one day."

"To confront him?"

"No, just to seethe. I had a lot of time on my hands, nothing else to do but stoke my bitterness. His career had soared at my expense. At Suzi Monroe's expense. I resolved to set things right one day."

"And today is that day."

"Not a day too soon, either." He parked at the curb on the next street and cut the engine, then reached across the console and caught Britt's arm before she could open the door.

He understood and respected her need to be personally involved in the solution to her problem. Her stake in this was as high as his, maybe ever higher because she stood to lose the most. She deserved a chance to remedy the wrong that had been done to her. In theory, he empathized.

But from a personal standpoint, he was afraid of something going terribly wrong and her getting hurt. "This could be ugly, Britt. You don't have to go along."

"I expect it to be ugly, and I most certainly do have to go along."

He nodded, acknowledging that she was capable of making her own decisions and had the right to do so. But knowing that didn't mitigate his fear for her safety. "This is a last resort kind of plan. We're taking a huge risk."

"Some risks are worth taking." Her quiet tone, and the way she looked at him when she said that, let him know she was referring to more than their ambushing Fordyce at home.

"Damn right." He hooked his hand behind her neck and pulled her toward him, giving her a hard, quick kiss before setting her away. He ran his thumb across her damp lower lip, then said hoarsely, "Let's go."

They followed the sidewalk around the block. It was an upscale neighborhood with its own police force and a crime watch co-op among homeowners. So as not to attract attention, they kept to a leisurely pace. A dog barked at them from behind an estate wall, and a jogger with iPod earplugs gave them an absentminded nod as he huffed past on the opposite side of the street. Other than that, they didn't draw anyone's attention.

When they reached the attorney general's house, they turned and started up the central walkway as though that was their morning routine. Britt had expressed some misgivings when Raley outlined his plan to her.

"He may have security guards," she'd said.

"He may. If so, we'll create a ruckus. Media would get on it. Even if we're dragged away in shackles, he'll eventually have to address why we came knocking."

"He could refuse to give us an audience."

"I doubt it. Not after what Candy told him. She hinted that I was at my wit's end and likely to do something crazy. I'm betting he doesn't want a public spectacle and would much rather meet me in private."

"But not quite *this* private."

"No. We'll definitely be an unwelcome surprise," he'd said.

Now, Britt remarked, "One less worry. I don't see any guards."

In fact, the house and property had an aspect of serenity. Automatic sprinklers had left the lawn looking dewy and fresh. The front porch, running the width of the house, had four fluted columns supporting the second-floor balcony. Large urns containing Boston ferns framed the double front door, which was painted high-gloss black.

Reaching it without being challenged, Raley looked at Britt. "Ready?"

"Get to the good stuff soon. This battery isn't fully charged."

She aimed the camera's lens at the door. Raley rapped the polished brass knocker three times. While waiting for it to be answered, he braced himself. For what, he didn't know. He tried mentally and physically to prepare himself for anything. An attacking Doberman? A formidable housekeeper? A child in Lightning McQueen jammies?

Surprisingly, the door was opened by Cobb Fordyce himself. He was dressed in suit trousers, shirt, and tie but wasn't wearing his jacket. He was holding a linen napkin. Apparently they'd caught him having breakfast.

Britt started recording.

He reacted as though the camcorder was an Uzi, staggering backward several steps. "What's this?"

"Good morning, Mr. Fordyce," Britt said. "It's been a while."

Identifying her as the newswoman cum fugitive, his eyes went wide. Then his gaze swung to Raley, and again he asked, "What is this?"

"This is the day you've been dreading for five years. We've come to talk to you about Cleveland Jones. Remember him?" Raley held up his files, which he'd brought with him. "If your memory needs refreshing, it's all in here."

The AG's eyes skittered beyond them, and he looked relieved to see that they were unaccompanied. Coming back to Raley, he said, "Cleveland Jones. Of course I remember. He was the man who started the fire at the police station."

"You're sticking to that story, then?" Britt asked.

Irritably, Fordyce raised his hand as though about to cover the lens of the camera with the napkin, then thought better of it and lowered his hand back to his side. "He set it just before he died of head wounds."

"Ms. Shelley and I think otherwise," Raley said. "And you *know* otherwise. So did Pat Wickham, Senior. So did Jay Burgess. That's why they're dead."

Fordyce's eyes shifted over to Britt. "She's charged with Burgess's murder."

"So arrest her," Raley said. "We'll wait while you read her her rights, and then when the police get here to take her into custody, they may be interested to hear what you were doing at the police station the very day it became a tinderbox and seven people died.

"Oh, and we'll gladly surrender this video recording so they can see for themselves the nervous perspiration that broke out on your lying face at the mention of that incident. Good morning, Mrs. Fordyce. Forgive the intrusion."

The attorney general spun around to

find that his wife had come to see who had interrupted their breakfast. Raley recognized her from Jay's funeral. She was a pretty, ladylike woman. Even at this early morning hour, she was in full makeup, dressed casually but well. She had a small purse hanging from her shoulder and a set of car keys in her hand.

Apprehensively she regarded the trio at her front door. "Cobb? Is everything okay?"

"Sure. Fine."

"The boys are due at baseball practice. Should I—"

"Yes. Go. Take them. Everything's fine."

Apparently she never questioned her husband, even when there was a fugitive from justice on her threshold. There was only the slightest hesitation before she turned and went back to the part of the house from which she'd come.

Fordyce faced Raley and Britt again. During that brief exchange with his wife, he'd regained his composure. Being a natural politician, he was ready to compromise. "I'll talk to you, but not here.

Not now. You were supposed to be at my office at eleven. I agreed to that. As far as I'm concerned, you're trespassing."

"Good try, but no dice," Raley said. "We talk here."

"My family—"

"They're on their way to baseball practice. Even if they weren't, we don't mean any harm to your family. Where would you like to talk?"

"I won't talk to a man with a weapon." He said it without fear, levelly, firmly.

Figuring this probably wasn't a point the AG was willing to concede, Raley said, "If you agree to talk, I'll surrender the pistol."

"And no camera."

"The camera stays on," Britt said. "This recording may be the only possible means I have of exonerating myself."

Fordyce mulled that over for several seconds, then said tersely, "Fine." He turned and motioned for them to follow.

The room to which he led them off the central foyer was a well-furnished and tastefully decorated home study, more for show than for actual work, Raley guessed. Fordyce moved behind his desk and sat down. "The pistol, Mr. Gannon."

Raley pulled it from his waistband and laid it on a square end table in the corner, within his reach but out of that of the attorney general. Then he sat down in a chair facing the desk. Britt took the matching chair. He noticed her fingers adjusting the focus on the camera.

Fordyce motioned toward the files Raley held. "What is all that?"

"The findings of my and Teddy Brunner's arson investigation. They're incomplete insofar as the seven casualties are concerned. I wasn't allowed to finish my investigation into the cause of Cleveland Jones's death. Brunner settled for the PD's explanation."

Fordyce stared at the file folders still crudely held together by a thick rubber band, then looked at Raley. "Do you refute that Cleveland Jones started the fire?"

"He was dead before the fire started."

Fordyce leaned back in his desk chair and folded his hands together beneath his chin. He may have been about to pray; he may have felt the need to. "What do you base that assertion on, Mr. Gannon?"

Raley talked for the next fifteen minutes uninterrupted. He showed Fordyce the copy of Cleveland Jones's autopsy report. "It was never ascertained how he got those skull fractures, but is it reasonable that head wounds severe enough to kill him would go unnoticed by the officers who arrested him? I don't think so. I was assigned to investigate, but I got nowhere."

He explained the police department's evasiveness. "I was stonewalled at every turn. At first I thought, Okay, they've had a fire that destroyed their headquarters and everything in it. They can't help but be a little scatterbrained and unorganized. Cut them some slack. On the other hand, there was a dead man who had died while in police custody, and not from smoke or burns. So I persisted." He paused to take a breath. "Before I could get any satisfactory answers, I was invited to a party at my friend Jay's house."

Not even his politician's poker face could completely conceal Fordyce's slight grimace at the mention of that. Raley guessed that the AG needed nothing to jog his memory of the incident, but he iterated the facts anyway for the benefit of the video camera.

He ended by saying, "No one—no one but you and the investigating detectives—ever heard my claim that I'd suffered a complete memory loss due to my unwitting ingestion of a drug. I was advised by my good friend Jay to keep that aspect of the story quiet. He said it would only make things look worse for me if I breathed a word about being drugged. People would think I'd been snorting coke along with Suzi Monroe.

"But when I heard Ms. Shelley say she suspected she'd been given a date rape drug that had wiped clean her memory of the night Jay was murdered, I knew we were victims of the same cover-up. And the motive—criminal lawyers like you are sticklers for motivation, right?—the motive of the perpetrators was to keep secret the facts of what happened to Cleveland Jones and who the actual arsonist was."

"Jay was going to tell me the night he died," Britt interjected. "If he did, I can't remember it. But I'm certain it was his need to unburden his conscience that got him killed."

Looking squarely at the attorney general, Raley said, "When Suzi Monroe died, you wanted me to take the fall for it. No doubt I would have, if not for Cassandra Mellors's intervention."

Fordyce frowned sourly. "Seems she's still your champion. Does she know any of this about Cleveland Jones?"

"I shared my suspicion, yes."

Fordyce dragged his hands down his face. After a moment, he lowered his hands and, looking like a man making a last-ditch effort to save himself, said, "If this is about payback, Mr. Gannon, please keep in mind that I didn't indict you. I spared you prosecution."

"Correct. But you might just as well have branded me guilty. I lost my job. I lost five fucking years of my life because you and the others set me up with Suzi

Monroe and then saw to it that she snorted enough cocaine to kill her."

Britt nudged his knee with hers, reminding him of the camera, and his promise to keep his temper under control. Nothing would be served if this came out looking like a personal vendetta. They were seeking justice, not revenge.

Fordyce glanced at the camera, then addressed Raley. "I'll admit that it never felt right to me, that girl's death. It bothered me that she died in Jay Burgess's apartment, a *policeman's* apartment. When Candy brought you to my office, and you told me that your defense was a short-term memory loss, my suspicion was further aroused."

"Suspicion?"

"Suspicion that something was out of whack. You were as clean-cut as they come. You were engaged to be married. Not that a diamond ring prevents people from cheating, but you didn't share your friend Jay's reputation for promiscuity. You had no history of drug use, your record was spotless, you were the fire department's rising star."

He held up his index finger. “But the real snag in my mind was that you were investigating the fire, and the detectives assigned to the Suzi Monroe case were the heroes of that fire.”

“So were you.”

“Yes.”

Raley hoped the camera was capturing the remorse evident in Fordyce’s face and voice. His shoulders no longer seemed so wide, his posture not so proud. He was staring at his hands as they rested on his desk. Was he having a Pontius Pilate moment, staring at the guilty stains on his hands, which only he could see?

Raley didn’t let himself be moved by the man’s penitent demeanor. “It felt out of whack, it had a snag, but you didn’t look too hard to find out why, did you?”

“No.” Slowly, Fordyce raised his head and looked directly into the camera. “I didn’t look too hard because the case involved policemen, decorated heroes of the police force, and I was about to announce my candidacy for the office of attorney general. An AG depends on the solid support of law enforcement agencies. I didn't want to alienate peace officers statewide by suggesting that a few were involved in a cover-up and very possibly murder."

Raley realized he was holding his breath. He glanced at Britt. She still held the camcorder steady on Fordyce, but she looked over at Raley to see if he realized the significance of the startling, self-indicting statement they'd just recorded.

She seized on it, asking, "What happened in the interrogation room with Cleveland Jones?"

Her voice, her demeanor, were gentle, nonthreatening, nonjudgmental, suggesting that she and the AG were the only ones present and that she had an earnest and unselfish interest in his cathartic admission.

So it came as a mild surprise to Raley when Fordyce said, "I don't know, Britt." He addressed her through the camera lens. "I shirked my duty on the Suzi Monroe matter because it was expedient. It was a self-serving evasion of responsibility that cost Mr. Gannon here dearly. I'm sorry for that. If I could, I would give him back those years of disgrace he's unjustly suffered, but I can't.

"But I don't know what happened in that interrogation room. Or how Cleveland Jones died, or who started the fire." When he saw that Raley was about to speak, he held up his hand, forestalling him. "You don't have to take my word for it. It's fact. You can check it out."

"Tell us," Britt said.

"I left my office in the courthouse a little before six o'clock, bound for the police station."

"Why were you going to the police station that late in the day?"

"To pick up some new evidence on a case that was coming up for trial. I was to meet the investigating officer at the reception desk. I was just about to enter the building when the fire alarm sounded. I rushed inside. There are survivors, people who were in the lobby at the time, who can support this.

"At first, we thought it was a false alarm. In that old building, something was always malfunctioning. Several people cracked jokes about it. Someone asked if it was a fire drill."

He paused, staring into space, as though re-creating that scene in his mind. "But almost immediately we smelled smoke and realized it was the real thing. I hustled people out through the main entrance and then ran along the corridors on the ground floor, shouting at people in the various offices to exit as quickly as possible." He paused again, shrugged. "You know the rest."

Britt said, "You're being modest. You went up the stairwell and began escorting people out from upper floors."

He nodded.

"So you truly were a hero," she said.

"That day, I did the right thing." Looking at Raley, he added, "It was later that I didn't."

Raley thought he must be the best liar in the history of the art, or he was telling the truth. "You've got witnesses who can testify that, when you walked into the police station, the alarm was already sounding?"

"Yes. Even police personnel who were at the reception desk that day."

"Had you been there earlier?"

"Earlier that day, you mean? No. That, too, can be substantiated. Even the district attorney has to sign in at the reception desk."

"The register was destroyed in the fire."

"I wasn't there earlier, Mr. Gannon. I didn't even leave my office for lunch, and my secretary can attest to that. It became a memorable day, so even minor details took on relevance."

"You never questioned Cleveland Jones?"

"No. I swear it. I didn't even know what he looked like until his picture, his mug shot, was published in the newspaper days following the fire."

Britt said, "We've heard from a reliable source that Pat Wickham, Senior, called you, asking that you go over there and threaten to throw the book at Jones if he didn't confess to assault."

Pat Jr. wasn't exactly what Raley would call a "reliable source," but Fordyce seemed to believe her.

He said, "Pat Wickham did call me. Earlier that afternoon. He said he had a skinhead in custody. A career criminal and general lowlife that they'd wanted to put away for a long time. But Cleveland Jones knew how to work the system, he said. He was dicking them around, and I quote. He said there was to be no plea bargain this time, that they had a chance to nail Cleveland Jones, but good.

"He asked me to provide some additional pressure that might result in a confession, which would save the state the cost of a trial. He wanted me to go over there, talk to Jones, lay it on thick how bleak his future looked. But I was busy and I couldn't get away right then. I told him I'd look in when I came over later in the day on the other errand."

He closed his eyes for a moment, as though searching his memory. "I remember wondering why he was obsessed with this assault charge. That's bad, but it wasn't like Jones was accused of battery rape, multiple murder, or child molestation." He leaned across his desk toward Raley. "What am I missing? Tell me."

"I don't have any proof."

"I haven't asked for any. What do you speculate happened?"

"I don't know who actually made the arrest," Raley told him. "That's one of the details nobody was willing to share. What our source has told us is that Pat Senior, George McGowan, and Jay Burgess were looking for Jones and were determined to see that he got hard time. Given that, I assume one or any combination of the three picked him up. Either during the arrest or, more likely, in the course of questioning him, they got rough, and it resulted in the skull fractures that proved fatal."

"You're saying they beat him to death?"

"Probably his death was an accident. But he died, and they panicked. They had to do something to cover the crime."

Fordyce frowned. "Fires are unreliable covers for murders. Those three would know that. Forensics would show that Jones didn't die of fire-related causes."

"True. What I suspect is that they set the contents of the wastebasket on fire in order to convince everyone that Jones went crazy in that room. They thought it would back up their lie of how irrationally he'd started behaving. They planned to put the fire out quickly. Create a little smoke, but nothing more. It would have served its purpose without too much harm being done.

"What they didn't count on was their small fire getting sucked into the antiquated ventilation system and spreading rapidly through the infrastructure. Before they knew it, the blaze was burning out of control, engulfing the stories above them, causing the building to collapse on itself."

"Realizing what they'd done, they saved those they could," Britt said softly.

"But there were still seven bodies to dig out of the rubble," Raley added.

"Jesus." Fordyce rubbed his forehead as though it had begun to ache. When at last he lowered his hand and looked at them, he said, "Three senior detectives questioning one skinhead punk? Why was that?"

"Turn off the camera." Raley knew

they had to tell Fordyce about Pat Jr., but he wanted to protect his confidence, too. Britt, knowing why he didn't want this part of their interview recorded, did as he asked.

"Pat Wickham's son is gay," he told Fordyce. "Jones had assaulted him in Hampton Park, broke his leg, busted his face. He sustained bad, disfiguring, permanent damage. Pat Senior wanted to give Jones some of his own medicine, and he got his buddies to help him."

Fordyce divided a look between them, then stood up and moved to the window that afforded him a view of his swimming pool. He gazed out onto the pool for several moments, then turned back to face them. "That's the piece that was missing. Now that I have it, it makes sense. They had two secrets to protect."

"There's more," Britt said, switching the camera back on. "We don't believe Pat Senior died in the line of duty." She related what Pat Jr. had told them about his father's steep decline after the fire. "He went downhill even further after

Suzi Monroe's death and his part in that cover-up."

Fordyce said, "He cracked under the burden of his guilt."

"A breakdown seemed imminent to those close to him," Britt said. "Apparently Jay and George McGowan were afraid that he would confess and then they would all topple. Raley and I suspect his slaying wasn't a random crime. Jay was diagnosed with a terminal illness. He wanted to clear his conscience before he died."

"So McGowan had to dispose of him, too," Fordyce said thoughtfully.

She raised her shoulder and gave him a significant look, letting him draw the logical conclusion. Then he looked at Raley, who said, "McGowan is the only one left breathing."

"No wonder he's been dodging my calls." The AG sighed heavily, then asked, "Do you have any proof whatsoever of what you're alleging?"

Britt answered. "No. But McGowan must be afraid that I do. My car is at the bottom of the Combahee River." She told him about that horrifying experience. "I would be down there with it if Raley hadn't been behind me. He saw my car disappear."

Fordyce turned to him. "You rescued her?"

"I got lucky. Another minute, she would have drowned."

"Well, that explains your 'disappearance,' " the AG said to Britt. "You were safe so long as you were believed dead."

"I was afraid I wouldn't live long if I came forward."

Raley assessed Fordyce. He appeared to believe them, but he was a careful man, whose courtroom win-loss record was impressive, partly because he never took anything at face value but filtered everything through the innate skepticism of a good trial lawyer.

"I hope you realize the seriousness of these allegations," Fordyce said. "By process of elimination, you're suggesting that George McGowan is an arsonist and murderer. And that he also made this attempt on Britt's life."

"We're alleging that he conspired in

all those crimes," Raley said. "Until just a few minutes ago, we thought you two were probably in cahoots."

Fordyce glanced at the pistol still lying on the table amid framed family photos and smiled grimly. "That explains why you came here armed."

"I think McGowan hired two men to take care of Jay and Britt," Raley said. "Not musclemen, not thuggish, but blend-in types. They searched my home and truck two days ago. Britt recognized one of them from The Wheelhouse, where she met Jay. The same two were at his funeral. They followed me from there, but I eluded them. We ran into them again last night but managed to get away." He didn't give the details of that encounter and was glad Fordyce didn't ask. "We're guessing they're the two who forced Britt's car off the road, although she can't swear to it." He paused, then said, "That more or less brings you up to date. That's where we are."

Neither said anything more, giving Fordyce time to assimilate everything they'd told him, which was a lot. During the silence, Britt switched off the camera, which was signaling her that the battery was failing anyway. It was fortunate that it had lasted this long.

Finally, Fordyce gave a slight nod of his head, as though having reached a decision. "At the very least, what you allege about Cleveland Jones and the fire demands reinvestigation. A full reinvestigation, and I want you to lead it, Mr. Gannon."

Taken aback, Raley said, "Thank you." But he wasn't going to let Fordyce off the hook just because he'd thrown him this bone. "And the Suzi Monroe matter?"

"Will also be reinvestigated. You have my word." He pointed toward the camcorder. "You have my admission that I was negligent the first time around. I intend to own up to that."

Raley gave him a curt nod.

Fordyce looked at Britt. "You're still charged with Jay Burgess's murder. I'm afraid I can't spare you the ordeal of answering to that charge, although, honestly, I thought it was preposterous. After I've had a chance to talk to the detectives investigating the case, I'm sure the accusation will be dropped. Without delay, I'll have George McGowan brought in for questioning. And I want these men who've been following you found and identified. I don't suppose you have names."

"Only a license plate number," Britt said.

Fordyce passed her a Post-it pad and pen. She wrote down the make of the maroon sedan and its license number, along with the location of the Holiday Inn. After having been seen there last night, it was unlikely the pair would remain at that location, but it would be a good place to begin the manhunt.

"Once they're brought in, separated, and questioned, I'll bet we can get one or both of them to give up McGowan," Fordyce said.

Raley doubted those two would be that easy to crack. But he kept that opinion to himself.

"Are you going to arrest me?" Britt asked.

Fordyce regarded her for several seconds, then smiled wryly. "I never dreaded seeing you in the press corps. You've always been tough but fair, and usually favorable in your reporting of me and the job I'm doing for the state. I've never doubted your integrity, Britt. So, I'm going to place you in protective custody rather than under arrest."

"I appreciate that."

Fordyce looked at Raley. "Both of you are extremely vulnerable. I'm sure you're aware of that," he said, again glancing at the pistol on the table. "You're key to making these felony cases against McGowan. If he would kill his own friends to keep them quiet, he won't hesitate to dispense with you. You'll need protection."

"For how long?" Raley didn't like the idea of being under guard, but he saw the necessity of protecting Britt.

"At least until George McGowan and the two men following you are in custody."

"We only know of two," Britt said. "Who's to say there aren't more? McGowan has a lot of money."

"I'll do everything within my power to protect you," Fordyce told her. To Raley he said, "Actually, Mr. Gannon, you were wrong when you said that this was the day I'd been dreading for five years. I've often wondered—daily in fact—if I would have been elected if not for the notoriety I gained from that fire. It's an uncertainty that's haunted me since I took office. I actually welcome this opportunity to prove, if only to myself, that I won on merit, not because of instant fame."

Then, shaking off the reflective thought, he said, "If you'll excuse me, I'll make some calls and get things rolling."

Britt and Raley stepped into the foyer, where she wrapped her arms around Raley's waist, hugging him quickly but tightly. "This is the best we could have hoped for!" she exclaimed with a soft gasp. "We have a powerful ally in our corner now."

"Yeah, but I hate being placed under lock and key."

"He doesn't want anything happening to you. Surely you can see the rationale. Believe me, I'd rather be out there covering the story as it unfolds. But more than that, I want to live. I want *you* to live."

"I feel the same. But I'd like to be there when McGowan realizes the jig is up. I know this isn't about getting revenge, but that would be a sweet moment for me."

"You'll have your moment."

Shortly after, Fordyce rejoined them. "A capitol security guard will be here momentarily and drive you . . . Wait. How'd you get here? I don't remember seeing a car."

"We left it on the next block."

"The men following you have marked it?"

"Yes, but I've switched the license plate a couple of times."

The AG smiled. "Even so, it's probably best to leave it there for the time being. The guard will drive you to the Marriott. It's nothing fancy, but you'll be comfortable."

Britt laughed. "Compared to the places where we've been hiding out, the Marriott will seem like a palace."

Fordyce tilted his head and divided a curious look between them. "One thing you didn't explain. How was it the two of you got together on this?"

"Uh, Raley . . . contacted me."

"I saw her press conference and was struck by the similarities of our experiences."

In stops and starts, omitting personal references, they told him that they'd joined forces and compared notes. The more they shared, the more convinced they became that Raley's hunches had been correct.

The brass knocker sounded smartly. Fordyce excused himself to answer the door. "Thank you for coming so soon," he said and moved aside to let the guard step into the foyer.

"You're welcome, sir." He proffered his badge. "I was intercepted on my way to the capitol. That's why I'm not in uniform." He glanced at Raley and Britt, giving them a nod. "Sir. Ma'am." Then back to the AG, "Is everything arranged at the hotel?"

"Yes," Fordyce replied. "They have adjoining rooms on the top floor. Stand post outside. Don't let anyone go in, not even a room service waiter that you haven't cleared first."

"I understand, sir. One of our men will also be in the lobby by the time we arrive. Another at the service entrance. More will be available if you request them."

"Excellent." Turning to Raley and Britt, Fordyce asked, "Can you provide descriptions of the two men who've been following you?"

"Yes," Raley said. "Fairly accurate ones, I think."

"Good. I'll send a police sketch artist over to the hotel right away." He shook hands with them in turn. "If you need anything, anything, call my office. If I'm not available, my secretary will accommodate you."

"We'd like to be kept informed of what's going on," Raley said.

"I'll give you periodic reports." He reached for Raley's hand and shook it a second time. "I wish that saying 'I'm sorry' was sufficient. I realize it's not."

"Make it up to me by getting George McGowan."

"You can count on it."

He motioned them toward the door where the guard was waiting. As they drew even with the foyer table, on which stood a large Chinese vase of fresh flowers, Britt grabbed the neck of the vase and swung it with all her strength at the guard's head.

With a sharp exclamation of pain, he reeled backward.

There was an explosion of china, flowers, and water when the vase shattered on the marble floor.

She yelled, *"Run!"*

Raley was stunned by what she'd done, but he trusted her. Without hesitation, he bolted after her through the open front door. She leaped off the porch, hurdling a flower bed, and struck out running full tilt across the grass, her sneakers slipping on the dew. She almost went down, but he grabbed her elbow and propelled her along the sidewalk.

He risked glancing back as they rounded the corner. Neither Fordyce nor the guard was coming after them. Possibly the guard was lying unconscious on Cobb Fordyce's floor. "The guard—"

"Was in Jay's town house that night," Britt panted, never breaking stride. "I recognized him instantly. I remember, Raley! I remember!"

CHAPTER 27

Raley drove as fast as he dared, wanting to put distance between them and the city of Columbia. He avoided main highways and kept to back roads that he'd come to know well during his exile.

He kept one eye on the rearview mirror, but if anyone was in pursuit, he hadn't spotted them. They weren't being chased by a convoy of squad cars running hot, but then he hadn't expected Fordyce to send police cars after them. More like innocuous sedans. A private posse.

"I believed that smooth-talking son of a bitch," he said angrily as they blew through a sleepy town with only a caution light at its main intersection.

"So did I," Britt said, "and I can usually detect when someone's trying to bamboozle me."

"Lying bastard."

"He seemed so contrite when he apologized to you."

"I'm sure he couldn't believe his good luck. His goons have been chasing us all over kingdom come, trying to kill us, and we showed up at his house! That so-called guard was probably lying in wait somewhere near the capitol, waiting for us to arrive at eleven o'clock. We would never have made it into the building."

"You were smart to deviate from that plan."

"But not smart enough to see through Fordyce's bullshit. Marriott, my ass," he snarled. "While we were standing in the hallway, grateful that we had an ally and protection, he was calling his hired hand, alerting him to a sudden change of plan."

"I may have killed him," she said shakily.

"I don't think so, but . . ." He gave her a glance. "But it might not be a bad idea for you to go to the police and turn yourself in. We have the videotape. We have Fordyce saying—"

"Nothing, Raley. Nothing substantive. The tape is useless. Fordyce played straight to the camera. On this video, our earnest attorney general was full of remorse and apology. We have contrition, but in no way, shape, or form did he incriminate himself in the matter of the fire, Suzi Monroe, or anything else."

Realizing she was right, he cursed.

"He knew exactly what he was doing," she said, "and we fell for his manipulation."

It infuriated Raley to realize how easily they'd been duped. "If we went to the police now, making accusations, Fordyce would say that we barged into his home, armed— Aw, *fuck*! I left the pistol on that table."

He berated himself for that oversight, but there was nothing he could do about it now. Besides, he doubted that he could ever actually shoot someone. But none of his enemies knew that, and he missed the false sense of security that came with having a loaded piece.

"Fordyce would say we told him a story that deserved further discussion, at the very least. But then when he summoned a guard to protect us until he could check into it, you—unprovoked—clouted the man with a vase."

"I can't prove that the guard killed Jay," she said. "But I know he was there."

"Do you remember seeing him at The Wheelhouse?"

"No. But I'm positive he was at Jay's town house, and that he had a partner."

"Butch? Sundance?"

"Neither. Another man."

"So we've got Butch and Sundance, the guy who came to Fordyce's rescue, and another we haven't seen yet. Four total, working in two pairs."

"I suppose," she said. "I'll be able to identify the fourth man when I see him again, because now I have a vivid mental image of him, bending over me—"

When she stopped abruptly, Raley snapped his head toward her. "A mental image of him bending over you . . . *What?* Did he rape you?"

"No, just . . ." She shuddered, took a

moment, then plugged the camcorder into the cigarette lighter again. "In case something happens to me, to us, this should be recorded."

It was a sobering thought, but Raley agreed with a nod.

She began. "Jay and I went into his apartment. I sat down on his sofa, where he joined me. He offered me scotch, but I told him that I wasn't feeling well, that the wine had hit me hard. He said he was feeling the effects of his drinks, too, and blamed his medications. We were more or less sprawled there, side by side, our heads back.

"He took my hand and told me again that he had a story that was going to blow a huge hole through the PD and city hall. I remember asking him to let me get my notepad out of my purse before he began, but I lacked the wherewithal to do it.

"He said, 'You won't need notes, you'll remember this.' I didn't argue. Actually, I was too far gone to care about accuracy, about anything. Jay took off my sandals, put my feet in his lap, and began massaging them. He asked if I was comfy because it was going to be a long story.

"I told him I was almost too comfy, that I could barely keep my eyes open. He laughed and said, 'Then how 'bout one last roll in the sack for old times' sake?' I said no thank you. He said, 'Ah well, I'm so drunk I don't think I can get it up anyway.' And I said, 'That's a first, isn't it?'

"We were still laughing over that when the two men walked in. The one we saw today, and another. They came in by way of the back terrace. One minute they weren't there. The next they were, as though they had materialized through the French doors.

"My first thought was to wonder why in the world they were wearing gloves on such a warm night. Then I noticed they were latex gloves, but that didn't particularly alarm me. I don't remember being afraid. Instead, I remember being *un*afraid. I felt euphoric, indifferent.

"But Jay was sober enough to be concerned. He stood up and confronted them. 'Who are you? What do you want?' The one who came to Fordyce's house said, 'We're here to party,' and pushed Jay back down onto the sofa.

"They ordered him to pour each of us a glass of scotch. They forced us to drink it. Then another. I remember feeling terribly sick. They didn't give me any more, but they made Jay continue drinking until most of the bottle was empty."

She stopped talking. Raley looked over at her; her eyes were closed. He reached out and took her hand. "Save the rest for the authorities. You don't have to tell me any more."

"Yes, I do." Giving him a wan smile, she held up the camcorder, reminding him that the whole story needed to be recorded. "Since that night, I have imagined horrible things that could have been done to me. I'm relieved to remember. It was bad, but it could have been much, much worse.

"They made us undress, first Jay and then me. They had to help both of us. Neither of us could stand on our own. I lost minutes of time I'll probably never get back, because I don't actually remember getting from the living room to the bedroom, but I remember lying naked on the bed.

"Then one of them—not the one who came to Fordyce's house, the other one—fondled me. Between my legs. It wasn't even sexual, it was . . . like the most demeaning insult. He leered down at me, saying directly into my face, 'It's a shame having to waste this nice—' "

She stopped, unable to go on. Raley squeezed her hand. He thought he might be able to shoot somebody after all. If he ever got a chance with either one of these creeps, he could kill them. Easy.

Britt looked away from him, out the passenger window, speaking softly. "His friend laughed all the time he was doing it. That's probably why I recognized him instantly. I remembered his grin, his obscene laugh. I don't know how I kept from crying out when he stepped through Fordyce's front door. I guess because I knew we had to get out of there. I realized if we didn't, we'd soon be dead. But if I didn't kill him with that vase, I hope I hurt him very bad. Anyway, back to that night, his partner told him he couldn't be a Romeo. 'One smear of spunk other that this guy's and the plan is blown.' "

"They knew better than to leave DNA evidence."

"That's probably what saved me from being raped. It certainly wasn't a matter of conscience."

"Was Fordyce mentioned by name? Or George McGowan?"

"No. I'm almost positive. These pros would know to be careful about that, too."

"What about Jay? What was he doing all this time?"

"He was lying on his back beside me. He didn't put up a struggle. I think he may already have been unconscious because of all the alcohol he'd consumed." She sighed and looked over at Raley. "The next thing I remember is waking up the following morning, thinking I had the worst hangover in history, but with no memory of any of this until Fordyce opened his front door to that sadistic bastard."

"Earlier you told me that, when you

woke up, Jay was turned away from you."

"I suppose after I passed out, they held the pillow over his face and then set the stage to make it look like a drunken lovers' quarrel that ended in murder." She stopped recording and turned off the camera but left it plugged in to keep the battery charging.

Raley wanted to go back and mop the marble floor with both Britt's attacker and Fordyce, but that would be a personally motivated, vengeful, and stupid action. Instead he had to focus on what they must do next. How could he bring Fordyce's treachery to the public's attention before Fordyce could have them eliminated? They were driving a marked car. They only had several minutes' head start.

And Fordyce had facilitators on retainer who responded to his summons at a moment's notice. There were at least four of them. They acted swiftly and lethally, then faded into the woodwork. They'd had less than one day to orchestrate Jay's execution, yet they'd carried out the plan perfectly.

This morning, if Britt hadn't recognized the man and acted swiftly, they would already be dead. By one means or another, they would have been expediently sanctioned. Fordyce could invent any story about how they came to be dead and he would be believed. He could say they'd attacked him, and he'd had no choice but to kill them in self-defense. Or that they had threatened him, and when he tried to defend himself, they fled, never to be seen again.

Whatever story he contrived, it would be believed. Their conversations with Candy and Pat Wickham, Jr., would substantiate that they were aggressively seeking revenge on those who, they believed, had wronged them. It would be surmised that their paranoia had made them dangerously delusional, so that, by the time they barged into the AG's home, they had lost all reason.

If they died or simply disappeared, Lewis Jones might smell a rat and create some noise, raise some questions. So might Delno Pickens. But who would listen to either of them, the neo-Nazi father of a reprobate and arsonist, and an unwashed old hermit who lived in the swamp?

With him and Britt out of the picture, the police station fire and all those deaths that came after it would remain in the history books as recorded. No one would ever know about the colossal miscarriage of justice being perpetuated as long as George McGowan and Cobb Fordyce were leading their lives with impunity.

Raley couldn't tolerate even the thought of that. He gripped the steering wheel and reminded himself that he wasn't dead yet. He might not survive, but as he and Britt sped along the narrow, two-lane road, he resolved that he would fight to his last breath to set things right.

Without the pistol, their only weapon was the video recording. As she had pointed out, it was hardly a signed confession. But it was all they had, so they had to make the most of it.

"Can you make a copy of that video?" he asked.

"I'd need two machines, and videotape only duplicates at real time. I don't have access to the machines and—"

"We don't have the time." But he'd begun to formulate an idea. "Actually, just the threat of the video might be enough."

"Enough to do what?"

"To get George McGowan to spill his guts." He glanced at her, saw that she was listening closely. "On the video, Fordyce doesn't implicate himself, but he doesn't refute my allegation that the three detectives were guilty. He even went so far as to venture that George had disposed of Jay. I don't think George will take too kindly to that."

"He won't want to take the fall all by his lonesome," she said. "He'll want to set the record straight."

"If I can coax something out of McGowan that would incriminate them both, then the video of Fordyce would be useful after all. We'd have caught him lying and trying to transfer blame." He motioned toward the camcorder. "Take out that tape and put in a fresh one. Has it been juiced up enough to run? Show me how to operate it."

"I'll do the camera work."

He shook his head. "I'll go to George. You have another chore."

She held his gaze for a moment, then said, "You want me to turn myself in."

"It's the only way you'll be safe, Britt." He outlined his plan to her. When he was finished, she asked, "What about Clark and Javier?"

"I don't trust the PD. I don't want you anywhere near police headquarters. McGowan and Fordyce have too many friends there. The tape might conveniently disappear."

"My lawyer?"

"We're not sure how trustworthy he is, but we know for certain he's got no balls."

She thought about it, then said, "All right, I'll do it. But it won't be easy. Especially today."

"If someone accosts you, you start talking fast, create a scene, draw attention to yourself if you have to do cartwheels up and down Broad Street. Produce that tape, make sure some of your media pals see it. Make yourself heard."

She smiled at him. “That I can do.”

“But can you drive my pickup?”

“Automatic shift?”

He nodded.

“Then I can drive it.”

The way their luck had been running, they were surprised to find the truck where they’d left it at the deserted airstrip. It was covered with a thick layer of dust but otherwise appeared not to have been touched.

“This spot is still our secret,” Raley remarked as he brought the sedan to a stop.

Britt unplugged the camcorder. “You’re clear on how to use it?”

“A three-year-old could do it.”

They got out of the sedan. Raley climbed behind the steering wheel of his pickup, started the engine, checked the gas gauge. “Half a tank, which should be plenty to get you into Charleston.”

She offered to take the sedan.

He shook his head adamantly. “Too dangerous. They’ll be looking for it. I only hope I can get to George before Fordyce’s heavies get to me.”

"They could be looking for the truck, too."

"They could, but it's meaner than the sedan. Harder for them to push off the road." Even though he'd said that, she read the worry in his expression as he got out of the cab, leaving the motor running.

"I'll be okay," she said.

"Are you trying to reassure me or yourself?"

"Both," she admitted. "But once I get where I'm going, I'll be safe. In handcuffs, perhaps, but safe."

He placed his hands on her shoulders and gave her a long, meaningful look. "Britt . . ."

She smiled gently and pressed her fingers vertically against his lips. "You don't have to say anything, Raley Gannon. I know you like me, and more than a little."

He pulled her against him and kissed her long and deeply, then released her and in a voice made gruff by emotion said, "Be careful. Promise me."

"I promise."

Before he could talk himself out of it, he boosted her into the cab of the pickup.

He followed her in the sedan from the airstrip to the main road, and then for several miles until their paths split. She waved to him from the driver's window. He gave her a thumbs-up, but for a full five minutes after they separated he was tempted to say *screw it* to this plan, make a quick U-turn, and go after her. He didn't want to let her out of his sight. He would much rather they stuck together no matter what.

But he kept to the plan. Each had an assignment, and both were equally crucial to success. The video recording of Fordyce empowered Britt. As long as it was in her possession, she would have a measure of protection and control. Raley was unarmed, except for the camcorder, which was nothing more than a stage prop, really. He hoped George McGowan would fall for it.

He wanted to ambush George before he had time to call the police, or his lawyer, or to prepare answers for Raley's accusations. Raley didn't want to give him time to summon Les and Miranda for backup, either. He wanted him alone and defenseless.

But, first, he had to know where to find him.

He stopped at a service station and used a pay phone to call Conway Concrete and Construction. When the receptionist answered, Raley gave her a fictitious name and told her he wanted to speak to George McGowan about a potential project. He only wanted to verify that George was in the company office and intended to hang up once it was confirmed.

Instead, the receptionist informed him that Mr. McGowan was feeling under the weather and, after having put in only a brief appearance at the office, he had gone home and was expected to stay there for the remainder of the day.

Even better, Raley thought.

He thanked the receptionist and was about to hang up when she said in a near whisper, “Actually, I think he was upset over the news about Attorney General Fordyce.”

Raley's hand was arrested in motion. Indeed, everything inside him went terribly and suddenly still with foreboding. "Attorney General Fordyce? What about him? What news?"

"Oh, you haven't heard?" Now there was an underlying excitement in her voice, the inflection of someone titillated by tragic news. "It's just *awful.* Cobb Fordyce was shot this morning in his home."

Raley's stomach dropped.

"His wife found him when she returned from an errand. She was hysterical, of course, but told the police that her husband had greeted the man and woman who shot him. They'd arrived unexpectedly, but he'd let them come inside. Mrs. Fordyce was wary, but he told her that everything was okay, for her to go ahead and drive their sons to baseball practice. She'll never get over leaving him alone with them, you can be sure of that. *And* she's almost positive that the woman was Britt Shelley. You know that reporter who's been missing? Her."

Raley squeezed his eyes shut and

leaned heavily against the telephone. "You said he was shot. Is he dead?"

"They haven't announced it officially, but he's as good as. He was shot in the head, and his condition is critical."

CHAPTER 28

Raley hung up on the talkative receptionist.

With shaking hands, he fed coins into the slots and punched in another number. He looked over his shoulder, feeling like the phone booth was a shooting gallery and there was a bull's-eye on his back.

"Hello?"

"It's me." He'd called Candy's cell phone in order to circumvent her secretary, and he intentionally didn't say his name.

"Jesus Christ," she hissed. "What have you done?"

"Nothing."

"I sent you to him. That implicates me."

"Is he dead?"

"There hasn't been an official announcement. It's touch and go. Media are camped out at the hospital awaiting word." Then, angrily, "That is, every reporter in the state except your new girlfriend. She *was* with you this morning, correct?"

"Yes, but—"

"Christ. First Jay, now—"

"She didn't smother Jay. You know I didn't shoot Fordyce in the head."

"Then how is it that he has a bullet in his brain? Why did you go to his house in the first place? Why didn't you keep the appointment I set up for you—which will mean my career and my ass if anyone finds out. Why a surprise visit to his house?"

"I wanted to catch him off guard."

She groaned. "Not a good answer, you idiot. Until you get a defense attorney, I advise you not to say that to anyone else."

"When we left him, Cobb Fordyce was alive and well. We thought he had double-crossed us."

"Another motive for shooting him."

"I didn't shoot him!"

"The police have the weapon. A Taurus .357. Will your prints be on it? Will hers?"

Raley rubbed his forehead, muttering, "Fuck me."

"In other words, yes."

"He must have used my pistol."

"He? *Who?*"

"She'll tell you. She's on her way to you."

"To me? Wha—"

"Listen! Listen to me. She doesn't even know about Fordyce unless she's heard it on the radio since we separated. I was to call and tell you to meet her where she interviewed you a few months ago. Do you know where she's talking about? She said you would."

"Yeah, okay."

"She'll be at the door where you let her in before. She's got a video."

"Of what?"

"She'll explain everything. Will you meet her?"

"Do you realize what you're asking? I have people—"

"I know this is a bad time."

"Bad? No, it's the *worst* time. Today of all days. Inconvenience and bad timing aside, you're asking me to break the law."

"She's coming to turn herself in."

"Great. I'll call the police, tell them—"

"No. No police."

"If I don't, it smacks of aiding and abetting, obstruction of justice, and—"

"I know all that, Candy. But you gotta do this, and you gotta do it this way."

"Why?"

"To save our lives." He let that settle, then said, "The man who killed Jay showed up at Fordyce's house this morning. Britt recognized him instantly." He was past worrying about using their names. "After we bolted, Fordyce was shot in the head. Now, do the math. We would have been killed, too, if we hadn't managed to escape. But we did, we can identify him, and this guy ain't gonna quit."

Subdued a bit, she said, "Who is this man? Why'd he kill Jay and shoot Fordyce? Does he have a name?"

"Not that I know."

"A description?"

"Britt will fill you in. Hopefully she won't be apprehended before she can get to you."

"She'll be half a block away from the courthouse. It's a circus down here. Reporters are camped out along Broad, waiting—"

"I know. She's taking a huge risk to get that video to you. Which should give you some idea of how vital it is."

"Why is it so important?"

"When you watch it, you'll know." A customer at one of the service station pumps was eyeing him. Probably he was just an average Joe whose Dodge Ram was running low on fuel, but Raley didn't know what the fourth hit man looked like. Until he did, he would regard every stranger as a potential assassin. "I can't talk any longer. I've got to move."

"Wait! Where are you? Why aren't you with Britt?"

If he told Candy that, he would be creating for her another impossible choice, because she would be duty-bound to dispatch police to the McGowans' estate. Sidestepping her question, he said, "Britt's on her way. For godsake, Candy, be there." He hung up before she could say anything more.

A silver Navigator was parked in the circular drive in front of George McGowan's mansion, indicating that he was at home, but Raley saw no one around. Several sleek horses grazed in a paddock about fifty yards from the house. Otherwise the place looked deserted.

Taking the camcorder with him, Raley alighted from the car and walked up to the front door. He didn't ring the bell, didn't knock, just turned the knob and, finding the door unlocked, walked in.

He closed the door soundlessly, then paused to listen. The house was as still and silent as a tomb.

He started down the central hallway, his footsteps muffled by a long, narrow Oriental carpet. He looked into the room on his left, a dining room. On his right was a formal living room with a marble fireplace and a crystal chandelier, both as tall as he was. Oil paintings in gilt frames. Heavy drapes made of shiny material. Collectibles. Rich people stuff.

Murder had been profitable for George McGowan.

Raley continued down the wide foyer on tiptoe, halting when he heard the clink of glass against glass coming from a room on his right, behind the staircase. He approached stealthily, hesitating when he reached the open doorway, then cautiously peering around the doorjamb.

George was seated behind a large desk, a bottle of bourbon in front of him. A full highball glass was in one hand, a nine-millimeter pistol in the other. He saw Raley immediately and smiled.

Waving him in with his gun hand, he said, "Come in, Raley. I've been waiting for you."

"I have every confidence that my appointment will be approved by the Senate."

Despite the upsetting call from Raley, Judge Cassandra Mellors didn't postpone her scheduled press conference. The room was crowded with reporters jockeying for the best positions, but it wasn't as well attended as it might have been.

The attempt on Cobb Fordyce's life had divided the press corps. Many reporters who would have been here covering her all-important day were instead keeping vigil outside the hospital in Columbia, awaiting word on Fordyce's condition.

"I spoke with the president just a few minutes ago," she told her audience. "He assured me that the vote taking place later today is a formality. I hope he's right." She staved off the chorus of questions. "Naturally, my excitement has been overshadowed by the tragedy that took place this morning at the home of our attorney general, a former colleague and a man I consider still to be a friend. My thoughts and prayers are with Mrs. Fordyce and the boys, as well as with the medical personnel who are valiantly trying to save Cobb Fordyce's life."

A reporter asked, "If he survives, will there be permanent brain damage?"

"The extent of the injury and its residual-effects haven't been determined. At this point the doctors are trying to keep him alive."

"Have you spoken to the detectives who are investigating the crime scene at the AG's home?"

"No. Regarding that, I have no more details than you."

"Have you spoken to Mrs. Fordyce?"

"No. Her brother is acting as spokesperson for the family. He's said that Mrs. Fordyce is at her husband's side and has requested all our prayers."

"Is it true that Britt Shelley and Raley Gannon are being sought for questioning in the shooting?"

"I have no comment on that."

"Mrs. Fordyce identified—"

She raised her hand. "That's all I have time for now."

She turned quickly and left them hurling questions at her. When she reached her office, she asked her secretary if there had been any messages. "Nothing, Judge," she said.

"No word from the hospital?"

She shook her head. "Or from Washington." Sheepishly, she added, "In spite of what happened today to Mr. Fordyce, I can't help but be excited for you."

Candy smiled. "I've got butterflies myself. Which is why I need some downtime. I'm going to the other office to rehearse my acceptance speech." That was a plausible excuse to leave, and her assistant didn't question her.

Because of all the interruptions and constant demands on Candy's time when she was in her courthouse office, she often retreated to a sanctuary where she could concentrate, focus, and sometimes rest between sessions on the bench. Only her assistant knew about it, and that was the point. No one could find her there unless she wanted to be found.

"I have my cell. Call me the moment you hear anything."

"Certainly, Judge."

She slipped out a back door, taking a familiar path through connecting alleyways that allowed her to cover half a block of Broad Street without ever having to be on the street itself, except to cross it. She emerged from an alley between two buildings and checked to see that the coast was clear. A delivery truck rumbled past, but otherwise there was a break in the traffic. A horse-drawn carriage full of tourists was turning the corner away from her. The media were still assembled in front of the courthouse, but no one was looking in her direction.

She walked swiftly across the street and ducked into an alley that bordered an abandoned office building. It was wedged between its neighbors, but unlike those buildings, it hadn't been renovated and was in a state of disrepair. It had six floors, but like many other structures in Charleston, it was only one room wide, so unless one were looking for it, the narrow building could easily go unnoticed.

It was so old and neglected that ferns sprouted from cracks in the mortar holding the ancient bricks onto the exterior walls. The judge was the single tenant and was allowed to occupy one small office only because of a favor she'd done the real estate agent who had been trying for years to unload this listing.

At the back of the building was a scratched and dented metal door. Waiting for her there was Britt Shelley, dressed in blue jeans, T-shirt, and baseball cap. She looked like a coed on her way to the ballpark to cheer on the home team, not like a woman accused of murder, fleeing both the law and a purported bad guy.

When Candy appeared, the reporter's relief was plain in her wide smile. "Thank God Raley reached you." Sounding breathless, she flattened her hand on her chest. "I was so afraid he wouldn't get through. I've come to surrender to you."

"Let's get inside first." Candy used a key to unlock the dead bolt, then hustled Britt into the musty, dim, damp interior. Reaching around her, she flipped on a light switch so they could see their way across a littered floor to the metal staircase.

Britt handled the climb better than Candy, who was panting by the time they reached the sixth-floor landing. The same key opened the office she had furnished with a desk, a couch for power naps, and a massage chair.

As soon as the door was closed behind them, she said, "Britt, have you heard the news from Columbia?"

Her dire tone didn't escape the newswoman. Apprehensively, she said, "If you talked to Raley, you know we didn't wait for our eleven o'clock appointment. We went to Fordyce's house."

"Yes, well, there's more, I'm afraid." Candy nodded toward a chair facing her desk. "You'd better sit down."

George was obviously drunk. Raley hoped he was too drunk to shoot straight. Surreptitiously he flipped the record button on the camcorder as Britt had instructed. Even if he didn't get a good picture, the audio would be there.

He stepped into the study. The first thing that captured his attention was the framed photograph of the four heroes of the fire hanging in a prominent place on the wall. If Fordyce didn't pull through, then George would be the only surviving one. The last keeper of the secret.

"Nice picture," Raley remarked.

George didn't lower the pistol aimed at Raley, but he gave the photo a glance. "Yeah. Made me a fucking hero." He gestured at the room. "Look at what all my heroism got me."

Raley walked to the chair across the desk from George and sat down. When he did, he saw the object on the desk near the bottle of whiskey. A vintage cigarette lighter with a lurid picture of a naked woman on it, a hologram. Formerly owned by Cleveland Jones, a gift from his grandfather, souvenir of a carnival.

George's eyes were bloodshot, his face florid, indicating recent and ample consumption of the bourbon. Unfortunately, however, his gun hand was rock steady. He'd been a cop. He couldn't miss at this range.

Raley said, "You're no hero, George."

The man gave a bitter laugh and quaffed the glass of bourbon, then poured himself another. "She thought so."

"She?"

"Miranda."

"Is she here?"

"She's out."

"Out where?"

"Just . . . out. Who knows? Who gives a shit?"

"I think you do, George."

Another laugh, as bitter as the first. "Yeah, well. My lovely wife. Wouldn't you agree she's lovely?"

"And then some."

George grinned as he took another sip of his fresh whiskey. "You know what it's like to have the hottest, richest girl around come on to you full throttle?"

"Must be nice." Raley was glad George was rambling drunkenly. It gave him time to think. He was wondering if he could wrest the pistol away without getting shot in the process. Had the liquor slowed George's reflexes enough for him to grab the gun before the former cop could react?

Had Britt made it safely to Candy? Was she, even now, pouring out the bizarre story of the crime George had helped orchestrate?

"Our first date," George said, "Miranda went down on me. In my car, no less. I was driving. Nearly killed us both when I came, but it was one hell of a rush."

"I can imagine."

"First time we fucked, guess what I discovered."

"She wasn't a virgin."

George laughed for real then. "That's a good one, Gannon. You have a sense of humor after all. Yeah, that was a good one. But seriously . . ." He took another slurp from his glass. "No, what I found was this itsy-bitsy gold stud in her clit. Man, you talk about a turn-on. Thought I'd died and gone to pussy heaven."

He paused to offer Raley a drink.

"No thank you."

"You sure? Kentucky's finest."

"I'll pass."

"Suit yourself. Where was I?"

"Heaven."

George belched. "Right. We hadn't dated a month before Miranda started talking marriage. Course I was all over that idea. She's hot and her old man's loaded. What's not to like, right?"

"Right."

"So down the aisle we went. Honeymooned in Tahiti. Swam naked in the surf. In fact, Miranda stayed naked most of the time. Practically wore blisters on my dick. I thought, *George, you lucky bastard, you have hit the jackpot for sure.* She had beauty, money, and a button that stayed excited twenty-four/seven on account of that little gold stud."

His eyes went vacant for several moments, then he squinted Raley back into focus. "She killed my kid, you know." Seeing Raley's shock, he said, "Yeah, you heard right. She came back from the honeymoon pregnant. I was thrilled, and for weeks strutted around here like a goddamn peacock. But I noticed she wasn't getting a tummy on her, and when I remarked on it, she started laughing and said, 'And I never will, darlin'.' She'd got rid of the baby and hadn't even bothered to tell me."

Raley felt a twinge of pity for the man, and had to remind himself of the lives George was responsible for taking.

"But my consolation prize was all the sex," George continued. "She's all about fun and games. Knows every trick in the book. Guess how she knows."

"I don't want to guess, George."

"She's been doing them for a long time, that's how. Technically, she was a virgin until she was twelve, but long before that, she and Les—"

Involuntarily Raley recoiled.

"Surprise!" George exclaimed. Then it seemed his entire face collapsed and was held on to his skull only by the loose skin. "I was sorta surprised myself, finding out that Miranda was daddy's girl in every sense of the word. That little gold charm I liked so well? He's the one who suggested it."

Raley swallowed his revulsion. "She was a child, a victim. Why didn't she tell someone?"

"Victim?" George said, scoffing. "No, Gannon, no. She liked it. She *loved* it."

"What about Mrs. Conway?"

"Probably suspected," George said with a negligent shrug. "How could she not? But one day when Miranda was about fourteen, her mother caught them in flagrante delicto. And *not* the missionary position. That night Mrs. Conway washed down a bottle of pills with a bottle of vodka and half of another. It was ruled an accidental overdose."

He finished the whiskey in his glass and poured more. "I'll bet you're wondering why I haven't left Miranda." Raley had been wondering that. He'd also been wondering if Britt had played the video for Candy yet and if police officers were being dispatched to arrest George. As disgusting as the conversation was, if he could keep him talking long enough . . .

"I've threatened to pack up and leave dozens of times, but she knew I never would. For one thing, I liked the money and the sex and the whole package that came with marrying Miranda Conway. But the big, major, number one reason I couldn't leave her was that she knew I was no hero. She knew about Cleveland Jones and how he died and how the fire started."

Raley's heart gave a little bump. "How did she know?"

"This . . ." George started laughing again. "You're going to like this, Gannon. I told her. I admitted it in what you might call a moment of weakness. Well, my brain was weak. My dick was a Louisville Slugger. See, we were playing a sex game. Leather restraints. Massage oil. Blindfold. It became kind of a truth-or-dare thing. We'd swap our deepest, darkest secrets, she said."

He leaned forward and whispered. "You ever had a candle pushed up your ass while your dick is being sucked?" He sat back and grinned drunkenly. "She wouldn't let me come until she had the whole story. Kept teasing and teasing, and, well, the truth spilled out along with my seed. To borrow an Old Testament phrase.

"Anyway, after, when she removed my blindfold, I reminded her that it was her turn, truth or dare. Then she smiled this gloating smile I'll never forget and told me who'd taught her this naughty little trick with the candle. She said, 'It's one of Daddy's favorite things we do.' "

Suddenly tears filled his eyes and ran down his bloated cheeks. "I wish she would have just castrated me then and there. Because she and Les have been sawing away at my balls every day since, stripping me of my manhood a little bit at a time. They know their secret is safe with me so long as mine is safe with them."

He considered the bourbon in his glass but pushed it away without drinking any more. Instead, he hefted the pistol in his hand as though trying to guess its weight. "I've been waiting on you, but you're earlier than I expected. I figured I would beat you to the punch, save you the trouble."

"Save me the trouble?" Raley asked.

"You know about Pat Junior, right? Being a homo?"

Raley nodded.

"Now you talk about a sorry excuse for a man," George said. "Cruel irony that all this started with that sniveling little faggot. And Cleveland Jones?" He made a sound of disgust. "He needed killing if anybody ever did. Lawless, cocky son of a bitch. Thought he was above the law. Had a real contempt for authority. Smart guy. Tough customer. You know the type.

"Pat was mortified about his son being gay and all, but this Jones character had almost killed him. Pat insisted on getting a confession out of Jones and putting him away for years, someplace he'd do hard time, where he'd be raped a coupla times a day. Punishment fitting the crime, see?

"In hindsight, we should've just popped him where we found him, let it be blamed on gangbangers. But no, we stayed within the law. To that point anyway. We hauled him to the station, then took him to a room where nobody could see in and started working him over. The four of us told him he wasn't getting out of there until he'd signed a confession, and we didn't care how long it took. In fact, we hoped it would take a nice, long time."

Raley said, "He didn't have skull fractures when you arrested him, did he?"

George wiped his wet cheeks and gave Raley a look that said the question wasn't even worth answering, but Raley had asked it mostly for the benefit of the camera.

"Who actually dealt the deathblow, George?"

More tears streamed from his bloodshot eyes. "Hard to say. Pat maybe. Jay got in a few good belts, but he wasn't that strong. Might have been me. We were taking turns. Jones was on the floor, and I think it was Jay who first noticed that he was no longer moving. Jay called the rest of us off. He felt for a pulse." George ran his arm under his nose, mopping up the mucus dripping from it with his sleeve. "Jones was dead."

He lapsed into silence, so Raley prompted him. "Then what happened?"

"What the fuck you think? We freaked, especially Pat, because we'd just killed a man, all on account of his queer son."

Raley nodded down at the lighter on the desk. "You started the fire with his lighter."

"I was the one who'd emptied his pockets when we checked him in. I kept the lighter. Don't know why. Maybe to bring home and show Miranda, thinking she'd get a kick out of it. I don't remember. Anyway I had it, and it came in handy."

"You wanted it to look like Jones had

just enough life in him to start the fire before he died."

"That was the basic plan. We were all panicking, yelling at each other, cussing, trying to sort it out. As I said, freaking out. Jay, of course, kept the coolest head. He said we'd tell everybody that we'd noticed his head wounds but thought they were superficial. That it wasn't until later, after we were pressuring him with questions, that he started acting weird and we realized he was out of his head.

"The rest of us agreed it sounded like a plan. Jay said to light the stuff in the trash can, so it would look like Jones had gone crazy. I set fire to some paper. We left the room, thinking the fire would soon burn itself out. A minute maybe. We counted on the smoke alarm going off, then rushing in and pretending to be shocked to find Jones dead. But the fire . . ." He dropped his chin on his chest, mumbling, "You know the rest."

Raley could barely contain himself. The camcorder had just recorded George's confession, although George seemed unaware of it, or indifferent to it.

Keeping his voice low, Raley asked, "Why did you keep the lighter?"

The man shook his large head mournfully. "Like when priests flog themselves? The lighter is like a whip. I take it out every now and then to remind myself of what I did."

He was quiet for a moment, and Raley counted the seconds. How long before the police would arrive? Britt would have told Candy about the night at Jay's house, the attempt on her life, the man this morning who obviously had shot Fordyce after they fled.

Fordyce.

Something niggled Raley's brain, but he didn't have time to address it before George continued.

"We were trying to act normal, waiting for the smoke alarm. But all of a sudden the fucking wall of that room was on fire, burning from the inside out. Then we really panicked. We didn't bother with Jones. We knew he was already dead. We started trying to get all the other people into the stairwell and out of the building. In all the confusion, with the smoke, nobody could see anything. No one could locate the keys to the holding cell." His chin began to tremble, and a sob shook his large body. "I can still hear those men trapped in the cell screaming."

He wiped his nose again. "It came as a shock to us that we were made out heroes," he said with a laugh that was negated by the tears rolling down his face. "We thought that, as soon as the fire was out, we'd be arrested. So you can imagine how we felt when . . . Well, you know how it was. That photo," he said, looking at the picture on the wall.

"We told ourselves there must be a reason for it turning out the way it had. A higher purpose, Jay called it. Some such bullshit," he said scornfully. "Anyhow, we made a pact. No one would have to know. No one could tell. Ever.

"We thought we'd be okay. We thought we'd get away with it. Brunner seemed satisfied with our explanation about Jones." He sighed and looked across at Raley. "But you were stubborn as hell and too fucking good. Jay tried stalling you, but on the issue of Cleveland Jones, you just wouldn't give up and let it go. You had us scared shitless."

Slowly Raley nodded. "So you devised a way to discredit me."

Britt wanted to know what the latest news from Columbia was, but the judge insisted on hearing what she had to say first.

So for the past ten minutes, Candy Mellors had listened as Britt gave her a rushed, almost breathless account of the last few days, beginning with her meeting with Jay and ending with her and Raley fleeing the attorney general's house. Knowing the constraints on the judge's time today, she had economized on words, divulging as many details as she could as concisely as possible.

She finished by saying, "Raley and I got the hell out of there."

Candy sat back and took a deep breath, as though she'd been the one doing all the talking. "Sweet Jesus. I understand now why you'd be hesitant to surrender to the police."

Britt nodded.

"Where is Raley?"

"He hopes to bluff George McGowan into thinking that Fordyce ratted him out. He took the camcorder, thinking he may get McGowan on tape admitting his role in all this, and incriminating Fordyce at the same time."

"Any such recording wouldn't be admissible in court."

"I realize that, and so does Raley. But having it is better than not."

"You have the tape of your interview with Fordyce?"

Britt pulled the small cartridge from the pocket of her jeans and handed it over. "Fordyce doesn't actually own up to his participation. But if Raley can get George McGowan's admission, then the AG's role will be exposed, and we'll have him on video lying about it, which would at least strengthen any prosecutor's case against him."

"It's a high body count," the judge said, shaking her head. "I'm dumbfounded by the extent of their perfidy."

"Even more astonishing is that they've got away with it for these five years."

"The man who responded to Cobb

Fordyce's summons this morning, the fake security guard, you're certain he was in Jay's town house that night?"

"Positive. My memory came back the instant Fordyce opened his front door and I saw him there on the threshold. Some of my recollections are still hazy. Segments of time are missing, but I remember him with perfect clarity because he laughed while his partner was molesting me."

"Molesting you? You didn't mention that before."

"It's not easy to talk about." Speaking woman to woman, Britt described the experience.

The judge frowned with distaste. "That must have been awful for you. You're certain that if you saw this man again you could identify him?"

"Without question."

"Would he look anything like that?"

Britt, puzzled by the question that was seemingly nonsensical, turned her head, following the direction of the judge's nod.

He had entered the room unheard and was standing with his back to the closed door, leering at her, just as he had when he violated her.

"Britt," the judge said, "I believe you're intimately acquainted with Mr. Smith."

CHAPTER 29

George seemed to have lapsed into a stupor. Without his noticing, Raley set the camcorder on the edge of the desk, left it recording, and gave George a verbal nudge. "You had to stop my investigation, so you set me up with Suzi Monroe."

George took a heavy breath and released it slowly. "Jay's idea. Two birds with one stone, stop you from finding out what we did to Cleveland Jones, and give ol' Jay a free shot at your fiancée." He winked a bloodshot eye. "His plan worked, too, didn't it? That was our Jay. Everything always went his way."

Raley recalled the morning he'd

awakened to find the girl dead beside him, how Jay had been calmly drinking coffee and reading the Sunday newspaper. Remarkable, that he could be that blasé after having sacrificed a young woman's life.

"Did Jay kill her?"

"She killed herself."

"He just supplied the dope."

"Pat and me, actually." George's reply was matter-of-fact. "Jay was to get the girl, we were to get the coke. That was our deal. Jay wooed her into slipping you the Mickey. Told her it would make you last all night, and it damn near did. Finally you passed out. Then we gave her the coke. Urged on by Jay, she . . ." He sobbed again. It took a moment for him to collect himself enough to go on.

"Next morning she was dead, and it worked out just like Jay had promised us it would. Your life went from sugar to shit. We were off the hook." George had begun to slur his words, but he was fully aware of what he was saying. He focused his bleary eyes on Raley. "How long before you figured it out?"

"A while. At first I denied it was possible. I didn't want to believe my best friend could do that to me. Not then, not now."

"But once you caught on, you didn't get over it."

"No, I didn't get over it."

George sighed. "Well, I can't say as I blame you. In your place, I probably would have done the same. Truth be known, I wish you had started with me."

Maybe George wasn't as lucid as Raley had thought. Perplexed, he said, "Started what with you, George?"

"Your vendetta."

"My—"

"I'm relieved, you know. Ever since Pat Senior got popped in that alley, I've been waiting for my turn, wondering how you were going to take me out, and when. Gotta hand it to you, the way you dispensed with Jay. That was poetic, man. Using that newswoman and giving her the drug like we gave you. Very clever. Sent us all a message that caused some puckered sphincters, let me tell you.

"After Jay, the rest of us knew we were screwed, that it was only a matter of time. Even Miranda and Les have been nervous, and those two are never rattled. But I can sense it. They're on edge, wondering if their relationship will be revealed once I'm exposed as a fraud. See, having a big, strapping hero for her husband is the perfect cover for them. And Pat Junior has been about to have a stroke. Of course, he's as frightened of everybody learning he's gay as he is of your revenge."

"George, what the hell are you talking about?"

But by now the man had become lost in the boozy maze of his mind. Raley's interruption didn't draw him out of it. "One thing I can't figure, though. Why'd you cap Cobb Fordyce this morning? He wasn't even there when we did Jones. He was the real hero of the fire, the *only* hero. He had nothing to do with Suzi Monroe, either. He even gave you a pass on that. So why'd you do him? No, no, don't bother answering. Screw it. I don't really care."

Suddenly, he raised the pistol and poked the barrel under his chin. Reacting instantly, Raley vaulted over the desk and caught George's wrist just as he pulled the trigger. The bullet went wide and bored a hole through the paneling.

The desk chair with both of them in it went over backward, crashing into a trophy case. Shattered glass rained down on them. Trophies attesting to George's athletic ability tumbled from their display shelves. A heavy silver cup hit Raley hard on the head, but he barely felt it. He was intent on his struggle over possession of the pistol.

George was much heavier than Raley, but Raley's coordination wasn't affected by bourbon. He wrested the pistol from George's hand, but George got in a punch, his meaty fist connecting solidly with Raley's eye. Inside Raley's skull, new suns were born in blasts of light, but he held on to the pistol.

"Let me do it! Goddamn you!" the man sobbed. "Let me do it."

"You said the *four* of you worked Jones over. But then you said Fordyce wasn't there."

"Give me the pistol." George was blubbering, stretching and flexing his fingers toward the gun that Raley held well beyond his reach.

"Who else was in that room, George?"

"Please," he whimpered. "I'm tired of it all. I just want to die."

With his free hand, Raley grabbed him by his collar and jerked him up until their faces were no more than an inch apart. "Who was the fourth person, George?" He shook him hard, causing his burly head to wobble. *"Who?"*

"Candy, of course."

Raley's breath came out in a gust. He stared at George's ruddy, contorted face, but didn't see any deceit in his sagging expression, only abject misery. He let go of him as though the fabric of George's shirt had stung his hands. When George's head hit the floor, there was a crunch of glass, but he seemed impervious to the shards that pierced his scalp. He rolled onto his side, assumed the fetal position, and continued to cry like a baby.

Candy. Of course.

Tightly gripping George's pistol, Raley surged to his feet and turned, ready to dash for the door. Instead he drew up short and froze.

Standing just inside the room, cradling pistols in their hands and in firing stances, were the two men he'd last seen partially dressed, racing back into their hotel rooms. Butch and Sundance. Both had their pants on now, and their expressions were taut with angry resolve.

"Drop the pistol, Gannon! Drop it *now*!"

Raley thought of Britt, whom he'd sent to the enemy, to Candy, his supposed friend, the one person in the world he'd trusted with his life. With Britt's life. He'd sent Britt to Candy for protection, not knowing until now that it was from Candy that Britt needed protection. It was too late to save her. Too late to save himself. Too late for every damn thing. He had absolutely nothing to lose by trying to shoot his way out of this.

These thoughts whizzed through Raley's mind with the speed of a comet as his finger tightened on the trigger.

Butch shouted, "Drop it! Don't do it! FBI!"

• • •

The man Candy had introduced as Mr. Smith had entered the room with the same silence and aura of hauteur and menace with which he'd walked into Jay's town house. Making a choking noise, Britt shot to her feet.

Candy laughed softly. "I see you *do* recognize him. He was ordered not to touch you that night, yet you say he did some fiddling down there. Which of you am I to believe, hmm?" Her cell phone rang. "Would you two please excuse me while I take this call?" The judge removed the cell phone from the pocket of her suit jacket and flipped it open.

As she did, Britt screamed bloody murder, hoping that whoever was on the other end of the call would hear her and come to her rescue, or that someone in a neighboring building might, miraculously, pick up the sound.

Smith responded immediately. He rushed forward and clapped his hand over her mouth and nose, pinning her arms against her body, making them useless.

The judge, frowning at her, calmly returned to her call. "Yes, that was Ms. Shelley, trying to make her presence known. She's taken care of. Your job is to get Gannon."

Britt listened with dismay and rising fear as Candy assigned the caller to find Raley and George McGowan and eliminate them both. "Don't leave any witnesses. Do whatever you have to, but make it look like Raley was responsible. And don't disappoint me. You've fucked up once already this morning."

She closed her phone with a decisive snap and returned it to her pocket. Britt's lungs were burning for air. At a small nod from the judge, Smith relaxed his hand, allowing her to breathe but holding her chin. She knew he could break her neck in an instant if he wished. She rasped, "I don't understand."

"No? What don't you get?" Candy asked.

"You were in on it all along?"

"From 'all along,' do you mean from the day of the fire?"

Britt nodded.

"Yes. From that day, when Jay called

and asked me to come to the police station. He, McGowan, and Wickham were interrogating a skinhead, and they needed someone from the DA's office to help scare a confession out of him. Fordyce wasn't available, so I grabbed my briefcase and trotted over."

"You were there when Cleveland Jones . . ."

"Had his skull bashed in, yes. We never were clear on who struck the deathblow."

The scene that this respected judge calmly described left Britt temporarily speechless.

"We managed to keep the secret," Candy continued, "but for the past five years I've kept close tabs on the men. Women are stronger, you know. Much stronger. Anyway, I paid careful attention to my—"

"Coconspirators," Britt supplied.

Candy smiled. "For lack of a better word. I monitored their lives, looking for any signs of change or weakness. When Jay was given his grim prognosis, that was a serious heads-up. I put a tap on his phone. Good thing, too, because I knew immediately when he called you for a date. Red alert. He was dying and got afraid of going to Hell. I knew what he wanted to confess.

"So I quickly put together a plan to make sure he didn't tell our secret, or if he did, you wouldn't remember it. I should have had you killed, too. I realize that now. But at the time, I thought you'd be of better use to me alive. You would appear to be one of Jay's many jilted lovers who'd finally had enough of his shenanigans and smothered him in his sleep. The plan was to make you the prime suspect, so the police wouldn't be investigating anyone else. Everything went according to plan." Her insidious smile faded. "Then you pulled your disappearing act."

"Raley kidnapped me from my house."

Taken aback by that, Candy stared at her, then laughed. "You're kidding. By-the-book Raley Gannon? He kidnapped you?"

Britt nodded.

"What do you know? Those years spent in the woods must have brought out some dormant primitive instincts," the judge said with amusement. Winking at Britt, she asked, "Do those animalistic urges take over in bed, too? We know about Jay's sexual talents, because he boasted of them. But I always wondered about Raley's. He doesn't kiss and tell the way Jay did. He's the strong, silent type."

Shaking her index finger teasingly, she said, "I've long suspected there were some strong undercurrents beneath the surface. Am I right?" Britt just stared at her, trying to keep her face expressionless while her mind was scrambling to devise a way out, a means to survive.

"Not gonna share?" the judge said. "Oh, well. Doesn't matter." She glanced at her wristwatch. "I've got to hurry this along. Where was I?"

"Raley's primitive instincts," Britt said. "Which served him well when he dived into the river and saved me from drowning."

"Ah. The rescuer. Now *that* sounds like the Raley I know. How did he know you went into the river?"

"I—"

"Never mind. I don't have time for a long story."

"I apologize for putting a crimp in your busy schedule."

"Don't resort to sarcasm, Britt. It doesn't flatter you." The judge paused a moment, then said, "I wasn't surprised to hear that Raley came out of hiding to attend Jay's funeral. Considering their lifelong friendship. I wasn't too bothered to learn that he was there, except that he had singled out George, and some of what he insinuated made George very nervous. Then your resurrection came as a shock. I thought I was finished with you."

"You intercepted the telephone conversation with my lawyer?"

"We'd tapped his phone, yes. When I heard you tell him that Jay's death and the police station fire were connected, I had to act swiftly. Mr. Smith here was responsible for your dip into the Combahee."

"Which, if I were ever found, would look like a suicide."

"That was the plan, but I see now that

too much was left to chance. I assumed we had succeeded and didn't know you were still alive until you and Raley paid a visit to Pat Junior's house."

"He reported that to you?"

"Immediately after you'd left. He's scared of me, you see. Because even when he was still in the hospital with his jaw wired shut, I warned him that if he ever told anyone I was in that interrogation room with Cleveland Jones, I would expose his homosexuality, which his father had looked upon as a disgrace, and had killed a man in order to keep it secret.

"And periodically, I would remind Pat Junior of that warning, just in case he was under the misconception that I'd forgotten it and he was safe from me. On his wedding day, I told him that, if he ever betrayed me, I would ruin his phony marriage. When his babies were born, I took teddy bears to the hospital and threatened to hurt the children if anyone ever found out that I'd been there when Jones died and the fire was set."

"You made yourself believed," Britt said. "He didn't tell."

"Bully for him."

The longer Britt could keep the judge talking, the better her chances were of escape. But how? Smith felt as unmovable as a wall behind her. Even if she could break his hold on her, she couldn't possibly make it to the door.

Could she go forward? The room had only one window, and it was directly behind Candy. It was a fixed, single-glass pane, without any metal or wood framework. But they were on the top floor of a six-story building. If she could, by some miracle, escape Smith long enough to ram past Candy and throw herself through the window, could she survive a fall from that height? Probably not. But she wasn't going to survive anyway, so perhaps it was worth taking the chance.

Not yet, though. Not until she had the complete story. Getting the story. That was her job, wasn't it?

Raley had said she didn't give herself enough credit, that she could be a star anywhere. She would do this last interview for him.

"The day of the fire, how did you escape the building?" she asked.

The judge guffawed. "Jay set the fire, and we left Jones in the room alone. I didn't need to stick around, so I took my departure then. By the time I was half a block away, I could smell smoke and the fire alarm had begun to sound. I joined the crowd of spectators who were rushing toward the building to watch the blaze. Nobody realized I'd just left it."

"And your companions weren't going to tell."

"Not without incriminating themselves."

"You helped engineer the Suzi Monroe incident."

"I hated doing that to Raley. I truly did." A vertical line appeared between her heavy eyebrows, making her contrition almost believable. "When we were kids, he was always nice to me. I wasn't pretty, wasn't one of the popular girls. He and Jay teased me a lot, but Raley's teasing wasn't cruel like Jay's could be. Raley always treated me kindly."

"And that's how you repaid his kindness? By ruining his reputation and destroying his life?"

The line on her forehead disappeared and she shrugged. "As I said, Britt, I never won any popularity contests. And I had to advance my career. No, I had to *make* my career."

"Even if it meant killing people," Britt said. "Cleveland Jones. Suzi Monroe. Pat Wickham, Senior. At least I assume you staged that fatal shooting in the alley."

"He was breaking down, falling apart. I was afraid that he would confess." She shrugged, glanced behind Britt toward Smith, said, "I did what was necessary."

"What did Jay and McGowan think of that timely fatal shooting?"

"I don't know. I never asked. They might have thought it was an awfully lucky break for them. They might have suspected me of having something to do with it, but in any case, we all pretended that it was a tragedy and never discussed it among ourselves."

Trying to buy more time, Britt said, "So the secret remained intact another few years. Then Jay got sick. Did you consult George on what should be done about Jay?"

Candy shook her head. "George drinks too much. I couldn't trust him not to get shitfaced and tell Miranda. So, I acted alone again. Well, alone except for Mr. Smith and his partner, Mr. Johnson."

"The man who came to Fordyce's house."

"That's the one. Although I doubt his name is really Johnson."

"Did you find them in the yellow pages? On Craigslist?"

Candy chuckled. "Call it underground classifieds. They're very handy when you need them. They flew in from St. Louis on the day you met Jay at The Wheelhouse."

"And this morning Johnson responded immediately to Fordyce's summons."

"We'd tapped the AG's phone and heard him call his assistant, asking that she send a capitol guard to escort you and Raley to a hotel. Lucky for me, he didn't specify to her why he wanted to keep you under lock and key. Even luckier, Johnson was waiting at the capitol building for you and Raley to arrive for your eleven o'clock appointment. He rushed to Fordyce's house and impersonated the requested guard."

Britt remembered Raley saying they would've been ambushed before they entered the capitol building, and she recalled Johnson explaining why he wasn't in uniform. But she was confused. "Are you telling me that Cobb Fordyce believed Johnson to be a capitol guard?"

"Jesus Christ, Britt," the judge said with asperity. "Aren't you getting it yet? Cobb Fordyce had nothing to do with either Cleveland Jones or Suzi Monroe. Everything he told you and Raley is the truth." She smiled as she dropped the small video cartridge into her pocket. "Too bad no one will ever see this video of yours. It probably captured one of our AG's crowning moments. Which is kind of poignant, when you think about it. He'll die—"

"Wait!" Britt exclaimed. "What do you mean he'll die?"

"Oh, jeez. In all the excitement, I forgot to tell you that Johnson shot Fordyce in the head after you ran. You and Raley are being sought for his attempted murder."

Britt listened with mounting incredulity as the judge described Cobb Fordyce's precarious medical condition. He *had* told her and Raley the truth. He *had* wanted to protect them until he could get to the bottom of the whole ugly story.

Then he had opened the door to his would-be assassin, sent by Cassandra Mellors.

Candy continued. "The real capitol guard arrived at the house to find Mrs. Fordyce in the foyer, cradling the AG's bloody head in her lap and screaming hysterically. It made for a dramatic news story. It's a shame you weren't available to cover it. But you still have celebrity status, Britt. You and Raley are the new Bonnie and Clyde.

"Even if Fordyce survives, there'll doubtless be significant brain damage. No one will ever know that Johnson shot him. By now he's probably dealt as effectively with George and Raley."

Britt gave an involuntary whimper.

"Does this spoil a budding romance?" Candy asked, her lips pursing with regret. "That's too bad."

Just then the judge's cell phone rang again. She took it from her jacket pocket. As soon as she flipped it open, Smith clamped his hand over Britt's mouth again.

"Yes?" Candy said into the phone. She listened, her face breaking into a wide grin. "That's wonderful news! When is he due to call? Fine. I'll be right there." She closed her phone. "The Senate just voted. I'm the new federal district court judge."

She spoke the words in a whisper, as though she barely believed the news. Then she met Britt's gaze. "You understand. Surely as a career woman, you understand, Britt. It's a man's world. I did what I had to do."

Britt jerked her head, and Smith's hand moved away from her mouth. Trying to keep her voice steady, she said,

"You won't get away with this. You're bound to know that. Eventually—"

"Excuse me, Britt. I'd love to hear what you think will happen—eventually—but the president is due to call with his congratulations in five minutes, and the media are gathering in my office to cover the event." She smiled sympathetically. "This would be a big story for you. I'm sorry you won't be there among your colleagues. I mean that sincerely, because basically I liked you and admired your work ethic. If only you'd told Jay you had other plans that night."

It didn't escape Britt that she was referring to her in the past tense. Her heart began to hammer with fright.

But the judge was the epitome of composure as she moved toward the door, saying to Smith as she went past, "Do it quietly. We'll take care of the body tonight."

She opened the door to leave, but her exit was blocked by two men.

As they barged in, Britt couldn't have mistaken them, although they were wearing black bulletproof vests over their golf shirts, shouting for everyone to drop to the floor, sweeping the room with drawn pistols, and identifying themselves as federal officers. Rushing in behind them were several SWAT officers of the PD, in full assault gear.

Bringing up the rear was Raley, also wearing a bulletproof vest.

Smith let go of Britt. She dropped to the floor as instructed by the men waving assault rifles. Smith didn't drop, or freeze, but instead went for the gun at the small of his back. One of the SWAT officers rushed him and knocked him to the ground, then flipped him facedown and yanked his weapon from the holster. Another of the men in black knelt beside Smith and, planting a knee between his shoulder blades, put restraints on his hands.

Raley ran straight to Britt. She felt his strong hands on her arms, pulling her up. "Are you all right?"

Dazed, she nodded, then stammered, "Y-yes."

Candy Mellors was screaming invectives at the FBI agent who had her face against the wall and was patting her down. “Are you crazy? The president is about to call me. The Senate—”

The man Raley had nicknamed Butch turned her around to face him. “The president isn’t going to be calling with congratulations, Judge. He got a call from my boss a couple of hours ago. The director advised him to withdraw your nomination, telling him that a full explanation about your alleged criminal activity would be forthcoming. The president took his advice.”

Her eyes were wide, wild, as she gaped first at him, then at Raley and Britt, then back at the agent. “But they approved my appointment. My assistant called just now and said—”

“That call was a ruse, to cover our approach,” the agent told her. “There was no vote today. There won’t be a vote. Ever.” He began reading her her rights.

Raley was still supporting Britt, caressing her upper arms as he held her close. “Is he the one who messed with you?” he asked in a quiet voice. She followed his hard gaze to the man she knew as Mr. Smith.

“Yes.”

Gently, Raley moved her aside and strode purposefully toward the man.

"Raley?" she said apprehensively.

Sandwiched between two SWAT officers, Smith must have felt safe from retribution. He saw Raley coming, but all he did was give him an insinuating smirk.

He was totally unprepared for Raley to swing his foot up and kick him between the legs, a kick hard enough to raise him off the floor a couple inches. There was a second or two delay before the agony slammed into his system. Then his whole body shook, he screamed like a girl, dropped to his knees, and toppled face-first onto the floor.

"That's enough, Gannon!" Sundance barked. "Back down."

But Britt didn't think Raley heard him. Or if he did, he didn't heed him, because instead of backing down, he lunged after Candy, who had used the distraction to break free from the agent. She threw herself against the window Britt herself had considered using as her escape and plunged through the shattering glass.

Raley went through it a nanosecond behind her.

Britt stared in horror at the empty window.

CHAPTER 30

Raley leaped from the window and landed on the surface ten feet below.

He knew this old building because he and fellow firefighters had run practice drills in it. In this block of Broad Street, one of the oldest in the city, the buildings were jammed together, the backs of them converging to form a labyrinth of brick walls and a patchwork quilt of rooftops. He knew that a mere four inches separated this building from the one abutting it, and that a jump from the six-story window would put him on its rooftop.

The roofing material was old and spongy and made for an easy landing, but it didn't provide good footing as he scrambled to stand up. Candy was already teetering at the edge of the roof when he shouted her name.

"Stop. Let's talk about it."

She turned toward him, putting her back to a drop he knew was straight down, fifty feet, give or take. "There's nothing to talk about."

"Only everything."

The FBI agent had extended her the courtesy of cuffing her hands in front rather than behind her back. Raley saw that they were bleeding, lacerated by window glass. Pieces of glass were caught in her hair. Landing on the rooftop had shredded her stockings and left her with scraped knees. If she was even aware of these injuries, she gave no sign of it.

"There's nothing more to talk about, Raley. You know everything. What you don't know, your girlfriend does." She hesitated, then said, "I'm sorta glad, you know. About you. Her. You deserve a break, after what we did to you."

"Why'd you do it, Candy? *How* could you?"

"Because, dammit, Raley, you just

wouldn't stop with the questions about that goddamn fire. And the skinhead. Short of killing you, too, we had to do *something.* You wouldn't give up."

"You didn't give up, either," he said quietly. "You had all of them killed. Pat Senior. Jay. Your *friend* Jay."

She smiled wryly. "Once I was in, I had to protect myself, my career."

"You can give up now." Not wanting to spook her into jumping, he moved closer an inch at a time, none of his gestures or movements threatening.

Her gaze jumped to something behind him. He took a glance over his shoulder. Two SWAT officers had rappelled out the window and down the side of the building and were crouched against the exterior wall, their rifles aimed at Candy.

"Stay back!" Raley shouted. Neither moved, but they didn't lower their rifles. "Let me talk to her," he pleaded in a softer voice. Turning back to Candy, he said, "Don't give these guys the satisfaction. Surrender now. It's over."

"They don't think so," she said, looking down over her shoulder.

He couldn't see over the edge of the roof to what was going on below, but he could imagine. He could hear police shouting for curious onlookers to move back. Sirens announced the arrival of emergency vehicles. Reporters and cameramen would have been jostling for advantageous spots from which to do their stand-ups.

Confirming what he guessed, Candy said, "This wasn't exactly the news story I had planned for today."

He heard the shift of boots behind him and knew that the SWAT officers had moved stealthily closer, but they weren't charging forward. They were giving him a little more time to talk her out of jumping. But how much more time before they rushed her? How much more time before she decided to end their conversation on her terms?

"From a presidential appointment to this," she murmured.

"I'm sorry it turned out this way for you, Candy."

She came back around to him, her expression scornful. "Not really."

"Yes, really. I *am* sorry. About all of it,

starting with Pat Junior being assaulted in the park, the victim of a hate crime."

The clap of rotors alerted them to the helicopter's approach. She looked out across the rooftops, spotted the chopper coming in low, spotted other SWAT officers taking position on neighboring rooftops.

She turned back to Raley just as he froze in place. Using her distraction to his advantage, he'd taken baby steps toward her and was now only six feet away, almost, but not quite, within arm's reach.

"I can't escape, can I, Raley?"

He shook his head and dared to take another step. "No, but you don't have to die."

"No, see, I do. Everything I've worked for is gone. So what's the point?"

And with that, she leaned backward.

Raley lunged. The humerus of his left arm snapped when he landed hard on the edge of the roof. The pain caused him to cry out. Or was it a cry of joy, because with his right hand, he was able to catch Candy's left hand. Ignoring the pain in his arm, he held on. He looked over the edge and saw her kicking thin air, kicking the brick wall, trying to wrest her hand free.

"Let me go, Raley," she shouted up at him. "For godsake, let me go."

The SWAT officers moved to either side of him. One dropped his rifle and extended his hand toward Candy's arm. But she was out of his reach. It was up to Raley to hold on. The cuts on her hand had made it slippery with blood, nearly impossible to hold on to, and yet he maintained his grip.

"Raley, please," she groaned as she doubled her efforts to pull free.

Blood-slicked skin slipped a fraction of an inch against his palm. His shoulder socket burned with the effort of holding her. His left arm was useless, the pain searing in its intensity. But he gritted his teeth and held on.

"Let go!" she screamed. "I ruined your life, you fool!"

In that instant, he couldn't think of a single reason why he shouldn't open his hand.

Their eyes connected. In hers he saw the hopelessness he'd experienced when his life was shattered by her treachery. Driven by single-minded ambition, she had destroyed his life and, for a time, robbed him of all hope.

He held her gaze, staring straight into her eyes as he felt her hand slipping, slipping, slipping, out of his grasp.

Special Agent Miller of the FBI said, "It think that's it." He silently consulted his partner, Special Agent Steiner, who gave a nod of agreement.

Miller, a.k.a. Butch, switched off the camcorder. "Thank you, Mr. Gannon. I appreciate your willingness to do this tonight. It could have waited until tomorrow."

"I wanted to get it over with," Raley said.

"Gentlemen?" Miller turned to Detectives Clark and Javier, who'd been invited to sit in on Raley's deposition. Between them they hadn't said a dozen words throughout the whole proceeding.

Clark asked, "When do we get a copy of the video?"

"First thing tomorrow," Miller replied.

Javier stood and, without a word, headed for the door. Clark gave them all a curt nod, then followed his partner out.

"Assholes," Raley said under his breath.

"They get perturbed whenever we horn in on their case," Miller said, seemingly unfazed by the detectives' sullen rudeness.

Raley wondered what the two federal agents would think of the nicknames he'd given them. Oddly, each name fit the man—at least as the pair had been portrayed in the movie. Of the two, Miller was more easygoing. Steiner was more sinister. His eyes were sharp and seemed to miss nothing. On appearance alone, he could easily have been mistaken for a hit man.

Steiner had been studying Raley closely for the last several minutes. Now he said, "You don't look so good."

Raley knew that to be true. They were sequestered in a small room in the FBI office on Meeting Street, just blocks from where the dramatic events of the afternoon had taken place.

Before the lengthy interview began, he'd caught a glimpse of his reflection in the window. His skin looked pasty. His left arm was in a cast and supported by a sling, his palms were abraded from when he'd landed on the roof, and there were several cuts on his face and arms from broken window glass. George McGowan had given him a black eye that was swollen and tender.

He didn't even resemble the man he'd been a week ago, but not all the changes were the results of today's physical ordeals. They also went beyond shaving his beard and trimming his hair. The real change was internal. It had to do with finally settling the matter of all that had happened five years ago. And a lot to do with Britt, who was sitting beside him, close, attentive to his weakening condition, attentive to everything.

"Are you holding up all right?" she asked now, her concern showing.

"Yeah." He squeezed her hand, which he'd been holding throughout the deposition. For almost three hours he'd talked into the camcorder, telling the FBI agents and the two Charleston PD detectives the whole story, repeating what he'd babbled in a verbal shorthand on the race from George McGowan's estate.

There in George's study, it had taken him several seconds to assimilate that the two men whom he'd mistaken for assassins were actually federal agents. He'd dropped George's pistol as instructed, but he'd made certain they understood, in a very short amount of time, that Candy Mellors was the instigator of several murders—which he was surprised to learn they had already deduced—and that Britt's life was in imminent danger.

Reacting swiftly, Steiner had offered to wait for other officers to come and take George into custody. Meanwhile Miller had sped toward downtown and, along the way, notified the police of the crisis situation and coordinated an operation to end it, they hoped without casualties.

Raley had insisted on going with Miller and said he would only follow in his own car if the agent refused to take him along. Miller had conceded. It was during that drive—which had seemed agonizingly long—that Raley had told him a sketchy version of everything George had confessed.

Over the last one hundred eighty minutes, he'd given a more detailed account, providing answers to the agents' many questions. Miller had another, which he asked now. "How did you and Ms. Shelley join forces?"

"I kidnapped her."

Miller and Steiner glanced at each other with raised eyebrows. "Care to expand on that, Ms. Shelley?" Steiner asked.

"Is it relevant?"

"You tell me," the agent replied. "Is it?"

"No."

The two agents looked at each other again. Steiner raised his shoulder in a shrug. Since Raley and Britt were sitting shoulder to shoulder and thigh to thigh, Raley doubted the agents would arrest him for committing that federal offense.

"I have a question for *you,*" Raley said. He was ready to get out of here. His arm was throbbing, his eye was making his whole head hurt, he badly needed another pain pill, but he didn't want this meeting to conclude until the agents had all their answers, and he had his. He didn't want to wake up tomorrow morning dreading another go-round of Q and A.

"How did the FBI get in on this?"

Miller explained. "Routine investigations are conducted when a judge is nominated for the federal district court. Cassandra Mellors's judicial record is commendable, noteworthy even, which is why she was nominated in the first place. No one expected to find anything out of whack.

"But one of our sharper data analysts brought to our attention that her name was tangentially linked to the investigation of one Suzi Monroe's death. From that we learned about the fire, the heroes of it, and—oops—the arson investigator's connection to the girl's lethal overdose. We learned that, a year after the fire, one of those same heroes was fatally shot in an alley, which remained an unsolved murder.

"So now we have two mysterious deaths, and interestingly, the same people were involved. Again tangentially, but we thought it was hinky. So we dug a little deeper and started looking at Jay Burgess and George McGowan, along with Judge Mellors."

"That's what you were doing that night in The Wheelhouse."

Miller nodded at Britt. "We knew Burgess was sick and didn't have long to live, but we were keeping him under surveillance all the same. We followed him to the bar. The two of you met, seemed compatible, left together, went to his house." Chagrined, he looked at Raley. "Steiner and I figured the guy deserved time with a pretty woman, so we knocked off for the night."

Raley sensed how deeply the agents regretted that decision.

Britt asked, "After Jay was killed, why didn't you come forward and let the local police know that you were conducting a covert investigation?"

"Well," Steiner said, "for all we knew, you'd had a lovers' quarrel with Burgess and snuffed him, just like the police suspected. It could have had nothing to do with the other matter. It was CPD's jurisdiction, their homicide, their investigation."

"Besides," Miller said, "we didn't want to tip our hand. If Judge Mellors was involved, we didn't want her to sense she was being investigated and start covering her tracks. And Burgess was a cop. Men in blue can get funny about protecting their own, even their dead own. If they thought we, the bleeping Feebs, were trying to pin a conspiracy on one of their heroes, how much cooperation do you suppose we'd have got?"

"But then you went missing," Steiner said. "That threw us."

"You didn't assume that I'd run away to avoid arrest?" Britt asked.

"It crossed our minds, but by then we'd done further background on you. Clean as a whistle. You didn't seem the type to skip out, any more than you seemed like a lady who'd smother a guy."

"Thanks for that," she said.

"Frankly, we feared the worst," Miller said. "We were afraid someone had removed you from the scene permanently."

"Was I among the someones you suspected?" Raley asked. Neither agent picked up that gauntlet, but he wasn't going to be deterred. "You came looking for me when Britt disappeared. Why? Why did you search my cabin?" He and Britt had already admitted to seeing them there.

"We wanted to talk to you about your old friends Jay and Candy, get a feel for you, get a read on how you felt about them."

"My ass," Raley scoffed. "If you'd only wanted to talk, you would've stuck around till I showed up."

Caught in the fib, Miller blushed. Steiner coughed behind his hand. "Okay, we suspected you might have had something to do with Burgess's murder."

"And Britt's disappearance," Raley said.

Steiner nodded. "That, too. After everything we'd read and heard, we figured you might want vengeance against all of them, including Ms. Shelley. You had motivation, we wanted to check out your opportunity."

"Did you have a search warrant that day?"

"No, but we had probable cause to go inside."

"How's that?"

"We looked in the windows and I saw the women's clothing scattered across your bed. New clothing. Some of it still in shopping bags. None of our research into you included a woman currently in your life. So when we saw the clothes, we thought we'd better go inside and check it out."

Drolly, Steiner said, "Turns out our instincts were right. You'd kidnapped her."

Raley glanced down at Britt, who smiled up at him, then addressed the agents. "Once Raley explained to me how he'd been set up with Suzi Monroe, much as I'd been set up with Jay, we formed an alliance to get to the bottom of it."

"We figured maybe you two had joined forces," Miller said. "We saw no signs of struggle. And if a man is about to kill a woman, he doesn't usually buy her new clothes first."

Britt said, "We would have explained everything if you'd stayed and identified yourselves. Why did you leave? Raley's truck was there, you knew we had to be close by."

"The funeral. We had to get back in time for it. We wanted to see who turned up, gauge reactions and such." Miller looked at Raley askance, a bit of egg on his face. "We didn't know you'd marked us until you left the cemetery and it became obvious that you knew we were following you." Then he looked at Britt. "Nice trick with the tires, by the way."

"Thank you."

"When you came charging out of your rooms after her, why didn't you identify yourselves as FBI?"

"Would you have believed it, raised your hands, and surrendered?" Miller asked.

Remembering him chasing after Britt wearing nothing but his underwear, Raley smiled. "No."

"I shouted 'FBI,' " Steiner said, "but you gunned the car. I didn't have my ID, my weapon, nothing to convince you, and you were aiming that cannon at us."

"Lucky I didn't shoot."

"Yeah, lucky. Today, too."

Reminded of when he'd faced off against them in George's study, Raley asked, "What'll happen to George McGowan?"

"Well, we've got the video of your interview with him, but a good defense lawyer will argue it's not admissible. Except for that cigarette lighter, all the evidence is circumstantial. He's got big money behind him, so he may be able to buy himself an acquittal."

"Or maybe he'll stick to his confession," Steiner mused aloud.

"Why would he?" Miller asked.

Raley knew why. George might prefer prison to the hell on earth he was living with Miranda and Les. Either way, the man's situation was pathetic.

"Pat Wickham has said he'll back up Raley's statement," Miller said.

"He no longer has to be afraid of retribution from Candy Mellors," Britt said. "She had him living in fear for himself and his family."

In his deposition, Raley had related how he and Britt had ambushed Pat Jr. outside the gay bar and admitted to seeing the agents there. Miller had explained that they were acting on the same hunch that Pat was hiding his sexual orientation and that his secret was somehow linked to the other events.

He and his family had been located at a lake resort in Arkansas. At present, he was in custody, charged with obstruction of justice. Raley felt sorry for him actually, and hoped that, if he was convicted, a merciful judge wouldn't send him to prison. Raley felt even more compassion for the younger man's wife and children, perhaps the only real innocents in the whole affair. Their lives would be affected by the scandal; there was no way to avoid it.

"Johnson was apprehended on his way to McGowan's place," Miller informed them. "He and Smith are well known to the bureau, by a variety of names. They've been flying under the radar for years, protected by people in high places for whom they did dirty work. We're glad to have them. Neither will ever know another day of freedom."

"At least Johnson won't have Cobb Fordyce's murder on his résumé," Britt said.

A hospital spokesperson had announced earlier that evening that the attorney general's condition had improved. Following surgery to remove the bullet, he had regained consciousness. He had recognized his wife and had even spoken her name. Doctors were cautiously optimistic. It remained to be seen how much impairment he would suffer, but at least he was alive and, for the time being, stable.

"As for Cassandra Mellors . . ." Steiner paused and looked meaningfully at Raley before continuing. "Her superficial wounds have been treated, but the doctors are concerned about her state of mind. She's being kept at the hospital for observation. She's under suicide watch. There's a guard outside her door, a nurse and a policewoman inside the room with her."

Raley nodded.

A heavy silence descended over

them. It was finally broken by Miller. "Nobody would have blamed you, or second-guessed you, Mr. Gannon. The SWAT officers would have attested to your effort to save her. They said that, even at risk to yourself, you refused to let go."

"He would never have let go," Britt said. Raley looked at her. Her eyes were soft and liquid. "Not in a million years."

His throat seized up with emotion over her understanding. He could no more have let go of Candy's hand and sent her to her death than he could have sprouted wings and flown off the roof. So he'd held on against impossible odds, fighting the relentless pull of gravity and his own physical limitations, maintaining his grip on her slippery hand, and gradually, painfully, pulling her up until the SWAT officers could catch her arms and haul her onto the roof to safety.

And arrest.

"Brave, you jumping out that window after her," Miller remarked.

"Not brave at all." Raley explained his familiarity with the building. "I knew when I went through the window I wouldn't have a long fall."

"Well, still . . . ," Miller said, "nobody else jumped through it." After another brief silence, he stood up quickly and made himself look busy by stacking his file folders. "That's all for now. Those detectives may want to take their own deposition. You'll probably be subpoenaed to testify in the upcoming trials. But as far as we're concerned, we're finished for now. Go home. Lie down before you fall down."

With an effort, Raley stood up. Britt helped support him as he shook hands with Miller. "I'm glad I didn't shoot you."

The agent grinned. "Me, too."

Steiner offered to drive them wherever they needed to go, and they accepted. But as they exited the building, the agent drew up short and exclaimed, "What in the Sam Hill . . . ?"

CHAPTER 31

Standing on the curb in front of Frankenstein was Delno Pickens. He'd put on shoes for the trip into the city, but only one strap of his overalls was hooked, leaving most of his upper body bare. Under the streetlight, the sprouts of woolly white hair created a weird-looking aura.

Raley could well understand Steiner's astonishment. "That's my friend."

"*Our* friend," Britt said.

Delno eyed Steiner up and down as the three of them approached. He scowled his disapproval of the agent, then spat tobacco juice into the gutter.

Raley asked, "What in the world are you doing here, Delno?"

"I came to bust y'all out. I saw on the TV y'all being escorted out of the hospital emergency room by the feds." He gave Steiner another baleful look and snorted with disdain.

"We're not under arrest." Raley explained that he'd been giving a deposition. "We're finished and on our way home."

"Well, that's good then," Delno said. "I can give you a ride."

Raley hesitated, then said, "Thanks. That would be great."

Steiner seemed reluctant to release them to Delno. Raley assured him that the old man looked stranger than he was. "He's harmless. Basically."

The agent shook hands with them in turn and wished them good luck—looking like he meant it—then returned to the building.

Raley helped Britt into the passenger side of Delno's contraption and climbed in beside her, saying softly, "Be afraid."

Britt gave Delno directions to her house, then she and Raley talked him through the events of the last couple of days. Raley concluded by telling his neighbor that what had started five years ago was finally over and relegated to the past, where it would stay.

Delno grumbled, “Good. Maybe your disposition will improve some.”

Despite the remark, Raley knew Delno shared his relief that it was, at last, over. As did his parents. He’d called them while waiting for his broken arm to be set, fearing they would hear headlines even in Augusta and fret. He’d told them that there was a lot to tell, but the upshot of it was that he’d been vindicated, and those who were responsible for Suzi Monroe’s death would be punished. His mom had cried. He thought maybe his dad had got choked up, too.

Turning onto Britt’s street, they were relieved to see that no media were staked out at her house. When Raley remarked on it, she said, “It’s been a heavy news day. First Fordyce, then Judge Mellors. The arrest of George McGowan. No one’s interested in me.”

As Delno clambered out and helped her from the vehicle, he said, “Don’t go being modest. I heard you're scheduled for a TV interview in the morning."

"I accepted the invitation, but only if certain conditions were met."

"Well, this is one viewer who'll be watching."

She clasped both his hands in hers, then leaned forward and hugged him. "Thanks for the ride, Delno. Thanks for everything."

He whipped the battered straw hat off his head and placed it over his heart. "My pleasure." Then he nodded toward Raley's arm sling and asked if he was going to be all right.

"The doc said it was a clean break, should heal in a few weeks."

"It's a wonder you didn't get yourself killed. Jumping out of a window. Damn fool thing to do." He spat again and wiped his mouth with the back of his hand. "You coming back?"

"To the cabin?"

"Now that you're a big shot, I thought maybe you'd be moving up, leaving the neighborhood."

Raley was touched. He saw past his neighbor's thorny exterior and knew the old man would miss him if he no longer lived nearby. "You can't get rid of me. I'll be back. And while I'm away, don't set any traps where I'm likely to be walking."

Delno's maw was brown and sloppy with chewed tobacco, but it was an earnest grin. He climbed back into the amalgamated vehicle, and with a dozen distinguishable grinds, clatters, and clangs, it bounced down the street.

Raley, almost too exhausted to move, followed Britt up the walkway and into the house. After the front door was locked and the shutters closed, he asked, "How did Delno know you're going to be on TV in the morning?"

"From the moment I agreed to the interview, the station has been promoting it all afternoon and evening."

"What were your conditions?"

"First, a public apology from the general manager for putting me on leave when I was innocent of any malfeasance. Then my old job back, but with a hefty raise. Hour-long special features programs, no fewer than three per year, my choice of topics. A private office and an assistant. And all in writing."

Raley whistled. "You're tough."

She gave him a saucy smile. "I'm in demand."

"You could name your salary." After a strategic pause, he added, "Anywhere."

"Probably, but—"

"Fear of failure?"

"No. After today, what could I possibly fear?" she said softly. "The truth is, I don't want to leave Charleston. It feels like home now, and I think I can do some good work here." She tilted her head as she looked up at him. "What about you? The fire chief came to the emergency room while you were being treated. According to the people I talked to later—"

"Always following the scent of a story, aren't you?"

"—he was clamoring to talk to you. You refused to see him. Why?"

"I guess I want to be courted, too. Let him stew for a day or two, then I'll agree to meet with him."

"And if he offers you your old job back?"

"I'll turn it down."

Her smile collapsed. "Oh."

"I'm going to hold out for the promotion I was promised. There's a veteran who took over when Brunner died, but he's ready to retire. I want to be made senior arson inspector for the whole department, for every firehouse, citywide."

"Oh," she repeated, this time in a different tone.

"I could do good work here, too."

"I believe that."

They smiled at each other, and then she walked into his embrace as he curved his right arm around her waist and drew her to him. She looped her arms around his waist. He whispered into her hair, "I'm not hurt that bad. Hug me tight."

She did, whispering back, "I just want to feel you, smell you, make sure you're here." There was a catch in her voice when she continued. "I've only known you for a few days. But when you jumped through that window, my heart stopped. You can't imagine—"

"I don't have to imagine. I know. I felt the same way when I realized that I'd sent you straight to the culprit who'd tried to kill you once already. If something had happened to you, I'd just as soon those feds shot me." He tipped her head up and touched her lower lip with the pad of his thumb. "Has it really only been a few days?"

"Impossible as that seems."

All the emotions they had experienced that day were unleashed when they kissed. It was deep and lasted forever. When they finally pulled apart, they were feverish with longing and reminded of the night before. He cleared his throat. "Britt, last night—"

"I know."

"I shouldn't have."

"*We* shouldn't have."

"Especially after I'd made such a big deal of it the first time."

"You were being conscientious."

"I was being a jerk."

"Sort of a jerk," she said with a soft smile. "But last night was different. It just felt right."

"It felt bloody great."

"So you're not . . . You don't regret it?"

"God no," he said huskily.

He had woken up with them spooned together, and for a time her nearness was enough. But then the sweet pressure of her bottom fit snugly against him, and the softness of her breast beneath his hand, had caused the predictable reaction.

His arousal woke her. She stirred. Lifting his hand to her mouth, she kissed his palm, gently sucked his fingertips, then lowered them to her nipples. With feather-light strokes he brought them erect, making her catch her breath. She rubbed against him in silent invitation.

He was hard and heavy, stretched to bursting. He intended to caress her with just the tip. But when he touched her, she was receptive and warm and very wet. He pushed himself into her, she enveloped him in her heat, and for a mindless, endless time, they mated with the merest of movements, rocking against each other in motions as fluid as a calm surf.

He withdrew only long enough to turn her onto her back before sinking into her again, then pressing himself deeper still. He barely had to move, he didn't want to, because she sheathed him so tightly, so completely, the pulsing of their bodies, his inside hers, brought her to orgasm. He held her hips tightly between his hands and felt each sweet contraction.

Being unprotected, he knew he should pull out, but his willpower to do so abandoned him to his pleasure. And not only to the pleasure, but to his need to meld with her in this most elemental way. She tilted her hips up as though reaching for more, her hands on his back were restless and urgent, and understanding what those entreaties implied, he came inside her. And came. And came.

When it was over, he slid his tongue into her mouth and they kissed, sexily and meaningfully in equal measure. For a long time they made love just by kissing. Until sleepiness overcame them again. They resumed their original position, he hugging her close, nuzzling her nape, tasting the fragrant skin beneath her hair, until they drifted back to sleep.

Neither had spoken a word, but it had been an intensely sexual and intimate experience, ripe with promise, implicative of a future. Words hadn't been necessary. And they weren't now.

Taking her hand, he led her into the bedroom.

AUTHOR'S NOTE

The fire in this novel is purely fictitious. In order to tell my story, I took creative license and invented a police station and the blaze that destroyed it.

I was well into writing this book when the deadly fire at the Sofa Super Store in Charleston occurred on June 18, 2007. It was an unsettling coincidence. For months, I considered changing the location of my story, fearing that it would appear insensitive to set it in a city that had withstood such a catastrophic loss.

But I changed my mind. That fire prompted reviews by numerous state and federal agencies, resulting in stricter safety measures and more effective fire-fighting procedures, which since have been adapted by fire departments all over the country. Hopefully this positive outcome will prevent another such devastating loss to a community, and to the individuals whose loss was much more personal.

Sandra Brown

ACKNOWLEDGMENTS

The Charleston Police Department moved into its present headquarters in 1974. I became acquainted with that facility when I wrote *The Alibi.* Prior to its relocation, the department had occupied a venerable stone building at the corner of St. Philip and Vanderhorst streets in the historic district. Within a year of being vacated, that building was demolished. I appreciate the help of Amie Gray of my staff, along with Jan Hiester and The Charleston Museum, for providing me with information and photos.

Special thanks, too, to the three citizens of Yemassee, South Carolina, who on a quiet Sunday morning directed my husband, Michael, and me to the Combahee River, which wasn't where it was supposed to be according to our map of the back roads. Once we assured these gentlemen that we weren't property developers, they were friendly, hospitable, and most generous with their assistance.

When lost, I've often ". . . depended on the kindness of strangers."

ABOUT THE AUTHOR

Sandra Brown is the author of numerous *New York Times* bestsellers, including *Play Dirty, Ricochet, Chill Factor, White Hot, The Crush, Envy,* and *The Switch*. She lives with her husband in Arlington, Texas.